THE PINCH

The Pinch

A History

a novel

STEVE STERN

Graywolf Press

This publication is made possible, in part, by the voters of Minnesota through a Minnesota State Arts Board Operating Support grant, thanks to a legislative appropriation from the arts and cultural heritage fund, and through a grant from the Wells Fargo Foundation Minnesota. Significant support has also been provided by Target, the McKnight Foundation, Amazon.com, and other generous contributions from foundations, corporations, and individuals. To these organizations and individuals we offer our heartfelt thanks.

Published by Graywolf Press
250 Third Avenue North, Suite 600
Minneapolis, Minnesota 55401

www.graywolfpress.org

Published in the United States of America
Printed in Canada

ISBN 978-1-55597-715-3

2 4 6 8 9 7 5 3 1
First Graywolf Printing, 2015

Library of Congress Control Number: 2014960045

Cover design: Kimberly Glyder Design

Cover art: Mario Bacchelli, *The Pinch, Memphis 1948*. Copyright © 2015 by the Estate of Mario Bacchelli.

for Sabrina

Contents

1. Welcome to Xanadu   3

2. Welcome to the Pinch   15

3. Champion of the Oppressed   35

4. A Local Apocalypse   49

5. Bolivar   73

6. Afterglow   89

7. Flashbacks   115

8. Beale Street   121

9. Hide and Seek   133

10. The Pinch: A History   143

11. Man without a Country   235

12. Before the Revolution   247

13. The *Floating Palace*   255

14. Artist in Clover   275

15. Party in the Park   281

16. Hostage to Destiny   293

17. Envoi   339

THE PINCH

◄1► Welcome to Xanadu

In the beginning was the book. I found it in a dusty used book shop on Main Street where I was working, so to speak. The book was called *The Pinch* and subtitled *a history*. It was a bible-thick doorstop in a cheap cloth binding, its title and author—one Muni Pinsker—stamped on the cover in faded gilt lettering. I was shelving books for my boss, Avrom Slutsky, when he told me I was about to misplace it.

"It says 'a history,'" I countered, pointing to the subtitle.

"So don't believe everything you read," replied Avrom, who'd been watching me from between the stacks of books on his desk. A veteran agoraphobe, the old man never left his shop and the cave-like apartment behind it, which is why he'd hired me in the first place. I was basically a glorified gofer who fetched his coffee and fried egg sandwiches from a nearby greasy spoon; I took his smelly laundry to the coin-op and got his prescriptions filled. I also shelved his recent purchases, an activity he seemed to think was a privilege, so he watched me like a myopic hawk through his Coke-bottle lenses.

"If it's not history, what is it?" I asked.

Avrom shrugged as far as his red suspenders allowed. "It's a hybrid work."

"Okay, where's the Hybrid shelf?"

"So file under Fiction."

"Fiction." Again I examined the dull beige cover, opening the book's deckle-edged pages at random. What I saw, adjacent a page of ordinary typeface, was a garishly colored illustration. The plate, pasted onto powder-gray paper, depicted an oddly familiar urban street whose dowdy brick and wooden facades—their chimneypots resembling organ pipes—overlooked a parrot-green canal. There were a number of boats in the canal, as well

3

as assorted sea serpents and semihuman creatures at play in the foam-flecked water. Venice it wasn't.

"What's the Pinch?" I felt compelled to inquire.

"It's where you live," said Avrom, wringing the end of a scraggly beard that often absorbed coffee and soup like a wick.

"What do you mean?" I figured he was being deliberately enigmatic. It was an aggravating habit of his.

"The Pinch. It's what they called the neighborhood around North Main Street. Used to be the old Jewish ghetto."

North Main Street was indeed where I lived, more or less, in a run-down railroad flat. It was to my knowledge the only occupied building (and I the only occupant) on an otherwise blighted street of abandoned structures and weed-choked vacant lots. At that point I began to fan the fawn-colored pages, browsing the weird illustrations and reading a line here and there. I could see at a glance that this was no conventional history. The language, for one thing, was fairly crude, the syntax somewhat out of whack, and nearly every phrase my eye lit on described some implausible event. Then, as was my custom, I flipped toward the end of the book. I began to peruse a passage in which a guy in a used book shop—a scrawny, hook-nosed dude named Lenny Sklarew—chances to open an undistinguished volume entitled *The Pinch*. I slammed shut the book.

"I'm a character!" I gasped.

"This is news?" said Avrom, dredging a hairy nostril with his pinkie.

"In this book. I'm a character in this book . . ."

Avrom thoughtfully inspected the matter on his finger while, trembling, I reopened the cover to the copyright page, which was absent. But on the title page, under the name of some press I never heard of, obviously a vanity outfit, was the publication date of 1952. It was currently 1968.

My heart was beating like a speed bag.

I had a thing in those days for offbeat books, especially ones written by outlaw authors hell-bent on destroying themselves at an early age. While that wasn't exactly my plan, neither did I rule out the possibility. Having washed out of college, I was waiting to be drafted and sometimes thought, mawkishly, that I might do for myself before the army got its turn. I was living a dead-end lifestyle, subsisting on cornflakes and beer and no end of illegal substances. A closet romantic, I liked to think I was putting myself in the way of wasting diseases, flirting with disaster. But somehow that piece of my generation's program to live fast and die young—the one where you succumbed to the ravages of wanton debauchery—continued to elude me. Though not technically a virgin, I tended to have a self-defeating line with the ladies, owing I supposed to a rabbity heart.

Anyway, I'm still standing there paralyzed in Avrom's shop.

"You can take it with you the book if you want," the old gent advised me.

Like I needed his permission. I'd already filched a whole library's worth of books (albeit under his nose) from his establishment, called a bit infelicitously The Book Asylum. They lay in toppled stacks along with the odd orange rind and reefer roach on the floor of my apartment.

"You don't seem to get it—" I began, since he was determined to ignore the colossal freakishness of my discovery.

"What's not to get?" he interrupted, infuriatingly.

"Avrom, I'm in the motherfucking book!"

"So nu?"

"So what does it *mean?*"

He pulled his Old Testment expression, the one where the wrinkles in his brow made a V like sergeant's stripes. "If you knew what means these things," he intoned, "you would rip down to the pupik your clothes for the grief of having lost in the first place this wisdom."

I gaped at him. "Oh, very helpful."

Avrom relaxed. "Boychik, you ain't in your farblundjit life doing squat." His pecan-shell eyelids were shut, which made me wonder if he was talking in his sleep. "So maybe in the book you're a hero."

Lying atop the heap of paperbacks on the floor of my apartment, that lackluster volume acquired a kind of hoodoo significance, like the sword in the stone or the bow that only Odysseus could draw. If I tried to open the book again, I might find the covers as immovable as the jaws of a trap. Then again, the jaws, yawning wide, might snap shut to swallow me whole.

It was February in the city of Memphis, matte gray and damp, the city stinking to high heaven in the throes of a garbage workers' strike. Plastic bags were piled in embankments on the sides of the streets like the body bags I'd have seen on the nightly news if I had a TV. Since much of my garbage was likely to accumulate in the apartment, and I was the only resident on the block, North Main Street was spared the mountains of refuse that burgeoned in other quarters. It smelled bad enough anyway, my street, what with its unflushed gutters and the fishy odor rising from the turgid river at the bottom of the bluff. The narrow two-story building I lived in, with its empty retail space on the ground floor, had been untenanted for years and probably should have been condemned. It stood on a corner next to an empty lot that bordered the jungle ruin of an old firehouse. My landlord, who was also my dealer, had purchased the building along with several others in the neighborhood with a view toward redevelopment, though nobody believed that would ever happen. In the meantime he'd had the street hooked up once again to the city's power grid, so I had faucets that coughed cold water, radiators that exuded no more warmth than expiring animals, lightbulbs that flickered like distant stars. For these amenities I was charged only pennies a month, as long as I also showed myself willing to peddle the landlord's unlawful wares.

The landlord, yclept Lamar Fontaine, liked to think of himself as an impresario. Toward that end he'd opened a seedy bar in another of his dilapidated properties directly opposite my apartment. My building and the bar were the only remaining signs of life on the street, unless you included the occasional raving derelict or river rat the size of a medicine ball. Because it had no name, the bar was referred to by its street address, the 348 North Main. Thanks to its reputation as a clearinghouse for all manner of illicit drugs, the 348 was a favorite port of call for what passed as the bohemian population of our provincial city. On any night of the week you were likely to see them: the knock-kneed, waifish girls with petals in their serpentine hair; the unshorn boys in leather vests and wire-rims, their glassy five-mile stares still visible through tinted lenses. You'd see me there too, guzzling Dixie beer and not-so-discreetly hawking Lamar's merchandise.

"Acid, mescaline, grass," I advertised sotto voce, though my voice tended to rise a decibel with every item I pronounced. "Nembies, bennies, crystal meth." I was a walking apothecary.

"You sure this stuff is pure?" my potential customer might ask, inspecting the tab of orange sunshine or windowpane in my sweaty palm.

"Pure as morning dew," I'd affirm, "if the dew was cut with a little strychnine." I couldn't tell a lie. But to reassure them I might pop a tablet into my mouth and chase it with a swig of beer.

Then I would look askance at Lamar, slouched at a table against the wall surveying his domain. He wore tropical suits even in winter and sported a drooping mustache, goatee, and shoulder-length chestnut hair like General Custer. A gentleman alcoholic, he drank whiskey from a silver hip flask, since the bar was only licensed to serve beer. A less scrupulous supervisor than old Avrom, he didn't seem to mind my unprofessional salesmanship; for all his pretensions he was a lousy businessman himself. He preferred being thought of more as a philanthropist than a merchant, so long as it was understood that I was his creature and the drugs had their source in him. Descended from old money, slaveholders, and cotton barons, Lamar liked to give the impression that his funds were unlimited. Whatever I rendered unto him when I turned out my pockets at the end of an evening, he considered gravy. Still, I made an effort after my fashion. I was grateful to him for the goods I was allowed to sample free of charge, to say nothing of the excuse the job gave me to approach the ladies.

On the night in question I'd already alienated several. When, for instance, a Pre-Raphaelite-looking young woman failed to guess my name (she hadn't actually tried), I introduced myself as Rumpleforeskin, to which she replied unamused, "Funny man." I asked another if she would like to swap her honor for some magic beans, and got a similar response. I knew, of course, that my brand of patter (call it a tic) was more apt to offend than intrigue, but if I disqualified myself first, you couldn't say I'd been outright rejected by the girl of the moment.

I had chased an assortment of pills with a couple of beers and was feeling pretty frisky when I saw her. She was a touch more put-together than the usual run of hippie talent in the bar. Her nose was of the chiseled variety (think Nefertiti), her umber eyes given to a feline narrowing when she spoke. Her hair was that shade of blue-black called "raven" in gothic novels, its texture fine as record vinyl. It was done up in a schoolmarmish twist, unlike the free-flowing tresses of the liberated types that swayed near the jukebox or conspired at the tables. Also, this one—when she'd removed her coat—was wearing a burgundy dress, a slinky vintage number at odds with the prevailing hip-huggers and miniskirts. A tourist, I concluded dismissively. She was engaged in lively conversation with a compact character in a navy blazer and a loosened necktie. He was smooth-shaven, with a shock of strawberry hair that hung like a breaking wave over an earnest eye.

I had hair like a burnt shrub.

"Acid, mescaline, grass," I interjected.

"No thanks," the dude replied, scarcely bothering to look in my direction. To his date he continued asserting, "Mayor Loeb will never cave in to their demands."

"But don't you think the mediation of the clergy will have an effect?" she wondered, batting her eyes contrarily. "They've got a pressure group that includes ministers and priests, even a rabbi—"

"The strike is illegal, Rachel. The city can't negotiate with the union until the men go back to work."

"Blue cheer, purple haze . . ." I persisted, which finally got the guy's attention.

"Excuse me, we're having a private conversation here."

I nodded in sympathy till he turned away, but still couldn't bring myself to stop eavesdropping on their exchange.

"Who cares if it's legal, Dennis?" the girl Rachel was saying with some impatience. "I'm talking about fundamental injustice."

"And I'm talking about strikers in contempt of the Chancery Court. Their union is outside the jurisdiction of the National Labor Relations Board—"

"There used to be a slave auction just down the street," I offered. I had this tidbit on Avrom's authority and thought it somehow demonstrated evidence of my social conscience.

Dennis turned back to me with a poisonous glare. He was very self-possessed for such a runty guy. "And this is relevant to what?" he asked.

"Also a tree that was used for lynchings." The tree was my own invention.

Rachel tilted her imperial head inquisitively.

"Exactly what part of 'fuck off' don't you understand?" wondered Dennis.

"Sorry," I said, but something about the girl (her flaring nostrils? the hand on a slightly canted hip?) kept me glued to the spot.

When I didn't move, Dennis feigned interest. "Just what kind of a nitwit are you?"

"I'm a pair of ragged claws scuttling across the floors of silent seas."

Dennis sniffed. "Oh, an English major," was his derisive verdict. He turned away again, satisfied that he'd effectively put me in my place.

Continuing his defense of the municipality, he cited various health hazards that rotting garbage might breed: "Typhoid, cholera . . . ," counting off diseases on his fingers as Rachel made an effort to listen. But I could tell she was growing annoyed with him. As he persisted in ignoring

my presence, I took the occasion to revise his original judgment, aware
that I was crossing beyond a point of no return.

"Lapsed," I said.

He never looked at me, but Rachel did, once again staring quizzically.

"Lapsed English major," I clarified for her sake. Then I thought I saw
the ghost of a smile flit across the girl's soft-hued face. That was all it
took to light a pilot in the hollow of my rib cage. The unembellished barroom held a complementary warmth that made me feel as if its occupants
were sheltering from a storm, though there was nothing but an icy drizzle
outside. A lemony, fin de siécle–style ambience enfolded the place: I saw
absinthe drinkers at the tables, the barmaid a dead ringer for the one in
the painting by Manet. The chemicals were being gentle with me tonight.

"Reform takes time," Dennis was explaining, his tone level and in-
structive, but his voice broke off abruptly when he noticed that Rachel was
no longer listening. He followed her gaze toward the object she seemed
to be taking the measure of, that being myself. "And until the strike is
resolved," he said, raising his voice to make sure he was heard, "trash like
this"—indicating me with his chin—"will remain uncollected."

"And rats like you will grow fat from the swill."

The remark cleared my lips without premeditation, and while it admittedly didn't make much sense, it nevertheless had the ring of a rapier-
like rejoinder in my ear. Not always so fast on my feet, I was pleased with
myself. In the event, I didn't anticipate what came next, which was that
Dennis, pint-sized as he was, knocked me down. He dispatched me handily with a one-two punch that consisted of an uppercut to the solar plexus
and a roundhouse to the skull: I saw asteroids and imagined exes marking
the spots that were my eyes, as the floor rose up to smack me as well.

What followed after that didn't figure in any category of possibility I
understood. Because, when the pain had dulled enough to let me draw
breath again, I found that my head was cradled against Rachel's genu-
flected knees. I heard sharp words exchanged between her and her date:
he telling her in effect that she must choose between him and me. "What
cornball script are you reading from?" she barked back at him, after which
he flung a parting oath and was apparently gone.

Then, before a dozen onlookers who probably assumed I'd gotten what
I deserved, she offered an apology. "I'm sorry," she said, releasing an essence like vanilla roses. The bar had grown silent but for the jukebox playing

a rock anthem by Iron Butterfly. "He's a bit of a hothead sometimes," she explained.

Despite my acute discomfort, I felt jealous: *I* wanted to be the hothead. At the same time, humiliation notwithstanding, I was enjoying the humid warmth of her thighs through the thin fabric of her dress. The blood that pulsed so percussively in my temples throbbed as well in remoter parts. I opened wide the eye that wasn't already beginning to swell shut and asked her, God help me, if she'd ever been mounted by a troll. The cushion of her thighs was abruptly removed from under me as she got hastily to her feet, leaving my head to bounce on the sticky hardwood floor. Seeing that I was still prostrate, however, she relented, and with a charity that surpassed understanding leaned over to drag me upright and back to my feet.

With the drama ended, the bar's clientele had retired to their tables, while Rachel and I remained facing each other awkwardly in the center of the room. When she released my sleeve, I began to teeter perhaps more than my actual dizziness warranted, so that she grabbed me again to keep me from keeling over. Then, having steadied me, she let go and wiped her palm on her dress as a prelude—no doubt—to washing her hands of me entirely. I started to teeter again. Out of the corner of my good eye I caught sight of Lamar, whose shit-eating smirk I interpreted as a kind of benediction.

"Could you maybe help me across the street?" I asked her, having as I saw it nothing to lose.

"What are you, blind?"

"I live across the street."

"Nobody lives around here."

I made a face to suggest that it wasn't exactly living.

With a put-upon sigh, she fastened an arm round my shoulder and escorted me out of the bar and over the road; then having come that far, she assisted me the rest of the way up the steep flight of stairs to my apartment. My brain was pounding like a tom-tom, my ribs bruised if not broken, but the rubber legs were pure theater. At the top of the stairs I pushed open the unlocked door with a knee.

"Welcome to Xanadu," I said contritely.

What hit you first on entering the apartment was an odor of gamy clothing so keen it stung the retina. When your eyes grew accustomed to their watering, you could make out the few items of furniture I'd salvaged from sidewalks and dustbins in the vicinity. In fact, the garbage strike had provided me with some odd late additions: a cardboard wardrobe, a slashed bucket seat. For all the radiator's Gatling-gun clamor, the place remained chilly. There was an unshaded bulb hanging from the concave ceiling, a fleabag mattress on the floor near the windows, and the tumulus of books in the middle of the room. They looked, the books, like a pyre awaiting the burning of a heretic.

Rachel dumped me unceremoniously on the mattress. I fully expected her to disregard my unsubtle groaning and depart, but instead she began to pick her way toward the kitchen. The *shush* of her stockinged calves brushing against one other was the rhythmic respiration of an angel. She returned with a dirty sock full of ice cubes that might have resided in that ancient refrigerator since the Pleistocene age. She offered me the sock (whose stiffness she may have detected) like you'd dangle a dead mouse by the tail.

"Hold this over your eye."

I sat on the mattress with my back against the windowsill, amazed at having lured a mortal woman into my digs. Affected though I was, I felt a little like her guilty captor, and as her captor it was my reluctant obligation, now that her duty was done, to let her go. Still she lingered in her tweed coat buttoned to the throat, observing the mound of books like an obstacle she had to climb over to reach the door. She nudged them with the toe of her boot as if stirring embers.

"Is it just a coincidence that so many of these authors killed themselves?" she wanted to know.

I smiled my idea of a dangerous smile. "I like your accent," I said. "Where are you from?"

Her expression was the perfect mixture of curiosity and disdain. "Are you trying to make conversation?"

Something in her tone of voice opened a tiny porthole of lucidity in my brain, through which I spied my little life in all its squalor. Then the porthole slammed shut and I smiled again, albeit sheepishly.

"I have to go," she announced abruptly though she continued to study the pile. Then she stooped to pick up a book, *the* book. "This one looks like somebody's bound dissertation."

"Don't touch it!" I blurted, starting up from the mattress but constrained by my aching ribs.

She dropped it like a live coal.

"It's a cursed book," I alleged.

"What are you talking about?"

"It's . . . I stole it from the library of a satanist."

With absolute confidence she assured me, "No you didn't."

"He was rumored to perform human sacrifice," I added. She rolled her eyes and I promptly changed the subject. "So, what do you do?"

Rachel peered at me as if trying to decide what species I belonged to, then shook her head in perplexity. "You're some piece of work," she concluded matter-of-factly. Then just as flatly she told me, "I grew up in Larchmont, New York. I came to Memphis on a grant from the Mid-South Folklore Center to research the roots of the Southern Jewish community. Dennis is my fiancé, sort of, and I only stayed with you because I was mad at him. So why am I still standing here in this pesh"—for she'd had some wine this evening—"pesthole?"

Ignoring her question, I submitted, "*I'm* a Jew," though the fact had not occurred to me for some time.

"Oh well," she said, her voice dripping irony, "that makes all the difference." There was a moment when her eyes narrowed like Lauren Bacall's, her mind gnawing a thought. Then she seemed to have reached some kind of decision, because she unbuttoned her overcoat, allowing it to drop onto the floor among the empty medicine vials. She began to walk toward me as far as the edge of the mattress upon which she knelt, raising a small cloud of dust. Unclasping a barrette, she shook out her hair so that it spilled like India ink over her forehead and shoulders. She had almost no waist at all. "So you'd like to defile me?" she teased, alluding, I guessed, to my unfortunate pickup line from the bar.

I tried to swallow but it seemed that my Adam's apple was caught in my windpipe. Watching me, her large eyes grew even wider.

"You're scared of girls, aren't you!" she declared, obviously delighted. She shoved me backward onto the mattress, paying no attention to my injuries. "Ouch!" I cried as, laughing, she wrested the soggy sock from my hand and twirled it coquettishly before tossing it over a shoulder. Asterisks of light from the unshaded bulb played in her glossy hair. When she lifted the hem of her dress to straddle me, I saw how the mauve stockings stopped at the top of her tender, goosefleshed thighs. There was a rustling, a fumbling, my heart pumping warm molasses in place of blood.

All of creation seemed to have gathered in my pants, which had been shoved to my ankles. Then a mournful cry escaped my lips as my excitement ranneth over.

"Oh dear," said Rachel, and daintily patted her mouth in a yawn.

I awoke sometime in the night to the sound of the rain tattooing the filmy window. Outside there was neither joy nor peace nor help from pain, while here beneath this sagging roof I held a live woman in my arms. "I will love you till I die," I whispered experimentally in her ear. Whether she heard me or not I can't say, but she stirred and asked herself sleepily, "What am I doing here?" Then she bolted from the bed dragging the blanket along with her, which left me naked and shivering. Cursing under her breath, she stumbled about the room in the dark retrieving her stray clothing. I hugged my knees to my chest and, recalling the subject of her research project, informed her with some urgency, "This was the old Jewish ghetto." "It's called the Pinch," I said, though she hadn't asked. "This neighborhood, the Pinch."

Hesitating, her spectral silhouette framed in the open doorway, she wondered aloud, "What's your name?" Then on second thought: "Never mind, I don't want to know."

When she'd fled the apartment I got up and switched on the overhead light, its harshness turning the room aggressively real. I wrapped myself in the blanket that still carried her fragrance, sat down on the slanting floor, and opened Muni Pinsker's book to its beginning. Then I started to read for the purpose of gathering information that might interest Rachel in case I should see her again.

◢2◣
Welcome to the Pinch

On a sweltering August afternoon in 1911, Muni Pinsker, listing from the weight of his battered grip, entered Pin's General Merchandise on North Main Street in Memphis, Tennessee. He was bedraggled and bone weary, having journeyed to America all the way from the mica mines of Nerchinsk in eastern Siberia, where he'd been exiled. The store smelled of pickles and kerosene, its floorboards creaking as did the ceiling fans. Shelves spilled quilting and cotton petticoats; sock garters and suspenders hung like limp rainbows on wooden racks. There was a display case containing a regiment of back scratchers, cutthroat razors, and hand-carved briar pipes. Behind a counter stood a shortish man in a waistcoat and apron, with a distinctively hooked nose and coarse, sandy hair. He was closing the drawer of a gilded cash register beside which stood a jar of hard candy, when he squinted over his nickel spectacles at the wayworn newcomer. Then he peered beyond the newcomer at a gangle-shanked character in bib overalls, who had shambled into the store behind Muni. The man grinned a gap-toothed grin, his eyes dull as pearl onions, while the contents of the burlap sack that was slung over his shoulder appeared to be squirming. He shouted something in the native tongue that Muni had only begun to learn and started to empty his sack, out of which tumbled a braided black clump. The clump plopped onto the sawdusted floor, where half a dozen serpents uncoiled and began to slither in all directions like runneling oil.

"Rabbi Eliakum," called the shopkeeper in a marvelously unexcited voice.

A stout old man with heavy-lidded, bloodhound eyes and a beard like a grizzled gray broom left off inspecting a lightweight union suit to turn around. He studied the snakes a moment as if attempting to discern a message in their undulations, some signal from the glint of their fangs.

Then he pronounced in a throaty Hebrew, "Woe unto the man who meets up with a venomous lizard," and in an earthier Yiddish, "and woe unto the venomous lizard that meets Eliakum ben Yahya."

Whereupon the rabbi lifted his eyes toward the beaten tin ceiling and passed a palsied hand above the serpents, which abruptly ceased their slithering, becoming ramrod stiff. They were converted in fact into a clutch of perfectly serviceable walking sticks, which the shopkeeper, coming from around his counter, gathered up and dumped into an umbrella stand alongside several other mahogany canes.

The gangling man let loose a hysterical whoop and slapped his knee before exiting the store. The old rabbi, perspiring freely beneath the fur shtreimel he wore despite the August heat, patted his forehead with a folded hankie, said "Good Shabbos," and departed as well. The shopkeeper turned back to the newcomer, who had fainted dead away.

Muni came to in a kitchen chair in the apartment over the store to which the shopkeeper and his wife had dragged him. The shopkeeper, his brow deeply furrowed, was fanning Muni's face with a rag, as his wife came forward to offer the young man a cup of tea. Muni stared at the steaming liquid on the table and wondered: Where were you when the wind had teeth? Because that insufferably stuffy kitchen was not conducive to the partaking of hot beverages. Thanking her nonetheless, he drank and the bitterness began to revive him.

"Oy," he sighed, "iz doos a mekhayeh." Which, roughly translated, meant: I forgot I was alive.

That was the cue for the shopkeeper to drop into the chair beside him, falling upon Muni's neck and jerking the young man's tousled head to his breast. "Your uncle Pinchas welcomes you to the Pinch," he cried. "Katie, give a keek on my dead brother's son, Muni Pinsker, that he looks, thanks God, like his mother."

Muni peered out from his uncle's headlock at Pinchas's wife, who smiled a tight-lipped smile, winked a jaunty eye, and tucked a strand of auburn hair fading to gray behind an ear. She admonished her husband to give the boy space to breathe, then spooned some mashed concoction from a pot on the coal-burning range into a bowl which she placed before the wanderer. Almost too tired to eat, Muni took (once his uncle had released him) a few gummy bites out of courtesy, while Pinchas apologized for the scene his nephew had witnessed below. "The goyim, they like to play on us tricks," he said, though Muni was already vague regarding the reference; his head was much too full of actual memories to admit the inadmissible. "They like to see the rebbe do his kishef, his magic."

"Magic," repeated Muni, testing the word on his tongue as if it were also a morsel of food. He made a face as if the word were not to his taste.

Ignoring his wife's token appeals to give the boy time to gather his wits, Pinchas peppered him with questions concerning his odyssey. But whether from aversion or fatigue, his nephew was frustratingly taciturn in his account: "I walked, I rode, I sailed, I rode, I walked," he shrugged. "I arrived." Though he had as yet no real sense of having reached a destination.

Then it was evening and they showed him to the closet-sized room they'd prepared for him, the first room of his own that Muni had ever known. He expressed his appreciation for everything, because he did indeed owe them everything, and collapsed onto the narrow camp bed, but he could not sleep. His heart was still keeping time to his interminable forward progress, and the suffocating heat pressed the air from his lungs with a whine like a squeezebox. Stripped to his drawers, he told himself that his sweat was the arctic rime melting from his bones, but he was ashamed to be thus saturating the clean sheets. He tried to comfort himself with the thought that at last he was beyond the long arm of the czar's police, but unable to relax, he rose and went to the open window to try and catch a breeze.

The full orange moon above the alley illumined a girl dancing in midair. Muni, however, was not deceived; he was accustomed to hallucination, having seen many things that were not there during the long hibernal ordeal of his travels. But look again and he observed that, rather than treading air, the girl—her dusky hair done up in a loose topknot, the strong limbs visible beneath her flimsy chemise—was bobbing barefoot on a rope. It was a slender, sagging rope, perhaps a clothesline, and the girl was balanced precariously upon it, wobbling a bit under the open parasol she was holding. She was staring at him, eyes wide and mouth open in an astonishment that Muni took exception to, since he was the one that ought to be astonished. Then he remembered that he was nearly naked and dove back into the bed.

"This Pinch is a primitive place and all its citizens pig-ignorant," Pinchas Pin informed his long-lost nephew over the kitchen table, but Muni was paying scant attention. He'd heard the appraisal often enough over the course of the past few days, and besides, he was busily involved in eating a fresh bialy from Ridblatt's Bakery. The roll was so warm and fragrant, its texture airy as cobweb, that he might have thought it had a holy component—that is, if he'd still set any store by holiness. "There ain't no superstition that they don't accept it's true," continued his uncle, speaking mostly in Yiddish for his nephew's sake, though the English locutions kept creeping in. "They don't none of them share the progressive views of scholars like me and you."

Muni ceased chewing a moment to register the compliment with a wistful smile. There was a time when he might have been flattered to be included in Pinchas's exclusive circle; his uncle was after all not without a degree of learning. But now this estimation only amused him. Having returned to society after so many years in perdition, Muni no longer knew what views he held. He only knew that it was a relief to stop awhile and catch his breath, even in such a malarial swamp as Memphis, America. For Muni one swamp would do as well as another, and the bite of mosquitoes was a fair enough exchange for the vicious bite of the frost in the taiga east of Irkutsk. Still, Pinchas's running catalog of complaints was a mixed invitation.

"It ain't bad enough you got in their sheets the yokels that are scaring the pants off the schwartzes," he went on, his English edging out the Yiddish until Muni could scarcely comprehend, "but these Yossel-come-latelies, I'm talking now the Shpinker Hasidim, they got yet to go and monkey with the fabric of time. In most places the days of the week that they follow one after the other, but here you get sometimes a Tuesday contains also elements from Monday and Wednesday. You get the minute that stretches like taffy candy to an hour. This is not chronological; it ain't any kind of logical."

Muni scratched his scalp in a show of thoughtfulness and felt how his once thick pelt of hair stood up now in stiff licks and patches since his aunt Katie had trimmed it. Though she was technically his aunt, it was hard to think of the tall, comely woman (a head taller than her husband) as a relation. This was due in part to the fact that she was a gentile, in part because she still seemed so girlish despite her years. There was a mischief, if somewhat laced with melancholy, that played about her zinc-green eyes. With such reckless impetuosity had she flicked her scissors through his hair that he feared she might remove the top of his skull like an egg in a cup. Like the yarmulke he'd exchanged for the worker's peaked cap in his student days. When he glanced in a mirror afterward—his first glimpse into a mirror in recent memory—he saw a stranger whose weather-seared features appeared as if mocked by a crown of cropped liver-brown feathers.

"A cockleburr," his aunt had judged, standing arms akimbo behind him.

As for Pinchas, he was entitled to think what he pleased; he was after all the pioneer Ashkenaz of North Main Street. What's more, he had in large part footed the bill for Muni's flight from the Siberian waste; he'd provided him with a destination, however unrpromising, and even a job. At first the nephew had protested his uncle's extravagant generosity; he owed him too much already: "You got here your hands full just to make ends meet."

But Pinchas pooh-poohed him. "Es mach nit oys, don't think that by you I'm doing no favors." In the first place he couldn't afford to pay the greenhorn a regular salary; all he could offer him was an outsize closet to sleep in and Katie's stodgy meals. "The truth of the matter is that you will be my slave."

As servitude was a condition that Muni understood, he took the joke seriously, vowing to stay and work off a debt that his uncle dismissed as null and void. He made himself more than useful, humping sacks of flour and grinding coffee, unpacking denim overalls until his fingers turned blue from the dye. Sometimes, when his uncle was otherwise engaged, he even waited on customers, some of whom had entered the store out of curiosity. They were eager to catch a glimpse of the immigrant who'd come to North Main from the shores of oblivion. (Once when Muni had alluded to feeling like a bit of a spectacle, Pinchas chided him: "You ain't so special. Is alive, the Pinch, with people used to be dead.") He ate his aunt's clotted variations on boiled potatoes and slept the troubled sleep that had yet to relieve his weariness, interrupted as it was by trips to the window to watch the girl who walked on air.

He saw her in the street as well, but there she was different. Sinewy and slight, she still managed to be somehow ungainly, clopping heedlessly along the sidewalk in her apron dress and button shoes. Sometimes she grazed the lampposts and failed to dodge passersby. He spied her through the plate glass of Rosen's Delicatessen, where she waited tables, spilling seltzer and colliding with customers so often that she apologized in advance. Her name was Jenny Bashrig, an awkward girl who had nothing in common with the one that danced on the wire. With her tapered nose, sardonic lips, and the unraveling skein of her sable hair, she seemed altogether earthbound. In fact, Muni wouldn't even have recognized her had he not caught her staring back at him from the other side of Rosen's window with the wire walker's sloe-black eyes. Then he wondered if she was clumsy or just careless when at large on a planet whose surface she saved all of her grace for rising above.

She was an orphan, Jenny, whose parents had drowned in a steamboat accident near Helena, Arkansas, en route to Memphis from the city of New Orleans. (This much Muni had learned from his aunt, of whom he'd inquired about the girl while at the same time feigning disinterest.) Fished from the river more dead than alive, the child had regurgitated, along with the turbid water from her lungs, a single syllable, the one she'd heard on her parents' lips since they'd left Zlotopol: "Pinch," she squeaked, and after much consternation on the part of her rescuers, who passed her from hand to hand, it was suggested that her utterance implied not an action but a place. Ever since, she had been a virtual ward of North Main Street. But while the entire neighborhood claimed her, Jenny had struck the attitude from early on that she belonged to no one but herself. The Rosen family, distant relations who'd anticipated the Bashrigs' arrival, had provided the girl with a roof and, when she was old enough, a nominal livelihood. But though she demonstrated her gratitude through dutiful drudgery, she never suppressed her independent streak; she remained a creature apart, barely educated and prone to undomestic habits. Muni supposed their status as outsiders was not so dissimilar, which was perhaps why she held a certain fascination for him. But while the interest seemed to some extent mutual, he had so far resisted any real exchange with the girl. With the exception of his aunt and uncle, the greenhorn still kept himself aloof from one and all.

On a sultry September morning, after they'd finished their breakfast, Muni and his uncle went downstairs as usual to open the store. Fastening his apron strings behind his back, Pinchas took up his familiar refrain.

"The Shpinker rebbe, old ben Yahya—a crackpot," he groused. "The man claims to go each evening in heaven where with the Baal Shem Tov he studies Torah." Persisting in his censure, he no longer troubled to translate the words his nephew was gradually becoming acquainted with. Muni was learning as well to take his uncle's grievances with a grain of salt. Hadn't he observed how the storekeeper found such frequent excuses to draw the rebbe into religious disputes? True, they tended to be one-sided arguments, since Rabbi Eliakum largely held his peace. The old man seemed bemused by the freethinker's capacity to remain unbelieving in the face of such practical demonstrations of the indwellingness of the divine. Today, however, after unlocking the front door, Muni was seized by a rogue impulse to call the proprietor's bluff.

"So Uncle, why do you stay?"

Pinchas Pin, né Pinsker, the suffix having dropped off like a vestigial tail since his arrival on North Main, was taken aback. "Stay where?"

"Here in the Pinch."

Pinchas looked at his nephew as if he were mad, and in one of those per-plexing statements that Muni was growing so accustomed to, declared, "There ain't no place else."

Shortly after, a colored man entered the store. Despite the caveats of the local Klan lest they set an unseemly precedent, the so-called Jew stores along North Main Street had no policy against trading with Negroes. Business was business. Most of the city's colored clientele, however, did their shopping south of the Pinch on rowdy Beale Street. So it wasn't unusual that, when a schwartze came into a North Main establishment, some irate customer might raise an objection. Such was the case this morning, when a pear-shaped matron left off sampling a bolt of percale in order to alert the proprietor to the fact that "there's a nigra in your store."

Pinchas looked up from replacing the drawer of his till, which he closed with a pleasing *click-ching*. He squinted over his eyeglasses at the black man, who was also wearing spectacles, round ones with smoky lenses, while tapping the floorboards before him with a rattan cane. In a stage whisper the storekeeper replied to the woman, "This one is blind, so maybe he don't know he's colored."

Shooing the little boy in her charge out the door in front of her, the woman indignantly exited the general store.

Muni had to laugh, a rare occurrence. During the weeks in his uncle's employ, he'd seen Pinchas indulge any number of drifters and bindle stiffs, some of whom he invited to stay for a plate of Katie's glutinous spuds. Muni recalled the Old Country custom of suspecting that every stranger might be the prophet Elijah in disguise, and so entreating him to share a Shabbos meal, but Pinchas was the sworn enemy of all such grand-mothers' tales.

"What for you can I do?" the storekeeper inquired of the Negro, who had stationed himself between the fabric counter and a flatware rack. He was an old fellow in a floppy hat, his hollow cheeks fretted with cracks like muddy sinkholes. He wore a collarless white shirt gone dun-drab with age and an ancient spiketail coat that gave him the aspect of a draggled crow. Muni, for whom black people were still a novelty, calculated that the man was old enough to have been born into bondage.

"Do y'all got a mite of catgut?" he asked in his sandpaper voice.

Pinchas had all kinds of gut, as well as yarn, twine, mason's and fish-ing line, kite string and shoestring, plaited rope. He asked the man how much he needed and was told " 'bout a footstep," which the storekeeper proceeded to unwind from a spool and snip with a pair of shears. He held out the curling catgut to the Negro until he remembered the man couldn't see. Approaching him, he took the cane from his fingers, tucked it under the man's damp armpit, and folded the gut into his leathery hand. The man thanked him kindly and, clenching the gut between his couple of buff-yellow teeth, reached into the gunnysack he carried in his other hand. He withdrew what looked at first glance like a hunk of driftwood but proved on closer inspection to be a violin, a rough and rustic relation of the original instrument. Feeling for the edge of the counter, he laid the instrument tenderly atop the hill of fabric, like an infant he was preparing to diaper. Then the blind man deftly replaced the missing string, turning the pegs at the scroll end to tighten it, plucking it until he was satisfied with the sound.

"Let's see can I play y'all gentlemens a tune," he said, stooping to remove a bow from his sack. Bracing the violin under his bristly chin, he began to saw the strings, while loose hairs from the bow tossed like the mane of the horse they were shorn from.

Muni's experience of fiddlers was limited to the vagabond musicians he'd heard at shtetl weddings as a boy, and so he expected something lively. Perhaps a jig with a foot-stomping rhythm that expressed the vi-tality of a people who, common wisdom had it, were a fundamentally happy lot. But this tune, if you could call it a tune, was achingly sorrowful. There were brief melodic moments, but no sooner did you begin to relax with a lyrical phrase than the music turned plaintive again. Muni wondered if the musician had simply failed to master his instrument, a judgment his uncle—clapping his hands over his ears—seemed also to have made. In rejecting the serenade, Pinchas appeared to disregard as well the presence in his store of the blacksmith's shifty son Hershel, a well-known ganef, a petty thief. Muni had been told to be on the lookout for the kid—a needle-nosed gowk in knee pants and jockey's cap—but he was too diverted by the music to pay him any heed. Though the fiddling transported him to a place he didn't especially want to go, he was helpless to resist being carried away.

Then the Negro ceased playing as abruptly as he'd begun and asked the storekeeper what he owed him. Pinchas made a dismissive sign—the recital was compensation enough—but as the blind man was insensible to signs, the storekeeper came forward to escort him ("Name's Asbestos") from the premises. Behind them, his shirt bulging with pilfered loot, slipped young Hershel Tarnopol.

Thereafter the blind man with the unlikely name became a fixture in the neighborhood. Novak the pawnbroker, who ran a shop on Beale Street, remembered having seen him playing on various corners down there. So why relocate from the district where he belonged to one where he was plainly, so to speak, out of tune? Did he mean to provide, with his unearthly oratorios, a kind of somber complement to the otherwise vibrant commercial racket of North Main? Because the blind man's music served as a frequent counterpoint to the three-toned horn on Sam Alabaster's touring car; it challenged the clangor of the trolley bells and the palaver of Leon Shapiro enticing passersby into his emporium to be measured for a suit of clothes. It was an antidote to the ecstatic ululation of the disciples of Rabbi Eliakum ben Yahya, gathered of an evening in Market Square Park to say the blessing over the new moon. And though he couldn't have said why, Muni Pinsker never passed him without dropping a little spare change if he had any into the fiddler's felt hat, which was generally brimming with coins.

"It says here," cited Pinchas from behind his upraised journal, spectacles sliding down the slope of his nose, "they got in the new State Duma in

Saint Petersburg deputies that they represent four Jewish parties." Pinchas tried conscientiously to stay abreast of events in his mother country, subscribing to a paper he had sent all the way from New York. In this way he had followed, if some weeks after the fact, the failed Russian revolution of 1905 and the ensuing pogroms, the trial for blood libel of the brick maker Mendel Beilis. When he wasn't griping about the intrusion of the uncanny into the quotidian life of the neighborhood, he was hopeful about prospects for the downfall of the czar. He looked forward to the impending establishment of an international socialist utopia. It was clear, however, that he was disappointed when his nephew, despite his own afflicted history, did not readily share his uncle's political enthusiasms. Muni showed little more interest in such goings-on, in fact, than did his aunt Katie, who merely smiled indulgently at her husband's theorizing as she carried on peeling potatoes.

Still, Muni was sorry that he couldn't find it in himself to better accommodate his uncle Pinchas; there was a time when he would have responded zealously to the shopkeeper's concerns. Hadn't he tried, during his imprisonment in Minsk and later Moscow, to stay informed about the seditious happenings in the streets? But privation and hunger and the coffled march across an icebound continent had distanced him from the once overriding importance of the Marxist dream. Now he felt not the least temptation to take down the fat volume of *Das Kapital* from his uncle's overstuffed bookshelf; nor was he drawn to the other staples of his insurgent years: neither Darwin nor Auguste Comte or the Yiddish editions of Tolstoy and Edward Bellamy, which elbowed aside Pinchas's copies of *The Ethics* and the Shulkhan Arukh. Of course, if Muni were honest, he would have had to admit that a thirst for social reform had never been his original impetus. It was perhaps simply his guilt over the lack of a passion for change that had compelled him to act so audaciously, to declare after refusing legal counsel at his trial, "I am a member of the Jewish Revolutionary Federation, and I will do everything in my power to overthrow the czarist autocracy and its bloody henchmen!" Which had thus sealed his fate.

Muni could hardly remember the person who'd shouted those words so defiantly in that Moscow courtroom. Bereft now of ideology, even curiosity, he felt nothing when looking back but a deep lassitude. There was little that engaged his interest—though now and again some character out of the cavalcade that passed through the general merchandise might briefly capture his attention. He might look up an instant from sweeping the floor to observe Mrs. Gruber the bootlegger, accompanied by her flame-bearded familiar Lazar der Royte, as she waddled in to purchase a sack of corn. Or the chapfallen Mr. and Mrs. Padauer, widely regarded in the Pinch as objects of pity, holding the hand of a toddler who resembled a wizened old man. Or Jenny Bashrig, upsetting a pyramid of butter churns as she gazed at Muni with unblinking black satin eyes. (Once or twice she had inquired of him concerning the use of a nickeled emasculator or fly powder in a bellows box, items whose utility Muni had no knowledge of nor Jenny any intention of purchasing.) There was Hershel Tarnopol, scamp, liar, and thief, whose petty pilfering was largely tolerated in deference to his talent for sleight of hand; and Rabbi ben Yahya and his disciples, some of whom entered the store trailing bits of rope they'd neglected to remove from their ankles. These were the strands they tied to furniture and doorknobs during prayers lest they levitate beyond a height of easy return.

It was nearly sundown on the first evening of Rosh Hashanah, the beginning of the Days of Awe, and the population of North Main was heading en masse toward Catfish Bayou. A stagnant inlet of the Mississippi only a few blocks north of the Pinch, the bayou was the site where Irish refugees from the Great Potato Famine had beached their johnboats decades ago. They had dismantled the square-ended boats to build makeshift shanties, some of which still stood, or rather leaned, though they'd long been abandoned by their previous tenants and taken over by destitute Negroes. The Irish had since emerged from the muck around the bayou to become the original inhabitants of North Main Street, which was then a lawless corridor atop the river bluff called Smoky Row. Their pinch-gutted countenances were the source of the neighborhood's eventual name. Muni had been cajoled by his uncle to come along and enjoy a spectacle that Pinchas regarded as yet another example of his neighbors' quaint delusions. Katie held Pinchas's hand as they walked, sashaying more like a sweetheart than a veteran wife, though her winsomeness seemed a trifle subdued to her nephew tonight.

"In this hekdish, this sink, was my Katie raised," explained Pinchas, indicating the marshy banks surrounding the brackish body of water; for the dredging of the river had reduced the once broad bayou to an overgrown cowpond. But Katie was quick to contradict him, recalling the hand-to-mouth childhood that Muni had heard her ruefully allude to more than once. "It was a paradise."

Their neighbors had come together to perform the tashlikh ritual, which involved emptying one's pockets of the breadcrumbs you'd stuffed them with and casting them upon the waters. The crumbs were meant to symbolize the sins you'd committed during the past year. It was supposed to be a solemn ceremony, but the cadre of citizens parading past the old auction block at Jackson Avenue had about them a carnival attitude. They gossiped and joked (Mr. Sebranig to his wife: "How about a bissel henky-penk after?" His wife: "Over my dead body." Mr. Sebranig: "How else?"), accompanied by the Widow Teitelbaum's windup gramophone, which she hauled behind her in a little wagon. The gramophone played a medley of Victor Herbert standards plus the Jazarimba Orchestra's exotic rendition of "Ain't We Got Fun." When the music began to drag, the broad-bottomed widow would pause to crank her machine, looking as she leaned toward the speaker in her blowsy apricot frock like a bee at the mouth of a trumpet flower. Rabbi ben Yahya and his knot of disciples in their holiday gabardines brought up the rear, beating their shallow breasts and singing wordless niggunim.

"Ay yay bim bom yiddle diddle do . . ."

Once they'd arrived at the bayou—the mud along its bank alive with polliwogs, ooze sucking at the soles of their shoes—some began reading psalms by the failing light. The five Alabaster children were enjoined by their papa to sprinkle generous portions of crumbs on the water, as if a multitude of sins were a proof of their prosperity. Old Ephraim Schneour scattered, instead of pumpernickel crusts, the ashes of the wife he'd abused for half a century, spreading them like a man sowing seed. Looking forlornly at one another over the head of the ill-favored child that stood between them, Mr. and Mrs. Padauer heaved a mutual sigh, having perhaps decided to throw bread in place of the boy. Jenny Bashrig tossed a few crumbs, only to have a breeze blow them back into her face, which she turned toward Muni, her soft eyes beginning to tear from the motes that had settled therein.

Hershel Tarnopol hopped excitedly in his patched plus fours beside his bullnecked father, whose volatile temper seemed uncharacteristically restrained this evening. He was carrying a lump of dough the size of a bowling ball, which, without ceremony, he flung toward the murky pond. The dough was still in the air when a huge pewter fish with scales like a coat of mail broke the surface, stretching its mouth impossibly wide to swallow the ball then diving back into the water with a mighty splash. "Mazel tov, Papa!" shouted Hershel, doing a squelchy hornpipe while the blacksmith, slumped in his undershirt, looked as spent as if he'd rolled aside the stone from his tomb.

At a signal from their baggy-eyed rebbe, the Shpinkers released from their slingshots a blizzard of ryebread crumbs that caused an equivalent storm of hungry blackbirds to swoop toward the bayou. "Grandstanders," sneered Pinchas in disgust, swatting a mosquito at his neck with his open palm. Then his eyes strayed beyond the water to an out-of-step phalanx approaching from the Shadyac Avenue side of the bay. It was in the nature of a counterparade that turned out to be, as they drew nearer, a delegation of local members of the Ku Klux Klan. They were decked out in their Halloween finest, white robes and pointed hoods, several of them carrying a large wooden cross horizontally on their shoulders like pallbearers. Muni's stomach tensed at the mob's resemblance to one of those Old Country Easter processions that were often the prelude to a pogrom, but the North Main Streeters retained their holiday mood, seeming if anything more amused than afraid. In fact, they began to make a game out of identifying the men beneath the robes.

"There's Joe Hankus Munro," said Mr. Bluestein. "I sold him the sheet he wears that it's cut on the bias." It was a signature feature his fellow citizens would recognize, as Mr. Bluestein, the tailor, was also a mohel.

"That one's Early Dewlily, the chandler, and that's the druggist Lyle Sugg," cited Leon Shapiro, asking the assembled to note the quality of the material they wore. "You can't get from Pin's Merchandise linen like that," he boasted for the benefit of chafing his business rival.

Pinchas took the bait: "It's shmattes compared to the muslin Ernest Poteet that he buys in my store." He pointed to the silk-trimmed robe with its elaborate insignia at the head of the procession, its wearer daintily lifting the hem to keep it from being soiled.

They continued their sport of spotting the individuals behind their getups, this one by his tumescent belly, that one by his pigeon toes, even as the klavern came to a halt before the Jews.

"Howdo, Ernest," said the neighborly Sam Alabaster to their leader, who replied, "Hidey, Sam," before clearing his throat. Then he commenced a formal address to the North Main Street gathering in his capacity as Grand Syklops of the North Memphis Chapter of the Invisible Empire of the Knights of the White Kamelia. It was a mild, moonless twilight, the rustling of the Klansmen's robes abetted here and there by Hershel Tarnopol, who stole among them lifting their skirts to reveal trousers rolled above hairy calves.

"As the symbol of our struggle to scourge our beloved Southland of the mongrel element that would contaminate our bloodline and pollute the purity of our womenhood," declared the Syklops, a lawyer, in his syrupy drawl, "and as a warning against their satanic chicanery, we hereby plant the holy standard of Caucasian Christendom."

A burly fellow in a crumpled white cowl stepped forward with a posthole digger and punched a hole in the sludge. Then the team of cross bearers inserted the foot of the tall cypress cross into the hole, swiveling it as if turning a giant screw. Still the cross leaned at a precarious angle, and no amount of shoring it up with more mud and stones could keep it from tilting. Making do nonetheless, they doused the cross liberally with a canister of kerosene. One man struck a match and lit a stick of punk, which, at a word from the Syklops, he touched to the base of the cross. Instantly it was ignited, flames climbing the spar and fanning out along the transverse arms until the whole crackling rood was blindingly incandescent. Though it was not yet dark out, the brightness of the blaze banished the rest of the world to its obscurest perimeter. Everyone stood admiring the burning cross, some of the Jews even offering their compliments to the Klan—one of whom had just had his hood snatched by the impish Hershel. Exposed as Hiram Peay, a sleepy-eyed slinger of hash, the man raised his skirts and made stumblingly to give chase.

Then a grumbling was heard among the ranks of the masked intruders, some having grown impatient with symbols, however impressive, and a tension set in between the two opposing camps. Dr. Seligman mopped his brow with a monogrammed hankie and suggested it was maybe time to disperse, which was the cue for Rabbi Eliakum ben Yahya to step resolutely forward. He shuffled near enough to the fire to endanger his beard from the sparks and removed a small bone box from his caftan. Opening the box, he took a pinch of snuff, stuffed it into his tuberous nose, and inhaled, after which he sneezed robustly and wiped his schnoz on his sleeve. "Gezuntheit!" chorused his disciples, as flames from the fiery cross shot high into the cobalt sky. The rabbi took another pinch, inhaled it into his other nostril, and sneezed again. "Gezuntheit!" went up like a cheer, and the flames rose even higher. From their vantage on the soggy embankment it seemed to the gathered parties that the conflagration had risen to the height of the clouds, igniting their fleece as surely as the punk had kindled the cross. A towering tree of flame now ascended from earth to the firmament, its trunk funneling like a cyclone that threatened to suck all and sundry into its swirl. Whipped by that incendiary wind, Jews and gentiles alike had to hold on to one another to keep from being swept away. (The exceptions being the lunatic Hasids, who tempted fate by joining hands to dance round the fire.) Soon the cypress cross was completely consumed, its torch absorbed into the billowing clouds that glowed an intense crimson hue before being doused by the night.

There was a general exhalation on the part of everyone in attendance. Some of the Jews muttered a hushed "Aleinu," while the Klansmen, who may have secretly hoped to provoke just such a spectacle, yipped and slapped their thighs. The entire company seemed to share in the thrill of having witnessed indisputable evidence of an age of wonders.

Then Pinchas leaned toward Muni as if to whisper, though he made certain his voice was in earshot of one and all. "The rebbe," he scoffed, "a showboat."

Muni woke the next morning with a feeling akin to bliss. After all, he was no longer shackled to a plank bed alongside a dozen malodorous convicts in the prison barracks east of Irkutsk. Strangely, though, this was the first morning since his escape (had he really escaped?) from penal servitude that he'd been able to fully appreciate the fact. This was not to say he was entirely at peace with finding himself in the bosom of North Main Street on the first day of the Jewish New Year; the religious calendar had long since lost all meaning for him. Nor was he particularly sanguine about the future: measured optimism was his uncle's department, who followed the doings of every international Jewish or Zionist congress with rapt attention. Muni had no stake in the future. It was just that this morning he was pleased to be waking to a room whose window was not glazed in ice, a room from which he was not harried in fetters into a hellishly cold dawn to mine mica schist. If he'd yet to make his peace with living in the Pinch, where the membrane between what was hidden and revealed seemed exceedingly thin, he was at least grateful to be shed of the past.

Moreover, the work he did for his uncle gave him a certain satisfaction, if only because the labor wasn't forced. Staying busy kept the memories at bay, and when things were slow around the general merchandise, Muni solicited odd jobs among Pinchas's neighbors, which he undertook for a little pocket change. He moonlighted for Saccharin's Buffalo Fish Company, unloading refrigerator cars down at the depot at Poplar and Front, and sorted scrap metal in the overflowing compound of Blockman's Junkyard. Initially the street had been wary of the gaunt-featured greenhorn, perhaps even a little afraid, for who knew how to welcome an immigrant fresh from the capital of koshmarin, of nightmares? Of course most had suffered bad dreams of their own; they understood what it took the newcomer to approach them trustfully, and his willingness to work soon put them at ease. Some even began to vie for his services.

On his free evenings Muni sat in a folding chair under the awning outside the store with his aunt and uncle. Now that the High Holidays had commenced, the neighborhood was swelled with the North Main Streeters' relations, who had traveled to the Pinch to be within walking distance of its several synagogues. After services they too sat out on the sidewalks inhaling the heady aromas of strudel and pastries from Ridblatt's Bakery. They listened to the gramophone the Widow Teitelbaum perched on her windowsill, playing marches, arias, and tangos such as "Too Much Mustard," and watched the Shpinker Hasids chasing sparks from the passing trolley.

"Their rebbe tells them that at the Creation the Lord poured into the vessels that form the universe his divine light," explained Pinchas. "But the light is too powerful for them to contain it, the vessels, so they plotz, *kaboom,* which scatters sparks throughout the world. These sparks, says ben Yahya, must be recovered and returned to the original source before can come the Messiah. So the nincompoops, they chase every flicker they see." This included the lightning bugs coruscating in the alleys among clematis and morning glory vines. The Hasids netted them and carried them back to their shtibl above the feed store in pillow slips that flickered from their contents like desultory lanterns.

Muni knew the legend of the breaking of the vessels from his yeshiva days, but it hurt his brain to remember. It was a feeling like when he swallowed too fast the crushed ice in a cherry dope.

Sometimes in the evenings Jenny Bashrig would entertain the street with her wirewalking. Wearing a nainsook nightgown over drawstring pantaloons, her bare toes gripping the cable as the wisps of her midnight hair came undone, she gamboled above the alley between Rosen's Delicatessen and Pin's Merchandise. "La Funambula," she called herself, as she bounced on the braided cord suspended from twin pulleys; she jumped rope and juggled lit candles with fingers that often seemed, at sea level, as if slathered in butter. In the past she'd performed to the Widow's gramophone standards, but lately she was accompanied by the eldritch music of the Negro Asbestos standing in the alley beneath her. Muni had observed the girl bringing stuffed turkey necks and bowls of bay-leaf stew to the blind fiddler on his corner. From time to time his instrument was heard to echo the notes of the shofar from the nearby Market Square shul. He had even played teasing descants on the solemn "Kol Nidrei" as sung by Cantor Bielski, whose clarion voice rang the synagogue rafters. Some thought it blasphemous that the panhandling black man should ape the sacred music, but none seemed able to stop listening; nobody, with the exception of Pinchas Pin, held his ears.

Having situated his chair alongside the others in the street where the cobbles showed through the worn asphalt, Muni watched Jenny's feats of equilibrium. In his gut he experienced a queasy sensation whose source he could not at first identify. Was he afraid she might fall? Then it came to him that he was jealous, not wishing to share a performance that should have been reserved exclusively for him.

Then it was Yom Kippur, the Day of Atonement, and the businesses along North Main Street were closed until sunset. Muni, having done penance enough in his day, was feeling unquiet, so he wandered south across Poplar Avenue to Nutty Iskowitz's Green Owl Café. But even Nutty's louche establishment, its interior papered with posters of main events at the Phoenix Boxing Arena, was emptied of its regular clientele. Its horse-faced proprietor was slumped in a booth, coughing thickly into a handkerchief, while across from him sat a stubble-cheeked gent smugly sipping his beer. Upon Muni's entrance Nutty launched into a complaint in Yiddish: the goy—he nodded toward the teamster, who emitted a contented belch—claimed it was more than his job was worth to unload the delivery wagon himself. "There's four bits in it for you," he offered, "and a plate of trayf on the house."

Muni was thankful for any respite from his aunt Katie's cooking.

In the alley behind the café he set to work unloading the beer wagon, whose pair of crow-bait nags stood in their traces nickering and flicking flies with their tails. Alcohol was technically illegal in the city of Memphis, but the dry law was rarely enforced, only when saloonkeepers failed to pay their monthly sops to Mayor Crump's myrmidons. Muni rolled the heavy wooden barrels backward down a sagging two-by-four ramp from the bed of the wagon, then wrestled them into the hatch of a second incline that sloped into Nutty's cellar. It was the kind of laborious task to which his body had become habituated during his exile, and while it revived a thousand dormant aches, the work nevertheless soothed his brain. Although it was late September, the summer was making a blistering last stand, and sweating buckets, Muni removed his dank broadcloth shirt. He noted in so doing the similarity of his own to the panpipe ribs of the draft horses—this despite his aunt's starchy diet—and wondered when he might regain even the meager weight of his student years; though flesh, he reflected, was the least of what he'd lost in his trials. At the bottom of the ramp, Muni rested his hands a moment on his knees. He began slowly to straighten his sore back, when his blood surged from the touch of strange fingers along his spine. Coming sharply to attention, he turned to find himself face-to-face with the fiddler Asbestos.

"Vos machstu! What you doink?"

"Bend over again," came a husky contralto (though the fiddler's lips had yet to move) and from behind him stepped the whip-thin Jenny Bashrig. She was wearing one of her formless dun-white smocks, which contrasted rather fetchingly with the shapeliness of her athletic limbs. Gazing at her, however, Muni was still unable to square the ungraceful waitress with the daredevil who danced on a string. "He wants to feel your stripes," she said.

"Vos ret ir epes?"

"Say it in English," she urged, as if to encourage his facility with the American tongue—though why should she care?

"What are you talking?"

"He wants to feel the stripes on your back."

Suddenly Muni was self-conscious, acutely aware of the wounds he'd suffered over the fearful years. The "stripes" she referred to were welts raised by the knout employed arbitrarily by prison guards—the knout being a treated hide thong embedded with metal filings and a hook fastened to its supple end. It inflicted such pain, tearing flesh from bone in strips like peeled bark, that the victim usually lost consciousness by the third stroke. Muni had of course never seen his own wounds, but he imagined them as a sort of topographical map leading back to the torments he'd fled. Sometimes he asked himself if you could judge an escape successful when its itinerary remained etched in your skin.

He continued to look at the girl in utter bewilderment.

"That's how he makes his music," she explained, which was no explanation at all.

"Nu?"

Her voice had a hint of the honeyed inflection of a native speaker. "He reads the stripes on the backs of former slaves and makes from them his musical compositions." She told him he had exhausted his stock of the old freedmen living down around Beale Street and had come to North Main looking for Israelites who still bore the signs of their captivity. "That would be you," she submitted.

Muni tried to think of an argument against allowing the blind man to fondle his scars. It was some kind of rude violation, wasn't it? To say nothing of the bizarre proposition that such ugly excrescences could be translated into musical scores. But the girl looked at him so appealingly with her serious, doe-soft eyes that he thought he might be willing to do a thing or two to oblige her. He might do things for her that made no earthly sense. Such as kneeling in the unpaved alley, leaning over the top of a barrel and hugging the plywood staves, as the fiddler's cool mocha fingers began to describe the marks on his back. The sob that welled up in his chest had nothing to do with physical pain; there was no pain, only a stirring of unwelcome recollections.

"Why is he called Asbestos?" asked Muni, in a bluff effort to suppress the intensity of his feelings.

This time he was answered by the man himself, chuckling breezily as he spoke: "'Cause I playing as best as I can."

Later that night Muni was slogging across the frozen surface of Catfish Bayou, following tracks left by the blades of dogsleds, leaning into the biting wind. He could no longer feel his feet, and the numbness that crept up his legs would soon engulf the rest of him; it would stall his progress and leave him to become another changeless feature of the frozen landscape. With each faltering tread his boots fractured the jade-green ice, the cracks sending out branches in all directions, the branches sprouting tendrils until the whole bayou was a lacy fretwork of rupture. Then the entire expanse of the pond collapsed beneath him like a breaking mirror. But instead of plunging into the icy depths, Muni hung suspended, held aloft by a pair of strong arms. He opened his eyes to find himself in the firm embrace of La Funambula. The strains of a nearby violin released splinters of sound that shot across the night sky like comets, their peacocks' tails showering sparks over the couple below. Muni nuzzled Jenny Bashrig's spice-scented hair, felt her small breasts crushed against his chest, and was proud to be holding her as staunchly as she held him. Then the music became more tempestuous, and Muni was abruptly aware that he'd been sleepwalking. Fully awake now, he was standing with the flesh-and-blood girl on her tightrope above the alley. A dizzy dread overcame him, and, tottering dangerously, he lost his balance, while Jenny, attempting to steady him, held on to Muni as he fell.

◢3◣
Champion of the Oppressed

"So where did it come from?" I asked Avrom at my next opportunity. Of course there were nothing but opportunities in Avrom's shop, since hardly anyone came in to browse. Downtown Memphis had entered its slow economic decline. Main Street's perennial holdouts, the department stores and old movie palaces—baroque facades like layer cakes left in the rain—were giving way to discount clothiers, quick lunch counters, and wig emporiums. Full of vacancies, the office buildings were largely occupied by bail bondsmen and jackleg lawyers with tufty sideburns and plaid pants. Besides, the Bluff City, as it was called, would never be mistaken for a bookish town.

"From outer space it came," replied old Avrom, his cough like a rooster's ragged crow. "Where did what come from?"

"The book," I said, trying my best to maintain an even tone.

"The Book? It was given to Moses on Mount Sinai. Who wants to know?"

I sighed. "I thought I was the wiseass here."

"Get in line, boychik."

He liked playing these games with me, Avrom, as what else did he have to amuse himself with? Think of him, if you want, as some hermit sage dwelling in his cave of esoteric tomes, but in the end he was just an exasperating old fart. But since he was fossil enough to remember something of the local history—only recently had it occurred to me that the city had a history—I persevered.

"You know what I'm talking about—*The Pinch*. Where did it come from?"

"Are you talking the place or the book?"

"The goddamn book."

Reclining in his cracked leather office chair, he raised a crooked fore-finger. "But the book and the place are one." The springs of his chair screeched the way it must sound to tug at a mandrake root.

"Swami Bullshitzky," I said, "you're such a pill."

At that the old geezer actually tucked his thumbs in his suspenders. I suppose he was only giving me back some of my own medicine, which today left a bitter taste. I fished in my pocket for one of Lamar's antidotes.

Then he deigned to answer my question. "From where you think comes the book? It comes from the author that his name is on the cover."

"Muni Pinsker. So who's Muni Pinsker?"

"Was proprietor of a general store on North Main Street. The place is empty now for years, but I believe there's living above it still a tenant?"

"And that would be . . . ?"

A perfunctory nod in my direction.

"Is he still alive?"

"Who?"

I made a fist and he raised his mottled hands in mock surrender.

"Too many questions," he complained. "You're giving me already a headache. Since when do you got questions? You who don't care from nothing."

"That's right," I replied a touch defiantly. "Like Zappa says, 'What's there to live for?'" Turning on my heel. "'Who needs the Peace Corps?'" Sloping off into the stacks where I pretended to be busy. My whole situation at Avrom's Asylum was predicated on make-believe, as my practically imaginary salary attested. I was as much Avrom's charity case as he was mine. *Luftmensch* was the word he used to describe himself: a man who lived on air; and I supposed his minimal support of his employee was by way of passing on that condition from one generation to the next.

Unable to keep up the charade any longer, however, I stepped back up to his desk and cried, "But I'm *in* the book!"

"You think that's strange? Back in my town of Zhldze a piece buttered toast once fell on the unbuttered side. Good on you that you should be someplace, because by me you are no place at all."

His eyes behind his thick lenses floated like jellyfish in twin aquariums, and I knew the conversation was over. But while it hurt my pride to belabor the subject, I inquired with all the humility I could summon, "What am I doing in it, the book?"

"Sweetheart, we are all people from the Book, which it got a long time ago lost, and now every book is from the lost book only a dim imitat-zieh." Then changing his tune, he snapped, "Have *I* read it? How should I know?"

Sorry I'd asked, I slammed out the door.

I had anyway an errand to run. Avrom had given me earlier the scrip for some medication meant to relieve one of his revolting afflictions. I was to get it filled at the Rexall drugstore on the corner of Main Street and Beale. I'd always heard Beale Street touted as the infamous Negro tender-loin, but you couldn't have proved it in broad daylight. By day the closed nightclubs and dives were upstaged by the barbershops, funeral parlors, and dentists' offices that shared the same blocks. All you could anyway see of the street from the corner at Main was a row of pawnshops run by superannuated Jews—the trios of brass balls hung above their doorways giving rise to bad jokes.

It was toward Beale that I assumed the small army of black men trudg-ing up Main Street past Goldsmith's Department Store was headed. They were a wintry throng in porkpie hats and doleful shoes, some wearing clerical collars and singing hymns. I knew enough to identify them as an alliance in support of the striking sanitation workers whose protests were all over the news, which I heard through the distortion of Avrom's antique wireless. The hotly debated topic of the strikers' demands had earned them a mention in the national press, which was noteworthy; since seldom was anything that happened in farthest Memphis brought to the national awareness.

Having exited the Rexall, I crossed Main in front of the crowd and stationed myself against a Goldsmith's show window full of new spring fashions to watch the proceedings. It appeared to be an orderly march, pa-troled on the street side by black-and-white squad cars crawling alongside the procession to keep them in line. But the cars, with their revolving red lights slashing the mole-gray fabric of the afternoon, kept edging into the crowd, forcing the marchers to bunch up against the curb and spill onto the sidewalk. There was grumbling in the ranks at the provocation, and at one point a parading lady—one of only a pair in that company—perhaps thinking that her gender might afford her some respect, indig-nantly reproached the police. Immediately thereafter, as the squad car inched forward, she screamed, "He runned over my foot!" and crumpled to the pavement. Several men broke ranks to assist her, one of them, a boy really, stooping to tug down the woman's skirt which was rucked up to her girdle. The veil of her pillbox hat still shadowed her face. Angry others, youthful members of the demonstration, attacked the vehicle that had injured her and began to rock it back and forth. Stone-faced cops poured out, more of them in fact than I'd have thought the car could contain, wielding truncheons and aerosol cans. Sirens began to blare.

Abandoning any pretense of discipline, the police erupted in a paroxysm of furious aggression, clubbing and Macing everyone they could reach. Bloodied men fell to the pavement and were beaten where they lay, some dragged semiconscious into the back of a waiting Black Maria. There were shouts of "Don't rub your eyes!" though big men bawled, cursing as they staggered in circles. A woolly-bearded old minister was on his knees with his hat in his hands as if offering up his skull to be cracked. People were trying desperately to take shelter inside the department store only to find that the doors had been locked. Riveted by the sight, I stood with my back to the plate-glass window, which suddenly shattered from the combined weight of the marchers shoved up against it. A niagara of shards cascaded about me, a mannequin in a garden-party dress toppled onto the sidewalk, and a cop began heading my way. His partly unbuttoned tunic revealed his undershirt and a bit of hirsute belly beneath, his mirror glasses reflecting myself as he must have perceived me: nigger lover, agitator, pervert, and freak. That's when, terror-struck to near paralysis, I nevertheless managed to goad my feet into motion. I beat it with the other demonstrators who had scattered across Main Street and were retreating east on Beale. Sprinting among them, I had a healthy portion of their shock and nausea, my eyes and lungs smarting from the clouds of gas drifting our way. But I also experienced a heart-stirring exhilaration, a sense of pride as if I'd been an active participant in the march: Lenny Sklarew, champion of the oppressed. Then, chagrined at the thought, I remembered that the whole affair was none of my concern. Having fled as far as the postage-stamp park with its verdigris-stained statue of W. C. Handy, I peeled off down an alley and made my way back toward the opposite end of Main.

That night I wanted to get trashed. I wanted to find a like mind to talk treason with, and thought again of the girl who'd shared my bed the week

before. Together we would decry the death of the soul, then jump holding hands from the Harahan Bridge. Then I remembered I was a loner;
I burned with a solitary gem-like flame. I read the tales of brain-fevered
authors who were similarly lit, though their works sometimes distracted
me from my own combustion. In any event, instead of going to the 348 to
peddle the goods I hadn't already smoked or swallowed, I opened the book.

I'd been reading it since my encounter with the lady folklorist, absorbing information I might regale her with if I ever saw her again. I'd begun
at the beginning, reading leisurely, lingering over the lush but uncooked
illustrations. I resisted the temptation to skip ahead, reluctant to spoil an
ending in which I myself might play an unwonted part. For that reason,
whenever I opened the book I felt myself caught in a tug-of-war between
curiosity and fear, and I confess that fear often seemed to win the day.

Avrom was wrong about *The Pinch;* it was an authentic history, at least
in its grim prologue, which recounted the arrival of the first Jew at the
site of what would become the city of Memphis. This was in the year
1541 and his name was Rodrigo (né Ruben) da Luna, a Portuguese secret
Jew, or Marrano as they were called. Having eluded the autos-da-fé of
the Inquisition, he'd hitched his fate to that of the Spanish conquistador
Hernando de Soto. De Soto had traveled via a circuitous route up from
Florida with a way-weary brigade of lancers and musketeers. In their train
were the ever-thinning ranks of carpenters, clergy, camp followers, and
tailors (to which latter group Rodrigo belonged). These, if they hadn't already perished from the flux or the poisoned arrows of native tribes, were
disillusioned by an expedition more inclined to pillage than colonize.
For de Soto was determined to push on in search of the Seven Cities of
Cibola, as described in the depraved hallucinations of the explorer Cabeza
de Vaca. The author Pinsker chronicled the moment when the rapacious
conquistador, sitting astride his Barbary steed atop the Chickasaw Bluffs,
looks across the broad expanse of the river that separates him from the
golden cities; while from the ranks Rodrigo da Luna is thinking you could
go farther and fare worse. He would have liked to try and trade with the
natives—maybe swap a starveling mule for fresh fish and persimmon
bread—rather than slaughter them as his captain preferred. He thought
that maps made a more enduring means of marking a trail than de Soto's
method of paving it with corpses. And wasn't the real estate atop these
rust-red bluffs eminently well situated for civilized habitation? After all,

what was to keep the indigenous folk, once they pointed their weapons in another direction, from becoming the tailor's devoted clients? ("Allow me to custom-fit you for a nice suede breechclout.") But already the soldiers and carpenters were constructing the barges that would ferry them across the river, and rather than be left behind, Rodrigo da Luna would travel with them into an even more hostile landscape and obscurer death.

Then give or take a hiatus of three and one-third centuries and the next Jew makes his frontier debut. This one is the educated peddler Pinchas Pinsker, who arrives in Memphis from Eastern Europe in 1878, just as the town is in the throes of an epidemic that has transformed it from a vital river port to a pesthouse.

Nearly a century and a few nights later I'm in the 348 listening to live music, when in walks Rachel sans fiancé. It frightened me how glad I was to see her. Over the week since our encounter I'd given up expecting her to return; I'd even stayed away from the bar so that I wouldn't have to experience the disappointment, at the risk of missing her while I was truant. She was wearing her long herringbone coat and a knit tam-o'- shanter that gave her an Anne of Green Gables sort of look. Then she removed the cap and her dark hair, unpinned tonight, spilled out as from an opened sluice. She was with a couple of girlfriends who took a table not far from Lamar's, where he sat like a grandee in his brocade vest. A weeping-willow-looking girl leaned against him, her languid arm draped over his shoulder. If she was looking for me, Rachel gave no indication of it. She and her friends—chunky and petite—were convivial, their heads nearly touching in an effort to talk over the music. From my stool at the end of the bar I waved a hand to get her attention, but when she eventually caught sight of me, she merely squinched up the corners of her mouth in the parody of a smile. Like a curtsy of the lips in which her eyes did not participate at all. Crushed, I turned back toward the band.

They were the house band, Velveeta and the Psychopimps as they called themselves, a jokey name signifying nothing: there was no Velveeta, no dictionary definition of *psychopimp*. But comic sobriquet aside, they played infectious music, their own subversive blend of raunchy, gut-bucket blues and straight-ahead rock 'n' roll. Much of their repertoire was inspired by classic Delta bluesmen, neglected old duffers whom the band would seek out and recall from extreme destitution. Students of musical history as well as accomplished musicians, the band members venerated these old men, some of whom were in advanced stages of illness and disability. They bought them whiskey and dispatched willing groupies to wash their bunions (and sometimes drink the water like broth). They were a diverse bunch, the Psychopimps, versatile, streetwise, and racially mixed, a fact that consolidated their singularity among Southern players. A chief supplier of their recreational stimulants via Lamar, I was a tolerated hanger-on of the band, something in the nature (I liked to think) of a mascot.

You better tell McNamara, tell Curtis LeMay, J. Edgar Hoover, and LBJ, they sang, *we gonna pitch that wang dang doodle all night long* . . .

With their combination of electric and traditional instruments, they made a joyful ruckus that turned your intestines to live wires: Elder Lincoln alternating effortlessly between keyboard and kit fiddle, Jimmy Pryor scratching his washboard like a breastplate with fleas, Cholly Jolly vexing the strings of his guitar with a bottleneck to set your teeth on edge. A cause célèbre among regional blues buffs, the band nevertheless disdained record deals, as if success would dilute their authenticity and betray their mentors. They sang about kingsnakes, hellhounds, dead presidents, and crosscut saws, items that mingled with the ingredients of the mild chemical cocktail in my brain to giddy effect.

As the music conspired to reverse my ill humor, a quaint phrase wormed its way into my head: "Faint heart ne'er won fair lady." Did I really want to win her, and what would I do with her if I did? But the fact that an alternative life—unexamined though it was—perhaps awaited me in Muni Pinsker's book made firsthand experience seem somehow less hazardous lately. So damning the consequences, I approached Rachel's table and stood there some seconds before I was noticed, when I had to shout over the din to be heard:

"Was I just some degrading episode you had on your to-do list?"

I hadn't meant to sound so hostile, but as all three ladies cupped their ears, I was forced to repeat the question at even greater volume. Rachel's friends looked to her, as did I, for an answer, and saw an angry crimp in her satiny brow. I read her lips more than heard her reply: "Don't flatter yourself."

I made an effort to grin to stave off what emerged as a full-throated sob.

Rolling her eyes toward the string of colored lights overhead, Rachel let go a querulous sigh then excused herself. Rising, she callipered my arm with her fingers and escorted me through the jangling music to the front of the bar. I half-expected her to shove me out the door and slam it behind me, but while she did push me onto the sidewalk, she stepped outside as well. She was wearing a shaggy cable-stitched sweater and a pair of distressed blue jeans, which on her looked a little like a costume, as if she'd dressed for a night of slumming. The wind whipped strands of her hair across her face, which she brushed away as if swatting locusts.

"What's wrong with you?" she hissed.

I wiped my snuffling nose with the back of my palm and straightened in an effort to recover some dignity. "I don't need your pity," I said.

She exhaled. "Does this look like pity?" she asked, presenting an implacable expression—tight ocher lips, hard hazel eyes—illuminated by the streetlight. "Do you think showing your vulnerable side makes you more appealing?"

I decided her pity might be preferable after all.

The scent of rotting refuse that pervaded the city, even despite the February chill, had drifted as far as North Main. The power station down the block was winking like a wrecked constellation, and from inside the bar you could hear the band singing, *Hello, Central, give me no-man's-land* . . .

"I guess I'm a little fragile," I admitted, and searching for a reason: "since I saw the cops maul the garbage collectors. They were marching up Main Street when the cops started clubbing them bloody and dragging them away."

She studied me in earnest a moment then smirked. "You're clearly a sensitive guy."

I began to make a case for my political engagement, which she cut short.

"You embarrassed me in front of my friends."

Inclining my head I inquired, "You're ashamed that you slept with me?"

"Damn straight—and don't make it sound like more than it was," she reminded me. "Sleeping was the extent of it."

I felt another sob coming on.

"Oh for God's sake," sighed Rachel. "Would you like me to call your mother?"

Again I endeavored to rally. "I don't have a mother," I told her. "I was raised by wolves in the fastness of the Caucasus Mountains."

"I'm going back inside," she said.

Desperate to detain her, I changed course. "Do you know when the first Jew came through here?"

She hesitated despite herself, succumbing to a sudden professional reflex. "There were German Jews in Memphis in the 1840s," she grudgingly replied. "Goldsmith's Department Store was founded just after the Civil War."

"I'm talking about the first Jew in the Pinch."

"I know about the Pinch," she stated as if I'd challenged her. "I've already conducted some oral history interviews with people who lived there."

"You mean *here*. So how did you learn about the Pinch?"

"You told me." The admission must have cost her something, as her fidgeting seemed to imply. "After you mentioned it I did some homework," she continued. "The Pinch was an Irish neighborhood until the Russian Jews started trickling in during the eighteen eighties and nineties. The Irish eventually moved on, and the district was Jewish till after the war."

"Did anybody tell you about the earthquake?"

"What earthquake? People talk about the synagogues, the shops—the Pinch was like every other ethnic urban ghetto. Nobody mentions anything about an earthquake."

"It happened; it practically swallowed the neighborhood. The epicenter was in Market Square Park, just over there. I can show you."

"You're batshit."

"It's just a block or two away."

She cleared her throat somewhat nervously. "I'd have to get my coat."

I was afraid that if she returned to her friends she might never come back. Remarking that she was indeed shivering from the cold, I took off my own overcoat, a worn-to-threads rag with no lining, and draped it over her shoulders. I hoped she would be impressed by the gallantry of the gesture.

She eyed me with grave suspicion. "This better be quick."

On the way I congratulated myself for having once again exploited Rachel's gullibility; her resistance was not nearly as intractable as she liked to project. The truth was that in all the months I'd spent on North Main Street I'd scarcely noticed the park myself. It was there opposite the old Ellis Auditorium: an acre of unattended crabgrass bordered by a Catholic church, a low-rise housing project, and some empty lots from which the structures had been recently razed: the kind of poky city vacuum that nature can't abide. As we entered it Rachel asked me, incidentally, what was my name, and I told her Captain Blood, a.k.a. Lenny Sklarew. Hers was Rachel Ostrofsky. Such a doughy Slavic mouthful for such a svelte American girl.

Of course I knew there would be no sign of the great tree that Muni Pinsker had described, the one that capsized into a hole during the quake. It was clear from the first that the author of *The Pinch*, however much he drew from actual events, could not be considered a reliable narrator. Still, his version of the past seemed so much truer than the present tenantless decay.

"You can see how the ground gives way in the middle of the park," I said, playing at cicerone.

"I don't even see a park," said Rachel, looking a little like a refugee—which became her—in my fluttering overcoat.

The patch of land that was all that remained of the original park resembled so many other orphaned tracts fallen victim to so-called urban renewal, tracts designated for face-lifts that never happened.

"But look, Rachel," I said, aware of calling her by her given name for the very first time. "See the way it dips . . ."

There did in fact seem to be a slight depression in the sparse grass, a concavity I marched into in my effort to make the point. In so doing I slammed into a solid object snout-first. Stunned, I fell backward onto the hard ground with a throbbing head, my nose oozing blood. Opening my eyes I expected to see—what? Maybe a swag-bellied cop or Rachel's battling fiancé? But there was nothing there.

The girl was standing over me, this time not bothering to kneel. "What are you on?" she asked.

"Methamphetamine, Tuinal, alcohol, caffeine, but that's got nothing to do with it."

"Do you think these kinds of theatrics are endearing?" she wondered, since my lying prostrate and bleeding was where we'd begun. Regardless, there was enough moonlight for her to perceive that my nose was indeed hemorrhaging, and just how did she account for that? How did I?

"Rachel," I said, trying to sound prophetic despite being flat on my back, head tilted to reverse the flow of blood, "there are more things in heaven and earth than you dreamed of in your folklore classes."

"No doubt," she replied without conviction.

"Rachel," I confided in a voice that trilled a bit from the fluid draining into my throat, "I walked into a tree."

"Uh-huh," she breathed, hovering impatiently above me, the wind waving the showy black standard of her hair. "Listen, Lenny, my friends will be wondering what became of me." Whereupon she removed my overcoat and spread it over me with the care she might have bestowed upon an invalid or a corpse, then set off in the direction of the bar.

The next day on the way to the Book Asylum I barged into a rack of vintage kangaroo-calf bicycle shoes, pleased at my ability to identify them even though they weren't there. The rack clattered noisily nonetheless as it toppled in front of me. Of course I was an old hand at confusing what was there with what was not. An intrepid psychic traveler, I'd crossed thresholds into unexplored regions encountering dragons and bugbears of every stripe and paisley (keeping the Thorazine handy in case I couldn't vanquish the dragon on my own). So what was the big deal about occasionally crossing over from what passed for real life into the pages of a bogus historical chronicle? Never mind that I approached the book with an ostrich-egg lump in my throat, since, in reading *The Pinch*, I was conscious of also approaching a rendezvous with myself.

Apprehension aside, the past put the present in the shade. The world from my North Main Street window was a toilet: the government was sliding toward fascism, the planet dying from neglect, and my lottery number put me in line to be shipped off on short notice to Vietnam. There, if I escaped the rockets and jungle rot, I would doubtless stumble into a man-trap and be impaled on envenomed stakes. Moreover—to offset the mind-fucking effects of *The Pinch*—I'd begun to read the newspapers, which reported that negotiations were at an impasse and no end in sight for the garbage strike. Undiscouraged by police harassment and the mayor's inflexible stance, however, the sanitation workers persisted in marching every day. Their ranks had been joined by students, clergymen, and ordinary citizens, a few of them white.

In that atmosphere Avrom's Asylum was as good as its name. The crowded shelves provided insulation from the unrest beyond its door, and there were times, I confess, when I thought I might like to hunker down in that dimly lit shop till the hard rain that was coming passed over. Then

I reminded myself that I belonged to a reckless tribe, who ran out to greet the winds of change with open arms; I remembered that I was, albeit at my own speed, in pursuit of a beautiful girl.

"Avrom," I said, as he gummed his fried egg sandwich (mine was pimento cheese), "I keep sort of stumbling into the past."

I wasn't really expecting an answer, though Avrom, his mouth crusted with yellow yolk dribbling into his beard, offered an offhand response: "Rabbi bar Hana that he once bumped into a frog as big as Mount Tabor, and like the eyelids of the morning were its eyes."

As usual I wondered why I even bothered to confide in the old kocker, as he sometimes called himself. But for all his double-talk I suppose I invested in him a degree of authority, if only by virtue of the blue tattoo on his wrist. Surely someone who'd been where he'd been must've returned with some kind of momentous insight to impart. Though I admit I was reluctant to ask him about that particular journey, or what he might have lost along the way. I had after all my own concerns, and besides the old man never gave me a straight reply. "Better you should be your own shamus," he would advise me, like he had the answers but thought it would be more educational if I found them myself. The thing was, before discovering Muni's book I hadn't really thought of what the questions might be.

Today's was "Who's Tyrone Pin?" That was the incongruous name to which the illustrations were attributed on the title page of *The Pinch*. Slouched in the understuffed armchair catty-cornered from Avrom's desk, I braced myself to hear the obvious: "He made like it says the pictures—" Imagine my surprise when, instead of the usual runaround, Avrom said simply, "Why you don't ask him?" It was a particularly unsettling reply given his previous assurance that all persons connected with the book were "gone with the wind." That was Avrom's phrase, which he seemed to think was original with him.

"And where would I find this Tyrone person?" I inquired, again expecting to be handed a riddle. By now it was apparent that Avrom was better acquainted with the book than he was willing to let on; like I said, he enjoyed making mystery. But since the answer was disturbing enough in its own right, the old man seemed to relish divulging it.

"He's since the war an inmate by the Western State Mental Hospital at Bolivar."

The information shook me to my socks. That the illustrator was living gave the book a kind of manifest presence in the world, made it more than just some indefinable artifact. But Avrom wasn't finished. "He grew up in the Pinch, Tyrone—Katie and Pinchas Pin's boy, a delicate kid, so I'm told."

Hoping to further exploit his confidential mood, I pressed him. "Did you know them, the Pins?"

"Me, I'm a Shlomo-come-lately, who do I know? By the time I get here everyone is—"

"Gone with the wind—so you said."

Later on I'm wondering what would be the point of making a trip to some ghoulish institution—which was Western State's reputation—to talk with a lunatic. Reading the book was a daunting enough experience in itself, especially now that I'd begun running into North Main Street's long-extinct merchandise. I stepped on an unreal roller skate and coasted a few hair-raising moments before I went sprawling; I barked my shin on the phantom fender of a 1908 Packard motor carriage and even glimpsed some ectoplasm in a serge waistcoat, watch fob, and gartered sleeves. Such occasions, despite the panoply of bruises I was collecting, were tantamount to waking up in a dream. I might have written off the incidents as acid flashbacks, but since I'd become so absorbed in the book, I was less inclined to sample the psychoactive stuff in my pantry. I used to declare with Stephen Dedalus the wish to wake up from the nightmare of history, but nowadays I had to struggle just to rouse myself enough from *The Pinch* to take notice of current events. Not that I struggled very hard. I was thus straddling two worlds when Rachel Ostrofsky came back into the 348 all alone.

◄ 4 ►
A Local Apocalypse

Until the earthquake, when North Main Street rippled like a beaten carpet and rolled like a wave, things had been relatively quiet. Of course, owing to Rabbi Eliakum ben Yahya and his followers' infernal tampering with the cosmos, there had been instances of what might be deemed the miraculous. But such events had been minimal, a mere trickle compared to the flood that followed the quake—which events included, incidentally, a flood.

But on the day that Jenny Bashrig was discharged from the St. Joseph Hospital, all that was yet to come. Muni had not visited her during her convalescence, and it was with shame that he watched her hobbling on crutches through the door of Rosen's Delicatessen. When they'd tumbled together from the rope above the alley, the girl struck the ground first with Muni landing on top of her. He'd heard the bone snap and seen the leg's unnatural angle as he rolled off, shaken but unharmed, onto the gravel, convinced she had deliberately broken his fall. While she lay moaning and convulsed in pain, Muni cried for help, alerting Mrs. Rosen, who hastened in her billowing nightclothes to fetch Dr. Seligman. The bathrobed doctor, after a swift inspection of her injury, phoned for an ambulance to come and haul her away. Attendants lifted her onto a stretcher and Muni averted his glance from her sloe-eyed stare and the bandy state of her splintered limb beneath the rumpled blue gown. He dodged Dr. Seligman's questions as to how he happened to be abroad at that hour in a torn nightshirt, and avoided what he perceived as the accusatory gaze of the blind fiddler on his corner. To say nothing of the neighbors who'd begun to poke their heads from their second-story windows. That was the last he'd seen of Jenny until he glimpsed her a week later from behind the plate glass of Pin's General Merchandise, as she was being helped by Old Man Rosen from the rear of the Argo Electric ambulance.

He couldn't say exactly why he hadn't gone to see her in the hospital. Of course it didn't help that, since the "accident," he and Jenny had become the chief topic of gossip in the Pinch. And the more people talked about them, speculating on the nature of their relationship and shushing one another when he came into view, the less Muni felt disposed to communicate with the girl. The intimacy he'd experienced with Jenny that night on the wire was an anomalous event; it had occurred almost entirely outside his consciousness and therefore beyond his control. The thought of it frightened him, as did the intense desire he'd felt when he held her pliant form. Having only recently reclaimed a kind of impromptu identity for himself, Muni was not yet prepared to make that self susceptible to the devices of another. The sensations the girl evoked in him were disturbing, and if he weren't careful they could shatter the fragile peace he'd fashioned for himself since coming to North Main.

"You're a cruel lad," judged his aunt Katie, who was not ordinarily meddlesome. The remark stung. He admired his aunt for her playful nature and comely looks, though he seemed to have arrived just as those looks had begun to fade. Before his eyes the blush of her high cheeks had turned from ripe to raw, and her dense auburn hair was recently knitted with silver. All her handsome features had entered their autumnal phase.

Muni was also aware of his uncle's unease over her aging. Didn't Pinchas protest overmuch in his running commentaries that his Katie was the same girl who'd rescued him decades before from a common grave? It was a tale he told at the least opportunity: how he'd succumbed to the plague of yellow jack upon his arrival in the city and, but for the intercession of a poor Irish lass, was given up for dead. Their marriage had condemned Katie to the lot of an outcast rejected by her own dissolute clan; it would have caused a scandal in Pinchas's community as well, had there been any community to speak of. But Pinchas Pin was the first Hebrew to set up shop in the Pinch. By the time others of his persuasion had begun to straggle into that rough-and-ready neighborhood, his business had become an institution, as had his marriage to the pretty colleen. It had not been a perfect union; their childlessness was a constant source of regret, but Katie's native exuberance had remained largely unflagging throughout. So it was with alarm that her husband observed how his wife had turned a corner into her climacteric, and was lately given to bouts of crankiness.

Once in Pinchas's presence Muni ventured to speculate that his coming to stay was perhaps responsible for putting undue stress on his uncle's wife. He was surprised by the vehemence of the merchant's response.

"You?" Pinchas fairly shouted. "Shtik goy! Ain't nobody else can make my Katie unhappy but me myself."

Muni never broached the subject again, though he couldn't shake his remorse over his aunt's disapproval of his apparent lack of concern for the fallen acrobat.

Still he continued to lie low after Jenny's return. The girl, for her part, never tried to seek him out but neither did she attempt to avoid him, and it was inevitable that their paths would cross again. For the time being, however, Muni ducked into doorways or retreated to the rear of the store if he saw her coming, swinging her weight along on crutches with the agility of a monkey ranging through trees. Some noted that Jenny seemed to negotiate the crutches better than she had her own two left feet before she'd fractured her leg.

Meanwhile life on North Main Street proceeded apace. Construction was under way for the Idle Hour Theater, which would serve as a venue for touring theatricals as well as the projection of the photoplays that were making the arc-lit nickelodeons obsolete. The theater was viewed with civic pride by the Reform congregation of Temple Israel, though the less secular-minded Market Square Synagogue was opposed to the impious project. They were as dismayed by the Idle Hour as by rumors that sons of the Pinch were seen frequenting a floating casino moored under the bluff at the Happy Hollow fishing camp. Further fueling a communal sense of opprobrium was the news that Mrs. Gruber had once more refused to pay tribute to the agents of Boss Crump's machine, and so was collared again for making moonshine. Bemoaning her disgrace, the street nevertheless turned out in a body for her trial, which was on a Friday afternoon in November. Called to the witness stand, Mrs. Gruber's colleague Lazar der Royte remarked through a window that the sun, whose color rivaled the red of his beard, had begun to set. Ignoring the prosecutor's questions, Lazar wrapped himself in his tallis and began to chant his Sabbath prayers.

The neighborhood was less cacophonous since the gramophone in the Widow Teitelbaum's window was no longer in competition with Asbestos's fiddle. Instead, when she played such popular ditties as "Peg o' My Heart" or "Yaddie Kaddie Kiddie Kaddie Koo," the blind musician executed variations upon them, turning the sprightliest tunes into dolorous threnodies. In Pin's General Merchandise it was business as usual, and business, Got tsu danken, was generally good. There was a run on rubber collars and oxblood Shinola was flying off the shelves, nor could novelty items like bagpipe balloons be kept in stock. Mr. Bluestein bought twelve yards of calico, and Mrs. Padauer—while her husband, a drummer in ladies' foundation garments, was away on a business trip—came in to buy her geriatric child a winter coat. Pinchas was busy with a supplier, so it fell to Muni to take down the naval reefer that Mrs. Padauer had selected from an overhead rack. He helped the little manikin (whom she referred to as "my peanut") on with the coat, which dwarfed his shriveled frame. While his mother was distracted in her inspection of a plaid mackinaw, the diminutive creature, Benjy by name, croaked in a voice like a belch, "I hope they don't bury me in this shmatte." When they'd left with their purchase, Pinchas, having observed the transaction out of the corner of an eye, answered the question on the tip of Muni's tongue.

"I would say that he was born, the peanut, around the time of the destruction of the Second Temple." He breathed on his spectacles and wiped them in his apron. "I got it also on the authority from Doc Seligman that he ain't entirely a human person."

Another subject of local interest was Hershel Tarnopol, who was on a spree. Ever since his father, Oyzer, had heaved his several pounds of sin into Catfish Bayou and gone thereafter into an inconsolable funk, Hershel had run amok in the neighborhood. Before, there had been a general tolerance for his escapades; after all, he'd stolen only essentials of the sort that the blacksmith, whose business was failing due to the tantrums that drove his customers away, neglected to provide their household. There had also been a certain admiration for the boy's stealth, and the sense that Hershel in his baggy plus fours was a necessary evil. It was as if the merchants believed that, as long as the jug-eared scamp was allowed his petty thefts, the street might be immune to greater incursions. But lately he'd been given to pure mischief, stealing items he could have no real use for: single shoes from the show rack in front of Sebranig's Custom Footwear, cattle dehorners from Hekkie's Hardware & Feed, an ormolu clock, a taxidermied owl, canvas puttees. So far no one had actually caught him in the act, but Hershel always made his presence known before merchandise vanished, lest others be given credit for his crimes. What's more, his pranks, which had thus far been relatively harmless—mixing colored gelatin in water closets, tossing a garfish into the ritual bath—had taken a more destructive turn. Cartridges exploded on the trolley tracks as the cars rolled over them, firing salvos that threatened the lives and limbs of passersby; and while no one had witnessed Hershel's direct involvement, his conspicuous glee left little doubt as to who was responsible.

An emergency meeting of the North Main Street Improvement Committee was convened to address the issue of the boy's delinquency. Leon Shapiro proposed they send a delegatz to Tarnopol's forge to register their grievances concerning his son: who knew but they might even discover their plundered goods stashed there in plain sight. But no one was willing to risk provoking the blacksmith's wrath. Neither, interestingly, did a single member of the committee recommend contacting the police.

One morning Hershel appeared in Pin's Merchandise with the bill of his jockey's cap pulled to the bridge of his nose, deceiving no one. Then demonstrating a remarkable lack of prudence, he lifted from its shelf an unwieldy Dandee clothes wringer with a reversible water board, and lumbered away with it in full sight of the proprietor and his menial. Muni looked to Pinchas, who merely shrugged: the kid was an occupational hazard. But in the face of such a flagrant offense to his uncle's place of business, Muni was seized by a righteous impulse, and flinging off his apron he chased the culprit out the door. In the street Hershel had not made much progress: he'd managed to lug the heavy appliance under the Rosens' striped awning and just past the soaped show window of Dlugach's Secondhand, when Muni emerged from the store. At the rate the ganef was plodding, Muni would easily overtake him—and then what? He would teach the boy a lesson. What lesson? Hadn't he just spent years in a place where your best chance of survival was commensurate with your skill at theft? But here things were different; here there was right and wrong.

Muni was already at Hershel's heels and about to grab hold of his collar, when the boy, looking back, dropped the wringer and neatly leaped over it. Not so Muni, whose foot snagged between the twin rollers, sending him sprawling headlong onto the sidewalk in front of Elster's Discount Furniture. This got a chuckle from Mr. Elster, seated in his doorway in a rotary-back veneer-seat rocker, priced $4.25. There the pursuit might have ended; the goods recovered, the employee could return triumphant to Pin's. But Muni was still dissatisfied, and having added to his incentive the need to save face, he was doubly determined to apprehend the blacksmith's son. He yanked the wringer like a sprung trap from his shoe, examined his torn trousers and the bruised knee beneath, and raised himself again to his feet.

Unburdened of his spoils, Hershel had accelerated his lath-legged pace. Already he was beyond the display racks outside Shapiro's Dry Goods and the alley that led to the livery stables behind which stood the blacksmith's forge; he'd passed Blen's Pharmacy, Schloss's Greengrocery, and Makowsky's Butcher Shop, picking up speed. Far outdistanced, Muni nevertheless stirred his limbs into motion. Heads turned as he sprinted across Commerce Avenue past the old auction block that served now as a wagon yard; he crossed Jackson Avenue where the trolley line veered east toward the car barn. He was beginning to enjoy the chase for the sheer sport of it, feeling somehow as if he were outrunning the weariness that had dogged him for so long—the weariness falling away like a splint no longer needed to mend sore bones.

The blacktop along North Main gave way to the old paving stones underneath; the stones petered out into gravel then earth as the track crossed the desolate stretch that separated civilization from Catfish Bayou. It was a blustery morning: liver-brown leaves from a few withered elms skittering across the barren ground, a chevron-shaped skein of geese honking overhead. Having increased his breakneck stride, Hershel Tarnopol sped down the slope toward the bloated pond; he raced across the crunching shingle and launched himself, legs still cycling, in an arc above the wind-riffled water. Arrived at the brow of the slope, Muni was just in time to see the mammoth pewter-gray fish leap out of the bayou, its whiskers waving like ganglia, its jaws stretched to a cavernous width to receive the boy. As Hershel dropped into its mouth feet first and was swallowed whole, the fish dove back beneath the oily surface with a splash and was gone.

Almost as astonishing to Muni as the event itself was the lack of surprise his tale of Hershel's fate generated in the community. Sightings of the big fish had already been reported: it was, as Rabbi ben Yahya's followers described it, a prodigy grown fat on the iniquities of the Jewish people. Nearly as large as Leviathan, the fish was an unmistakable harbinger of the coming of Messiah, et cetera. As for Hershel Tarnopol, it was fitting that the scourge of North Main Street should have come to such a biblical reckoning as to be swallowed by a whale.

"Was a catfish," Muni assured them, proud of his growing ability to recognize local fauna.

"Nifter shmifter," they replied. "A fish is a fish."

"Don't split hairs with these clowns," his uncle Pinchas cautioned him. "You'll end up meshuggeh as they are." Pinchas was squeamish whenever the rebbe's disciples milled about his store inspecting items they could never use. They fingered catchers' mitts and razor strops like connoisseurs, argued over the kosherness of an ink pen or hot water bottle, but seldom bought anything. When they did make a purchase, Pinchas would bite their coins to ensure their legitimacy. Where did their money come from anyway, since none of them had ever been seen to engage in work? Rumor had it they received remittances from the godforsaken Lithuanian village they hailed from, its inhabitants happy to pay them to stay away. But Pinchas wouldn't have put it past them to mint their own currency.

The only person appropriately disturbed by the disappearance of the neighborhood scapegrace was Hershel's father, Oyzer, who had since allowed his livelihood to languish. The blacksmith (the wags called him Oyzer Destroyser, though never to his face) had surrendered his mad fits of temper to an ominous brooding, and could be seen early each morning shambling with the rod and reel he'd purchased at Pin's in the direction of Catfish Bayou. There he would sit on the bank until sundown.

Then there was enough of a nip in the late autumn air to remind Muni Pinsker of the ravening winds that had blown him to this river city, and he knew he ought to count his blessings. But he was restless, possessed of contradictory emotions that he'd thought were forever defunct; and he was haunted by the girl he continued to evade. The visceral charge he'd experienced during his heated pursuit of the thief, to say nothing of its stupendous conclusion, had yet to dissipate. In chasing Hershel, Muni had felt strangely as if he were chasing some renegade piece of himself just out of reach; his inability to apprehend the boy—or to save him from his impetuous plunge—had left the immigrant lastingly frustrated. For all his gratitude toward his uncle, he'd begun to feel constrained in Pinchas's employ, no longer satisfied with sorting merchandise, taking inventory, and performing odd jobs. In the midst of stacking flour sifters or pricing jars of disappearing cream, Muni might find himself frozen in place, trying to recall some elusive version of the youth he'd once been. He might emerge from his trance to observe that the clock had advanced perhaps a quarter of an hour—fifteen lost and irretrievable minutes.

It was during one of these woolgathering episodes that Pinchas tapped him on the temple and wondered if he might be so bold as to intrude upon his nephew's meditations. "They need from us, the screwballs, a sack chickpeas." Muni obligingly shouldered a forty-pound bag of the beans that Pinchas ordered specially for the Shpinkers and toted it round to their shtibl on Commerce Avenue above Hekkie's Hardware & Feed. He trudged up the long flight of rickety stairs to the sanctuary of Eliakum ben Yahya and his disciples, which Muni had never entered before. He was greeted at the head of the stairs by a fish-faced young Hasid, who took the sack without offering any gratuity and told the delivery boy to put it on their tab. Muni might have turned abruptly and departed had he not been a little spellbound by what he beheld. The large room with its warped floorboards and potbelly stove, the grimy windows admitting shafts of light viscous as honey, bore a marked resemblance—notwithstanding the extreme behavior of its occupants—to the study houses of his tender years. But as those years were mainly shrouded in shadows, the scene before him captivated him afresh.

The skullcapped fanatics yammered and swayed over a raft of open texts heaped atop a trestle table, at the head of which their portly rebbe appeared to be sleeping. Some of the disciples were seated, some standing, and among the standing were those involved in various acts of penance. They flagellated themselves and each other with the leather straps of their phylacteries, one beating his head against a wall until plaster fell. Here and there were materials bespeaking necromantic activities: the armless trunk of a lay figure fashioned out of clay in the process of being molded or abandoned, foundering in the wallow of a galvanized washtub. There were improvised ritual furnishings: a standing wardrobe that functioned as an ark of the Torah, a hearing trumpet that doubled for a ram's horn, a tricolored map tacked to the wall that, on closer inspection, laid claim to revealing the geography of the World to Come.

A disputation was in progress under their slumbering rebbe's nose over how many parasitic cherubim might colonize the nest of his beard. Quotations were cited from Yakov Yosef of Medziboz and *The Kumquat of Sfat,* assertions made and contradictions submitted until the room was in an even greater uproar. Then Rabbi ben Yahya's goggle eyes snapped open. Rising slowly to his feet with a melancholy sigh, he began to pace around the table, bonking with a closed fist the head of the odd disciple until that disciple sat back down. He bonked those who rose to replace them, themselves replaced when they sat by some of the formerly seated who stood again. It was a bizarre exercise that cast the rebbe in the role of a diabolical musician pounding the keyboard of a human carillon, though no music beyond the hosannas of the faithful was available to Muni's ears.

Who were these cranks that lived largely on air supplemented by a diet of chickpeas? They ate them boiled, fried, tossed them uncooked into their yawning mouths and chewed them to a pithy puree. The chickpeas no doubt accounted for the Hasids' chronic flatulence, which vitiated the atmosphere of their shtibl. But their flatus was also deemed conducive to a useful upthrust during prayer, and the beans themselves provided the nourishment essential for pursuing their occult experiments. Experiments that played havoc with the commonplace reality of North Main Street. The mystery for Muni was why they had chosen the Pinch for their laboratory, when there were so many other places where Jews of their feather were much thicker on the ground.

"Because," Pinchas had explained, though the notion clearly offended his sense of propriety, "they have calculated that will be dead center, the city of Memphis, of the coming apocalypse."

The rebbe was back in his cushioned chair, his beard obscuring his ritual garment like the bib of a hair shirt. Serenely he began holding forth on a subject that rang a distant bell in Muni's brain.

"From the Angel of Forgetfulness we know that under the nose he tweaks you when you were born, so the soul don't remember what once it knew in Paradise. But comes the real tweaking when you forget what since you were born you think you remembered. Then you will stop looking within yourself for HaShem. Also will you stop looking for Him without or above or behind or beside yourself either. So where you should look?" The disciples shifted their eyes, lifted and let fall their shoulders in unison. "Nowhere is where! When you are in your body nowhere, you are everywhere in your soul. Let go already from everywhere, you should exchange it for nowhere and nothing."

His followers wagged their heads as if they understood what he was talking about. One with a fluttering eyelid, flush with exaltation, exclaimed, "So sublime is nothing that no thinking about it can do it justice!"

But Rabbi ben Yahya was quick to put him in his place: "Look at who thinks he's nothing." The retort was greeted with wholesale sniggering.

Muni thought he had heard enough, but just as he turned to leave, the rebbe, indifferent to his lingering presence, began discoursing on multiple worlds. "Like dreidls on twin axes they spin, heaven and earth," he proclaimed, "and when the letters from the dreidls that they make a match, the two worlds kiss and Messiah comes."

Again a distant bell tolled.

Muni was still sleeping fitfully, rising from his cot during the night to look out his window. But there was never anything on the wire between its fixed pulleys except perhaps Mrs. Rosen's bellying bloomers or a pair of her husband's dropseat longjohns that she'd forgotten to take in. Sometimes there were slighter garments that Muni tried to ignore, just as he did the silhouettes he saw behind the drawn shades of the apartment above the delicatessen. Was it his fault that La Funambula might never perform again? Somehow he couldn't help but think that yes, it was. But he'd sidestepped her for so long now that the distance across the alley had become for him as great as the distance from, say, the mines of Nerchinsk to America. So much time had elapsed since their shared tumble that it was too late to change his tack; it was impossible that he should ever speak to her again.

At the same time he knew an encounter was unavoidable. There had been so many near misses on the street and in Market Square Park; and when the electric lights came back on after the maiden screening of *Calamity Anne's Inheritance* at the new Idle Hour Theater, there she was. Jenny walked with a cane since the plaster cast had been removed from her leg, limping with a dignity she'd never evidenced in her former knock-kneed stride. The cane was one of those serpent-headed walking sticks from their nest in the umbrella stand at Pin's. (She'd also acquired one for the schwartze Asbestos, who was seen to twirl it with surprising dexterity.) No longer attempting to hide from Jenny Bashrig's approach, neither could Muni meet her eye, though stealing a peek he might detect the trace of a smile playing upon her primrose lips. Then it seemed to him as if the girl were actually enjoying his consternation. Once, as he watched her making her way past Plesofsky's dentistry on Overton Avenue, she suddenly clenched the cane between her teeth and kicked into a handstand. With her petticoats hiding her head and her ribbed lisle knickers fully exposed, she rounded the corner inverted into North Main Street.

Several days later, on a raw and windblown February afternoon, Mose Dlugach, looking suspiciously droll in his oilskin slicker, asked Pinchas if he could borrow his nephew for a while to beat some rugs. His own worthless sons were over at the Neighborhood House learning the turkey trot and he couldn't afford to leave his shop any longer. The rugs were oriental carpets that had been gathering dust for years alongside the assemblage of curios in the attic-like environment of Dlugach's Secondhand; they could do with a good airing out. Though he couldn't see what was so urgent about the job that it demanded his immediate attention, Muni nevertheless appreciated the diversion. One at a time he lugged the columnar carpets down the back stairs and into the drab little yard behind the shop. There he unrolled them, draped them over a drooping clothesline, and walloped them with a two-by-four. It was a more strenuous task than he'd anticipated, but Muni, exorcising unrealized frustrations, took pleasure in mercilessly swatting the stiff fabric, raising thunderheads of dust from the pile. Even more than lambasting the rugs, however, he enjoyed watching their intricate patterns unfolding as he spread them over that bald scrap of ground. Then it was as if he were transforming the backyard, with its board fence, rusted wash boiler, and outhouse, into a parti-color caravansary.

One bulky carpet, though, proved to be heavier than the rest. Finding it too difficult to hoist onto his shoulder, Muni dragged it instead out through the rear of the premises and tugged it bumping down the wooden steps. In the yard he used his foot to kick it into a trundling rotation, and as the carpet began to unroll, it released from its dwindling cylinder a hidden girl. It was Jenny Bashrig, who spilled out of the rug as from the curl of a wave, hugging the cane to her chest like a scepter as she continued rolling over and over across the beaten earth. She fetched up against the fence where she lay motionless in her peacoat, while Muni held his breath until she opened her eyes. Then she got a bit stiffly to her feet and stood there, leaning on her cane with one hand, brushing herself off with the other, and all the while laughing fit to burst. The wind discomposed her pitchy hair, strands of which lashed her cheeks until she peeled them away still laughing.

Muni was stunned: of all the marvels he'd witnessed since coming to the Pinch, this one seemed the least credible.

Jenny tried to swallow her laughter with an unladylike snort. She pulled a knit cap from her pocket and tugged it purposefully over her head, then let go of another mutinous guffaw. After which she wiped her nose on her sleeve. "You don't got to be scared of me," she said.

He began automatically to deny the charge, then realized that it was true. "I'm sorry what happened to your leg," he offered finally.

"I can tell you're sorry," she replied, admitting a smile he feared might break into hilarity again, "because of how sorry you look."

He was aware that she was teasing him, and while it made him no less uncomfortable, her tone suggested she had forgiven him his part in her injury. He didn't deserve to be forgiven, and for a moment Muni thought of handing her the bat, which still lay at his feet, that he might receive his just punishment. But nothing in the girl's rosy demeanor suggested she was in a punishing mood. Muni wished he could respond to her banter with some lighthearted riposte of his own; the situation seemed to call for it, but frivolity was never his strong suit. He made a stab at it anyway, offering a random tidbit he recalled from some newspaper item that Pinchas had offhandedly related.

"Did you know that they're putting now in the Cracker Jack box a prize?" His blush at the sheer insipidness of the remark inflamed his ears.

Jenny looked at him with a patient expression that bordered on pity, which made Muni squirm. "And this has what to do with the price of lox in Zhitomir?" she asked. But his nervousness seemed to have infected her as well, both of them struck dumb by the realization that, despite their familiarity, they were still perfect strangers. Jenny ultimately broke the silence: "I had to bribe Mr. Dlugach with a half dozen of Mrs. Rosen's boolkies," she volunteered, though her voice had lost its prior self-possession. "Clever, no?" Muni conceded that she was clever, after which he was speechless again. The bashfulness that had overtaken them both might have held them there till petrifaction set in, had not Jenny summoned the temerity to propose that they take a walk. Muni opened his mouth to make his apologies; he had work to do—but found that he was already following her.

"Is painful for you, the walking?" he managed, but she assured him that movement was always beneficial; then she set a pace, bobbing in her rhythmic limp, that Muni found hard to keep up with. They crossed Front Street, both still taciturn, and strolled down the rutted drive that led out along the river bluff, at the foot of which was the packet boat landing. So far during his tenure in Memphis Muni had paid little attention to the fact that the meandering Father of Waters flowed just below the Pinch; but on that brisk afternoon he was roused by the sight of a pair of low-lying steamers, their smokestacks puffing salt-and-pepper clouds as they took on goods and passengers. Docked beside them a showboat like a two-tiered wedding cake, a paddle the size of a carnival wheel at its stern, was piping minstrel tunes on its calliope. Barrels, potato sacks, and produce crates were piled in pyramids all about the levee, its stones pocked—as Jenny pointed out somewhat formally—with minié ball holes from Yankee gunboats.

"What kind holes?" inquired Muni, but the girl had already moved on.

Colored roustabouts, perspiring despite the bitter wind, heaved bales of cotton end over end up the groaning gangplanks, filling the lower and upper decks until the boats themselves became giant floating cotton bales. Old lady vendors hawked fish from trick buckets warmed by live coals; huddled stevedores sucked whiskey from jugs bristling with straws. Tin lizzies, driven by cotton and hardwood factors in fur-collared ulsters, joggled and backfired over the cobbles on tours of inspection, spooking the horses pulling baggage drays. Across the narrow channel the lanterns were being lit in the squatters' shanties tethered to the bank of Mud Island on pontoons—"So they can ride out the floods," Jenny had Muni to know, still dispensing information by the stingy morsel. As if she sensed that her companion had a delicate constitution that could only tolerate spoon-feeding. Despite the paucity of her conversation, however, Muni, who'd scarcely uttered a word, had the impression that the girl was mistress of all she surveyed.

Beyond the island a burnt-orange sun was beginning to set, as the pilot lights came on along the Arkansas shore. Such were the sights that lay at the doorstep of the Pinch, and while Muni had viewed them before on solitary walks, he thought he'd never seen them till he glimpsed them today through Jenny's wide-awake eyes; though she wasn't necessarily thrilled by what she saw.

"Did you know there's a curse on this city?" she said, tying tight the strings of her cap under her chin.

"In curses I don't believe," said Muni, adding a "kaynehoreh" against the evil eye.

Jenny sniffed. "Asbestos told me," she said, as if that settled all arguments, and Muni could have sworn he heard strains of the Negro's strident fiddle in the air.

The girl began speaking more freely, either from a release of nervous energy or an increasing comfort in the greenhorn's company. She recounted something of the city's history, breezily compressing centuries into the space of a paragraph: a Spanish conquistador had once passed through on a quest for gold, butchering Red Indians along the way, and later settlers had bilked the selfsame Indians out of their land. In departing their hallowed bluffs the Indians had flung a curse on the heads of the white men who'd displaced them. There was debate over the nature of that curse, and some said the yellow fever epidemics of the last century were retribution enough—"but I think," pronounced Jenny with blithe confidence (she was again the mischievous maidl who'd engineered their encounter), "the worst is yet to come."

Then pensively pointing north with her index finger: "It's six hours by train to St. Louis," and south—beyond the railroad bridge recently broadened to accommodate motorcars—with her thumb: "Eight hours to New Orleans. In between is nowhere at all. I would like," stated Jenny, with that vestige of Yiddish syntax that still sometimes invaded her speech, "to kick from my heels the dust of this town." Then she voiced her intention to join the circus.

The threat of her leaving gave Muni a touch of vertigo, made him realize how, for all his restlessness, he clung to the Pinch as to a raft in rough waters. "Uncle Pinchas says," he injected, "that in Palestine the Arabs are butchering Jews . . ." Jenny eyed him as if wondering if he could only speak in non sequiturs, but Muni felt compelled to remind her that things could be barbarous out there where history was happening. He continued enumerating events he'd mostly ignored when his uncle rehearsed them over the breakfast table. ". . . and they got on trial in the state of Georgia the Jew Leo Frank for a murder nobody believes he did it."

Jenny frowned as if to show herself proof against such distractions. "The other girls," she said, "they don't think about nothing but who will dance with them at the next Menorah Institute mixer. Me, I need," she rummaged her brain for the word, "experience."

Muni tried to remember if he'd ever felt a similar call to adventure. "I had in my life enough experience," he told her, but he had to admit that the longing became Jenny Bashrig.

On subsequent walks, often at dusk since each had their duties during the day, the girl was forthcoming about her past. Much of what she revealed, though, Muni was already familiar with from the Pins' account of her history: he knew, for instance, that she was an orphan, and was pleased to inform her that they shared that singular distinction. He knew also that, while the Rosens had taken her in, she had been throughout her childhood fundamentally the ward of the street, the entire community contributing to her upkeep. That he too was beholden to a community that had helped fund his flight to freedom was a topic he was not so anxious to discuss. While he had no thought of absconding, he still didn't like to recall a debt that bound him in obedience to the Pinch, though no one else seemed to acknowledge the liability. In the ghetto tsedakah, or charity, was regarded a sacred duty that entailed no obligation on the part of the recipient. And in time, as Muni grew easier with Jenny, he became less oppressed by what he felt he owed North Main Street.

Although she was full of curious facts about the neighborhood and the city at large, Jenny's education had not advanced beyond grade school. "Me and my teachers, we didn't ever see eye to eye," she confessed, almost proud of her virtual illiteracy. She boasted of her recalcitrance, her refusal to submit to the tyranny of Miss Christine Reudelhuber, the severely coiffed, talcum-reeking principal of the local school. Declared incorrigible, she'd begun her haphazard waitressing career at Rosen's while openly developing her acrobatic skills. Having found her body something of an impediment at street level, she set out to discover how it might function more nimbly aloft, for such was her reasoning. Following instructions in a mail-order pamphlet on the science of equilibrism, she hung a slack rope near to the ground in the Rosen's backyard; eventually she graduated from the rope to a woven cable purchased from a ship chandler's down at the river wharf. That was the wire with which she'd replaced the clothesline strung across the alley between the Rosens and the Pins. She'd made no secret of her ultimate ambition to join a circus and travel the world. Never once, however, did she allude to the fact that her injury had grounded her, perhaps permanently, and Muni tactfully avoided the subject altogether.

"Now you," Jenny said to him, demure again after one of her lengthy disclosures. They'd been sauntering along Main Street proper, past Court Square with its burbling fountain, peering into the dressed windows of the department stores owned by German Jews. These were the Jews who'd come to America with money and culture, and so bypassed the unventilated tenements of the Pinch.

"Me what?" wondered Muni, stalling, because he knew perfectly well what she meant: it was his turn to impart a detail or two of his own past. It was a past that had obviously intrigued the girl since his arrival, had even given him something of a heroic cachet in her eyes. So why was he so reluctant to revisit his history? It wasn't that he was ashamed—why should he be ashamed? Hadn't he survived the unspeakable against all odds? But his memories had been lost and found and lost again so often that he was no longer sure of the veracity of those that remained. Sometimes it even seemed to him that his past didn't count; his own life had not yet started. Or rather, it had started once, been aborted, and was only just beginning again.

"Sure, the boy was fetched from out of the bulrushes," Muni's aunt Katie had informed the girl, mocking her nephew's diffidence. "He fell from the moon."

She was relentless in regaling Jenny with spurious facts about Muni's origins, whenever their neighbor, who needed no invitation, dropped by at dinnertime. Jenny brought with her cold cuts and blintzes for which Pinchas was especially grateful, such a welcome change from Katie's spuds. Lately Katie had tended to sling their suppers at her men with a growing irascibility, her humor prickly to the point of making her unapproachable. Moreover, she was unresponsive to any questions from her husband concerning her mood. At a loss, Pinchas fluctuated between hurt and solicitude, worried about the physical toll Katie's temper was taking— the scooped cheeks and broken capillaries, the plum bruises beneath her eyes. But when Jenny was around, Katie perked up: she became garrulous, dispensing apocryphal versions of her nephew's biography as confounding to her husband as to Muni himself. Jenny, however, was amused by Mrs. Pin's fancies, and Katie would giggle as well, the two females retreating into a corner to conspire in whispers. Though he had no idea what transpired between them, Pinchas was glad to see his spouse animated again, though as soon as Jenny left, Katie reverted to her sour aspect.

Their outings took Jenny and Muni ever farther afield; the city had its points of interest. There was Beale Street with its barrelhouses cheek by jowl with funeral parlors, where the casketed dead were showcased in windows as examples of the mortician's art. (On Beale they also saw the colored men rounded up by gaitered police for the offense of fraternizing in public.) There were the Italianate mansions along Adams Avenue, and the tree-lined Parkway, where you had to dodge cantering horses bearing smart equestrian ladies in riding pants. It was on the bridle path in the Parkway's median that they sighted the first purple crocuses nudging their heads through the leaf-moldy loam. But for Muni, nowhere else in the city had the liveliness of North Main Street itself, at least as it was interpreted through Jenny's back-fence tales. She told him how Mr. Crow, the locksmith, would have his wife committed to the county sanitarium by day, only to return at night to plead for her release; how the local hero Eddie Kid Wolf got his glass jaw routinely shattered in the Phoenix Arena over at Winchester and Front. Tantalized by her loshen horeh, her gossip, Muni sometimes felt that the shops and apartments above them, the narrow frame houses along the side streets, existed solely by the grace of the girl. Still he was slow to connect his increased affection for the picturesque ordinariness of the street with his feelings for his talky companion. It made him uneasy that he and Jenny Bashrig were already considered an item by their neighbors, since there was nothing in their association thus far that signified a romantic attachment.

After all, they had yet to even hold hands. Meanwhile everyone smiled benevolently upon the young couple. The fiddler Asbestos, whose blessing they also seemed to have secured, encouraged their intimacy with a purling adagio whenever they passed. They passed him often, as there were days when he seemed to occupy every street corner at once. As aggravated by the blind man's familiarity with the girl as he was arrested by his music, Muni paused once to address him: "Don't you got someplace else you need to be?"

"I am someplace else," replied the Negro with his yellow-toothed grin. Then he added mysteriously, "I ain't what you think I am."

"Frankly I don't know what I think you are," said Muni, thus terminating their exchange.

Was Jenny pretty? Her nose was slightly crooked, her stripling figure wiry to a nearly unfeminine degree, but her eyes—those lamp-black
puddles—had their own gravitational pull. Looking into them, Muni felt
a tidal response in his kishkes, as if his very insides were being drawn
toward the girl. At some point Jenny had discarded her cane, and while
she still limped, might limp forever, her jerky movements had become so
adapted to her gait that Muni hardly noticed. He was selfishly thankful that her handicap kept her anchored to terra firma, that she didn't
attempt to mount her rope or tinker with the reels that held it taut.
Also, she'd stopped talking so much about leaving town, though when
she mentioned it Muni fought an urge to hold her back physically. He
wanted to hold her. Once he went so far as to remark that her coat was
too thin for the climate, imagining she might then nestle against him for
warmth. Would he have the courage to enfold her with a cautious arm?
He remembered the shameless flirtations of the Labor Bund girls back
in Minsk: how he would stammer in embarrassment, his belly a furnace,
until deportation put an end to desire. But the weather had turned and a
new season was afoot: japonica, forsythia, and sweet jasmine grew out of
the cracks in the sidewalk; creepers climbed the alley walls. The perfume
of growing things vied with the fulsome odors from Sacharin's fish market and the nearby river, and energies Muni was unaware he possessed
were quickened by his proximity to the girl.

But even while the whole street seemed solicitous of the match, Muni
refrained from any conduct that might be perceived as courtship. At the
same time he knew that mere friendship would never entirely content him,
though he sometimes felt he and Jenny were still separated by mountains and frozen wastes. Then one mild April evening, during the agitated days just after the sinking of the *Titanic*, they took a walk through
Market Square Park. A number of other strollers were also abroad in that
ill-lighted public space, its gas lamps not yet replaced by electric lights.
Leaving the path Jenny had bolted ahead of him out across the patchy
lawn, lurching in her uneven stride toward the towering oak that was
the park's centerpiece. This was the tree under whose broad boughs in
summer, when the tenements became ovens, the population of the Pinch
would bring hampers, picnic on blankets spread over the grass, then bed
down for the night.

Despite the faint glow of her eggshell frock Muni lost sight of the girl in the shadows; she was a ghost and then she was gone. Having followed her beneath the branches, he stood there stymied among the sinuous roots peering this way and that, when a pair of strong hands grasped him under the arms and hoisted him into the air. Kicking and twisting, he struggled to regain his equilibrium, even as he was set astride a nodding bough—from which, looking up, he saw Jenny hanging by her knees. Moonlight filtering through the new leaves revealed her braid dangling like a bell-pull from under the skirt draped over her head, leaving her umbrella-style drawers fully exposed. Then, skinning the cat, she dropped neatly onto the limb that supported Muni, and leaned forward to plant a wet kiss on his lips.

The contact, brief as it was, left Muni so light-headed he thought he might swoon; he might have slid from the branch and broken his head had not Jenny held on to keep him from tumbling. The canopy of leaves cast harlequin shadows over her expectant face, and he felt compelled out of gratitude (if not challenged) to return her favor in kind. But while he still lacked the nerve to give back the kiss, there was something he thought she might even prefer. A piece of his past was the least of what he owed her for her attentions, though reaching into that grab bag could be like thrusting a hand into embers.

"When I was brodyag," he submitted, "that it means a fugitive fleeing the katorga, the labor camp, I came one time in the wilderness to what I think—I'm that weary—is from a wrecked sailing ship its hull. But close up I can see that it's instead the rib bones and tusks from a old-timey monster."

Meager as was his offering, the girl received it like a gift and was moved to give him another more protracted kiss. Again Muni's giddiness threatened to dislodge him from his perch, and grabbing him to steady his wobbling, Jenny was tickled, her laughter approaching a noisy hilarity. Then it was Muni's turn to take the initiative, clapping a hand over her mouth to mute her cackling lest the strollers discover them in their leafy roost.

After that the progress of their touching was a hole-and-corner affair, conducted exclusively in the tree that became their regular trysting place. Jenny was always the provocateur, assuming a sauciness on high that she would never have dared on earth in broad daylight. Given the right circumstances—stars, redolent breeze—she might bite Muni's ear-lobe or peck his brow. Certainly her lambent attentions were prompted by a genuine fondness, but there was another more expedient motive behind them. Because for every kitsl or stroke he received, Muni felt it incumbent upon him to divulge another memory in return. Squeeze his hand and he might recall how even words froze in the Siberian immensity, so that you had to wait till the spring thaw to hear what was said months before. Buss his cheek and he told you that compared with what they were fed— brined cabbage garnished with a single goosefoot ("So tsedrait were we with hunger that we licked from the wheelbarrow the axle grease")— his aunt Katie's black pudding was a feast. Their cleavings and caresses, however, remained confined to their nocturnal fastness, untranslatable to solid ground where they maintained a discreet acquaintance.

Nevertheless, the electricity between them when they were together was palpable. Though they feigned nonchalance, no one was fooled. Jenny's expression remained fixed in a kind of cat-that-ate-the-canary simper, while Muni wondered if people could tell that his veins and arteries were flushed with quicksilver. Amused by his nephew's distracted manner, Uncle Pinchas pretended impatience with him in the store, while his aunt might suspend her crabbiness long enough to pinch his cheek in passing. And once, with a dreary sigh, she said, "Faith but I'm not half jealous of you and yer flame." There was a beat before Muni realized that by "flame" she meant Jenny.

Then night would fall and he and the girl would withdraw into the branches of the oak. They went separately to the tree to ensure the clandestine nature of their meetings, and one would always find the other waiting among the lower branches. Then they would climb ever higher, scooting farther out along the nodding boughs, Jenny assisting Muni, who lacked her simian skills. They clung to aeries that afforded broad vistas over the tar-papered rooftops of the Pinch and the river, with its riding barges spangled in hurricane lamps. "I can see from here the Statue of Liberty," Jenny might insist, "and the Eiffel Tower and the Wall of China." While Muni: "I can see the depot at Poplar and Front," which was only a few blocks away, but farther than that he didn't care to look. Then they would kiss, kiss and embrace, and despite their dizzy swaying Muni learned to retain his balance. He trusted the girl to keep him from falling even as his dazzled brain remained steeped in a broth of wanting. How was it, he wondered, that things done in the tree seemed never to leave the tree, their consequences not extending past the reach of its branches?

Muni understood that Jenny was no ordinary girl, and that by coaxing him into empyrean altitudes, she introduced him to a new order of being. Above the earth they were beyond the range of the rude world's conventions. The fear he felt the first time she placed his hand over her breast gradually dissolved into an ambrosial delirium. And when, tentatively, she drew his fingers under her dress until they rested on the stocking fabric above her knee, he could believe that the warmth that infected his vitals was somehow holy. The sounds that reached them at that lofty height—train whistles and automobile klaxons—were muffled by the wind, though a measure from the blind man's fiddle might still be audible. Although his music was not made a whit more cheerful for being tempered by tenderness.

"Are we bad?" Jenny would whisper to Muni, who honestly didn't know; he'd traveled too far from his largely forgotten youth when he had the statutes of the rabbis by heart. But while it may have been merely self-serving, he maintained that the rabbis had no jurisdiction over their aerial petting.

Their conversation was still more conspicuous for what they didn't say than for what they did: Muni continued doling out his somewhat unreliable memories, while Jenny invoked a wanderlust she was increasingly less invested in. Once or twice Muni asked her what she and his aunt Katie shmoozed about, since it was only in Jenny's company that his aunt appeared untroubled these days. "Girl stuff," Jenny assured him with a wink, as if he would know what that meant, and Muni nodded like he understood before admitting he didn't. But in the language of their arboreal bundling each was becoming fluent. Muni could now reciprocate Jenny's clippings and claspings with equal fervor if not virtuosity. The more graduated was his exploration of her person, the nearer he felt to inhabiting the place he'd been living in for a solid year. He needed only Jenny Bashrig's express invitation to finally arrive.

It came on a midsummer night during the first real heat wave of the season. The jaundiced sky above the Pinch contained the humid swelter like a bell jar, impelling neighbors to flee their airless apartments. They lolled about under the boughs of the great oak in Market Square Park, swapping complaints and fanning mosquitoes away from their sleeping children, while high above them Muni and Jenny disported themselves. Fireflies flickered in an intermittent semaphore answered by flashes of heat lightning over the Arkansas floodplain. Jenny sprawled among the rustling branches as if relaxing in a hammock while Muni straddled the fork of an adjacent limb, admiring her languor.

Then he did something he hadn't done before: unprovoked, he volunteered a memory—though the accuracy of his hindsight was always in question.

"When I'm in the taiga a runaway," he began, "the dogsleds are on my heels. They might be a party of trappers or they might be peasants out to capture and collect on the fugitive his bounty—" but he couldn't afford to wait to find out which. Whips cracked, oaths were shouted, and Muni took off on his clodhopping snowshoes over the glassy expanse of the steppe. Ahead of him was a cloud bank he hoped to reach before the sleds overtook him. Hobbled by the broken racquets attached to his feet, however, he stopped to tear them off, but the snow's brittle crust only slowed his progress. Then for all of his panic, he was aware of a stunning phenomenon: a burst of sunlight had turned the rolling steppe golden, illuminating the cloud bank before him in a celestial nimbus. At the same time the ground itself had begun to stir under him. "Comes a loud noise like, excuse me, the firmament is breaking wind—" then the ground beneath Muni's feet erupted and he was catapulted into thin air.

Despite the evening's dimming half-light Muni could see that Jenny's mouth hung open, and for once he felt like the seducer and savored his power. He assured her the event was no less remarkable for its logical explanation: that a grove of dwarf pines, bent horizontal by its burden of snow since the previous autumn, had been stirred by the first warm sunshine of spring. The trees were further alerted by Muni's footfalls, which had cracked the ice that embalmed them so that they snapped in a sudden snowquake to attention. Thus did the reawakened trees fling the fugitive like a shot from a sling into the gilded fog, where he landed toches-over-teakettle on the frozen surface of Lake Baikal, the inland sea.

"Jenny," said Muni, his heart lifting heavy wings to confess, "when together we smotsken, I am flying again in the air." His next utterance might have been to ask her to marry him, had she not spoken up first.

"So what are you waiting?" she replied, smiling brazenly. "Ravish me already."

Muni knew better than to take her seriously. It was her talent to sound in deadly earnest even as she teased him, this time with a phrase she might have borrowed from some dime novel. After all, both of them were aware in their bones that the trespass they entertained was more than the Law (which who could remember?) allowed. Nevertheless, as Jenny still lay carelessly cradled by the pitch and sway of their perch, Muni was further inspirited by her boldness, intoxicated by their perilous altitude. Above their heads the Milky Way spiraled like cream stirred in black coffee and the blind man's fiddle could be heard playing some incidental melody of the spheres. Leaning forward, Muni gingerly lifted the dust-ruffled hem of her skirt, as Jenny, biting her lip in concentration, fumbled with the buttons of his fly. She reached into his pants the way a naughty child steals into a jar to snatch a macaroon, only to find that she's pulled out a serpent instead; but fascinated more than alarmed, she couldn't let go—while Muni, submissive to that part of his anatomy that had leached the blood from his spinning brain, cried aloud as he seized the girl in an ultimate embrace.

The initial shock of their coupling nearly jettisoned them from the top of the tree, each hanging on exclusively to the other. Muni's rapture purged him of every concern that wasn't Jenny. Released from the familiar world, he dangled in a hanging garden of sensations that were utterly strange in their sweetness, convinced that no one before him had ever known such bliss. But the seismic tremors they shared at the nether extreme of their passion had roots that troubled the depths of their fears as well. Because their shuddering embrace, Muni suddenly realized, had generated a contagion that prompted in its turn a universal trembling. Opening his eyes he saw from Jenny's expression that she had reached the same frightened conclusion: they had gone too far and the impact of their union had unseated nature itself. Or was it the reverse? Nature was settling scores with the wayward lovers. Whatever the case, the great patriarch oak had become unstable; tilting slowly, it groaned as if mortally wounded, wrenching its roots free of the planet to which it was moored, and with a sound like a nail pried from the vault of heaven, it started to topple. The lovers, holding on to one another now for dear life, declared their mutual devotion even as they rode the tree down its windy decline toward the earth, which gaped open to receive them.

◢5◣
Bolivar

On the night Rachel turned up again at the 348, I had come back only a short time before from a band rehearsal in midtown. Lamar Fontaine had received a shipment of high-grade Owsley acid from California, and I'd made a delivery to the once genteel neighborhood where Velveeta and the Psychopimps had set up their ménage. Before going I'd scooped the powdered LSD into gelatin capsules, which I invariably made a sloppy job of; I dropped more on the floor than I got into the caps. A portion of the spilled powder was transferred via a licked forefinger from the floor to my tongue. So I was pretty wasted by the time I hitched a ride out to Madison and Cooper with the newly criminalized drug. My destination was a gaily painted turn-of-the-century pile known as Beatnik Manor, headquarters of the Psychopimps and their circle, among whom I counted myself. I was as much drawn to the atmosphere as the music. The place was regularly filled with young people faithful to the watchword of the *poètes maudits*, to be always drunk "on wine, poetry, or virtue," give or take the virtue. They were originals, the tenants of that steep-gabled manse, and I felt that by association so was I. Traveling between Beatnik Manor, Avrom's shop, and 348 North Main, I moved from one safe house to another, passing only briefly through the fallen world. Though lately, between sanctuaries, I often risked slipping into the past.

The freaky aura of Beatnik Manor had spread to the tree-arcaded neighborhood, where a coffeehouse, a head shop, and other signs of incipient bohemia had begun to appear. Inside the house, thanks to my sprung psyche, I had difficulty in distinguishing between the natural and supernatural beings; I ran a gauntlet of gorgons and magi and even a North Main Street matron in a shirtwaist and patch wig before the band came into focus sitting around their smoke-filled parlor. They were jamming with a one-legged old blues legend named Bunky Foote. In keeping with their ethnological mission, the band had resurrected the gin-soaked Bunky from a North Mississippi swamp, redeeming his flat-topped "ax" from a Beale Street pawnshop along the way. He sat in a ladder-back rocker as he played his guitar, his prosthetic limb—which he'd detached to further his relaxation—leaning against the wall behind him. (In departing he would strap on the limb, lift the cap from his woolly tonsure, and declare, "Now y'all can call me Bunky Feetes.") Beside him Jimmy Pryor with his Prince Valiant do alternated scratching his washboard with blowing into a ceramic jug. Between sets he would dart into his basement shop to work on his puppets, returning with caricature effigies of friends and historical figures, sometimes combining them with eerie effects. The fair-haired Ira Kisco fingered his prized twelve-string guitar, a joint stuck in the capo and a Claude Lévi-Strauss paperback folded over his knee. Sandy Eubank, the curly-locked chanteuse in a loose-fitting smock whose translucency left little to the imagination, improvised dance steps she called the Eubanky Stomp. Meanwhile assorted hipsters came and went. They got stoned and added, between trips to a nefarious upstairs, lurid colors to the surreal images that lined the interior walls. Beyond those walls Moloch and the military-industrial complex ruled the day, but the scene at Beatnik Manor remained a bulwark against their incursions.

They generally greeted me as one of their own: "Candy Man Lenny!" "Twenty-Three Sklarew!" "Breath 'n' Britches," this from Elder Lincoln, de facto leader of the band. Even their groupies would seem pleased to see me, at least until I'd made a few typically churlish advances, after which their eyes glazed over. I didn't mind, having lately conceived a fidelity to Rachel Ostrofsky.

Taking my place on the floor among the other devotees, I listened as the band sang in fiendish harmony along with Bunky: *Jelly roll done killed my pappy, drove my mama stone blind* . . . They played a song that itemized all the things Mr. Crump, the deceased political sachem who'd run the city of Memphis for decades, didn't 'low, which included easy riders and "protonihilistic boogie blues." Their traditional instruments—fiddle, Dobro, mouth harp—mingled in an unholy alliance with Cholly Jolly's electric guitar, its sound the snarl of a tomcat in rut. Then the band took a recess, and, snapped back into an awareness of why I'd come, I broke out the contraband, for which they passed the hat. My gentleman landlord,

Lamar Fontaine, self-appointed benefactor to the Psychopimps, was content with whatever token donations they made.

The band members then began to talk shop, and I was impressed as always with their musical sophistication, having none of my own. Sometimes I thought they spoke a secret language. Sweet-scented hash pipes floated from hand to hand while Cholly Jolly, his sorrel eyebrows thick as his walrus mustache, praised Bunky Foote to his face. Bunky's broad grin contracted, however, as Cholly included such rivals as Furry Lewis, Sleepy John, and Mi'sippi Fred in his canon. The grin expanded again when Cholly, in a burst of muggle-fueled fellowship, insisted, "Everything comes from you guys. You say more in a bent note than Clapton can in the whole twelve-bar scheme. The inside stuff, Cap'm, the shades of light and dark in your sliding chords, that's where the sweet spots lie."

The classically trained Ira Kisco seconded Cholly's assertion. "I thought I knew my way round a blues progression pretty good, but I didn't know diddly 'bout the structures: the thirteen and a half bars and the whole gonzo cabala of modal tunings and turnarounds—"

"Show-off," from Sandy Eubank, her loose limbs displayed to good advantage in a beanbag pouf.

Having returned from the basement with an odd new puppet, Jimmy Pryor recalled the first time they'd had Bunky over to the manor. "We threw you a banquet like the one Apollinaire and Gertrude Stein made for Henri Rousseau. That one was a sham soiree, really, which they intended to rag the old naïf, but the Douanier received the honor with such courtly dignity that he turned the tables on his hosts. The Bunk, he did the same with us."

By now Bunky Foote, without losing his grin, had begun to writhe in embarrassment. Elder Lincoln, silent so far behind his keyboard, his mahogany jaw set and tense, finally spoke up. "Yeah, y'all white folks sure been good to us 'sploited coloreds."

There was a moment when the room seemed duly chastised. Elder, by dint of his golden throat and expertise with a range of instruments, was the Psychopimp's front man; he was respected as well for his hard-won street creds, and commanded an authority whenever he spoke. Given to radical mood swings, he had ample reason to be moody lately. The week before, out walking in the neighborhood with the lily-white Sandy—a decidedly provocative act—he was stomped by the cops. The bruises and a royal goose egg on his brow still bore witness to the assault. But Cholly seemed to suspect there was another cause of Elder's flare-up.

"What's eating you, man?"

"Man," said Elder acidly, "I'm sick of this chickenshit town. The mayor and his stooges squat in their counting house, refuse to even negotiate with the union, while the garbageman," he struck a sour note on the keyboard behind him for emphasis, "he still qualifies for welfare on a full-time salary."

Though the strike was on everyone's mind, I was surprised to hear the issue noised about at Beatnik Manor. The Psychopimps were notorious for their grand schemes, their projected Dada events and dream carnivals, some of which even materialized. Cosmic revolutions they might entertain, but local politics seemed too pedestrian a topic to cross their radar.

Of course nobody was inclined to argue with Elder. "Mayor Loeb ain't about to give a inch," affirmed Sandy.

"'Just like a tree that's standing by the water,'" Elder bitterly intoned.

"Chandler and James and them on the city council," submitted Jimmy Pryor, dandling the little puppet on his knee: it was a miniature bald-headed monk in a saffron robe, "they think," lifting the puppet with its stick legs dangling, speaking ventriloquially through its beak-shaped mouth, "strike is part of worldwide Commie plot. Reds are inspiring peasants to revolt." The Oriental singsong of Jimmy's pitched voice had an unsettling effect on his audience.

Ira Kisco, ever the diplomat, tried to strike an optimistic chord. "The union's bringing in some pretty big guns. Roy Wilkins turned a lot of heads the other night with his speech at the Mason Temple."

"I know all about it," Elder harrumphed. "He warned folks not to foul their own nest. Tell that to the local chapter of the Invaders: Black Power, baby; them young bucks are ready to burn the city down."

That was the cue for Jimmy Pryor, kicking back the carpet, to place his little monk on the floor, strike a match, and set fire to its robe. The whole room flashed on those images of the Vietnamese monks who'd immolated themselves in protest against the decimation of their country. The flaming puppet crumpled and fell face-forward in a stinking mess of melting rubber, felt, and fleece. Then I sensed how the chilly menace of headline events had filtered through the walls of Beatnik Manor, which I'd previously thought were impenetrable.

Everyone's attention remained glued to the greasy spot where the puppet had been; which was when, egged on by the chemical buzz in my brain, I decided it was up to me to break the spell. "I was with the marchers that got Maced at Main and Beale," I announced. "We had to run like hell to keep from being beaten to bonemeal. My eyes are still stinging from the spray." And as no one seemed properly agog: "You had bodies lying in the street just like sacks of uncollected garbage." I realized, however vaguely, that the image was inappropriate; I'd confused the incident with the condition of the streets during the Yellow Fever epidemic as described in Muni Pinsker's book. Still I throbbed with anticipation, waiting for the room to recognize the largeness of my experience and pepper me with questions. But beyond a polite grunt on the part of Ira Kisco, I was mostly ignored.

Elder Lincoln, the plastic pick stuck in his 'fro like a half-buried cleaver, was still nodding his head over Jimmy's monk flambeau. "Martyrs," he opined, "that's what the movement needs all right. Specially martyrs that take a few pigs along with them."

After the immense effort it had taken me to formulate my speech, I struggled against a tail-spinning temptation to sulk; I summoned the waning effects of the acid to see myself as "tameless, swift, and proud," rather than just a boorish drug mule endured for the sake of the booty I brought.

She made a beeline toward me across the barroom, and while my heart hummed like the Lorelei, I tried to assume an air of careless unconcern.

"Red devils, yellow jackets, blue angels . . . ," I offered.

"I want to talk to you," said Rachel, who'd yet to remove her corny tam-o'-shanter. A few tendrils peeked from beneath the cap to caress her downy cheek.

"Maybe you'd prefer some crystal meth for the business lady's trip?" I said, as she was behaving in such a business-like manner.

"Can you please be real for a minute?" she asked.

I pondered the question: since having found myself a character in a book, I had, understandably, an ever more arbitrary sense of reality. "Where's Dennis?" I inquired, pretending to yawn.

She frowned. "That's none of your business." It gratified me to have provoked her, though her dark eyes were already softening, nostrils unflaring.

"Dennis and I decided we needed some time apart." I must have shown some relief, because she cautioned me: "Look, Lenny"—I savored her invocation of my name; I enjoyed looming over her by half a head, though her slenderness made her appear taller than she was—"that night with you, it never happened, okay? Call it an out-of-body experience."

I winced, my eyes involuntarily traveling over the body I'd remained outside of. "More's the pity," I muttered.

She gave me a look lest I forget my unspoken shame. "Like I said, it never happened," she reiterated. Then she sighed, rolled her eyes toward the ceiling: this was not how the conversation was supposed to go. Here she'd come down all alone to the city's seedy underbelly to find a guy who should have been flattered by the gesture but was instead being childishly difficult. Meanwhile the place was relatively quiet for a change. Lamar, in his bottle-green frock coat, was playing at master of ceremonies; he had pulled the plug on the jukebox, mounted a projector on a table, and was showing, through a dust-filled cone of light, an animated pornographic film: Snow White serially violated by industrious dwarves. I fluctuated between relishing Rachel's embarrassment and concealing my own.

"Can't we just be friends?" she asked.

Didn't she know that those were the most dreaded words a woman can say to a man? On the other hand, it was a kind of touching if pathetic request that must have hurt her pride to make. But I was resolved to stand as firm against her humility as I did against her condescension. Remarkably clearheaded despite (or thanks to) the evening's stimulants, I asked her point-blank, "What do you want?"

"I want to hear what you really know about the Pinch."

I blinked: she'd pronounced the open sesame that relaxed all hostilities, instantly rendering me a helpless conduit for the particulars of Muni Pinsker's world. "I know," I began, "that the night they turned on the electric lights for the first time, Lily Altfeder found her long-lost parrot, stiff but still upright on top of her hall tree. I know that Emile Grossbart, the watchmaker, was accustomed to wearing his truss outside his pants. I know that Eddie Kid Wolf performed feats of strength onstage at the Idle Hour Talent Show. He started by lifting a longhorn calf over his head and continued through all the months it took the calf to grow into a steer. Then he kept it tethered in the yard behind his family's rag shop till it drowned in the flood—"

"What flood?"

"The flood that followed the earthquake."

"That's what I wanted to talk to you about." Because it seemed that a sampling of Rachel's oral history informants had referred to some nameless event that occurred on North Main around the eve of the First World War. "That's what they say, 'Something happened.' Of course they were just kids at the time, but while none of them seem able to specify exactly what took place, they all agree it was momentous and afterward nothing was the same. When I ask them about an earthquake, nobody remembers. Either they know something they're not telling me or they're suffering from collective amnesia."

Whatever the case, Rachel was determined to put together an accurate time line for the history of the Pinch. She'd gone to the public library to check old newspaper records and discovered that there had indeed been seismic activity along the New Madrid Fault in the summer of 1913. But apparently the temblors were barely perceptible and damage to the city minimal. She'd looked high and low for references to physical consequences around North Main Street but so far had turned up zilch.

I enjoyed watching her grow animated as she described her vocational sleuthing and at one point exclaimed, "Nancy Drew!," which she ignored. Then coming to the heart of the matter she asked me, "Do you know of any local documentation about the quake?"

A grin unzipped itself across my face. "I've got pictures," I said.

Rachel actually clapped her hands in excitement, and the sound reverberated in my insides like rosy thunder.

In my apartment we knelt on the knobbly floor and I opened the book to show her an illustration of the upside-down oak tree in the park. Its tortured roots were thronged like a grandstand with creatures running the gamut from ordinary citizens to grotesques with articulated wings. The colors were eye-popping but conformed to nothing under heaven.

"These are just fanciful illustrations," she complained, bewildered and disappointed. "I want photos, documents . . ." But when I affected offense and made to take the book away from her, she refused to let it go, her eyes still fixed on the images.

"He's still alive," I told her.

"Who?"

"The illustrator, Tyrone Pin, he's still alive."

Heaving a fretful sigh, she said I could perhaps introduce her to the artist sometime: who knew but he might fill in some of the holes in her investigations. She had yet to remove her cap or coat, and when I invited her to do so she said she had to leave. My throat contracted like Chinese handcuffs, the tip of my tongue aching to trace the orchid pink whorl of her ear; her scent alone was a volume of *The Arabian Nights*. To her back as she departed I murmured that I adored her, and scarcely turning her head she admonished me to get over it. When I followed her onto the landing, she called up from the bottom of the stairs, "And forgodsakes don't cry."

Driving east out of the city in Rachel's Buick Brontosaur, as she called it, I could hardly contain my high spirits. "We're just like Jack and Neal," I remarked, which earned me a mildly withering look from Rachel. The truth was, she had appeared a bit tense from the moment she picked me up that morning, which was crisp and sunny after days of overcast skies. Was her mood owing to the unlikely presence of myself in her passenger seat or to the questionable excursion we were undertaking? She was after all making a large detour from the geographical locus of her research, with nothing to justify it but wanton curiosity. Whereas I was determined to view the trip in the light of an adventure. I'd done my part, was proud of my yeoman endeavor in phoning ahead to the hospital to arrange a visit, apparently the first the patient had received in memory, and now felt entitled to relax and enjoy the ride. Also, I'd nibbled just enough of a peyote button to give the monotonous landscape a lucent edge. It was Rachel and my first outing together.

Of course she was right to suspect the legitimacy of our junket. Making a pilgrimage to meet some dabbler locked up in a lunatic asylum since 1947 (incidentally the year of my birth) was not, on its surface, a very promising proposition. Never mind that his paintings served to illustrate a narrative in which yours truly figured among the dramatis personae. With a drum-rolling heart I'd peeked ahead at the passage where Lenny takes *The Pinch* back to his apartment, opens it, and begins to read. But farther than that I was still reluctant to go. What, in any case, would I learn? Probably just that Lenny Sklarew finds a book in which he reads that Lenny Sklarew found a book, ad nauseum. Which is not to say that Muni Pinsker's North Main Street didn't feel like a welcome home every time I stuck my nose in those pages. This was despite the old Shpinker rebbe's caution to his flock that "it's impossible to come back to someplace that you never been there before." Tshuvah, he called it: return. But whenever I put down the book and looked out the window at the forsaken street, from which you could smell the stench of the planet's decomposition, it was then that I felt like a stranger. The whole business was enough to "strangle up your mind," as Dylan says.

I glanced out the car window at a herd of cows lowing in a red-dirt pasture. "What do you get when you breed a Guernsey with a Holstein?" I asked Rachel, who shrugged her disinterest. "A Goldstein," I said contemplatively.

Then looking for some neutral subject, I brought up the strike, which turned out to be anything but neutral. Since the confrontation with the cops in front of Goldsmith's Department Store there'd been boycotts and marches every day, the strikers carrying placards reading I AM A MAN. The signs were mesmerizing in their repetition, broadcasting the notion that, like independence or imports, manhood was something that needed declaring. At any rate the issue was a sore point for Rachel, since the strike had driven a wedge between her and her so-called fiancé. This much she affirmed, which I might have taken as a confidence if it hadn't sounded so much like she was simply dismissing the subject. Vaguely miffed, I pictured myself on the picket line carrying a placard reading *I Am a Hippocampus* or something like that.

"Dennis is probably right," she conceded, as if obliged in his absence to defend his side of the argument. "He says it's a legal, not a moral issue." She began outlining the details of the failed strike negotiations, about which she was well informed. "So he has a point when he says it's all about the union contract and the dues checkoff. You have to give the mayor and his council some credit. They're honorable men and they dealt in good faith with the union representatives."

I was imagining her Roman-nosed profile engraved on ancient coins that might be placed over my eyes when I died.

"Rachel," I said, trying to keep my voice level, umbrage threatening to override my infatuation, "do you have any idea what it's like to be a garbage collector in the city of Memphis? No place to wash, no place to pee, laboring in filth for a wage that won't even support your family." I was encouraged by the accidental rhyme. "The heavy lifting cripples your spine but you never see a penny in workmen's compensation. Comes a storm, you take shelter in the barrel at the back of the truck, where the antiquated compressor shorts out and the hydraulic ram starts up and the truck eats you, bones and all."

I was repeating almost verbatim things I'd heard Elder Lincoln say at Beatnik Manor, but in saying them I surprised myself by how whipped up I became. "The union made every reasonable argument, but the mayor wouldn't deal. Now he won't even listen. Labor leaders, national labor leaders, and ministers were Maced on Main Street!—and still Mayor Loeb sits in his chamber with his thumb up his butt."

Rachel patted my knee. "Calm down, Lenny," she said soothingly. "You're preaching to the choir."

To congratulate myself on having achieved such a pitch of self-righteousness, I pulled out a joint and lit it. Rachel grabbed it and threw it out the window, admitting a blast of cold air that reinforced the rebuke. Afterward, however, she patted my knee again as if to say no hard feelings. Nor did she object when I switched the radio from the soft rock to the alternative station, where the DJ was introducing the musical stylings of the Insect Trust.

We arrived in the town of Bolivar—shoddy Greek Revival buildings surrounding a courthouse square complete with Confederate monument and hanging tree. When we stopped at a gas station to ask directions to Western State Hospital, the pump jockey, wearing a sleeveless shirt in the thirty-degree weather, merely grinned at me. Then he turned his head to squirt amber juice through a gap in his teeth.

The hospital grounds, once we'd located them, were bare but for the sentinel poplars that lined the drive like umbrellas without canopies. The building itself, with its moon-gray turrets and gables, was the kind of place you were meant to approach on a stormy night illuminated by flashes of lightning. It was sinister to the point of laughable, appearing even in daylight as the haunted institution it was rumored to be. The interior, when we'd parked the car and crossed the overheated threshold, was no less oppressive, with its scuffed linoleum and walls of pea-green tiles. There was a poker-stiff receptionist, who seemed to seethe as she announced our arrival over a switchboard. Minutes later an officious individual in horn-rims and lab coat, whose status we never learned, padded forward. Gravely, he bade us follow him through a series of locked doors with wire-glass windows, his keyring clattering like a medieval jailer's.

I tried to break the tension: "You and me," I whispered to Rachel, "Hansel and Gretel," which fell flat, and after that our surroundings effectively neutralized any attempt on my part at humor. Rachel anyway kept her eyes straight ahead, laconically answering our escort's questions: No, we weren't related to the patient; he'd made some paintings she was led to believe might be a key element in her ethnic heritage inquiries, and so on. The lab coat's only response was an all-purpose Cheshire-cat smirk.

We passed through a dust-moted dayroom, its windows encased in steel mesh, where a nurse with a mastiff's face sat beside a potted plant in the spraddle-legged posture of a lavatory concierge. Oyster-eyed inmates in seersucker bathrobes and paper slippers were bent over incomplete jigsaw puzzles and zigzagging concatenations of dominoes. An old man with a shaved head, crosshatched with what I took for a lobotomy scar, stood fidgeting in place; another, obese as a human archipelago, deployed toy soldiers on a tray in his lap. A woman in a gown like a pillowslip manipulated the rabbit ears on the snowy TV as if grappling with the horns of a bull. I was beginning to feel a guilty identification with the bourgeoisie of previous centuries who visited asylums on Sundays to view the insane as in a zoo. They paid a penny and were given sticks to poke the inmates with to coax them out of their lethargy.

Having bypassed an empty ward, we followed our chaperone down a long ammoniac corridor toward the end of which he rapped on a closed door. "Though he has his walking privileges, Mr. Pin seldom leaves his room," he informed us, then had us to know it was generally against hospital policy to allow patients to keep to themselves. "But in Mr. Pin's case the staff feels his hobby is the best therapy." And having received no answer from within, he turned the knob.

No wonder the door had been shut. Because the riot of color that escaped the narrow horse stall of a room threatened to subvert the bilious atmosphere of that grim facility. If not contained, it might deluge the place in a brilliance that could wake up the loonies from their stupor and excite them beyond electroshock to flat-out mutiny. I don't know what I expected—maybe some poor gibbering soul chained in a catacomb, his palette hung round his neck like an albatross. Instead, surrounded by exotic panels plastered to every surface, including the ceiling, sat a slight, bird-boned man in his mid- to late forties. He had cheeks white as meerschaum, sleepy green eyes, and a crop of fine auburn hair. He was wearing a bulky blue fisherman's sweater several sizes too large, his moist lips mouthing a silent language as he stirred a brush in a yogurt container on a table scattered with children's art materials: a Winky Dink Magic Paint and Crayon set with a plastic palette, and a tin tray of Kopy Kat watercolors. The composition before him, slathered in rich, incongruous hues on a flap from a cardboard box, depicted, as did all the others, a phantasmal streetscape. The street was represented in every season, or rather all seasons were simultaneously evoked. There was the floating North Main, North Main Street populated with shopkeepers haggling with celestial messengers and fish with feet, Hasidim riding Torah pointers, wild Indians and peddlers with wagons harnessed to dragonflies, fiddlers and fox-faced pipers serenading a wedding in a tree. Snow fell on flesh-red magnolias in full blossom; children slid down awnings out of firetrap tenements that crumbled behind them into skirmishes of honeysuckle and wisteria. A girl frolicked on a wire over an open pit filled with higgledy-piggledy corpses blanketed in stardust. The only relief from that assault on the senses was the small window looking out onto an afternoon that was blessedly leaden by contrast.

I knew there were artists who cultivated such crackbrained visions, could even name some that might be cited as Tyrone's "masters." But this was the authentic *horror vacui*, and it was humbling, if not downright stupefying, to be standing there in the presence of a certified maniac.

Having seen us into the room, our minder entered behind us and shut the door, compounding the claustrophobia that already gripped my gut. We were now completely immersed in the painter's element, and I wondered: had Tyrone been spurred by his dementia into interpreting Muni Pinsker's fabulations, or had the fabulations themselves driven Tyrone mad? Meanwhile our escort, peering owlishly over his horn-rims, had turned curator: "He works in a number of mediums, mostly cheap watercolors, though in recent years he's used the tempera poster paint the Hadassah ladies send him." His intonation itself was as unctuous as oil from a tube. "They also provide him with preprimed canvases, though he still prefers cardboard and construction paper. The art is quite primitive, as you can see, without logic or perspective, but the blockish figures have a certain folkish charm."

I could have brained him with a brickbat. Did he think the artist was deaf and dumb? From Avrom I knew that Tyrone Pin had been born late in the lives of his parents, Katie and Pinchas, so late in fact that neither survived his childhood. Orphaned, he was looked after by his cousin Muni, who inherited him along with Pinchas's store, and at a relatively tender age the boy had gone to war.

The mirrored door of a small medicine cabinet hung on the wall above a sink, its glass smeared with enamel in the shape of a mask, with a beard like surf and a deep-creased brow. Looking into it Tyrone would see his own eyes peering out from the face of an Ancient of Days, into a cell in a madhouse appointed in the spitting images of those that decked the inside of his skull. "Hab rachmones," I heard myself say under my breath, a Yiddish phrase I'd picked up from my reading, meaning "Have mercy." I vowed then and there to curb my use of mind-altering substances.

Rachel, in the interim, had assumed her professional demeanor. Removing a small handheld tape recorder from her purse, she asked permission with the arch of a brow to switch it on. Then she edged closer to Tyrone and inquired of him calmly, "What are you working on?" I was proud of her for ignoring the curator or keeper or whatever he was, who cautioned her that the patient was beyond her reach. Tyrone continued daubing with his brush at the composition in front of him, his mouth still speaking silent instructions to his hand. He gave no indication of having heard his interviewer. "Do you know where you are?" she asked, again with delicacy, and in my mind I answered for him: "Somewhere else." The radiator twanged like a Jew's harp, the heat in that hermetic room intensifying the chemical taint of the assorted pigments. Rachel persisted softly in her questions, holding her device close to Tyrone's lips as if to catch a stray mumble or sigh, though the artist never showed the least awareness of her presence. But at one point the words he was mouthing became briefly audible.

"I can sleep in the window," he said, the statement half a question, "with the curly dog coats?" His voice was a rusty hinge.

"Yes," said Rachel, gently encouraging. "Sleep wherever you want."

He became a touch more declarative: "And tomorrow we'll go to the circus under Jenny's dress."

Rachel blushed a peachy pink. "Sure thing, the circus."

"When I would jump on the bed," he mused, still without looking up, though his lips twitched as if in an effort to smile, "my head got stuck in the ceiling and my legs would go . . ." Here he actually kicked his legs a bit under the table.

Rachel said she was sorry.

"One time I pulled the barnacle goose out from the ground by his beak," he continued, "and hid him inside the pendulum clock." We were all—even the keeper who'd cupped an ear—straining to make sense of his utterances, when he suddenly raised his head from its former focus with an expression of acute distress.

"My back aches where they pulled out the wings," he proclaimed. He looked at us then and began to snigger so uncontrollably that I wondered if he'd been putting us on all along. But just when it seemed that he might be in danger of coming undone, the tears streaming in freshets down his cheeks, he inhaled and abruptly ceased; again he bent toward his water-colors, muttering "The people there were made out of flies."

For the first time since we'd entered his room, Rachel turned toward me, her oval face stricken in an echo of the artist's agitation. By this time, however, his language had ebbed back into soundlessness, his face bent in its fixated attention to the picture at hand.

On the drive back to Memphis, still a little unstrung from the encounter, I only half-listened to Rachel expressing annoyance. "Well, that was a waste of time," she complained; she seemed to be talking to herself for my benefit. "What did I learn? Not to go chasing after wild geese . . . barnacle geese yet." Despite a moist eye she blew a derisive raspberry, then further irked by my enduring silence, persisted: "I know what *you're* thinking, Lenny." I wasn't aware of thinking anything. "You're thinking we're in one of those movies where the mismatched couple meets some holy fool and then bond over the experience?" She groaned at the very idea, while I, still trying to recall if I'd ever seen such a movie, said nothing: let her fume. I bit my tongue rather than tell her how much, at that moment, I wanted to kiss her neck.

It had turned bitterly cold outside, the delft-blue sky retreating from an onslaught of dark clouds. I caught a glimpse out the window of a scarecrow in a stubble of cornstalks, just as Rachel reached across the seat to squeeze my hand. My breath caught: the gesture seemed to effectively erase our previous intimacy—the night that never happened—and replace it with something more durable. I knew enough to stay mute, since any blurted declaration from me might undo the moment. A few seconds passed and she removed her hand anyway, having perhaps thought better of it. But the reason turned out to be purely practical, because it had started to snow, great saucer-sized flakes of a kind rarely seen in Tennessee. The fallow pastures and tilted silos were turned almost instantly into features out of Currier and Ives, an absurdly precious landscape that neither of us, hazardous driving conditions aside, were of a mind to disparage.

I told Avrom we'd visited the madman and he asked me what did I want, a Good Samaritan medal? But it was one of his talkative days and, after his habit of doling out information in short rations, he let it be known that Tyrone had been among the troops who liberated the camps.

"How do you know?" I asked, expecting the usual bull.

"Because I was in it, the lager."

I assumed that his reply was intended as a conversation stopper; any reference to that place usually was. But I had acquired, at least provisionally, a girlfriend and so considered myself a man of some substance, and on the strength of that credential pressed him to elaborate. To my astonishment he made a terse admission: as he lay fevered and anemic in the camp, he was the captive audience of a meshuggeh GI who hunkered beside his cot and hokked him a tscheinik; told him a tale no one who could walk away would have listened to. It had to do with a fabled place called the Pinch, which became entangled in the survivor's delirium, and when he recovered he (the survivor) conceived the desire to make the journey to see for himself.

"I came, I saw," said Avrom, picking a nit from his beard and flicking it; then a shrug conveying volumes of disenchantment. "I'm still here. Sitzfleish it's called."

I felt privileged to have received the disclosure but was damned if I'd let him know it.

Outside the shop the strikers were marching from Beale Street to city hall and from city hall back to Beale again, tramping through the slush left over from the deepest snowfall the city had known. All the world's woes had slept for a day under a white counterpane then woke the next morning to sunshine and took back the streets. Beyond Main there was a war on: place-names like Khe Sanh and Dien Bien Phu were dropped as commonly into conversation as one might say *Electric Kool-Aid*. I hadn't heard from Rachel in days, though how could I? I had no phone. Of course she might have called Avrom's shop or dropped by the 348, and I might have sought her out at the Folklore Center in its mossy mansion on Peabody Avenue. But for the time being I liked recollecting her in tranquility, isolating her constituent parts—the curl the size of a finger ring at the nape of her neck, her calves as slender as bowling pins, her occasionally envenomed tongue. I was also reading *The Pinch* at a page or two every night, advancing hesitantly the way you'd enter a cavern whose sunlit mouth you're afraid to lose sight of.

My besotted affection for Rachel somehow contributed to the intensity of my reading, or vice versa. Whatever the case, when I shut the book I was still flocked about by its contents; merchants, thieves, and errant souls continued to divert me from my own historical moment. I remained anchored to the past by the weight of the washbasins, lard presses, and canister mills in Pin's General Merchandise, which I dragged about in my mind like the clanking strongboxes that trailed Marley's ghost. Avrom would remove his dentures and clack them at me to get my attention; Lamar would poke a finger at my chest, exhorting me to raise the price of cannabis; he was apparently in some kind of trouble. Sometimes I was afraid my transported involvement in the book put Rachel out of reach as well, and I would try and resist reading further. I'd try to get back to the familiar desolation of North Main Street, leave the apartment and run downstairs as I did this morning, only to find myself waist-deep in a morass of floating sundries like Alice in her pool of tears.

6
Afterglow

"You shouldn't take it so personal," argued Jenny with respect to the havoc the quake had unleashed. She was dusting herself off at the edge of the crevasse they had just hauled themselves out of, inspecting her various contusions. So casually did she examine herself that you'd have thought she'd only taken a minor pratfall rather than dropped out of the sky into an abyss. But Muni, bruised, abraded, and shaken to the core, couldn't help but believe that their treetop liaison had touched off the calamitous consequences.

"We should have first to been married," he proclaimed.

Jenny gaped at him in disbelief. "From where did you get such a big head?" she asked him sharply, while beyond her their panicked neighbors scurried here and there in the altered landscape. "You think it matters to God what you did?"

"But Jenny—" he began, and was silenced by the disappointment he read in her face. When he found his tongue again he submitted glumly, "Your question that the rabbis have debated it for centuries." Then instantly he was sorry for his betrayal; he was ashamed that the event, its earthshaking proportions notwithstanding, had supplanted the unfathomable delight he'd experienced in their intimacy. Still he couldn't let go of the guilt he felt for having set the planet awry. Having done so, were they now supposed to bask in some dewy-eyed postcoital glow? Scarcely able to control the trembling of his hand, Muni attempted to dab with his shirttail the sickle-shaped scar on Jenny's chin, then gave it up. "How can I join with you in the fraylikheit, the gladness, after what we just been through?"

For the oak, in toppling, had not fallen onto level ground. Had that happened, its limbs might have absorbed the shock and the couple, still suspended in its branches, climbed down handily. Instead the entire tree, at the end of its long decline, had pitched top foremost into the chasm that opened beneath it and had caused it to fall over in the first place. Market Square Park had shifted like the head of an awakening colossus and yawned, its acorn-strewn turf developing jaws that gobbled up the oak in all its leafy luxuriance. Then with such gathered velocity had the tree tipped groaning into the hole that it was virtually upended; its broad limbs, thus inverted, were stuffed into the maw of the gaping cavity so that its unearthed roots now protruded above the ground. They approximated in their height and breadth, those tangled roots, the original tree. And perched among them were a company of improbable creatures who, uncomfortable with their sudden exposure, leaped onto the grass and scattered in their various directions.

Muni and Jenny had managed to hold on, riding the bough they clung to all the way down into its subterranean berth. Dazed and disoriented after the tree had come to its jolting rest—wedged upside down in the crevasse—they were amazed to find themselves still in one piece. Then came the task of climbing out of a stygian shaft that may have had no bottom, a chill sepulchral breeze wafting out of its depths. Clambering up the downed tree proved much harder than mounting the oak when it stood erect. The climb was especially difficult for Muni, who lacked Jenny's agility in the first place and was moreover in shock. But the girl, apparently as skillful at spelunking as at scaling heights, endeavored despite her bum leg to aid her young man at each stage of their ascent. She grabbed him by the wrist, hauled him by the shirt collar and the seat of his pants, even as the earth continued to hiccup and rumble, threatening to dislodge them from every hard-earned purchase. In this way they were able to grapple by degrees along the knotty trunk, sometimes squeezing between the branches and the bedrock laid bare by the eruption. Surfacing at last into an ocher-red evening, they discovered the park transformed, its previously horizontal lawn bunched like a rug. Hysterical neighbors tottered over the rolling paths while dogs stood frozen in their tracks. But instead of the exhilaration the couple might have shared at having survived their ordeal, they exchanged cross words. Then before Muni could speak again and add further fuel to the fire, Jenny put a finger to his lips, took his arm, and led him out of the park.

The neighborhood was practically unrecognizable. Wooden buildings, flimsy to begin with, leaned against each other at precarious angles, if they hadn't already fallen down. The sturdier structures, jogged from their foundations and further disturbed by mysterious flickerings from within, had shrugged layers of bricks and mortar onto the pavement, their cornices and moldings dropping off like rotten limbs. Most of the citizens had vacated their apartments and fled toward open spaces, but one or two were left hanging from windowsills while friends and relations hopped about underneath them with open arms. Taking in the scene from the raised sidewalk in front of Schloss's Grocery, Jenny and Muni squeezed each other's hands. Chimneys had collapsed and gas mains burst, releasing flames that rose from the streets like fumaroles illuminating a sulfur sky. Ruptured pipes spewed boiling water up through the asphalt, the water rushing forth to meet the stream that coursed from the breach that had opened at Catfish Bayou. The alluvial soil around the bayou, loosened by the quake, had slid into the frothing water causing the pond to overflow its banks. A channel was then created that forked around a stalled trolley and merged again to gush into North Main Street. Show racks and furniture were washed from their displays in front of the shops and carried before the flood, which swept all manner of detritus along with it: baby buggies, herring barrels, a loveseat, a bass viol. Rats, possums, and raccoons were also caught up in the surge, paddling desperately to stay afloat. Some had managed to scramble aboard the casket of a yellow fever victim disinterred from the sandy loam around the bayou. The whole floating menagerie poured past Commerce, Winchester, Market, and Exchange Streets, debouching into the basin of Poplar Avenue, where it swerved and cascaded downhill toward the levee.

One notable feature amid the general chaos was the portly Rabbi ben Yahya, flanked by his disciples and sporting his best beaver shtreimel as he waded into the flood. He was blowing discordant tekiot on an undulant ebony ear trumpet weeks before the holidays, while his Hasidim, dodging debris, danced an ecstatic hora in midstream.

Later, legend would have it that the current of the Mississippi River had reversed itself and flowed backward for hours, that tremors could be felt as far away as Nashville and New Orleans. People would claim to have witnessed portents: swarms of passenger pigeons had set upon cornfields devouring acres of crops; apple-green parrots, never before seen in these parts, had populated whole stands of catalpa trees. Cattle lowed in chorus and huddled together, as did other animals—bears, foxes, panthers, coyotes—not known for their camaraderie. The moon was pink; a forest had seen a mass exodus of squirrels; there were glades carpeted in a ropy weave of snakes. But for all these ill-omened sightings, the earthquake was not a far-reaching cataclysm: the rest of the city seemed to have been passed over, the damage confined almost exclusively to the Pinch.

Aftershocks continued to rattle the ground and ring the chimes of nearby churches, their clanging competing with the bells of fire stations all over town. A motorized steam pumper churned upstream into North Main and was briefly amphibious before becoming swamped. Firemen in steel helmets leaped into the waist-deep water and spread a net beneath the rotund Mrs. Gruber, who dropped from her fire escape like an overfed baby from the beak of a stork. The better part of the fire brigade, however, had been dispatched to the Phoenix Boxing Arena over on Front. That great barn-like structure, which was hosting the long-awaited rematch between Sailor Merkle and Eddie Kid Wolf, was in full conflagration. Its fractured gas lines, unintentionally ignited by an attendee's cigar, had caused the place to go up like a signal flare. At the first cries of alarm the spectators had abandoned the premises in a stampede that trampled several unfortunates under foot. The heat from the arena's flames cracked the windows of adjacent buildings, their glass panes breaking with the *pff-pff* of air rifle reports. In the backyard of Dlugach's Secondhand a geyser of mud and brimstone had erupted, and riding its crest (in his short pants and middy blouse) was Benjy the ancient child. From the window of their apartment above Dlugach's, Mr. and Mrs. Padauer, his presumptive parents, leaned out in a vain attempt to rescue the boy.

This was not the world in which Muni and Jenny had initiated their romance. Witnessing such pandemonium on the heels of an unconsecrated union left them both feeling woefully unbalanced—which was doubly disturbing in the case of the equilibrist Jenny Bashrig.

"It looks like curtains for the Pinch," she concluded, and when her companion didn't catch the expression, offered a sad "Kaput."

For reasons he couldn't identify, Muni resented her assessment. "So this is by you wishful thinking?" he wondered.

Jenny narrowed her eyes like gun ports but did not answer. Then they agreed that it was anyway time they should try to check on their people.

They made their way toward the river bluff, whose higher ground they'd been told the displaced population had retreated to, but along the way found themselves fighting a current of pedestrians headed in the opposite direction. The planet had not yet ceased its rumblings and already their neighbors were returning whence they'd fled. If they couldn't reclaim their tenements, whose listing walls and fallen masonry the police had cordoned off, then they would at least reassemble within the ghetto's Sabbath boundaries. Jenny and Muni about-faced with the crowd as it forded the torrent of North Main Street to regroup in the previously evacuated Market Square Park. Some, having salvaged oil lamps, groceries, and feather beds from their apartments, began claiming family-sized parcels of lawn. The favored spots were those closest to the crater from which sprouted the monstrous network of roots; because upright or topsy-turvy, the tree was still the focal point of the park that had so often served as a neighborhood dormitory. Where else should they take refuge on such a night?

Under a flapping marquee an advance guard of uniformed foot soldiers from the Salvation Army was already ladling soup, but a dispute among the local rabbis as to whether the stuff was trayf discouraged their congregants from partaking. The issue was anyway moot, since the refugees much preferred the day-old bagels the Ridblatts had begun to distribute. The butcher Makowsky, still wearing his blood-stained apron, passed out slices of pickled beef tongue, while Mr. and Mrs. Rosen were uncommonly generous with their Danishes. Children gamboled among the scattered lanterns like so many Jack-Be-Nimbles hurtling fairy lights, their parents greeting one another like long-lost relations. Despite their sudden grievously reduced circumstances, the mood of those gathered in the park bordered on festive.

With the exception of the Padauers' doddering child, who'd sustained second-degree burns from the fountain of sludge, and Mrs. Gruber, who broke a hip after falling through the firemen's net—other than them and the gentiles crushed at the boxing arena and the blacksmith Tarnopol, rumored to have been swallowed by quicksand at the bayou—all of North Main Street and its immediate environs looked to be present and accounted for. Miraculously there were no other casualties to report. Of course a few citizens had superficial injuries that needed attending to, but Doc Seligman and the starchy Miss Reudelhuber, his acting nurse, were sufficient to the task. (A Red Cross chapter would later arrive on the scene to find nothing to do.) Everyone was chatty and ebullient, which may have been merely a symptom of shock, though they seemed to have swapped their earlier dread for the hum of collective unconstraint. One and all behaved like passengers washed up on an island after a shipwreck, stunned but thankful to be still among the living.

Sam Alabaster's doting wife surrounded him with cushions like a pasha and elevated his gouty leg on an ottoman, while he assured her, "In heaven *you* will be my footstool." Their kids, having sprinted up and down a wavy patch of turf until they were seasick, upchucked in concert over the edge of the crevasse. Mrs. Alabaster shepherded them away from the precipice, only to find her husband risen from his bivouac and hobbling forward in his dressing gown to peer into the pit as well. As his wife drew him back from the brink, he was replaced by Mr. Bluestein, who'd toddled up in his nightshirt holding a candle like a ghetto Diogenes. He squinted down the long shaft of the inverted oak, which disappeared in darkness, and remarked to the Widow Teitelbaum standing next to him, "Maybe is now rightside-up, the tree, and it's we are heads over heels." It was an uncharacteristic remark from such a sober-minded man, but the widow, embracing her rescued gramophone, nevertheless nodded reflectively in accord. So did Nutty Iskowitz and his property, the palooka Eddie Kid Wolf, saved by the catastrophe from having been KO'd by Sailor Merkle once again. He was still wearing his shot-silk trunks and flowing robe, whose hem some prankish kids carried like a train. Mr. Sebranig had also advanced to the lip of the chasm, where he toyed with his fleshly wife, the two of them executing a light-footed foxtrot toward and away from the magnetic hole. They were accompanied by the bleating of the deaf-aid shofar from the Hasidic camp. Tired of blowing it, Rabbi ben Yahya had ceded the task to a follower. The shofar was dolefully complemented by the strings of Asbestos's fiddle, though the fiddler himself was nowhere to be seen.

Following his bittersweet parting from Jenny, Muni located his aunt and uncle, who were also among those standing at the rim of the abyss. After a warm reunion, at least on the part of his uncle—his aunt Katie only listlessly participating—Pinchas wasted no time in informing his nephew that, appearances aside, this was not a natural disaster.

"They did it," he declared, pointing in the direction of the clustered Hasids. "The knucklehead Shpinkers, they finally did it."

"Did what, Uncle?"

"They engineered from heaven and earth the nuptials."

"Nupshuls?" Muni understood the word if not its context. How did that old Talmudic adage go? "The world is a wedding." Funny that the word *wedding* should have had so little resonance for him till now.

"From heaven and earth," repeated Pinchas, lifting and inclining his chin toward each destination. "Or if not heaven, then sitra achra, what they call the Other Side. Now we got with the aftermath to contend." But although he didn't sound thrilled by this monumental turn of events, neither did Pinchas, for all his disquiet, seem unduly alarmed. While for his part Muni was relieved to hear that his responsibility for what had happened was shared by others.

It was already getting on toward morning, and the North Main Streeters, wilting from a surfeit of excitement, had settled down on their respective plots of ground to catch some winks. The sky was already beginning to brighten from indigo to salmon-pink, like the interior of an abalone shell, but the park was still relatively cool. People were strewn about on pallets as if they'd been haphazardly deposited there by the recent upheaval, though the prevailing attitude remained that of survivors rather than victims. Having shrugged his suspenders from his shoulders, Muni too lay back in the soft grass. He cradled his head in his intertwined fingers, giving ear to the earth's increasingly infrequent eructations, like belches after a hearty meal. Like his neighbors Muni felt a certain satisfaction at having endured such a major tumult, though for him the experience had broader implications than tonight's big event. He realized that, during all his time in America, he'd neglected to celebrate the staggering fact that he was still alive: not even his ardor for Jenny had roused him to that.

Jenny. She was bedded down somewhere nearby, he assumed, and while the very idea of her stirred in his belly a maelstrom of emotions, he reminded himself that she was not an idea but a girl. He thought he could smell the lilac-and-kosher-dill scent of her on the breeze, which lulled him; the park had become an inviolable zone of tranquility. Then even as he entertained the notion that he must have been spared for a reason,

Muni imagined how Jenny would tease him for the thought. "Where'd you get such a big head?" he wondered, chuckling aloud as he tucked himself comfortably under a patchwork of dreams.

He awoke minutes (or was it hours?) later to muggy sunshine, refreshed but somewhat disconcerted upon finding that his pocket watch had stopped. It was a recent purchase, a coin-silver hunting watch that Novak the pawn-broker claimed had a sixteen-jewel movement and would last till Messiah arrived. Muni had thought it might last until he could afford a better one. Then he observed that the walleyed Mr. Shapiro, ensconced on a crazy quilt a few yards away, was looking befuddled as he presented the open face of his watch to his equally puzzled wife. And Sam Alabaster was shaking the gunmetal case of his own moon calendar watch as if time could be bullied back into motion.

"Maybe they don't remember to wind them up," ventured Pinchas from his dew-drenched blanket; and winding the stem of his turnip with a show of confidence, he then began thumping it with his knuckles when the hands refused to move. Comparing watches, nephew and uncle noted that both had stopped at 7:36, which was approximately the time the temblors had begun the night before.

All about them the North Main Streeters were rising from their improvised bedding to greet the new day. They swiveled their heads like periscopes as if to get their bearings, orienting themselves by the compass points of familiar faces. Over there, as lean as the lamppost beneath which he swayed, was the pious bootlegger Lazar der Royte at his morning prayers. The pursy Mrs. Padauer shared a park bench with her weak-chinned husband in his felt crusher hat; sandwiched between them was their aged tyke, knee pants bulging from the diaper-thick bandages that swaddled his scalded tush. There was the merchant Pinchas Pin and his vinegary wife, and a headless figure molded from clay, with stumps in place of arms and legs, that came trundling precipitously along the gravel path. It tumbled over railings and flailed in its attempt to pick itself up, only to plunge thereafter, to the delight of all who saw, straight into a bench or shrub.

Muni turned to his uncle, the answer man: "Vos iz?" And Pinchas, rolling his eyes: "It's the golem that he didn't finish making it, the rebbe."

The laughter of their neighbors pervading the air seemed to clear it of the early morning haze. Many rubbed their eyes with the heels of their hands, trying to square the world they were looking at with the one they had woke to the day before. The difference wasn't so much that North Main Street was under water, the flood having submerged their businesses and made tributaries of the side streets. That much they could observe from the park, which was still above sea level. But the real difference was the way the devastated district had everything and nothing in common with the Pinch. The atmosphere was somehow tonic despite the heat, every object sharply defined but with a michutz, a little something extra. The roots of the upended tree writhed like tentacles; they waved like the batons of a hundred concert conductors; the fire plug in front of the stucco synagogue spun like a bobbin. The blackbirds that perched on the telegraph wires were notes in a musical staff whose melody even the most tone-deaf could read.

Watching his neighbors in the act of evaluating their situation, Pinchas offered this studied aside to his nephew: "I think we don't see things as *they* are so much as we see them as *we* are." Muni tried to digest the statement, whatever it meant, though it clearly did nothing to alleviate Katie's sour mood, and it frankly failed to rise to the level of the general intoxication to which Muni himself had succumbed.

People were performing their ablutions in the granite fountain, empty for years but filled now with a hot ground water that spurted up in sporadic jets through a crack. Children were using the fountain for a sailboat basin, their fleet of twigs rehearsing in miniature the flotilla their parents were beginning to launch for the purpose of reaching their front doors. For no sooner had they freshened themselves after their open-air nap, itself invigorating, than the North Main Streeters set out to reclaim their abodes. In this, they flew in the face of the injunctions the civic authorities had put in place overnight. There were sawhorse barriers, fire and police ordinances plastered to every doorpost declaring their habitations unsafe. The papers promised disaster relief: a distribution center would be established and necessities dispensed, arrangements made for temporary housing until reconstruction could render the tenements habitable again. But so far no such services had materialized. The city of Memphis made all the appropriate noises: the authorities intended to behave responsibly toward their citizens of Hebrew extraction. But other than the couple of independent organizations that had already come and gone, noise was what the city delivered; emergency measures seemed to have evaporated with the dew. And while the community didn't like to appear ungrateful, they nevertheless dismissed the municipal response.

They dismissed the prohibitions that would have kept them from their homes, and set out to take up residence again above their flooded shops. No one interfered with them; having fulfilled their duty toward the ghetto, at least in print, the municipality under the auspices of Mayor Crump (called, for his ruddy complexion, the Red Snapper) washed its hands of North Main Street. After all, the city proper was perfectly intact; the banks, theaters, and retail stores that composed the heart of downtown Memphis were unharmed by the misfortune that had visited the Pinch. That district had always been a flyblown excrescence anyway. Moreover, there seemed a common reluctance on the part of outsiders to enter the self-styled Pale north of Poplar Avenue. It was as if, since yesterday, an invisible wall had been erected; and after giving short shrift to the disturbance and boasting of the city's unstinting aid efforts, the local press for the most part forgot about the quake.

The water was not so deep that they couldn't have waded, but Muni's uncle, in order to spare his wife the immersion, ferried her along with their nephew back to North Main from the boat launch at Market Square Park. They held a course against the current toward Pin's General Merchandise by means of a flat-bottomed pirogue hauled up for a price from the levee. Their neighbors employed similar conveyances, navigating skiffs, dories, a jury-rigged raft buoyed on oil drum pontoons, which they paddled with tea trays, dustpans, and the occasional oar. Most of the vessels had been bought for peanuts or procured in exchange for stopped pocket watches from the fisherfolk down at the Happy Hollow shantytown. They were hauled up the bluff to the park by energetic North Main Streeters who then shoved them off in a body, like an armada setting sail on a voyage of conquest.

The Pins arrived at the sunken portals of their store to find that its front doors had made an ineffective floodgate. They disembarked into waist-deep water, Pinchas lifting his wife in his arms, though she complained all the while that she was capable of managing on her own. Their nephew yanked open one of the glass-paned double doors, admitting a surge that instantly increased the level of the water inside. A flotsam of wallowing fabrics, fly swatters, toy soldiers, hampers, and fans bobbed all about them. Rolling hogsheads spilled straw and china cruets onto the surface of the mercantile soup. Submersed to the navel in that sloppy element, Muni looked toward his uncle to gauge his reaction, and saw that Pinchas had gone ghostly pale. He wasn't taking stock of the shambles of his business, however, but peering over the spectacles that had slipped to the tip of his nose, he was studying the tight features of his wife's faded face. He was cursing himself for having previously failed to notice her frailty, realizing upon lifting her above the risen water that she now weighed little more than her bones.

"Uncle?" said Muni, too distracted by the aquatic disorder to detect the particular nature of his uncle's dismay. Unanswering, Pinchas was already sloshing through the swill toward the stairs at the rear of the shop, up which he carried his querulous bride.

Muni forged his way back through the cracked-open door and once again took in the ruined Pinch. It was a tragedy, was it not? But for the life of him he couldn't see it that way. From Muni's saturated vantage the world floated inside and out, and whatever wasn't waterlogged rode the surface of the flooded neighborhood like the buoyant sensations that floated free in his breast and skull.

Over the gunwales of their ad hoc argosy the families were assessing their sunken shops and homes. Fathers briefly left their wives and children to wade into their businesses and inspect the losses, only to slosh back out—heads shaking—to the comparative serenity of the boats. The pharmacist Blen sat in a rocking dinghy beside his pie-faced wife, gazing at the wreckage of his drugstore. The window had given way, allowing the water to liberate the large glass show globes, which in turn had discolored the flood with their red and green dyes. Mr. and Mrs. Elster in their leaky cockleshell watched a parlor suite (swarming with cats) that had escaped their discount emporium drifting by. Mose Dlugach and his shiftless sons, Sam Alabaster and his brood in their half-submerged skiff, old Ephraim Schneour wearing his bowler at an unusually rakish angle—all appraised their damaged livelihoods and weighed their options. Muni could hear their voices carrying across the narrows.

Sam Alabaster: "Commercial insurance we got, but only we paid for theft and fire, no?"

Mendel Blen: "That way, God forbid, we could get from our parnosseh a little something back in hard times."

Sam: "Tahkeh, but who didn't waive the clause that included coverage for floods?"

Nobody didn't. The Mississippi River, for all the deluges it had wrought north and south of the city, could never climb the bluff to their doorsteps— that was the conventional wisdom. And as for earthquakes, who ever heard of such a thing in this part of the world? Nearly everyone, as it turned out, except the residents of the Pinch, as the New Madrid fault line upon which the city of Memphis sat rivaled the most fretful on earth.

Afloat in their knocking vessels, the neighbors frowned in fitting apprehension, but no one was fooled; the frowns were forced. The harbor they were anchored in was an eminently safe one. So what if their buildings were crippled, some with toppled walls exposing entire cross sections of interior—such as the one in which an unveiled Widow Teitelbaum could be seen seated in her bath, turning faucets from which no water flowed? There was no gas and the coal cellars were swamped, nor was there any unspoiled meat or produce to be had in the inundated groceries and butcher shops. But never mind, a new dispensation was afoot. The feeling was infectious: they were participants in a grand regatta, and while ordinary life might be turned on its noodle—"mit kop arop," as the old folks said—the transformation of their neighborhood was an astronomically bracing sea change.

All heads turned to watch a downed sycamore sailing past at a respectable clip. It was straddled by Rabbi Eliakum ben Yahya's band of fanatics making for their Commerce Avenue shtibl. The rabbi himself, seated like a bosun astride the roots at the stern, exhorted his disciples manning brick trowels to put their backs into it. No sooner had they passed than a thickset creature caked in mud and brandishing a rod and reel came splashing along the street from the northern end. Children squealed: how many golems had the quake set free? But their parents assured them that this one was only the blacksmith Tarnopol emerged from the quicksand around Catfish Bayou.

All that afternoon and into the evening the Pinch was a hive of industry to which Muni gladly lent a hand. Boats sailed into the inlet at Auction Street, where the farmers sold live chickens and potatoes by the bushel in the muddy wagonyard; then laden with fresh cargo, the boats sailed back to the busy port of North Main. A bucket brigade transferred water from a working pump above a horse trough in front of the No. 7 firehouse.

Wriggling fish were snatched from the ooze of the largely drained bayou and brought to Mr. Saccharin and his minions to be pickled and smoked. In lieu of coal the wood from fallen lintels and windowsills was broken up and fed to cookstoves cobwebbed in soot. The population organized by lantern light, like a squadron of will-o'-the-wisps, a kind of triage with regard to the crooked structures themselves. With whipsaws donated by Hekkie's Hardware they cut down the cottonwoods growing in the back-yards and alleys, some of whose trunks were already split from the quake. They hewed the scrub locusts that the tremors had caused to twine like cadeucei. With them they boarded up and buttressed the walls of the canted buildings, left them leaning on crutches like wounded soldiers.

Though working after dark had its hazardous element, the neighbors were not fearful in the least. For one thing, they were aware of being aided in some of the riskier tasks by shadowy figures holding ladders and even driving home nails—that is, when those same bantam creatures weren't removing the ladders from under them and hammering their thumbs. They were also aware of an access to unusual energies and, despite their swag bellies and duodenal ulcers, a shared capacity for physical exertion forgotten since their distant youth. In the morning they would review their handiwork and find that it lent the street an extemporaneous as-pect, like the crazy town constructed by the legendary fools of Chelm. But tonight they were conscious only of the theatricality of their labors, as if they were at once the perpetrators and spectators of their actions. It was a consciousness they took with them to their beds—which slid along the sloping floors of foundered apartments—where they slept a righteous sleep above the moonlit lagoon.

Having spent himself in strenuous activity along with the others, Muni had also surrendered to a well-earned slumber, though he'd lain awake for hours on his cot. From his off-kilter room over the store he was still able to hear the hammers and saws (though their noise had altogether ceased) and the fiddle. Retiring for the night, he had himself witnessed the fiddler Asbestos emerging from the security of a floating steamer trunk, whose lid sprang open to release a mordant music. Not without a nod to melody, the blind man's fiddling remained a grave counterpoint to the evening's chimerical atmosphere. But while it might once have taunted him, tonight Muni thought the music was rather catchy; it bore him up the way it had Jenny in her rope-dancing days. Strange that he'd scarcely thought of the girl during his labors, as he dangled light-headedly from the shaky scaffolding he was helping to erect. Only at the brink of sleep had he recalled that he was a young man in love, dwelling in an extraordinary land. It was a condition he perceived as a memory even as the experience unfolded.

He was awakened by her tapping at what was left of the window sash. Opening his bleary eyes, he rubbed them until he was certain that he saw what he saw: Jenny standing again in midair. Her onyx-black hair was slipping out of its twist, her white cotton shift slightly billowing, her dark eyes possessing depths beyond sounding. But rather than bouncing on a rope, this morning she swayed a bit jerkily from side to side. When Muni had bundled himself in his sheet and shuffled still half-asleep to the window, he saw that her coltish legs appeared to have grown overnight to an inordinate length. There were many things he supposed he would have to get used to in this curious new order.

"Kiss me?" she invited, and though he hesitated an irresolute beat—for when had he waked to such a proposition?—it never occurred to him that he could do other than oblige. Poking his head out the window, Muni tasted her lips, hungrily as it happened, their saltiness reinvigorating the living current between them. Catching his breath, he looked down to see the twin tupelo poles extending from beneath her shift into the sodden alley below. Stilts. Resourceful girl, she must have manufactured them during the night. "Funny thing," she said, reeling a little herself from the embrace. "It's a new day but also the same one as yesterday. How can that be?"

Muni nodded at the assertion and knew it was true. That it was also impossible seemed somehow irrelevant. He made a mental note to ask his uncle to explain the phenomenon, as Jenny beckoned him to climb on board. "You nuts?" he wanted to know, which she confirmed. So he asked her not to look (though she did anyway) as he dropped the sheet in order to pull on his shirt and pants over his drawers. Then he clambered gingerly across the jagged window ledge onto the lyre-like curve of Jenny's back. With his feet he discovered the pegs on which her own bare feet rested and clasped his hands around her firm waist, amazed that such an unprecedented act should feel so natural.

"Shouldn't we be afraid?" he wondered.

"What's to be afraid?" Then she took a giant step pretending to stumble, which made Muni yip with fright.

En route she offered him a poppyseed pastry dug from the pocket of her shift, which he scarfed up with gusto though it was stale. All his appetites, it seemed, were wide awake. The street from their tottering elevation had the quality of appearing both authentic and illusory, the familiar buildings in their unplumb incarnations utterly strange. Old North Main Street was at the same time itself and a fanciful stage version of itself, its properties bolstered up and likely to fall apart at any moment. But the players, as they went about the business of attempting to salvage their goods, most of which were unredeemable, appeared unconcerned with the imminent collapse of their shops and homes. Several sailed the coppery lagoon in their makeshift vessels to no particular purpose, all of them clearly in a holiday mood.

The Days of Awe were still weeks away, but the quake and its dramatic aftermath had enforced, for better or worse, an interlude from the ordinary run of things—and there seemed to be the conviction at large in those irrigated streets that time was stalled. Of course there was as yet no real evidence beyond the stopped clocks that such a situation obtained. Yesterday morning had advanced into afternoon, afternoon ebbed into evening, and there was every expectation the same pattern would recur today. In fact, the exquisite clarity of this morning's robin's egg sky was the looking-glass image of the day before. It was safe to assume that the world beyond Poplar Avenue persisted as usual, commerce along the river was uninterrupted, and society east of Alabama Street adhered to its seasonal calendar. But the Pinch, no longer landlocked, was quarantined (it was generally agreed) by a species of time that had relinquished its linear progress.

Today (which was Monday?) could also be said to contain other Mondays, and Wednesdays, other years. Uncle Pinchas had early on advised his nephew that time was prone to a certain elasticity in the Pinch, due to the cabalistic meddling of the crackbrained fanatics in their midst. And this morning, as Muni and Jenny tramped on stilts through the altered landscape, they passed into and out of odd patches—beneath the shadow of a bridge ramp that trembled from vehicles passing overhead, past saddled horses tethered at a trough in front of a galleried saloon—that did not conform to the current scene. That scene involved whole families filling striped pillowslips with sand from the boils that had erupted around the bottomless pit in the park; these they piled in front of the shops to make embankments that would confine the lagoon to a canal no wider than the street itself. Some of the sandbags they transported by raft to the bayou to construct a dike across the initial breach. They worked, Muni's neighbors, with the steadfast diligence of pyramid builders, though their labors seemed also to partake of equal parts make-believe.

"Jenny," said Muni who needed her compliance, "we're having fun, no?"

"You," replied Jenny with feigned irritation, all the while manning her stilts like a natural extension of her legs, minus the limp, "you wouldn't know fun if it bit your hiney. Anyhow, after a flood doesn't usually come cholera and dysentery? So how is it we got instead a seagoing jamboree?"

Indeed, some of the neighbors navigating the channel could be heard shouting to one another in half-baked nautical terms. They cursed like sailors as they slung more bags atop the pillowcase parapet, behaving in their newfound swagger as prodigally as their offspring, whose summer vacation from school was now indefinitely extended. Some of the children, having captured the rebbe's headless golem, were using its hollow corpus as a flotation device, though it continued to show signs of a twitching animation. Others gawked at the play of their reflections in the shop windows, which had acquired irregular features such as halos and donkey heads. In his exuberance Muni took the liberty of nibbling Jenny's ear, prompting laughter that resulted in a dangerous wobbling. Self-conscious, he looked about to see who might have observed them, though a couple canoodling on stilts above standing water scarcely constituted a special attraction on such a morning.

They had taken a turn around the lagoon and arrived back at the entrance to Pin's General Merchandise. There Muni slid down the twin poles onto the rampart, picked the splinters from his palms, and waded into the broth that engulfed the store. Above him Jenny abandoned the stilts to step through an upstairs window. Inside, Uncle Pinchas, pants rolled to the knees, was bailing water with a brass cuspidor. He seemed to be making headway, since the previously boggy depth was diminished to a shallow sludge.

"Nu, Uncle," said Muni, but Pinchas scarcely acknowledged him. He tried again with a jovial Old Country greeting, "Uncle Pinchas, how fares a Yid?"

Pinchas paused in his activity to give his nephew a look through moisture-beaded spectacles. Apparently satisfied that the young man was as addled as the rest of his community, he said with a grim defiance, "How do you think?"

Muni took in the bowed walls and blistered counters already smutted with fungus, the warped glove cases and scrap albums fat with scalloped pages the proprietor was trying to flatten with C-clamps. Few commodities remained unspoiled: the dry goods were drenched, sacks of spuds sending runner-like eyes through their burlap—though (Muni found himself thinking) wasn't a ravaged business finally incidental in the scheme of things? Why did his uncle seem so resistant to the general levity? Pinchas had exchanged the cuspidor for a box of lumpy corn starch, which he began sprinkling over his dripping inventory as a dehumidifying agent. Muni gently grasped the arm that shook the box. "So, Uncle," he said, "explain me again what happened." For hadn't he always relied on Pinchas to make sense of this singular neighborhood? And perhaps in explaining, his uncle would snap out of his mood.

"What can I tell you?" he said. "The Pinch is the place where things that don't happen, happen. So maybe what happened, it ain't exactly takink place."

Which hardly qualified as an answer. When Muni continued to gaze at him expectantly, Pinchas sighed and said, "Come upstairs."

Over weak tea at the kitchen table Pinchas gave his nephew a further account of the pernicious kibitzing of Rabbi ben Yahya and his zealots. "The Shpinkers, they don't know from ruination and revelation the difference. They starve themselves and make their mikvah in ice water; flog themselves bloody and twist like pretzels their joints when they worship. They dress up in French underwear the holy scrolls and pray like demons in heat until what's above spins out from its axis and collides with below." He bumped his chafed knuckles together in illustration. "Then comes the cataclyzz: the earth opens and out pours the creatures from superstition, and time don't flow anymore but sits still like a stagnant sump. This they call mashiach tseyt, Messiah time, which it will herald Messiah himself. Everything is prepared for his coming. That's what they believe, the meshuggeners."

"But what do *you* believe, Uncle?" asked Muni.

Pinchas removed his spectacles, squeezed the hump at the bridge of his nose. "I believe my Katie is ill."

It was then that Jenny entered from the bedroom damp-eyed and distraught.

"I called in Doc Seligman," continued Pinchas. "He didn't even need to look at her; he knows already she's sick. I'm crying hospital, but the doc says, '*You* tell her; to me she don't listen.' Anyway, he says, she's better off now at home. What she's got, a hospital can't cure it."

Muni asked if his uncle had sought a "second opinion," a phrase he'd heard bandied about.

"I got already from Seligman a second opinion, and a third."

It made a kind of cloudy sense that the hospital had been ruled out, now that the Pinch had become an essentially isolated province, but why had Pinchas so readily accepted Katie's condition? "But Uncle," his nephew protested, though before he could press the issue further, he was distracted by Jenny, who, standing at his shoulder, had begun softly to sob. Muni turned to her, perplexed, since this drama surrounding his aunt seemed so fundamentally out of tone with the character of a burnished new world.

Still he made a point of visiting his bedridden aunt. Her hair, bleached of its carroty essence, was the gray of rain-washed shingles, her pallid flesh interlaced with blue veins like marble. Her eyes, with their gas-green flame virtually extinguished, were a milky opalescence. Seeming embarrassed by the depredations of her accelerated aging and the cloying odor she exuded, Katie nevertheless rallied the strength to tease him with the neighborhood gossip.

"Nephew and Jenny sitting in a tree," she intoned, "k-i-s-s . . . ," the letters dissipating in a throaty aspiration.

Unpleasant as it was, Muni was grateful that she gave him an audience, since almost all others, Pinchas included, were forbidden to enter the sickroom.

"Seligman says Katie is with me a shlecht vayb, a shrew, so that I won't miss her when she's gone," confided Pinchas from the kitchen chair that had become the seat of his distress. "But I know better."

"What do you know, Uncle?" asked Muni, who could barely stand to linger indoors while outside the people carried on like skylarkers in Eden. He was hardly paying attention when Pinchas replied, "I know that she punishes me."

This gave his nephew pause. "Beg pardon," he respectfully submitted, uneasy to find himself gainsaying his uncle, "but isn't it Aunt Katie that's the victim?"

"She punishes me," continued Pinchas, oblivious of Muni's challenge, "because I'm not anymore with her a man." It wasn't a confession that Muni would have invited, but his uncle wasn't done. "What's the point if we can't make together a baby?"

That the couple were well past their childbearing years seemed the least of what was wrong with Pinchas's argument. "I don't think that from spite nobody dies," Muni offered with a great lump in his throat.

"You tell that to my Katie," called Pinchas, for his nephew, who'd heard all he could bear to, was already halfway down the stairs.

Dr. Seligman came and went with his syringes and gentian blue vials, and Jenny was also much in attendance. She brought herbal infusions from the Widow Teitelbaum and soups from Mrs. Rosen, which the patient seldom touched. (The deli was operating out of the Rosens' upstairs kitchen, Mrs. Rosen lowering baskets of borscht and sandwiches into the passing boats from her fire escape.) When Pinchas poked his head into the bedroom, however, Katie spat a string of Irish curses until he withdrew, though he hung on in the doorway suffering her abuse like a warm spring shower.

But despite his aunt's progressive emaciation Muni still couldn't find it in himself to feel sorry for her. This, he knew, was unconscionable: she was after all the wife of the man who'd rescued him from affliction, and didn't he venerate her gentle person as well? Hadn't they both been in his eyes—that is, until his uncle disabused him—the very model of domestic harmony? But the giddy climate of North Main Street was unfavorable to your common-variety pity; it was an atmosphere that argued against even the remorse you might feel for not feeling pity. And anyway Muni thought his aunt was beautiful in her languishing: wasting away became her like a cameo on an ageless sepulcher.

That's how things stood in the old neighborhood: nobody and nothing was so base or inessential that they lacked some aspect of the sublime. Every gesture, from scrounging for foodstuffs to caulking rust buckets and emptying water closets with a sieve, seemed to take its place in the grand narrative. Viewing the scuttled street from an upstairs window, Muni would recall the concept of neshomah yeterah, the bonus soul the faithful are granted on Friday nights. He remembered how, back in his childhood cheder in Blod, even their sadistic old melammed would wax rhapsodic when speaking of Shabbos: how the Sabbath was a palace in time whose architecture contained both the immemorial past and the promised future. Now the Pinch seemed to occupy a perpetual Sabbath that encompassed a past as distant as Muni's childhood and then some. Every action echoed a chiddush nifla (Muni remembered the phrase), some wondrous event.

Every ladder was a type of Jacob's Ladder; every mired but still spinning bicycle wheel—a rainbow in its spokes—was a version of the wheel Ezekiel saw. The flood was a reprise of the Flood. During sanguine sunsets the canal of North Main Street became the River Sambatyon, beyond which dwelled the lost tribes of Israel. When Tillie Alperin's little Esther burned her tongue on a hot knish, Isaiah's lips were seared again by the angel's lump of coal. Jakie Belz proudly presented his soiled linen as evidence that he'd been visited in the night by the demoness Lilith. Every gas pipe, base burner, and bedpan contained a trapped soul demanding release. Ike Petrofsky complained (or was he boasting?) of having to wade through several past lives in the morning in order to get back to the here and now—"And tomorrow I can step if I want into today."

Muni supposed he might also get around to recognizing a future that infiltrated the present at every turn, but there was no rush. For the time being he was captivated by current events that were themselves still encrusted with the past, his own and others'. Memories once too painful to revive—of prison and the katorga and the hopeful time before—seemed as if refined into luminous tintypes in the alchemical air. When he'd read them as a child in cheder, the stories of the Torah were converted before his eyes into tangible experience. Now, though he was blindsided by the prospect, Muni's experience of the Pinch seemed to clamor for a translation back into text. He remembered how the tales from holy writ, conveyed through the medium of Hebrew characters, could filter the grayest shtetl light into a Joseph's coat of colors; so how much brighter would words make a light that was already resplendent. The neighborhood was tohu v'bohu, a mishmash of stories that needed only some designated scribe to apprehend and record them for all time.

"Somebody ought to write it all down," Muni told Jenny one evening, when they were huddled together among the Medusa's hair roots of the inverted oak.

Her reply was a suggestion she would regret till her dying day: "So why don't you already?"

They had picked up their affair of the heart more or less where they'd left off before the quake. Of course the entire community was now stricken with a kind of pandemic infatuation, a free-floating euphoria that perhaps lent spice to the lovers' feelings; though a gleeful Muni preferred to think it was the other way around: his passion for Jenny had enlivened the whole neighborhood. But whereas his spirits were practically lighter than air, Jenny, whose medium had been thin air itself, seemed to keep at least one foot on the ground. She almost resented that their affair was nothing special in a place where *everything* was special, and she worried about Katie Pin. She even admitted to feeling some guilt over being happy while Katie lay at death's door. "It isn't nice to be romantic under her nose," she cautioned, sensing that their amorousness may have served to aggravate Katie's lamentable state. Muni couldn't have disagreed more.

"Does her good, I think, to see young people in love," he insisted, unable to understand Jenny's reservations.

Then one night in the tree, in a burst of spontaneous sentiment, he'd confessed to a youthful folly.

He was gazing at her barefoot countenance, her slender form in an embroidered smock backlit by a red-orange dusk that caused the twisted roots to do a fair impression of a burning bush. Other couples occupied those wavering boughs as well, flirting with each other more boldly than they'd have dared on dry land, dry land having become a scarce commodity. Above them Muni also caught sight of an ill-shaped little entity in a brass hat, which, when he squinted to sharpen his focus, was gone. A grin wreathed his face as he wondered if all this immoderate gladness was merely a function of his desire for Jenny.

"You know," he was suddenly moved to confide in her, "I used to make poems." There was one he remembered—remembered for the first time in an age—about the prophet Samuel in a foul mood after being recalled from death by the Witch of Endor; there was another about the sheydim, the elementals, who wove elflocks into Samson's beeswaxed hair . . .

"And now you make what?" mused the girl, tickling his middle with an uplifted toe. "Whoopee?"

But instead of divulging another memory, as her touch had routinely prompted, Muni swatted away her foot like a housefly. "Be for a moment serious," he scolded, shocked at his own thin-skinned response. But he was not done mulling over his recollection of the poems, which were admittedly callow and immature though not without a certain . . . he searched for the word.

The girl had screwed up her face and crossed her eyes in a burlesque of seriousness, defusing Muni's mood. "We are not by you amused," he pronounced, his peevishness already dissolved into parody.

"Okey-doke," said Jenny, still playing along, commencing as if to climb down. "Drop me a line when you get a chance."

"Jenny—" Muni grabbed her wrist to detain her. Maybe this was it, the ideal opportunity to propose to her, but the very thought flooded his head with an excess of emotion that robbed him of speech. The girl slid fluidly from her perch into his arms, as though in pronouncing her name he held an empty garment for her body to slip into. She leaned against him, pinning him to the crotch of a dirt-caked root with the pressure of her small breasts and hips. They had yet to repeat the deed that preceded the quake, when their fused bodies tolled like a clapper in a bell. But now the heat of their contact, for all its urgency, served only to enhance for Muni the delight he took in observing the very rich hours of North Main Street. It was an appallingly pure sensation, the kind that begged to be recorded the way sins and mitzvot are inscribed on the Jewish New Year in the Book of Life; because nothing in experience was real—this was his thunderous conviction—until it was wedded to the word. That was the marriage over which Muni, with Jenny's blessing, felt a sudden blind compulsion to preside.

"Don't go away," he blurted, leaping clear of the abyss to hit the ground running. "I'll be right back," he shouted over his shoulder, though he was already out of earshot.

The grand canal of North Main was lit by lanterns, moths, and toy gondolas with guttering candles for masts, with silk tallises and celluloid shirtfronts for sails. The buildings that bordered the water, despite their hobbled condition, assumed such a look of stability that you'd have thought they'd always been so skewed, and the shops were open for business though there was little left to sell. As a result, commerce was more a performance than an actual exchange of goods and services, the citizens like children who played at being entrepreneurs. Only Pin's General Merchandise, once the flagship enterprise of North Main Street, stood in darkness; for these days Pinchas Pin remained mostly sunk in despondency at the kitchen table. He roused himself only to inquire of his wife's health from the visiting doctor or to receive the consolations of Jenny Bashrig, who came and went. But even the gloomy store, an aberration in that glimmering neighborhood, had for Muni an air of deepest mystery.

He foraged among the mildewed shelves, poked with matches into shadowed recesses until he found what he was looking for: a chirographic fountain pen with an automatic inkstand and a quire of white octavo stationery. The pen's tapered handle was split and the paper moldy, its virgin leaves cockled and water-stained but nonetheless sufficient for his purpose. Muni tiptoed up the stairs past the kitchen in order not to disturb his brooding uncle. He could hear Pinchas lamenting aloud and even caught snatches of his blaming himself for Katie's ailment, for the barrenness of his marriage. And while his uncle's plaint made no immediate impression, it nevertheless penetrated Muni's awareness, lodging in some remote corner of his brain from which it might work its way out like a splinter over time.

Muni took the pen and paper into his matchbox room, its only furniture the folding cot and squat deal dresser upon which stood a porcelain ewer and basin. He peeled off a single page from the stack and shoved the rest beneath the slopjar under his cot. From his uncle's bookshelf in the hallway he selected a substantial volume, the Yiddish translation of Kropotkin's *Conquest of Bread* as it turned out. He sat on his cot, placed the book on his knees, and spread the paper across its smooth cloth binding. Then with a galloping heart Muni took up the inkpen and prepared to begin: he had some vague idea of making notes for future reference, of quickly acquitting himself of his renegade impulse then hurrying back to Jenny; it was after all with her that the real inspiration resided. But he found himself paralyzed.

He hadn't actually indited anything to paper since the doggerel verse of his yeshiva days, though lack of practice wasn't the only reason for his hesitation. For one thing, he couldn't decide what language to write in: his Hebrew was rusty from disuse and he regarded Yiddish as the holy tongue's poor relation; nor had he yet taken full possession of his host country's idiom. But even if he were able to choose a vernacular appropriate to his undertaking, what precisely was his subject? Everything he observed was replete with meaning, and he stood ready to make of himself a kind of conduit: the postapocalyptic Pinch would speak through Muni Pinsker as its primary means of expression. But how does one distill *everything* into a cogent narrative? His uncle, quoting a favorite Russian author, once told him that all happy families are alike, and there was certainly a democracy of elation among the families of North Main. Some were as possessed as Muni, literally so, claiming that the voices of dead folk lately spoke to and through them. But those voices were not wanting for interpreters.

There was also the matter of the time that composition demanded, time that could be better spent in the company of your beloved. But wasn't there, given its apparent immutability, plenty of time to go around? Still Muni felt that what he contemplated amounted to a betrayal. What had come over him that he'd left his girl dangling alone among that mare's nest of undulating roots? He should hasten back to her at once and offer his most fervent apologies. "Jenny, sweet kichel, forgive me! Be my bride!" Conjugal fever was anyway in the air, several couples having already succumbed to matrimony since the flood. Hadn't the hidebound Rabbi Lapidus from the Baron de Hirsch Synagogue just been enlisted to perform a triple wedding? A barge had been outfitted with singing oarsmen and a pavilion-sized canopy for the ceremony. Muni decided on the spot that he and Jenny should be a part of the ongoing celebrations, which looked as if they might never end. A *scribe!* What had he been thinking?

He was at the point of running back to the girl when he heard his uncle's groan from the kitchen. It was a full-throated animal groan that was answered by the corrosive strains of the fiddle from somewhere outside. Since the quake and the numinous period that followed, Asbestos's playing had evoked more than ever a pathos at odds with the general gaiety. To be sure, other sour notes had been struck in the Pinch, other characters out of step with the prevailing high spirits. The blacksmith, for instance, still sat dejected with his bamboo rod on the bank of the bayou, which the dike had restored again to a shallow cove. And Mr and Mrs Padauer remained deeply unsettled by the resemblance of their child to the host of fey creatures that flitted in the margins of everyone's vision. Muni's uncle sat slumped in the kitchen like a husband banished from a room where a wife is giving birth; only, Pinchas understood it wasn't shtik naches, it wasn't a new life that Katie was being delivered of. Then there were the memories that persisted in bubbling up from Muni's own sorrow-laden past. Such contrary elements stood out like loose threads that wanted weaving back into the otherwise harmonious tapestry of the street; they called attention to themselves, in fact, with a needling insistence that superseded every other affection on earth.

◢7◣
Flashbacks

The next time I saw Rachel was at a concert at the Overton Park Shell.
The Shell was an outdoor amphitheater located in the forested midtown
park that also contained the city's zoo, and between sets you could hear
the yowls and screeches of beasts and rare birds. It was really a summer
venue, the Shell, with its broad stage arched over by a concrete crescent
like the mouth of a horn of plenty, but despite the nippy March evening
the concert had drawn a large crowd. Velveeta and the Psychopimps, at
Elder Lincoln's urging, had organized a roster of regional musicians, including old blues originals like Bukka White, Furry Lewis, and Sleepy
John; they'd engaged other popular local rock bands such as the trans-
gressive Mud Boy and the Neutrons, and guaranteed that the event's proceeds would go toward funding the sanitation workers' strike.

I would have invited Rachel to come along if I'd been able to contact her,
but my calls to the Folklore Center had gone unanswered and her home
phone wasn't listed. I admit I might have done more to seek her out, but
I was preoccupied with my own affairs. I had my hands full navigating
between the bookstore and North Main Street, where Lamar was pres-
suring me to become a more aggressive peddler of his bootleg goods. The
fact was, Lamar's merchandise sold itself; all I had to do was make it available and can the double-talk that tended to discourage the consumers.
But apparently Lamar's extravagant lifestyle—the philanthropic activities that supported, among other things, a small harem in his suite at the
Peabody Hotel—had caused bills to come due; and certain sinister parties
were proving impatient. Meanwhile I was finding it increasingly difficult to
negotiate between a past made manifest by my reading of Muni Pinsker's
book and the current scene; and to be honest, being in love with Rachel only
complicated matters. I had to struggle mightily to keep my wits about me.

I was standing in line outside the Port-O-Potty when I saw her. Though I'd been busy filtering among the benches pushing pills, I wasn't high on anything myself—oh, maybe a little Dex and some beer. But since I'd begun to divide my time between two worlds, my brain remained jazzed to the point of requiring no further stimulation. It was intermission and the line for the convenience was long, and in the quarter hour I'd waited to get to its head my need had become fairly urgent. Rachel was again without her fiancé, who had receded in my mind to nearly imaginary. She was accompanied by her two friends—the chunky one and the petite—from the bar, but spotting me she excused herself and broke away from her companions. Having gone native for the concert, she was wearing a macramé headband and a crocheted shawl along with a peasant skirt and boots. On the one hand, who was she kidding? While on the other, as she approached me beneath the staggered lamplight affecting a rangy stride, she looked like some spitfire Gypsy girl. What's more, she was smiling for a change.

"Hello, stranger," she greeted me genially, which was odd since the estrangement was largely owing to her.

I was about to apprise her of that fact when this biker dude strolled up, bear-like and piratical in his bandanna, earring, and nicotine-stained beard. He wore an embossed leather vest over a protuberant chest, bare despite the chilly night air. "Emergency, man," he muttered, stepping in front of me in line and waiting for the door of the necessary to open. "You don't mind, do you?" he said to me over his shoulder, the question purely rhetorical.

His shoulders were massive, but prompted by dire need, I tapped a hairy patch on one of them. "I don't mind," I said, "but they might," indicating the queue of restless characters behind me. Then turning I shouted, "This guy wants to know if it's okay to break in line?"

There was an instant uproar that included threats and flaunted fists, perhaps a brandished weapon or two. It was clear that the bladder-heavy column was prepared to turn into a mob at the least violation of protocol. The biker growled into his beard but waved his big hands in the air in a gesture of surrender as he slouched away.

Rachel stood agape, which gave me to realize what I had done. Lately the no longer so distant past had come to hold such sovereignty over the present that immediate events didn't always make a strong impression. I sometimes misplaced my faculty for recognizing danger until after the fact; then it would strike me, what had just happened, and leave me completely unnerved. "Good one, Lenny," Rachel applauded, which only served to highlight my foolhardiness. Her remark combined with a shove from behind caused me nearly to have an accident. Thankfully the Potty door opened and I bolted in after the previous occupant with a minimum of leakage.

When I emerged, still shaken, Rachel was waiting. She invited me to join her friends who, remembering my performance at the 348, received me warily: like a creature in need of housebreaking but otherwise harmless. We took our seats on the weathered wooden benches just as the show was beginning again. The Psychopimps had returned to the stage: Sandy Eubank flinging snaky curls and piping like the Queen of the Night, Elder Lincoln on his fiddle channeling Paganini via Congo Square. An illustrious local pianist in a magenta claw hammer was sitting in with them for the set, his fingers riding the keys like ocean swells. It was the kind of ensemble unique to the city of Memphis, which had birthed the blues and rock 'n' roll and presided over their incestuous union. The air was fragrant with a mixture of weed and patchouli, the beam from a lavender spot scintillating with fireflies. Tonight the Aquarian tribes had descended on the park as one nation, at a juncture where music trumped history and the hoofbeats of the horsemen of the apocalypse were reduced to a minor chord.

Then came an interlude during which the Psychopimps presented an example of the type of gonzo theater that had become a standard component of their performances. The puckish Jimmy Pryor introduced his latest dummy, a little Negro in bib overalls with a melon-sized head and exaggerated ethnic features. He was modeled after Hambone of *Hambone's Meditations*, a single-panel cartoon that appeared daily in the *Commercial Appeal*. Each day Hambone dispensed homespun wisdom, rustic chestnuts such as: "Mos' folks, dey loses at de mouf what dey teks in at de ears." Jimmy's figure had a sign around his neck reading I <u>AM</u> A MAN.

"Mayor Loeb," said Hambone, seated on Jimmy's knee (Jimmy himself was perched on a stool in a crushed opera hat), "Mayor Loeb, he say de wukker cain't have no checkoff fo' dues. I say don't need no Checkoff, nor Dustyevsky neither. Jes' need the union and a mite uv dignity."

Rachel touched my arm in a gesture meant to signify our shared sympathy regarding this issue: she'd come on board. I looked at the arm she'd touched and then at her soft aquiline profile, her jet-black hair in its stylized liberation, and felt a twinge of conscience, because I hadn't paid much attention to the headlines of late. Later on, when the concert was over and she took me aside to report some new findings in her research—did I know that Elvis Presley had been the Dubrovner family's shabbos goy?—I refrained from offering any information in return. Her dark eyes had gone somewhat lynx-like in their expectation, and I wanted in my soul to take her with me; I wanted to show her the ladies flicking chickens in the back of Makowsky's butcher shop or Hekkie Grussom's wife braiding flax into rope in the yard behind his hardware store. I wanted to watch her peek through the curtain of the women's gallery at the strange fire ablaze on the altar of the Market Square shul. But instead, in the face of her undisguised disappointment, I said good night and promptly turned away, intending to beat it back into Muni's book, though I lay awake until dawn without reading a page.

Of course I wasn't entirely unaware of what was going on. How could I be when the situation was all the talk at Beatnik Manor? Things were heating up, the strikers marching every day for their self-respect, though I wondered if there was enough of that article to go around. Strike leaders had been arrested for jaywalking, union officials jailed for contempt of court. A mock funeral was held outside city hall to mourn the death of freedom, and at night the horizon over South Memphis was coral-red from the trash fires the strike supporters lit. Moreover, it was rumored that the Reverend Dr. Martin Luther King Jr. himself was coming to the city to speak on behalf of the sanitation workers. The issue seemed to have become a cause célèbre. But when I wasn't obsessing over my missed connection with Rachel, I was literally absorbed in *The Pinch*, though I still managed only a page or two a night—because the effort involved in reading that particular volume could be as exacting as the effort of living on earth.

At first I might have discounted the experience as the aftereffects of hallucinogens, which I wasn't unfamiliar with. Such phenomena were common enough, especially when you'd stopped using the stuff as abruptly as I had: it left fluorescent echoes in the brain. But lately the echoes had more volume and substance than their original source. To read about the entertainments at the Idle Hour Theater, where every night was Talent Night, was to find myself in the audience among spell-struck neighbors. Onstage the citizens tried to outdo one another in performing wonders, though the miraculous had become relatively prosaic in those parts. Everybody was a magician. Harold Dlugach made a solemn show of lighting his brother Morton's poots, from which fabulous salamanders materialized in the resulting blue flames; the Shpinker Hasids extracted the souls of local suicides from mirrors and ladies' reticules, then released them like carrier pigeons with messages to God. (Muni wrote that, sequestered for so long, ben Yahya's Hasids were now ubiquitous, whereas their rebbe seldom entered society anymore and looked peaky whenever he did.)

Sometimes I confused what I read with what I imagined I'd read, or passed through, as when wide awake I dreamed that I sloshed into Pinchas Pin's General Merchandise: I climbed the stairs and padded down the short hallway to peer into the little cupboard of a room, where a gaunt man with pouched eyes sat on a bed in his skivvies inscribing the deeds of the neighborhood. What would happen, I wondered, if I nudged aside his shoulder, displacing his writing hand to make room for mine, instead of simply retreating back to my own half of the century?

◢ 8 ◣
Beale Street

When Jenny entered his room, stepping from her stilts through the window holding aloft a covered dish, Muni could scarcely bring himself to look up from his labor. She peered over his shoulder and he made automatically to conceal the writing with his hand. He needn't have: the cursive was nearly illegible, a combination of Hebrew-laced Yiddish and the English he was trying to domesticate with the help of a broken-spined dictionary. Besides, Jenny was virtually unlettered.

"It's a secret what you're scribbling?" asked the girl.

"Not altogether," said Muni, still abstracted, "but it's not yet ready for the public consumption."

"Neither are you," she teased, mussing his already unkempt hair. He had lost weight and his unwashed undershirt had a vinegar smell. She set down the plate of kugel, removed the half-eaten plate of buckwheat groats she'd left there before; then leaning over him, she pulled his face to her breast and brushed the crown of his head with her lips.

"You're crazy as a bedbug," was her whispered diagnosis.

With his nose tucked in the voile crease between her tsitskehs, he inhaled her essence of lilac and cold cuts, and wondered why he did not rise from the cot to take her in his arms. Desire aside, Muni didn't want to disappoint her; she'd been tolerant thus far of his elusiveness, never blaming him for running away. He was keenly aware of their deferred intimacy and wondered if his reluctance to hold her involved a portion of guilt; though whether or not their sins were permissible in this unorthodox climate was frankly immaterial to him now: his ache was acute and the moment opportune. So why was he still incapable of leaving off his employment for the sake of the girl? The answer was as inescapable as fate.

"Yenny," he said to her whisper-soft breasts, which muffled his words,

"I am by Norf Main Freet iss instrumum." Lifting his head. "When it speaks—and it don't never stop talking—I must listen and take down every word."

Jenny shoved him to arm's length, disburdened herself of a weighty sigh. "You poor deluded putz," she said, not without a tinge of genuine rancor, and barged out of the room to check on Katie Pin.

Attending to Pinchas's wife and helping the Rosens in their effort to feed a community that lived essentially on air was keeping her busy. She saw to the needs of the failing Katie, spoon-fed and sitz-bathed her, emptied her slops and read her articles on society scandals from back issues of *Harper's Weekly*. She kept the shades drawn to keep out the insult of the neighborhood's radiance and shooed her husband from the bedroom, though he protested, "Katie, I hate you already, God forbid! Now will you let me in?" Because he thought—this was his logic—that if she believed he no longer loved her, she wouldn't mind so much his watching over her decline. But Katie only screamed at him as Jenny explained before closing the door, "She don't like you should see her dilapidate." He watched anyway, peeking in while she was sleeping to ensure that there was still some indication of her breathing. Her once robust form was turning practically diaphanous in its degeneration, the only body in the Pinch that was visibly aging, and it seemed to her frantic husband that his wife suffered the martyrdom of age for all the others who'd been given a pass.

Eventually Jenny stopped invading the Pins' apartment through Muni's window. How many times could she be expected to endure the same rude reception? His absorption in his febrile occupation had become a completely hermetic activity; it was an exercise made further exasperating by the ambivalent face he showed her whenever she managed to get his attention, though on her final few visits she'd failed to arouse even that tepid response. Muni had barely bothered to look up from his hen-scratching. Unshaven, unlaundered, and increasingly thin, he looked much as he had on the day he'd arrived on North Main Street from overseas. Back when he was a sleepwalker and she a ropewalker—avocations that who would have thought so compatible? Now he was a delirious insomniac like so many of their neighbors, some of whom repeated after Rabbi ben Yahya that "sleep is the unripe fruit of death." The Shpinker rebbe's bromides were frequently on their lips of late.

Jenny wondered if Muni ever left his smelly cell anymore, strewn now with his uncle's books—whose formal devices he appropriated as needed—and the drift of pages scored with his fitful scrawl. For books Jenny had little use, and as for the writing itself, who did Muni Pinsker think he was? Were the angels dictating to him a new testament that the work should preclude all other concerns? It wasn't lost on her how the very environment that inspired his labor had also made him a shut-in—was he even aware of the irony? But her anger was mixed (she couldn't help it) with anxious concern. She worried about his well-being and even reserved some small part of her nature in which to admire his obsessive industry: how it displaced all else in his purview, including his regard for her. It was a passion that duplicated the charged atmosphere of the Pinch itself, which spilled beyond the boundaries of any given day to overflow the rest of existence.

"It's this stupid street that's drove you nuts," Jenny concluded on her last pass through his room, never asking why she herself remained proof against the neighborhood's questionable influence. And still receiving no response from her sometime hartseniu, her lover, she gave way to a livid "You're not a person anymore!"

He showed no sign of having heard her, though when she was gone he paused to shake a cramp out of his wrist. He gazed at his scrawl and marveled at how the words functioned like a prism, refracting the black ink and white page into an iridescence. "I'm a person and a bit," Muni reflected, thrilled at his own audacity.

She began to enter the apartment by the kitchen window, wearing a serving tray on a strap around her neck so it wouldn't interfere with her stilt-walking facility. From the tray she removed the dishes she brought for Pinchas and Katie. (Pinchas only picked an occasional noodle from the broth, which left a generous helping of table scraps for Muni, though the boniness of both men advertised their want of nourishment.) Jenny and Pinchas would exchange solemn nods before the girl went into the sickroom to nurse Pinchas's wife in her extremity. When she first experienced the morning queasiness with its accompanying dry heaves, Jenny wondered if Katie's infirmity was contagious, then dismissed her discomfort as a symptom of fatigue. She was working too hard in order to steer clear of disappointment. The missed monthly, however, was more difficult to ignore, though did any women have regular cycles since the clocks had stopped? But with the nausea came bloat and nipples as swollen as plums, and despite an abiding naïveté about such things, Jenny could no longer deny the truth of her situation.

Against all reason the girl felt joyful. Her first impulse was to share her news with the father-to-be, imagining how it might snap him out of his fervid single-mindedness. "We're going to have a happy event," she'd announce, and he would leave off his graphomania to lift her into the air as in a dance; though she knew he would more likely reply, "We had already the event," if he replied at all. Because what occurrence could possibly surpass his waking dream? Then Jenny didn't know whether she was more aggrieved over their imagined conversation or the one she knew they would never have. Why had the dumkopf never proposed to her? Didn't he understand that theirs would be a special child, the first to be born into the postdiluvian Pinch?

There was an evening when she peered into Muni's room, lit by a single yahrzeit candle, and saw the reams of pages that threatened to inundate or bury him alive. It came to her what an unwelcome intrusion the birth of a flesh-and-blood child would be in a world composed exclusively of words. After that Jenny began actively to resent the common dream that had inebriated the street.

She had an urge to confide in Katie but worried that her news might be the last thing that, in her contemplation of last things, the childless woman would want to hear. Then once at sundown, from the tar-beach rooftop of the Rosens' building, Jenny surveyed the brazen surface of the canal with its lamplit fleet. Rabbi ben Yahya had said that the water was derived from the perspiration of heavenly hosts singing the praises of the highest, and these days the rebbe's word was taken as gospel. The star-speckled evening stretched south toward antiquity, north toward the end of days. That it was no longer confined by its former diurnal horizons could also be attributed to the Shpinker rebbe, whose Hasids had prayed a hole in the membrane separating the fallen world from its opposite number. The Hasids themselves maintained, paradoxically, that they had repaired the rift between Olam Ha-ba and Olam Ha-zeh, above and below, thus allowing free passage between the two spheres. This meant that an angel might, if it wished, cohabit with a mortal and a mortal become likewise a citizen of Paradise. A boat could do duty as both a floating barbershop and a shivah shel-maalah, a celestial academy. Children plunged into the canal and surfaced with novelties: amphoras wreathed in blue algae, electronic gadgets that had yet to be invented, a rusalka (a mermaid) that they were made to throw back again. In the park some householders were turning on a spit a flayed red ox, which (though only partially visible) was as big as a mastodon.

From her vantage Jenny, heart-stricken, took in the broad expanse of that freakish street and rejected wholesale its garish goings-on. What kind of a normal childhood could be had in the midst of such humbug? The Pinch was finally no place to raise a kid.

She considered consulting the Widow Teitelbaum, who did a back-stairs business as kishef macher, a medicine lady. She kept a cabinet of herbal teas and patent medicines like Hardy's Woman's Friend that she sold over the counter, and was known to administer mercury and hellebore enemas to good effect. The Jews had no special problem with abortion—some proclaiming like the joker Asher Sebranig that "it ain't human, the fetus, till it gets its law degree." Circumstances sometimes warranted desperate measures. But the word itself left a nasty taste on Jenny's tongue. Besides, she knew there would be gossip; North Main Street was all about choosing life these days, and terminating a pregnancy would not have been consistent with the general air of festivity. So she decided to turn to the Negro Asbestos with whom she had a peculiar relationship, though he was lately hard to find. He came and went at a time when it seldom occurred to anyone else to leave the boundaries of the Pinch. Some even thought it impossible, so much had the district come to define their world. In this attitude (remarked Rabbi ben Yahya), they were like the population of the mythical city of Luz, the city of immortals, whose residents went outside the walls only to die.

Jenny came upon Asbestos as he was crawling from under a rust-cankered manhole cover on Winchester Street. When she accosted him, the fiddler explained that it was easier for a blind man to negotiate the underground city than to walk abroad on its surface. Wringing out a saturated pant leg, he alluded to a system of tunnels beneath downtown Memphis that predated the Civil War. "Folk'd use them to conduck your slave to Beulah Land." Jenny had heard it all before; had already gleaned from her dealings with Asbestos, who as the object of her charity had come to trust her, that such clandestine operations persisted to this day. Armies of indigent black men were daily arrested on trumped-up charges and indentured to forced labor in mines and lumber camps, and certain intrepid types conspired for their deliverance. Give him a little schnapps and the fiddler might allow that he himself, sightlessness notwithstanding, had a finger in such operations during his subterranean rambles. Ordinarily Jenny humored him—"Old man, you won't never die in bed"—but today all that business, if it really occurred, unfolded in a universe no longer even parallel to the Pinch.

Impatiently she interrupted Asbestos's discourse and appealed to him for help. As he listened, his prune face collapsed behind its smoked lenses and he cautioned the girl in his emery voice, "You ain't want to do that, honey." He was right, she didn't. Nevertheless she threatened to pursue independent means that included certain cunning medieval devices if he refused her. In the end the Negro downheartedly relented and agreed to arrange everything. A few nights later they set out for Beale Street by an overland route, since—thanks to the pillowslip ramparts—it was now possible to travel along buckling sidewalks all the way to Main Street proper.

Asbestos led the way with his tapping cane, and Jenny fatalistically followed the blind man. Despite his bias against aboveground travel, he seemed to know every lamppost and crosswalk on the way to Beale. Straggling together past the department stores and specialty shops, they raised eyebrows; a blind nig and a gimpy jew girl, they may even have invited some vulgar remarks. But Jenny, for all her trepidation, felt a slight sense of relief to be back in an ordinary precinct where everything was more or less finite. People window-shopped, trolley lines clacked, wires sang; the air smelled of horse manure and roasted peanuts. The weather was appropriately autumnal; there were newspapers with headlines announcing the opening of a canal in Central America and the imminence of a war in Europe. Everything proceeded according to rational categories without the least intimation of eternity.

After Asbestos had asked her for the umpteenth time if she maybe had second thoughts, they turned the corner onto Beale Street and proceeded under dangling pawnshop globes. A black man in a turned-around collar tipped his homburg to the fiddler and spoke his name, while Jenny wondered: Who tips his hat to a blind man? Farther along, a street-corner band—washboard, bull fiddle, and jug—left off the spirited number they were playing to strike up what sounded to the girl like one of the fiddler's own funereal scores. Pausing, Asbestos flashed a rare grin, took his instrument from its sack, and sawed a few collaborative chords. So it seemed that the schnorrer of North Main Street, upon whom Jenny had condescended to bestow her benevolence, was a dignitary here on Beale. Why was she not surprised? They pressed on through a fine mist of frying pigs' snouts from a vendor's oil drum grill. The pavement was crowded with peddlers hawking stink killers and hair straighteners, vials of Oil of Gladness and packets of Come-To-Me Powder. A couple of undertakers quarreled over a corpse being stretchered from a barroom into a horse-drawn ambulance. Through their open doors Jenny could see the yellow-skinned ladies gyrating to barrelhouse pianos, their buttocks rolling like juggled melons beneath the fringe of their hobble skirts.

Despite the many looks askance, Jenny didn't feel the fear take hold until Asbestos asked if they'd come yet as far as the Monarch Club. "See mens roll they bones in Pappy Haddum's horn," he advised. "Sign say, *No Dozen Here*." She peered through a smoky door toward a bar on top of which men were tossing dice into a large leather funnel, saw the sign above the bar, and confirmed that they had arrived. The fiddler directed her into an alley and up a steep flight of stairs on the outside of the building, where their knock at a paint-blistered door was answered in due course.

"Howdo, Mizriz Barbee," Asbestos greeted the imposing woman, who cordially invited them in. Her moon face was buffed cordovan, a hand-rolled cigarette dangling from a meaty lip, a knit fascinator tied toothache-fashion round her bulbous head. Her breasts inside the ging-ham housedress might have helped to fortify the North Main Street seawall—which was the last antic thought Jenny would entertain that night. Suddenly struck by the enormity of what she was about to do, she was reduced to the condition of a tongue-tied little girl.

"Chile, don't be skeered," said the midwife in a voice like warm butter-scotch. She waved a hand as if to introduce her patient to the reassuring tidiness of her apartment—the antimacassared armchair, the pot boiling on a wood-burning cookstove. But when she shambled forward on her thick ankles to pull back the curtain on the alcove she called her "surg'ry," acrophile that she was, Jenny grew queasy and fought against falling into a swoon.

There was a table with an oilcloth and, in the corner, one half of an upright packing crate, painted red, which could serve as a modesty screen. A portrait of a bronze-skinned Jesus adorned a wall whose floral paper was unfurling from the plaster to reveal the thin laths beneath. On a stool beside the table was an orderly array of items—crotchet needles, curling irons, a catheter—in an emulation of clinical instruments, though their pitilessness was salient. The midwife was wiping her hands in her apron in what the girl assumed was a sanitary motion, but when she held out a pink palm Jenny realized she'd misread the gesture.

"I take y'all's donation now," showing ivory teeth interspersed with gold, the cigarette remaining somehow glued to her lower lip.

Jenny fished in the pocket of her middy skirt and surrendered the agreed-upon sum, a wad of cash comprising a year's worth of tips. Mizriz Barbee fanned herself with the bills—as if the breeze whispered their amount—before stuffing them into her prodigious bosom. Obedient to his instincts Asbestos chose that moment to make a discreet exit from the apartment, while Jenny silently mouthed the word *coward*. A fly buzzed, a mouse skittered, the piano from the honky-tonk below played a syncopated rag. The girl was handed a clammy sheet with a hole in it to slip her head through and invited to undress behind the screen. Disrobed, Jenny glimpsed her tight belly, which had not yet begun to "show," unkneaded dough that would never rise.

When she reappeared, the midwife pressed a tin cup into her hands, saying, "Swallah this yere medicine." The words had a sacerdotal authority, and utterly passive now Jenny did as she was told. She breathed fire and began to cough from the scorching bite of the red-eye, while the midwife slapped her back and guffawed. Reclaiming the cup, she allowed the butt to drop from her lip into the liquid with a sizzle then swilled the rest of the contents herself. She enfolded the girl in her hammy arms and lifted her with an affable grunt onto the table. Still reeling from the whiskey, which had somewhat cut the fear, Jenny squirmed from the feel of the cold oilcloth on her bare buttocks. But if the dram did anything to diminish the pain of the midwife's procedure, you couldn't have proved it by the girl. The pain was its own voluminous province, with zones and latitudes and turbulent moods; her cries sounded like some far-off opera to her own ears. When she'd finally come through it, Jenny recognized the room and the woman with bloody hands, the fiddler returned to poke his head around the packing crate—which is not to say that she wasn't still lost and a long way from home.

She had sufficient focus to take note, once she was helped to sit up, of the pail at the foot of the table and the mess it contained, which caused her to retch down her front. On the streetcar rattling north toward the Pinch, white passengers in rush seats craned their necks to glower menacingly at the girl. It wasn't bad enough that she was seated beside a Negro in the Colored section, her head tilted onto his shoulder, but the scent of her sick was pervading the car.

And so Jenny joined the handful of citizens who remained impervious to the enticements of North Main Street's unending fling. The discontent she'd expressed over the years had been mostly for the sake of conversation; she understood that now, understood what it really meant not to belong. Her desperate action, she felt, had disqualified her from participating in the everyday life of the old neighborhood, not that much of the everyday had survived the quake. When she'd recovered her strength, Jenny was stony in her resolution. She took in the clothes that hung on the line suspended between the delicatessen and the general store, then clamped shut the lock securing the pulley and, barefoot in her muslin chemise, mounted the rope. It was neither entirely static nor loose enough to qualify as slack. The tightrope was for the classic equilibrist, the slack for the clown, but the unevenness of her legs since her accident had left her— the girl discovered—peculiarly suited to both types of performance. Once her joints were again lubricated by movement, it seemed to her that none of her gifts had been lost in retirement. She was versatile, could enact her routines with or without a weighted pole; she could balance on a chair, prance (notwithstanding her limp) like a ballerina. With gymnastic maneuverings she could swing in giant circles, executing twists and airborne releases. The transports she enjoyed upon experiencing once again her body's death-defiance of gravity rivaled, she'd have wagered, the loftiest spiritual acrobatics of ben Yahya's disciples. It went without saying that she didn't deserve to feel such exhilaration.

Of course nobody paid attention to her efforts, least of all the sedulous Muni Pinsker outside whose window she performed. Ineffable occurrences having become so commonplace in the Pinch, what interest had her neighbors in the perfectly natural phenomenon of a girl on a wire?

It was Asbestos, traveling back and forth at his leisure between the great world and North Main, who alerted Jenny to the fact that the circus had come to town. The news came as no surprise to the ropewalker, who'd seen the gaudy posters on hoardings during her journey to Beale. Hadn't they helped spur her motivation to take up her art again? This particular circus, Forepaugh & Broadway's Floating Carnival of Fun, had sailed downriver from north of St. Paul and was docked at the foot of the levee. Its quarters were composed of a steamboat that doubled as a menagerie, which towed an ornate wooden "palace." The palace sat astride a huge flat-bottomed barge and housed an extravaganza of several rings. If they knew of its arrival, the North Main Streeters, enjoying a floating carnival of their own, were not the least bit curious about such a flea-bitten exhibition. Though the piping of its steam organ could be heard in the Pinch, it was nearly drowned out by the music of the Shpinkers' improvised niggunim, their chants tweaked in turn by the blind man's soulful cadenzas. But for Jenny Bashrig, so out of place in the old neighborhood, the circus calliope was a siren song she had no choice but to follow to its source.

Lacking the price of admission, she avoided the matinee and evening hours and made her way down the bluff to the riverfront on a breezy October (was it?) morning. The wind was whipping up whitecaps on the surface of the mile-wide river, compared to which the grand canal of North Main Street—thought Jenny—was a ditch. The broad floodplain on the Arkansas side flashed light and dark beneath the scudding shadows of clouds like wandering atolls; and the girl felt her perspective beginning to shift, her own drama starting to shrink to a shameful inconsequence in the presence of the wider world. The sideshow tents erected at the foot of the levee flew banners displaying crude images of Siamese triplets and the monster rats of Sumatra. The trunk of an elephant and the neck of a camel protruded through the open portholes of the wallowing steamboat, its promenade deck perched upon by grooming chimpanzees. A lion shuddered the planks of the pier with its deep bass roar, and Jenny, brightening, couldn't help but think "Noah's Ark," though she rejected the thought as the kind of association her neighbors might make.

As the ticket booth was empty, she ascended the creaking gangplank onto the deck of the barge unobserved. She entered the so-called palace via a draperied companionway that led between tiers of bleachers into a tawdry, tabernacle-sized amphitheater. An animal pungency stung her nostrils. Painted tapestries, gilt mirrors, and carved woodwork ornamented the interior in a faded pastiche of Gilded Age splendor; raffish sunlight, invaded by flitting barn swallows, slanted through the high windows to illumine three sawdust rings. In the nearest a stocky equestrienne in a tatty leotard stood erect astride the back of a cantering steed. The spotted horse circled a midget with a whip, his stance duplicating the bareback rider's as he balanced upon a pig in full harness. The middle ring was vacant, but in the farthest from Jenny a pair of men in matching dressing gowns were inspecting a heavy net that lay folded in the sawdust and sand. Jenny'd seen the trawlers of Happy Hollow examining their seines with a similar diligence, but it thrilled her to think of the bigger fish this net was designed to catch. The rigging above them was hung with the properties of various aerial acts like a playground for weightless children; a rope ladder extended upward to a platform from which a taut cable was stretched.

Members of the ring crew were lugging in, anaconda-fashion, a large rolled tarp through the wide-open carriage doors. In the stands a bald man with a handlebar mustache was playing cards with a giantess in a pinchbeck tiara whose tights appeared to be stuffed with cannonballs. Could that be Professor Hotspur of Hotspur's Pantomimic Pachyderms, and the woman Madame Hortense the Female Hercules, as advertised on the panels outside? Jenny wondered even as she shed her peacoat, kicked off her shoes, and toddled over to the farthest ring. There she mounted the wooden curb, grabbed hold of the narrow rope ladder, and began to clamber up its jittery length.

Nobody noticed when she stepped from the lofty platform onto the polished steel cable, until a roustabout happened to look up and inquire, "Why ain't that gal wearin' her mechanic?" Another, shading bloodshot eyes, offered the stunned reply, "That'n ain't even with the show." Then the laborers shared a collective groan: they'd seen this kind of thing before—circus-crazed civilians sneaking in after hours to enter a tiger's cage or dangle from a trapeze. The bad ends they came to invariably spelled trouble for the whole company. Dropping their burden, the crew scrambled into the ring to begin frantically hoisting the safety net to catch the harebrained girl when she fell. The two men who'd been contemplating repairs to the net took their time in moving out of their way. Standing at the side of the ring, they began blithely discussing the girl's technique, commenting on the relation of her center of mass to her base of support. "Not too wide in her lateral acceleration," judged the taller, his arms shoved into the silk sleeves of his robe like a Chinaman. "Nor too narrow in her sagittal direction," remarked his partner, arching a brow over a drowsy eye.

"But that business of gripping the wire between her great and second toe . . ."

"Definitely out. We'll have to buy her a nice pair of buffalo hide slippers . . ."

". . . and slather the soles with molasses to limit the torque."

When the circus cast off from the Memphis levee to make for more southerly ports, almost no one in the Pinch was aware that La Funambula had gone with it. For them, anyone who strayed beyond the neighborhood was instantly lost to memory. Of course the Rosens knew she was gone, Mr. Rosen attempting to comfort his wife as she shed a torrent of tears over the nearly illiterate scrawl of Jenny's note. (The note, with its clumsy profession of gratitude, was so damp from the combined tears of Mrs. Rosen and her foster daughter that it was later pinned pennant-wise to the highwire clothesline to dry.) Pinchas Pin was also aware of her departure, since it was Jenny who'd informed him—cradling his inconsolable head in her lap before saying good-bye—that his Katie's suffering was finally at an end. But Muni Pinsker, in the fever dream of his chronicling, remained unmindful of her absence while dedicating every word he wrote to his precious girl.

9

Hide and Seek

I was carrying away a stack of books that comprised the better part of Avrom's Judaica collection, when his lizardy eyelids snapped open.

"It makes you feel good that you steal from an old man?"

"I'm borrowing them," I said, slightly chagrined. But Avrom's income came mostly from Social Security and the odd reparation from Germany; from his shop with its phantom clientele he got bubkes. Besides, I knew I had only to ask, but theft lent my relation to the books an element of intrigue.

Avrom squinted over his thick lenses in an effort to make out the titles. "What are you, becoming a yeshiva bocher?" How to tell him that perusing *The Pinch* meant resorting to no end of reference materials? That becoming Muni Pinsker's ideal reader involved the assimilation of a whole history and culture. "Maybe you should go instead in synagogue," he suggested, this from a skeptic who cursed God at every turn.

"I went already," I said (I was starting to sound like him). "They confirmed me at sixteen; I thought I was a Methodist."

Avrom studied me with rheumy eyes that seemed to be struggling to focus. Was I starting to disappear? "I'm laughing," he said, though he showed no signs of it. He hawked some phlegm into the coffee tin on his desk and peered inside to examine its contents.

I set down the stack of books, raising dust from the floor I'd neglected to sweep. "Avrom," I was suddenly moved to confess, "I don't hardly seem to live here anymore. It's like I learned another language and now I'm forgetting my mother tongue."

"'Thou art greatly despised,'" he replied. "Obadiah chapter one, verse two: 'for Rome possesses neither script nor tongue.'" "Come again?" I asked, when he fairly barked at me, "*Here* you didn't never live." He endeavored to raise himself upright amid the cushions that buttressed his rump. "Poor pisher"—saliva sprayed from his lips—"the lostest of the lost generation."

"That one was before my time," I countered, sorry to have made myself vulnerable to the old man. But he wasn't finished.

"What do you want I should say to you? I should give to you wisdom like I'm some lamed vovnik? I'm the prophet Elijah in disguise? Okay: for virility, mix with ground kohl a seven-hued scorpion; against a succubus say, 'Bar tit, bar tamei, bar tina, kashmaggaz . . .'" Then, with gnashing of dentures, "Tahkeh, from my own life I didn't learn nothing!"

I'd never known him to get so worked up. "Why are you being such a"—what was the Yiddish for "bastard"?—"momzer?"

"Because," he said, still exercised, squeezing his beard like a sponge; a molasses-like tear formed at its tip and plopped onto his desk, "because, Reb Pinocchio, you got in your life no strings attached, you can go where you want, even in Paradise. Me, I got only memories that by them I'm pinned in this farshtunkener chair."

His gouged face showed a ferocity that dared me to contradict him, and for a moment we were deadlocked in our feelings of mutual inadequacy. Then, defeated by his stare, I hung my head and made a mumbled effort to change the subject; I had to clear my throat to hear myself speak. "Are there other copies of it, *The Pinch*?" It was a question I'd been meaning to put to him for a while. There was after all no copyright, no Library of Congress number; I knew nothing of its provenance. Maybe a fellowship of readers were plodding even now through Muni's tangled narrative, encountering one another in and out of time.

Avrom sighed as if heaving a demon from his pigeon breast and reverted to his usual bemusement. It was, he attested, the one and only volume. "The meshuggener Tyrone that he gave me for safekeeping the manuscript. Then I gave with his cockeyed pictures to Shendeldecker the printer when they locked him up."

"So you were responsible for its printing?"

He didn't say no.

"But you said you never read it?"

"I opened," Avrom shrugged, his eyebrows like caterpillars rampant. "It's the same story that I heard it already from the horse's mouth, or anyway the nephew of the horse. I heard in the lager and wondered can you get to North Main Street from here. When I arrived, is mostly gone with the wind, the street. It's anyhow better I should reside here in this charming dacha."

He looked out through the glass door where a garbage striker with a sandwich board was passing.

"Avrom," I asked, ignoring his mood—as what could I do about it anyway?—"what became of Muni Pinsker?"

He turned back to me and belched softly, made a face at the ill wind he'd expelled. "Happened what always happens: he died there like everybody else. Mr. Hanover that he died there. Mr. Elster died there. Mr. and Mrs. Sebranig died over there. Everybody stayed and they died there. Didn't nobody just run away."

That night I'm involved in a business transaction at the back of the bar when the heat burst through the front door. They were wearing duty jackets and graven expressions, standard issue guts lapping over belts that drooped in turn from sidearms, radios, handcuffs, and pepper spray. For a few moments they seemed implausible, so out of place was their martial presence amid that ethereal crowd. Then the cold facts kicked in and I recalled that Lamar, so generous with his illicit gifts, had never bothered to secure a proper beer license for the 348. Moreover, the barroom was dense with muggle smoke and cellophane packets of legend drugs, a quantity of which could be found on my person. I remembered that I was a felon, a concept I'd never quite gotten my head around. Outlaw, yes, but felon?

I expected the cops to begin arresting every acid eater and underage drinker in sight. But instead, parting the patrons like tall grass, they made straight for my landlord, spruce in his plantation attire, his insouciant posture advertising his proprietorship. They yanked him out of his chair and read him his rights. He received the handcuffs as if he were being attended by valets, while an unripe nymph draped his coat over his shoulders like an opera cape. As the cops frog-marched him toward the door, I turned tail and made for the rear of the premises. If Lamar was busted, wouldn't his associate be next in line? With the draft hanging over my head and now the threat of police, it occurred to me I was a desperate character. I ducked into the musty storeroom at the back of the bar, which contained a pyramid of aluminum kegs and an oxidized toilet from a bygone era. Scrambling up the kegs—some of which rolled from under me to trip up imagined pursuers—I reached for the narrow casement window, yanked the rusty latch, and threw open the sash as far as it would go; then I slithered through the casement, tumbling headfirst into a paved backyard.

Beyond the brick wall was a coffee factory, its lights on and aromas emanating as they hadn't for half a century. Next door the sheitel-wigged Hattie Zipper stood on an upstairs landing behind her apartment airing out a featherbed; she was exchanging gossip with Tillie Alperin in the window of the neighboring building, brushing periwinkles from her daughter's tawny hair. From the bare branch of a chinaberry tree a creature with shaggy flanks and hooves (which I recognized from my reading as a millinery demon, a kapelyushnikl) hung by its knobby knees. A steamboat sounded its whistle, and a stringed instrument from somewhere nearby imitated its plangent moan. I could have hidden there circa 1900 in perpetuity, I thought, safe from cops and universal conscription. From where I stood, though, I could barely even remember Rachel's face—or rather, I could cherish the memory of her face from afar with a poignant longing. But was Lenny Sklarew some craven pitsvinik who lived on unrequited passions? Well, maybe. But touching the past, for all its allure, tonight made me want even more the solid portion that only my own place in time could provide. Ashamed of myself for hesitating, I climbed the wall and trotted along a back alley as far as Poplar Avenue. Still afraid to return to my apartment, however, I boarded a trolley and rode it until it dissolved into thin air, leaving me to walk the rest of the way to the midtown refuge of Beatnik Manor.

The house was flush as usual with "the mad ones, who never yawn or say a commonplace thing but burn like roman candles," at least those whose flames hadn't been snuffed out already by cynicism and substance abuse. A few of the Psychopimps were sitting around the parlor along with their customary hangers-on—some of whom shuffled in place to unheard music or contributed with colored markers to the kaleidoscopic walls. Hunkered among them was a small contingent of black brothers, the tag *Invaders* spray-painted in Day-Glo across the backs of their leather jackets. Elder Lincoln was holding forth from a rocker, his acoustic violin propped upright on his knee.

"My grandmama Abishag, she done come one time upon a lynched man after the mob have departed," employing the folk speech he reserved for storytelling. "Not a soul even standin' guard. The victim he was a old feller, a fiddler by the look of him 'cause his broken instrument have been hung round his broken neck. Got also no eyes lef' in his hade. See, my grandmama didn't have no chirren and her husband's long gone, so she look bofe ways and unbutton the hung man's fly to see do the legend be true. Then she look round, hitch up her skirt, ain't nothin' but a ol' nation sack, and scoot her booty smack up against his Johnson erectus. Tha's how my daddy that I didn't never know got born and how I come by my musical aptitude."

He grinned saucily as the hippies groaned, having perhaps heard this one before. The brothers, younger than the general run of freaks in the room, voiced their annoyance at such frivolous smoke. One of them, a razor part in his bushy 'fro, muttered, "Niggah, that's fucked up," while another, wearing a baseball cap with the bill turned sideways, said, "Yo, Elder, you down with us or what?"

Elder cocked his head in puzzlement, feigned or otherwise.

Then the third Invader, who commanded a certain air of authority (by virtue of his aboriginal brow?), said, "Bro, you gon' be our podnah in crime?" It had the ring of a rehearsed request.

"Ezackly what's on y'all's mind?"

The beetle brow shifted his sallow eyes to and fro. "It ain't for the ears of all these zebras."

"These zebras are my friends, Sweet Weeyum," submitted Elder.

Sweet Weeyum jutted his lower lip till it matched in protrusion his overarching brow. Still clearly suspicious, he nevertheless relaxed his guard enough to get down to cases. He spoke frankly, even boastfully, about sabotage, offhandedly alluding to items such as peashooters and Molotov cocktails.

The tension that permeated the room brought Ira Kisco to his feet. "Elder," he asked, "what you doing listening to these punks?" His voice wavered between accusatory and apologetic.

Elder frowned. "These punks are my brethren."

Ira hung his head in momentary surrender, then raised it. "What about the movement, man?" One of the Invaders wondered aloud what did a mothafuckin' Viking know of "the *movement*"? He spoke the words with a biting sarcasm, but while perhaps a touch embarrassed by his Nordic features, Ira persisted all the same. "Remember nonviolent civil disobedience? Gandhi and King and all that?"

At the latter name Sweet Weeyum remarked truculently, "Doctah Kang ain't nothin' but the president's house niggah. The man done had his day."

Ira forced a laugh and rested his case, but in the absence of a similarly dismissive response from Elder he left the room. He was followed soon after by a broad-toothed Cholly Jolly in his six-gallon hat, pumping his fist and shouting an ironic "Black power!" The remaining hippies, their spans of attention spent, fell to gazing at the roiling bubbles inside a glass bong.

Elder continued rocking thoughtfully as he gave ear to the Invaders stating their insurrectionary objectives. Their spokesman, Sweet Weeyum, had begun to list specific targets, businesses run by councilmen who'd been especially vocal in their opposition to the strike; perhaps even the councilmen themselves. At one point Elder noticed that I was still lingering at the edge of their conversation. Actually, I was fascinated, not so much by the substance of their parley as by Elder's indulgence of it. A gifted young black man who moved with relative impunity between both sides of the color line, Elder Lincoln was much admired by those who didn't deem him a traitor to his race. ("Oreo" was the word sometimes bruited about.) As a consequence, he was torn between two cultures, and being more or less in the same boat myself, I couldn't help but be intrigued by the guy.

"Yo, monkey man," Elder was suddenly addressing me, less hospitably than I was used to. "Can we hep you?"

Trying to hide my hurt feelings, I replied, "I ain't no ear hustler, know what I'm sayin', but y'all do be talkin' some off-da-hinges drama. Copacetee, my brothas," I assured them, rising from the ash-strewn carpet. "Holla back atcha boy Lenny now and then." And having exhausted all the street jargon I knew, I straggled out of the parlor to the tune of nasal sniggering behind me.

In the kitchen assorted Psychopimps and their camp followers were seated round a square table solemnly passing slab bottles and spliffs. "The cops raided the 348," I announced in my capacity as messenger from the world at large—though it came to me my more compelling message was from another world altogether. "They arrested Lamar Fontaine," I added, mentioning also that I was on the lam, but that wasn't heard due to the rumblings of general solicitude. Their concern, however, seemed not so much for the bar or its proprietor as for the ruptured chemical pipeline between North Main Street and the manor.

I thought their reaction unworthy of them. Where was the sympathy for their benefactor? Certainly Lamar had his idiosyncrasies, not the least of which was his sartorial pride in his antebellum heritage and penchant for adolescent flesh, but his largess toward the band and their outlandish projects had been princely. How could they be so unmoved? Of course, if I were honest I'd have had to admit to being almost as heartless: I was more worried about the threat to my livelihood and tenancy than I was about my landlord's incarceration. What did I really care about drug traffickers or maverick musicians, or for that matter garbagemen and foreign wars—when what I wanted most at that moment (peace, Rachel) was to get back to the book I'd left in my apartment, which I figured was still too risky to return to that night?

Knackered from the long evening, I went nosing about that funhouse looking for a place to crash. In most rooms, including the hallways, the sleeping bags wriggled from the bodies twining inside them like chrysalises about to hatch. Stepping over them, I eventually discovered at the dark end of the house a small conservatory, its walls and ceiling composed of weather-scored quartz glass panes. On one of the panes was a large orange thumbprint that I assumed was the moon. I settled into a canvas deck chair amid a jungle of unlawful plants and luxuriant ferns, squinting through them toward the vanished civilization I was homesick for.

In the morning I took a bus back downtown. The shop reeked of geriatric must, Avrom breathing like an accordion, hacking up unsightly matter into his Luzianne coffee tin. His color was the yellow of the skim on hollandaise. When I suggested he call Doc Fruchter, a Pinch alumnus who still made house calls, he told me, "A calamity in your navel." His curses often more riddle than sting. Still he ran me ragged with fetching the nostrums that the old quack had prescribed him and shelving the termite-bored library of a recently deceased entomologist. So it wasn't until my lunch break that I managed to get to a phone booth. I called the office of Lamar's attorney, Bernie "the Mouthpiece" Rappaport, and asked how things stood with my landlord. I braced myself to hear I didn't know what: he'd been tortured, electrodes applied to his genitals until he named names. For all I knew I was a marked man.

"He won't let me put up his bail," said Bernie, sounding insulted. I'd met the lawyer once at the 348, a baggy little man with a threadbare comb-over dressed in discordant plaids. His only concession to the unconventional lifestyle of the clients he tended to represent was a pair of rufous muttonchops.

"What's that?"

"He advised me against posting his bond." I thought I could smell his cheap aftershave through the phone. "He wants to stay in stir."

"Why, forgodsakes?"

"Let's just say there are people on the outside who pose more of a threat to him than the courts."

I knew that Lamar's finances were in disarray, that he purchased his stuff from nefarious sources, but he'd made such a haven of 348 North Main Street, to say nothing of his lavish suite at the Peabody, that I thought of him as untouchable. Besides, there was his thoroughbred family who for all I knew still held slaves. Couldn't their influence be brought to bear?

"You didn't hear they already disowned him, their disgraced scion? They're the type of family that got scions."

I wondered where his imminent trial and conviction would leave me.

Late that afternoon I returned to the scene of the previous night's flight. It was a somber slate-gray homecoming, North Main Street more deserted than usual, barren of its lately invasive long ago. The bar was padlocked, a hand-scrawled placard in the window reading *Closed Til Further Notice By Order of the Oinks*; the neon numbers above the door were extinguished, perhaps forever. What's more, there was a barge-sized aqua sedan parked across the street in front of my building, containing no doubt a plainclothes cop waiting to apprehend me. Then I remembered that the vehicle was Rachel's own rust-trimmed Buick Brontosaur, and the face in the driver's-side window, once she'd unrolled it, was the girl herself. Disheveled and dog-weary from sleeplessness, I nevertheless felt my whole countenance distorted by an imbecile grin. As I approached the car she got out and smiled as well, though inscrutably.

"I've been asking some of my informants about Tyrone," she began without preamble, infuriatingly matter-of-fact. "Seems there were a couple of years after the war when he was—what did they call him?—the shtot meshuggener, a kind of village idiot. He was everybody's pet, harmless until he began trying to harm himself." That's when the street intervened to have him committed to Bolivar. But now the old Pinch survivors, themselves living in a luxury often subsidized by their comfortable children (it seemed they hadn't all died "over there"), were in a position to help improve the artist's situation. With Rachel's prompting they might be willing to bring his plight to the attention of their respective synagogues: contributions could be made and funds raised to transfer him to the relative serenity of the B'nai B'rith Home, a well-endowed facility under the hawthorns across from Overton Park.

Oh, she was a pretty girl. She was wearing a short patchwork skirt and her perennial leather boots, a Navajo poncho with the hood thrown back. Her hair was woven in plaits like military braids. Every time I saw her she seemed to have graduated to some new stage of bohemianism. Could this be my influence?

"How long have you been waiting for me?" I asked, wishing for: *All my life.*

"I just arrived," she replied, looking confused by my obvious disappointment.

Then pretending it was only natural to do so, I invited her upstairs, and she followed as if custom dictated. My heart sank when I found the door to my apartment ajar, then remembered that I never bothered to lock it; I likewise balked at discovering that the place had been ransacked until I recalled that trashed was its normal condition. Once we'd entered I was acutely aware that Rachel Ostrofsky stood again in my drafty flat with its rancid odor for no other reason than I had asked her to. She seemed as awkward with this knowledge as I was, and for an immeasurable moment we could neither of us think of anything to say. I offered her the single chair, a rickety rattan job I'd scavenged from an abandoned toolshed strangled by creepers. Cautiously sitting, she crossed her shapely legs, which enflamed me all the more for the unshaven fuzz on her shins. Did I love her? I confess that she oscillated in my brain between the unassailable idea of her and the warm and fallible thing herself; though this evening she seemed emphatically three-dimensional, her presence a lodestar toward which a rudderless shlemiel might claw his way back from lost worlds.

Can I touch your aura? Jump your bones? "Would you like a beer?" I asked her. Not waiting for a reply, I went into the galley kitchen and opened the little fridge which was bare of beers, just a puckered apple and a dev-iled ham sandwich gone chartreuse with mold. When I returned to her empty-handed, Rachel seemed not even to notice but instead said to me diffidently, "Lenny, I've been thinking I'd like to do"—*all the most de-grading things we can think of*—"LSD."

I won't pretend to understand the feelings her request evoked in me. Certainly there was lust, an ache and a throb; there was the memory of the botched consummation we'd yet to repair. But there was something else as well—a gratitude that nearly choked me, sadness like a hymn. It was as if she'd asked to meet my imaginary friend. I reached down to pry her fingers from the arm of the chair and pulled her to her feet, ignor-ing her bewildered expression, which intensified when she felt how I was trembling. I led her over to the fetid mattress where I knelt and bade her do the same. I willed her to trust me, summoning an unfledged authority, praying she wouldn't suddenly come to her senses and cut and run. Then I took up the book that lay facedown on the rumpled sheets, its splayed covers like a rooftop in a flood, and began to read aloud from its pages.

◢ 10 ◣
The Pinch: A History

1878

Once upon a bone-dry July afternoon, a solitary pack peddler by the name of Pinchas Pinsker came down the road. Pushing a wooden handcart, which he leaned against at an angle almost parallel to the ground, he turned into an avenue of oaks that led toward a colonnaded plantation house. His cart was a low, two-wheeled affair that had recently belonged to a greengrocer in Crab Orchard, Kentucky, and for it Pinchas had swapped a quantity of sateen ticking that the man's wife had admired. He pushed the contraption by a pair of spindled handstaffs that he hoped one day to hitch to a horse's flanks. The cart contained the tarp-covered contents of a small racket store: razors, carpet slippers, snuffboxes, and tobacco; there were spectacles, kitchen utensils, candles, oilcloth, dress patterns, and yard goods; dolls for the children, kickshaws for the ladies. Though he wasn't born to this profession, when he removed the tarp from his merchandise, Pinchas—a short, bespectacled man with a nap of sandy hair under his bowler hat—felt like a conjuror revealing treasures.

As he neared the broad-porticoed house, he anticipated the servants and children coming out to greet him. That's what he was accustomed to. The occupants of sharecroppers' shacks and planters' mansions alike would trickle forth from their habitations to welcome the Jew peddler and sample his wares. It was why he'd been drawn to the South in the first place, having heard that the population viewed the Hebrew with reverence as a person of the Book. Never mind that in the years since his bar mitzvah, rather than holy writ, the book Pinchas had most cherished was a Yiddish translation of the first volume of *Das Kapital,* a copy of which was secreted in his cart.

It was his political sympathies that had compelled him to leave his family and the Russian Pale of Settlement one step ahead of the czar's police. But despite arriving in the New World with his ideals intact, Pinchas had since conceived a healthy tolerance for free enterprise. His pulse was quickened by the babel of the hagglers and shmeikelers along the jostling thoroughfares of the Lower East Side of New York. No stranger to labor himself, having served apprenticeships as a draper and grain broker back in Blod, Pinchas began peddling flour sifters and mousetraps from a stall on Ludlow Street. Restless with how his ignorance of the native language confined him to the ghetto, however, he took to straying into outlying quarters. He wandered among the arrant residents of the Five Points and the complacent burghers of Kleindeutschland above Fourteenth Street, picking up snatches of the American tongue along the way. Here was a mobility he'd been denied in the Old Country, and while he remained disapproving of their acquisitive values, Pinchas was nonetheless infected by the yeasty energies of these Yankee citizens. Addicted now to the habit of movement, he secured a small loan from Yarmolovsky's Bank on Canal Street; he purchased forty dollars' worth of goods from a nearby supply house and set off to broaden his orbit, taking a train as far as Cincinnati, whence he proceeded on foot along the sun-baked highways into Kentucky and farther south.

As he neared the big house, he wondered why no one had yet to appear. The hedges were neatly trimmed in elaborate topiary shapes, the kitchen garden weeded and pruned, but the house and grounds seemed otherwise abandoned. A gaunt hound with a panting pink tongue approached him, nuzzling his leg and whimpering pitifully; a lowing cow dragged her swollen udders through the tea roses. The air around the mansion, already oppressive in the afternoon heat, had a forbidding odor, miasmic like rotting silage. Pinchas marveled that he should have goosebumps despite his streaming perspiration. The whole day had in fact had a portentous quality about it, all the traffic along the rutted highway headed away from the city of Memphis toward which he was bound. The passengers in their traps and wagons piled with trunks and household furnishings looked distressed, some with sponges tied clownishly over their noses.

Curiosity overcoming his trepidation, he climbed the front steps and pressed his nose against the pane of a tall, rippled-glass window. The gallery overhead shaded the porch and shielded the glass from glare so that

Pinchas was able to spy the sumptuous parlor inside. Empty of occupants, the parlor was appointed with a marble hearth, brass firedogs, and a portrait of a saber-wielding officer in Confederate butternut above the mantelpiece. The porch planks creaked under his hobnails as Pinchas slunk around the corner of the house and peered through the window of another room. It took his eyes a few seconds to adjust to the dim interior of what turned out to be a high-ceilinged bedroom containing a nightmare tableau; for beneath the canopy of a disordered bed lay a man and woman, their silk-robed bodies snarled in an unnatural configuration—their eyes stark-staring, faces frozen in the rigor of their final agony, as if their souls had wrenched themselves free of their gawking mouths. On the floor below the bed was another pair of lifeless bodies, similarly entangled: two ring-letted little girls in their alice-blue nighties. The twin daughters along with their parents were wreathed in flies and blanketed in what appeared to be a lava of black caviar, some of which was also sprayed across the wainscoting'd walls.

Pinchas's first thought was irrational: the serfs had murdered their masters and children and fled the estate. Then he remembered that the serfs—the slaves? had there really been slaves?—were freed more than a decade before. "Vey iz mir," he gasped aloud, lurching headlong back toward his cart. He took up the handles and steered it blindly through a cloud of mosquitoes so thick it left a peddler-shaped hole where he'd passed through, and without looking back turned again into the open road.

Now he was alert to the signs that told him he had stumbled into the Valley of the Shadow. Shacks along the way featured men with shotguns sitting sentinel in their yards, flinty wives standing fiercely behind them in their Sunday bonnets. The current of traffic moving always in the opposite direction grew denser, occasional passengers calling out to him from their carriages what might have been warnings. But if Pinchas didn't exactly ignore them, neither did he take their words to heart—one of which ("yellow jack") was repeated with some frequency. He imagined Yellow Jack as a Goliath terrorizing the city whose outskirts he had entered, a giant with whom he was destined to contend. At the same time he understood that this was nonsense. What Jew heads deliberately upstream during an exodus? But Pinchas had been so often discouraged from crossing borders and thresholds due to this interdiction or that imperial ukase that he proceeded on the strength of sheer dogged forward momentum.

He was halted at a bridge over a powder-dry stream by a pair of militia-men in partial uniform.

"What bidness you got in Mefiss?" asked the apple-cheeked younger, his weapon at the ready.

Pinchas was forthright. "Iss to make a livink, mayn beezniz."

Said the slovenly older soldier with a sneer, "Seem like livin' ain't what folks're about round here." He spat. "Cross this bridge, Mister, and you might never come back."

But since they were posted there to stop the infected from leaving the city, a function they'd shown themselves wholly inadequate to perform, they made no effort to block Pinchas's progress. He soon wished they had.

The road was flanked by dismal shanties that gave way before long to two-story clapboard facades, decaying plank pavements, and a de-praved citizenry. Individuals staggering in the lime-dusted roadway and assemblages spilling out the doors of saloons appeared to be simultane-ously involved in acts of celebration and mourning; nor could you deter-mine where one left off and the other began. A drunk with a shock of corn-tassel hair tottered up to Pinchas with a clay jug dangling from his pinky finger, saying, "Used to, the milkman'd shout, 'Wide awake, all alive!' Now it's 'Bring out your dead!'" He laughed like a loon as he offered the peddler a draft, which Pinchas kindly declined. He forged ahead past some bystanders watching idly as a man with a canary complexion looked to be running in circles while lying in the dirt. They watched until one of the bystanders, removing a tiny pistol from a breast pocket, shot the man like a rabid dog, after which they all moved away. On a stoop a buxom lady lay collapsed in a nest of calico; a preacher with graying temples like the wings on Mercury's helmet mounted a barrel to declare that the plague was God's vengeance for the pagan festival of Mardi Gras. In an upstairs window a woman was singing in a plaintive contralto: "Dream, dream, grah mo chree / here on your mama's knee . . . ," while the air, riven with a general keening, provided a jarring disharmony.

The groceries and snack houses were largely boarded up—some with yellow cards and black crepe nailed to their doors—but the grog shops were thriving. Their clientele, as they exited, paused to inspect the fresh caskets that a company of kerchiefed Negroes were unloading from a fur-niture van. The empty caskets were then exchanged for the tenanted ones left on the doorsteps of stricken families. Some of the groggery patrons scrutinized the pine boxes as if shopping for their next berth, while others, pallid and less steady on their pins, looked as if they'd just crawled out of them. One box lay open on the curb as if for viewing: its occupant, marinating in a stew of tar and carbolic acid, was dressed in his full lodge regalia, his black tongue lolling like a slug.

There were drums of boiling creosote stationed along the curbs and burning bedclothes saturated in regurgitation. Asafetida bags tied around the necks of frightened citizens vied with the pungency of decomposing flesh. It was the stench that had preceded the city limits by several furlongs, and was suffocating in its intensity here. Making a mighty effort to place one foot in front of the other, Pinchas steered his cart around a bare-boned mule struggling to climb out of a sinkhole. The hole was the result of an overflowing basement privy, and rats as large as terriers rode the mule.

It was coming on dusk and Pinchas was near to falling down from exhaustion. Having slept these past weeks in haybarns and pastures, he'd looked forward to a night's lodging under a proper roof, where he could wash off the shmutz from the road and refresh himself. He'd been told that Memphis was a city of cheap rooming houses run by maternal widows, but here the peddler had straggled into a charnel house instead. Then he'd passed out of the ramshackle quarter into a soberer district of Federal-style buildings, fashionable shops, and electric trolley lines. But the street, for all its elegant window displays, was as desolate at this end as it was anarchic at the other. There was no traffic save the clattering coffin wagons and the carts from which ragged men, like devils pitching brimstone, shoveled heaps of disinfectant powder. The only pedestrians were the scurrying gent in a cutaway holding a rosewater pomander to his nose and a pair of nuns dragging the hems of their habits in the greenish dust. Cannons boomed, church bells rang, and Pinchas came to a full stop in order to scratch the angry mosquito bites that stippled his neck and arms.

It was then he was approached from both sides of the avenue by children or midgets: he couldn't tell which as all were in nightshirts and uniformly short of stature, their faces hidden by red bandannas. About the bandannas Pinchas wasn't so concerned, since half the population wore masks like ganefs; only these turned out to be ganefs indeed. For in a matter of seconds, before the spent peddler could even react, they had whipped the tarp from his merchandise and gathered up the entirety of his stock-in-trade from the cart. Spiriting away armloads piled as high as their heads with tinware, piece goods, garters, and pewter buttons, the thieves vanished as swiftly as they'd appeared; though one returned to snatch up the canvas tarpaulin and, as an afterthought, the volume of Marx.

Wanting despite his inertia to give chase, Pinchas was stymied by his inability to choose which of their several directions to pursue them in. "A plague befall you!" he called after them reflexively, chilled by his apprehension that the curse may already have been fulfilled. He patted himself to make sure that the roll of bills, his savings, was still pinned to the inside of his dank flannel drawers. Then, as he pondered his empty cart with a sigh like a stab, he was distracted by the sight of a young man choking sobs, lugging a body in a winding sheet down a flight of stone steps. Mechanically Pinchas wheeled his cart toward the curb, and without exchanging a word with the weeping man, took up one end of the body by the feet that protruded from the shroud. They were a woman's bare, spatulate feet with callused toes. Together Pinchas and the man lifted the corpse onto the cart, and tipping the sweaty rim of his bowler hat, the heartsick peddler continued on his way.

He wandered gaslit sidestreets past tall Italianate houses with turrets and ornate iron gates. Most were completely dark, though in one or two lights flickered like foxfire behind the hooded windows. Some of the more modest abodes had signs at the gate advertising rooms, but their haunted aspect told the peddler that strangers need not apply. Once or twice he sought to inquire of a rare pedestrian, who only quickened his pace at the peddler's approach. Even though evening had descended, there was no relief from the sticky heat, and Pinchas's legs, despite their habitual forward motion, were close to giving out. He was staggering before a boxy two-story house that, unlike its neighbors, was brightly lit from within. Watermelon vines spiraled the porch columns and a magnolia stood in the yard, its fragrance cutting somewhat the pervasive stench. On the porch sat a porcine woman in a rocker fanning herself with what looked like a raptor's wing. She was wearing a flounced silk wrapper and smoking a long-stemmed pipe, her platinum hair piled in a towering pompadour.

"You got maybe a room?" asked the peddler, before his knees buckled under him and he knelt on the broken board paving. He heard the woman bellow, "Dinah! Eulalie! A customer."

Ladies in rustling skirts, their cologne so acrid it brought tears to his eyes, grabbed Pinchas under the arms. As they dragged him up the front steps and through the front door, he couldn't tell whether he was being rescued or abducted. He was aware of passing through a furbelowed parlor, complete with pier glass, fainting couch, and the portrait of a naked female attended by putti. He was hauled up a steep, carpeted staircase and taken into a room off a narrow hallway. Unfolded across a brass bed, Pinchas felt cool hands caressing him even as they shoved a mercury thermometer between his lips and took his pulse. They unbuttoned his garments and toiveled his sunken chest with damp cloths. At length one of the ladies—Pinchas could tell she was only a girl despite the heavy rouge—pronounced authoritatively, "He ain't fevered, just tuckered out."

One of the girls had fetched a bowl of beef bouillon and begun to spoon-feed him, while another offered him a tot of brandy from a cupping glass. A third, arms folded across her blotchy décolletage, made a considered judgment: "I believe this here is a Jew feller." At that the two others resumed their clinical attitudes. "How can you tell?" asked the girl with the broth, inclining her sausage-curled head for a closer inspection. "Well," replied the one across the bed from her, setting aside the brandy, "he has got what you call the map a Jerusalem writ on his face." But the standing girl with the dappled bosom asserted somewhat listlessly that that wasn't sufficient proof. "Ain't but one way to be sure," she said, which sent the others into a fit of titters, upon which two pairs of hands made for the flies of Pinchas's underwear.

His energies in some measure restored by their ministrations, the peddler's first impulse was to protect his modesty and extricate himself from the room. The rabbis of his youth would have been scandalized. On the other hand, Pinchas had as good as abandoned his heritage, Isaiah and Jeremiah having been replaced in his hierarchy of prophets by Proudhon and Kropotkin. In his travels, once he'd neglected to keep the Sabbath, he never bothered to keep it again, nor did he make any effort to observe the dietary laws. Where women were concerned he had resisted temptation only because temptation had been scarce in his experience. And while these daughters of Lilith would be reckoned unclean by every category of the halakhic code, Pinchas realized with a wan smile that he wasn't picky. He was after all a Narodnik, a freethinker, despite his late commercial proclivities, and the despotic faith of his forefathers could not reach him here.

For all that, he was ashamed of his thoughts, which he might attribute to his weakened condition, though how to explain the rebellious stirring in his loins? Meanwhile the ladies had opened his drawers and uncovered his upstanding organ, which they leered at, having never before beheld the sign of the Covenant. "Thang's nekkider than nekkid," observed the girl on the peddler's left side, damask-cheeked and saucer-eyed. The one at his right, risen to her knees on the mattress, clapped her hands, which jiggled her curls like pendants on a chandelier. "I want a go," she resolved. "I ain't never rid one a these." She was lifting her crinoline when the other girl shoved her roughly out of the way, then positioned herself astride Pinchas's outstretched legs. A hilarious tussling ensued, during which the spectator girl, her maculate bodice glazed in sweat, began to slide down the wall in a swoon. The two on the bed ceased their frolic to stare at their fallen companion. The one straddling Pinchas looked in perplexity from her fellow on the floor to the peddler's peeled member. "It ain't all *that* peculiar," she reckoned. Then the fallen girl began to convulse, projecting a stream of bile like molten coffee grounds across the valance below the bedstead.

Pinchas watched in horror as the two girls, with amazingly unruffled efficiency, left the bed to attend to their companion slumped against the wall. They pressed a lace hankie to her mouth and watched as a crimson stain slowly spread. Galvanized by the scene and the fetor that made the air in the room unbreathable, Pinchas tucked his wilted manhood back into his long johns and slid from the mattress. Trailing the sheet he'd wrapped carelessly about his person, he shuffled back into the hallway, where he encountered two more painted ladies, who parted to let him pass.

Turning about, the addled peddler asked them, "Where am I?"

"Annie Cook's," they said in unison over their shoulders, then commenced to contradict each other, one cheerfully alleging that the establishment was a "bawdy," the other a "pest" house. Unenlightened, Pinchas proceeded down the corridor, passing closed doors behind which could be heard a medley of moans and shrieks; but whether from amorous exertions or the laments of the infirm, who could say? A door at the end of the hall, however, stood open, and through it Pinchas spied the ladies nursing a chap whose fallow flesh appeared to have been parboiled from the inside out. This house, he concluded, was a kind of sanctuary where the nafkehs doubled as sisters of mercy—and sometimes martyrs. Good on them, he thought, but an upright man such as he (in health if not virtue) had no business here. Woozy though he was, Pinchas had seen enough. He made his way down the back stairs and was in the street again before he realized that, still togaed in the bedsheet, he'd forgotten his clothes.

What's more, the money he'd pinned to the inside of his union suit was no longer there. "Mutzlekh!" Pinchas congratulated himself. "You got now nothing left to lose." He trudged on, thinking he might find an officer to accompany him back to the brothel and demand that his funds be returned. But after he'd turned a corner or two without spotting a cop, Pinchas doubted he would even be able to retrace his steps. Besides, he still retained his Old Country distrust of police; and given the state of the infected city, infernal in the light of the fever fires, he figured the police would have better things to do than to retrieve an indigent immigrant's purloined purse.

He'd found his way back to Main Street, which was desolate as an outpost. One step ahead of the fatigue that was threatening to overtake him again, he plodded on, crossing a street between palisades of rotting cotton and entering a park that overlooked the river's traveling expanse. A leaden sky marbled with moonlight illuminated a cluster of paddle wheelers (perhaps in quarantine) riding at anchor below the levee, their smokestacks contributing to the fouled atmosphere.

Pinchas coveted the few benches that crowned the bluff, but they were already occupied by silhouettes in various stages of tribulation. One hugged himself as he sat rocking furiously back and forth; another recited verses in Latin, and the peddler knew enough of gentile customs to assume the poor soul was administering some type of sacrament to himself. The petrified attitude of another invited an enterprising young thief, employing a hook and line to avoid contamination, to fish in his pockets for spoils. It occurred to Pinchas that, if he were willing to risk the contagion, he might secure a suit of clothes from a stiff, but his main objective at the moment was simply to lie down. His weariness had acquired a nauseous component; his head ached and his stomach had begun to cramp. This was possibly due to the onset of heatstroke, he reasoned, though that affliction did not commonly occur after dark. Still, he felt that his very skin was on fire, even as he'd begun to be racked with chills.

He steered his unsteady steps toward a mulberry hedge, behind which he hoped to find some privacy. Rounding the hedge he came upon a young woman lying supine on the ground, her features marmoreal, her gorged blue breast bared to the living infant that fiercely sucked at it. "Gott in himmel," gasped Pinchas, who believed in neither God nor heaven. In fact he was by then more prepared to expect the kind of intervention that directly took place: when a yipping, half-naked bedlamite, death riding the flapping tails of his gown, appeared out of nowhere to shove Pinchas to the ground; then scarcely breaking stride, he stooped to pluck the tyke from the dead mother's breast and carry it away.

His cheek pressed against the prickly grass, Pinchas understood that what he'd witnessed had no place in a sensible world—or was it the peddler himself who no longer belonged? He was almost grateful when he felt his griping gut uncoil, giving up along with his insides a vital spark at the quick of his being in a muddy emulsion of pitch-black blood. His last conscious thought was how convenient it was that his remains should already be swaddled in their graveclothes.

When reading aloud to Rachel from The Pinch, *I would glance at her from time to time, watching for signs that she thought the words were more than stories. Certainly she was receptive, often changing positions on the mattress to make herself more comfortable: she hugged her knees, stretched her legs to loll on her side, tilted her head to catch a peculiar turn of phrase; sometimes she admitted an inward smile, sometimes laughed outright. But I could tell that the book remained for her merely a book, the stories only stories, a whimsical gloss on the factual history of North Main. Occasionally her attitude infected mine, reducing Muni's chronicles to diversions for the gullible, fabrications that had little in common with the real life of the street. And honestly, there were times when it was a relief to share that perspective. Meanwhile I never let on that at some point in the narrative we would run into yours truly; then fact and fancy would collide or maybe blend into one and the same.*

Her unwilling suspension of disbelief aside: naked, Rachel was herself a catalog of enchantments. She was tickled when I undressed her, not from the undue exposure so much as from her amusement at my shaking hands and chattering teeth. "Such an enfant terrible!" she would tease me. "Scared of a naked lady." And it was true that no bogey I'd encountered during my pharmaceutical escapades had instilled in me such awe as Rachel's close-pored flesh. Her breasts, when I lay my cheek against them, were soft as spongecake, her belly like the trough of a salt lick I traced with my tongue. Her burnished thighs fluctuated like waves, parting to reveal a floating garden I swam toward from over the crest of a hip. Entering her I tried not to lose myself, and looked to her human face to gauge the rectitude of my progress; but the moods of her face kept changing till I didn't know whether I clung to a heroine or a whore or an impish child.

Okay, so the multitudes she contained gave me a fright—and then they didn't; because letting go (and I could let go tumultuously since Rachel was on the pill) I would find myself again in familiar surroundings. For there sat tailor Bluestein at the machine in the window of his shop, sewing garments with odd apertures for the mutant creatures that sheltered in the outhouse behind his building. The merchant Shapiro was advising Mrs. Grunewald that the fabric she fingered was a sample from the pargod, the curtain that surrounded the Lord's holy throne. "Note the irregularities that they're unborn souls stitched into the material like pinned butterflies." The butcher Makowsky sank his cleaver into marbled meat carved from a flank (or so he claimed) of the Messiah Ox, and the pot at Ike Taubenblatts' pinochle game was stuffed with forfeited shadows. Ridblatt delivered fresh challah to Rosen's Deli, where the alter kockers tore off pieces and stuffed their faces, the bread foaming like a benign hydrophobia in their toothless mouths. But Rachel lived elsewhere, and after I'd tarried a spell on North Main Street I made the journey back to my bed, where we would twine, my girl and me, like those vines that grew over the graves of legendary lovers.

And so I had for a time the best of both worlds.

He opened his eyes to darkest eternity. Of course Pinchas Pinsker had never supposed there would be an afterlife, and it humbled him to find himself in one, though this straitened confinement hardly qualified as any kind of a life. It angered him as well, his cramped situation, or at least he registered an emotion that might have risen to the status of anger had he had the strength for it. Because an afterlife gave the lie to the strict rationalist view he'd adhered to since rejecting the Torah of his student days; it vindicated all the narishkeit he thought he'd left behind him in the shtetl. His nose twitched against the stink of the effluvium that saturated his winding sheet. This must be Sheol, the inky perdition to which Jewish no-goodniks were everlastingly sentenced; though it seemed to Pinchas he'd scarcely had time in his brief life to earn such a bleak retribution.

Granted, his few virtues might not have merited Paradise—but Sheol? Had he really been so great a sinner?

He felt himself momentarily in motion, floating for a spell in a shifting, desultory manner until he landed *kerplump*. The demons of the left side of darkness were toying with him, Pinchas assumed, the pain in his restricted limbs compounded by the unhappy realization that death had made him superstitious. He thought he heard voices and concluded that he wasn't alone. Naturally there would be myriad others condemned to a similar solitude, fated to listen to one another's mumblings and blubberings without a hope of ever understanding or being themselves understood. Then it came to him that there was an alternative he'd failed to consider: maybe he wasn't actually dead. But that one seemed even less plausible than the other options. Again he heard muffled voices and decided it wouldn't hurt to cry out, but the best he could muster in his feeble state was a pathetic inaudible groan. He discovered, however, that he still had the use of his fingers, and so began to rap on the ceiling of his horizontal cell. No sooner had he done so than he felt himself floating again, tilting to left and right then sliding downward with a velocity that left his stomach behind. He continued his desperate rapping, gathering what energy remained to him to deliver a full-blown, close-knuckled knock. Banging away on the lid of his captivity, Pinchas was aware of his mortal thirst, of wanting now beyond reason to be let out already from this airless purgatorial box!

The voices outside his stifling space grew louder. There was a sound like the squeal of a sphincter and a coffin-shaped seam of light appeared above him; then the lid was prized all the way off, and lustrous human faces—one with a broken nose and prognathous jaw, the other with a conflagration of ginger hair—hovered over him in the torrid afternoon. Drained of energy, Pinchas lay back unmoving in his enclosure.

"It's a queer look that's on him for a man that's dead," said the plug-ugly fellow.

"Dada," exclaimed the redheaded girl, "he's alive!"

"Faith, how can you tell, Katie darling?"

"Look how his sorrowful eyes are upon us."

"Similar, I'm thinking, would be the eyes of any carcass."

"But this one's," she said, poking an obtrusive index finger into Pinchas's solar plexus, "are not past blinking."

Her father allowed that that was the case but cautioned her not to touch his revolting person again. Then an argument commenced between father and daughter over whether the man deserved redeeming from his current circumstance. The father was of a mind to leave sleeping dogs lie. "After all, we don't know where the filthy beggar has been." This opinion was backed up by the pair of thick-ribbed lads lumbering on either side of the father, though the girl shut them both up with a word: "Eejits." Then she protested that the man's animate condition made it incumbent on every Christian to do his duty. "Besides, the very fact of his breathing gives the proof he survived the distemper and is no longer a danger."

"But Katie mavourneen, we've our own grief to bear and it's no affair we have to be shouldering an extra burden. Look about you, daughter, and your mother still unburied in this hidjiss place where no priest would attend us."

For they were standing amid a congregation of knotty pine coffins in the broad gash of the open plague pit at the Elmwood Cemetery, where paupers were consigned to mass burial.

"My mother it was," said the girl with a flash of temper, "that you drove into this early grave with your wanton ways. For her the distemper was a mercy and even this dreadful place a welcome rest. He"—pointing to the invalid in the box, who was trying without success to mouth some defense of his own—"is the Lord's opportunity for you to do penance."

"It's a hard unforgiving lass you are altogether, Katie Keough, but when did your loving da ever refuse you? Neither the lame cur nor the mangy tom you were wont to drag to our humble door did I turn away."

Which was how the peddler Pinchas Pinsker came to be lifted in his casket by the two lumpish brothers and loaded onto a rattling donkey cart. He was hauled from the burial ground under the skirts of the willow trees to the squishy banks of Catfish Bayou, just north of the district called the Pinch. This was the gangrenous sink that had greeted the peddler on his entry into the city: the bayou little more than an open sewer, a putrid channel around which refugees from the Great Hunger had pitched their miserable hovels. The Keoughs' own dwelling consisted chiefly of the mud-plugged hull of an overturned johnboat, its kitchen a jerrybuilt postscript. Pinchas was installed in that kitchen on a rank pallet under a shelf that supported a flitch of dried pork, his presence forcing the eviction of the family hound that had so far escaped the city's mass extermination of pets.

His first coherent thought with regard to his convalescent residence was that he may have been better off in the casket. Despite here and there a feminine touch—a lace doily under a growler, a crocheted cozy over a rifle stock—the place was a sty. It was little improved by the fumes from the sour mash whiskey still operated by father and sons. The still, Pinchas would learn, supplemented a meager income from their cottage fishing industry, since the fish they netted in the swill of the bayou were only marginally edible. If the house was in mourning, the peddler never saw any signs of it beyond the daughter's fixed irritability toward her men. Nor did the family seem to heed the fever raging around them, which was carrying off their neighbors in droves. The smell of the bayou combined with the rancidness of their hovel did help to neutralize the universal putrescence that was a constant reminder of plague. But as he began, under Katie's care, to regain a semblance of his former vitality, the peddler grew more accustomed to his surroundings and started to view them in a different light. He ate with gusto Katie's spuds in their various incarnations, slurped the soup the girl called "fishyswaz," and began to think he'd awakened into some snug household tale. Like the one he'd once read in a Yiddish translation in which a sea captain's family lived in the rollicking warmth of a capsized vessel on a beach.

He was practically unaware of the hostility directed toward him by the patriarch, Cashel Keough, and his surly sons, Murtagh and Tighe. Bitterly they complained of the space Katie had appropriated for her charge in their already crowded quarters, never mind the amount of victuals he consumed. And to see the sapless intruder wearing his own bleached nightshirt, which ballooned about him like a baptismal gown, was almost more than the crapulent Cashel could bear. Adamant in her defense of the invalid, Katie alternated between cautioning her family not to interfere in her solicitations and assuring them their charity would be recorded in the annals of heaven. But Cashel was not as easily cowed by his daughter as were her brothers. He was suspicious of the way her patient mangled the Lord's own English. And when he heard the man ask Katie in his lingering confusion, "Didn't you paint it with lamb's blood the doorpost of your house?," Cashel knitted his bristling brow in contemplation.

"Pin-skerr? Is that by way of being the lad's heathen name?" Leaning closer to examine the hump at the bridge of the invalid's nose. "I do believe it's an Israelite we're after nurturing in our boozum." Tighe and Murtagh nodded their ungainly heads in accord with their da's sage judgment.

Smiling weakly, Pinchas himself concurred, anticipating more of the kind of hospitable reception he'd been used to receiving from the rural folk.

"And wasn't it his people themselves that poisoned the wells back in the day of your allover Black Death?" mused Cashel, his voice rising an octave with every syllable. Then he and his boys might have laid hands on the peddler, tossing him into the mire at their doorstep, had not the daughter of the house stepped between them. Katie shooed them away from the sickbed and refused to hear a discouraging word concerning her charge.

Her father sulked, her brothers groused, and Pinchas began gradually to come back to himself. Gradually, because he was in no hurry. He marveled that the affliction of a single night could have taken such a ruinous toll on his constitution. But then it was not every day that one dropped dead and was rescued intact from the other side; and while he didn't believe for a second that such a thing had actually happened, he felt nonetheless that he was somehow changed. After a few days he was able to stand with Katie's assistance and take some steps about the shanty's beaten earth floor. This was no easy feat given the clutter, the fishing gear and rat traps (some with the rats still in them) obstructing his path; for Katie was not a conscientious housekeeper. He was eventually able to sit at the table, enduring the dagger stares of the menfolk as they consumed their mounds of jacketed potatoes. The stares were doubly intense from young Tighe, in whose plaited shirt and trousers the girl had recently appareled her patient. But for all the tension his presence bred in the house, Pinchas was not anxious to leave. He knew well enough the grim necropolis that awaited a penniless peddler beyond their door.

But that wasn't the only reason Pinchas was reluctant to reveal the full extent of his recovery. He luxuriated in Katie's attentions, even when the measures she took to restore him verged on the heroic: for she administered regular doses of castor oil and calomel to reactivate kidney function and loosen the bowels, the effects of which Pinchas suffered in grateful humiliation. Reborn, he was content there should be a period during which he was reduced to the condition of a virtual babe in arms. When his body began to regain its previous vigor, his clearing brain acknowledged certain stirrings that had been—though unrecognized till now—a fundamental motivation all along. Because, beyond his need to escape the cloistered life of the shtetl and the incarceration his treasonous sympathies promised, Pinchas had yielded as well to a call to adventure. And adventure included an unspoken quest for romance. True, such a desire was not wholly compatible with his commitment to dialectical materialism, or to the cruder materialism he'd lately practiced. In fact, he was as vexed by this desire as he was by his inexperience. He derided his growing fondness for the girl even as he regarded her as the agent of his salvation, a notion her father affirmed in his cups.

"It's a mockery of our Lord's own resurrection you've made with this Jew man," Cashel was heard to mutter.

And Katie: "Put a cake in it, Da!"

The brothers, less vocal, satisfied themselves with pissing discreetly in the peddler's porridge and thumping him in places where the bruises wouldn't show. Pinchas was stoic in suffering their abuse, having endured worse at the hands of the girl herself, whom he was coming to adore.

He knew it was an impossible infatuation, not the least because he was a Hebrew and she the daughter of a popish clan who viewed him as essentially vermin. But such obstacles the peddler, perhaps delusional in his reinvigorated state, believed he could overcome. Added to these deterrents, however, was the further inconvenience of a fiancé. For it seemed that Katie Keough had been pledged to one Phelim Mulrooney, a barkeep who operated a dram shop over in Catfish Alley. It happened that the Keough men, averse to their own rotgut (whose side effects rivaled the symptoms of the plague itself), had run up an exorbitant tab at Squire Mulrooney's tavern. In point of fact, they were in default of a bill they could never hope to settle. The barkeep, though, had magnanimously agreed to waive their debt, and even to extend them a line of credit, in exchange for the hand of the fair but undowered Katie. The maid herself had not objected to the betrothal; its imminence was the trump card she held over her father and brothers, and played whenever the occasion called for it. To break off the engagement would have meant severing their lifeline, and by periodically threatening to do just that, Katie would have her way in most matters. Besides, the girl had been approached by worse suitors, and despite a face so infested with blackheads that he looked to have been peppered by buckshot, Phelim Mulrooney was a man of parts. The proprietor of a thriving business, he made a more or less honest, if disreputable, living. The Pinch had offered her no better prospects.

Pinchas had ascertained all this during the tavern keeper's visits. The man would appear on the gentile Sabbath, doff his stiff bowler, and greet them—often with wilting flowers for Katie—with a "God save all in this house." The Keoughs would respond with false enthusiasm, because it was clear none were overly fond of their benefactor. He would pay his shamefast respects to his intended, embarrassed by his own transparent carnality, and even inquire after the welfare of her patient, whom he regarded as the girl's innocent pastime. Then he would sit down with the men and, casting the occasional cow's eyes in Katie's direction, discuss items concerning the wedding. Impatient though he was, however, Phelim agreed there was nothing for it but to postpone the affair until the ongoing crisis had abated. For death still held dominion over the district.

"A feller can't unstopper a keg or raise a bucket from a well without he turns up a corpse," the suitor would repine. "They're after saying there ain't enough living to bury the dead and it's the niggers are having to do it."

Of course there was always the question, never expressed, of their own survival. Phelim himself wore as a charm against misfortune a moonstone amulet sold to him by a fishwife who was later stoned for a witch. "The world's gone plain medieval and no kicker." Eavesdropping from where he lay on his pallet, Pinchas silently maintained there was no impediment so great that he couldn't surmount it, as long as the girl felt about him as he did about her. But so far there was little evidence in support of that.

Perhaps the barkeep Mulrooney was right and he was nothing to her but an ephemeral pet. Living among louts in the absence of her mother, she was in need of a creature on which she could expend some tenderness, and in lieu of a broken-winged bird a sick Yid peddler would have to do. As soon as he was mended, she would set him free without a second thought. So he continued to call forth the odd fit of coughing and dissemble a frailty he no longer felt. Then he would try to count the freckles that sprinkled her cheeks like spilled nutmeg as she passed a saucer of rum vapors under his nose. He held his breath to glimpse the shady contours of her camisole as she knelt to give him a mustard footbath, and spied her emerald eye peeking at him from behind a helix of strawberry hair. Her hands, as she dried them in her apron, darted like sparrows in a bath; her slight breast lifted suspensefully before a sigh. Sometimes she caught him ogling her and they both blushed in mutual discomfiture, though he might think he detected the hint of a smile. Then he could believe that, along with the turbid light that filtered into her hovel from the hellscape outside, she had allowed herself to bask an instant in his adoration.

"Katie," he had resolutely confided in her, "the man I was before you have saved me I am no more." To which the girl inquired, "Are you then no more a man at all?" Ignoring her retort, he stood by his statement: because the previous Pinchas had had no tolerance for magical thinking; the credulity of the Russian Pale with its deathless prophets and hidden saints was a world he'd long since left behind. But how to argue with the fact that he'd been raised from his coffin by an angel? And now he felt his identity as erstwhile revolutionary and peregrine merchant was a casualty of that event. All that once defined him had been displaced by his overriding passion for the girl. "Katie, I am gornisht vi a vantz," he avowed, "nothing but a insect without you."

They tickled her, his singular confessions, which she occasionally countered with melodic Irish equivalents: "We say amadán, a fool." She seemed to enjoy listening to his fractured syntax, often correcting his speech, as if in healing his body she must also knit his broken tongue. Sometimes, however, his relentless expressions of gratitude seemed to get under her skin. Was it that she'd simply had enough of his malarkey, or had she come to feel the burden of a responsibility for his very existence? In his most hopeful moments Pinchas suspected that she knew he was malingering and was complicit in prolonging his convalescence.

He offered her tortured versions of biblical verses recalled from his cheder days, whose meaning he felt he'd only begun to understand: "Your eyes are toyvn . . . pretty doves / your hair a flock of goats—"

"A flock of goats!"

"Your teeth are ewes that they sheared already the fleece—"

"For the love of Jaysus!"

"Your breasts—"

"Shut your gob!"

But she hid her amusement in her apron.

Once, when the men were out peddling their poteen and he was alone with the girl, Pinchas dared to venture, "Katie, you are, I think, mayn bashert." He lay sprawled across the tattered quilt, his back against the bowed wall of the kip, eyes moist behind their small oval lenses.

"The cheek!" she exclaimed, though her potato masher remained poised in midflail; then in a whisper, "What does it mean, bashert?"

"It means a destined one."

Lowering the masher into the bowl, the girl became thoughtful. "We say m'anamchara, soul mate, or macushla machree, pulse of my heart." Her roseate complexion deepened as she returned to mauling her spuds, and Pinchas thought she glowed like a synagogue's everlasting lamp.

He wondered how he could want so much to worship and possess her at the same time, and how either option seemed to him equally holy. But no sooner had Pinchas realized that she was fond of him as well than he began to anguish over her well-being. Enslaved to a family of ingrates who conspired to sell her into the servitude of a loveless marriage, she was in dire need of being rescued from her fate. And that was to say nothing of the threat of the plague itself, which she might contract any day in her comings and goings—that is, if her wayward father and brothers didn't bring it back home to her from their knockings-about. Unable to contain his anxiety on her behalf, Pinchas found himself risen to his feet, taking hold of Katie's free hand. She again ceased pummeling her boiled tubers to level at him a dubious gaze.

"You saved me my life," he said. "Now you will please to let me"—he recalled the cardinal utterance of his profession—"settle the account."

She snickered, rolled her eyes, but made no effort to withdraw her hand from his. "Give an ear to who's talking salvation," she quipped.

"Katie, I got for you shpilkes," he admitted, "which it means I am afraid."

"Faith and didn't the Gypsy assure me I've nothing to fear from the distemper? It's other ills the years have in store for me."

But she could see he was far from appeased.

"Pinchas"—his name on her lips was pure music—"say after me: From tinker and pooka . . ."

"From tinker and pooka . . . ," he solemnly repeated.

". . . and black-hearted stranger . . ."

". . .and black-hearted stranger . . ."

"God keep"—here she squeezed his hand—"God keep my treasure this day from danger."

He completed the incantation and vowed to himself he would never leave her side.

It was a difficult vow to keep, given that his sham condition kept him from accompanying her into the perilous out-of-doors. He was torn, wanting at once to show himself as her protector and loath to reveal the extent of his fitness lest he be abruptly sent packing. Of course Katie would never turn him out, but the rest of her brood had become ever more voluble in expressing their discontent. Their neighbors were dying like flies, the virulence of the fever so great in their quarter that the remainder of the city claimed that it originated there. The Irish were a long-standing scapegoat, there being none lower on the social ladder but poor blacks, at least not until Pinchas had come along. But the Keough men had grown tired of the harmless persecutions—gluing his toes with molasses, painting his phiz with boot polish while he slept—they'd inflicted on the freeloader in Katie's absence; they were weary of appearing repentant in the face of their sister's wrath when she returned. They were ready to be rid of the Yid for good and all. His situation, Pinchas understood, was untenable and could not endure, but the love that steeled his resolve had also, he believed, made him cunning. It was time to devise a plan.

On an August evening—humidity so dense it curled the roof shingles—the brothers sat sharing a jar as they gutted a string of crappie. Fish innards slithered from the listing table, plopping onto the toes of their plow shoes and the floor. Across the room lay the peddler under a sodden sheet, pretending to sleep as he listened to their discussion of the topic that absorbed what little air was left in the room: for even her "gombeen siblings," as Katie called them, had begun to recognize that their days might be numbered. Who knew but their da might return this very night bringing the infection from the tavern, or their sister from her foraging?

"They say," reckoned Murtagh, his stubbled face flecked with bits of bloody intestine, "you can tell by his breath on a glass who's a carrier. Put a microscope to the glass and it's tiny bogeys you'll see."

His sheepdog eyes peering through a fringe of cornsilk hair, Tighe remarked, "Sure, and your carrier can make a gamecock go roupy by coughing upon it."

"That, I think, is moonshine," disparaged his older brother, "though your smaller bird will succumb."

Sentimental when soused, they fell to brooding over their fellows who'd been recently taken by Mister Jack: Rory Kavanagh, Spanker O'Malone—the list went on. "Fine lads gone too soon to glory and it's himself that survives," said Murtagh, tilting his square head in the direction of the recumbent Pinchas. "There's justice for you."

"Bang on," Tighe nodded in assent. "And there lies the Jew like a great-I-am in the place of old Finbar." For he still nursed a bitterness that the swayback hound, whose treble yelps he'd so savored when lifting it by the ears, had been banished from its pallet to the out-of-doors. Still feigning sleep, Pinchas manufactured a raucous snore.

Then Murtagh, who was not above goading his little brother, suggested that he might perhaps introduce a red pepper to the dosser's bony arse. Whereat Tighe, rising shakily to his feet, offered to go him one better and introduce the whole of the sheeny's anatomy to the night.

"Whisht, boyo, our Katie would be having your guts for garters."

"The biggety minx," exclaimed Tighe in a burst of pot valor, "she can start with these," plucking the entrails stuck to his trousers and flinging them at the wall. "The divil take Katie and her reasty rabbi!" Tottering forward, he leaned over the peddler and gave his shoulder a rough shake. "Here," he shouted, "it's time yer mushed along up the yard." Then a cuff to the back of the counterfeit sleeper's skull.

But Pinchas had provided for just such an eventuality. With the sheet pulled tightly over his head, he dredged with furtive fingers the reserve of ingredients he'd tucked into the deep pockets of Cashel's nightshirt. From the right-hand compartment he scooped the saffron pollen he'd collected from the overripe irises that Phelim Mulrooney had bestowed on Katie during his visits. He rubbed the pollen rapidly over his face, then took from the other pocket the pulpy blackberries he'd filched from Katie's larder and pressed them into his squinched-up eyes. He stuffed the fistful of tea leaves into his cheeks, so that before Tighe could tear the sheet from his head and haul him to his feet, Pinchas's skin was turned a saffron yellow and purple tears leaked from his nostrils and eyes.

"He looks a bad dose," judged Murtagh, giving a wide berth to both his little brother and the peddler, whom Tighe was attempting to march toward the door. Noises that seemed to have their source in Pinchas's diaphragm had begun to emerge from his throat. "Leave off your hold on his oxter, brother," Murtagh warned. "The man's about to spew." Then sure enough, announced by an animal caterwaul, a black substance began to issue from Pinchas's mouth like feathers from a punctured pillow. Tighe leapt away from his captive to join his big brother as witness.

"The feller's a fair volcano," he observed.

At that moment the door opened and Katie appeared, her arms evenly burdened with her produce basket and the earthen slop bucket. Dropping both, she cried, "Lord save us, he's that sick again!" She straightaway directed her brothers to help her get the afflicted back to bed, though neither would come near. Draping Pinchas's arm over her shoulder, she returned him to his pallet, where he lay floundering like an eel, alternating his tormented moaning with a racking cough. In the midst of his travail he was heard to ask for a rabbi.

"I fear there's no such creature in this town, my heart," Katie assured him.

"Then get for me a priest!"

Lifting a brow in consternation, Katie nevertheless turned to her brothers, who remained stock still. "You heard him, you fluthered elephants, get him a priest!"

Murtagh wondered aloud what the sheeny might be wanting with a man of the cloth.

"Thimblewit," barked his sister, "would you deny a dying man his last rites?"

Murtagh and Tighe exchanged looks, shrugged, then started for the door, clearly glad of an excuse to quit the wretched scene. As they exited the shanty, they were met by their pickled old man, who was stumbling in arm in arm with his future son-in-law, the barkeep Mulrooney. Florid-faced, Cashel Keough turned briefly to regard his departing sons, then back toward the misery on the pallet.

"What's all this ruction then?" he inquired.

"As you see," breathed Katie, with no will left to explain what should have been self-evident.

Pinchas yawped, yammered, and writhed, while Cashel winced and became defensive. "Sure it's no fault of mine," he said, though no one had accused him, "and didn't I tell you from the start he was crow bait?"

Katie paid no attention. She was up again and at the distillery in the corner, dousing a loofah sponge with a beaker containing the dregs of their vile poteen.

"Hold, lass," cautioned her father, "that's good shellac yer after wasting on a dead man." He made to interfere with his daughter, who pivoted in her fury and flung the tin beaker at his head. But her aim was

wild and the receptacle sailed past her da's shoulder to bounce off Phelim
Mulrooney's noggin. The barkeep touched the swelling node on his forehead, whose slope extended hairless to the crown of his meaty skull, and
tasted the blood. It did not seem to meet with his approval. "This isn't
the complaisant girl I was promised," he pouted, and turned to leave, but
Cashel held him fast by the rubber collar, insisting, "We had a bargain."

Again the door swung open and in lurched the brothers with a gosling-
headed party wearing a Roman cassock and collar in tow. Other than his
soiled vestments, there seemed little of the divine about him; in truth,
his pie-eyed visage with its wine-red snoot attested that he was as advanced in drink as Cashel himself. The sweat rolled off his wrinkled
countenance in rills.

"God and Mary to you, Father Farquhar," greeted Cashel somewhat
perfunctorily.

"Where lies the candidate for shanctification?" replied the priest.

The sad article whose thrashing and wailing arrested all other eyes and
ears was indicated to him. Squinting at Pinchas, Father Farquhar began automatically to recite his office from where he stood, the Latin purling from
his lips along with a thread of drool: "Miseratumtuiomnipotensdeush . . ."
Having thus acquitted himself of the sacrament, he made the sign of the
cross and turned to leave, only to find his way blocked by Murtaugh and
Tighe. Still functioning as their sister's agents, they were responding to
her appeal from the death pallet that Father Farquhar not depart without
first administering extreme unction. Dutifully they turned the priest back
around and shoved him forward toward the infirm.

Forced to his brittle knees by the brothers, the priest fetched a small
flask from his cassock. He uncorked it and extended a limpet-like tongue
to receive its contents, which were not forthcoming. "It appears I'm fresh
out of the holy chrism," he complained.

Katie offered some cooking oil, but Father Farquhar allowed as how
"your mortal soul favors bonded shpirits to attend its journey home." Katie
frowned, but in lieu of the poteen—the better part of which was dripping
from Squire Mulrooney's chin—she presented the sponge with which
she'd been bathing her patient's brow. The priest squeezed it, catching the
drops like a nectar on his tongue; then shuddering, declared, "Thish'll do."
Reinforced by the stimulating drizzle, he began again to recite his office at
the parting of the spirit: "Peristamshanctumunctionem . . . ," sprinkling

whiskey over the fever victim's forehead and hands. The aggrieved girl pressed her fingers to Pinchas's chest to try and still his agonies. The front of his nightshirt was coated in the lees of the ersatz *vomito negro*, and when Katie withdrew her hand bits of the awful matter remained stuck to her fingers, which she sniffed. Then her frightened face passed through several seasons of expression, from flummoxed to suspicious to the wry suggestion of a smile. Father Farquhar was merrily rattling off a litany of the sins the poor man must be excused of—sins of sight, hearing, smell, touch, taste, and carnal delectation. He was interrupted, however, when the afflicted sat suddenly bolt upright and cried in a voice that caused pismires to fall from the rafters, "Katie, mayn gelibteh, marry me!"

Then he fell back and recommenced his spasmodic moaning, giving every indication that he was half-dead already. But the reverent mood of that crooked house was broken, the onlookers stunningly disconcerted. As they awaited the peddler's last gasp, which was surely impending, Pinchas sat erect again. "Marry me," he pleaded, "so from your kiss I can die!"

Having entwined her fingers with the peddler's, the girl made an effort to arrange her sheepish features in a show of solemnity. "It's in the way of being his final wish," she proclaimed to the priest, as if no other argument could be entertained.

His knees worn out from genuflecting, the befuddled Father Farquhar rolled backward onto his haunches in a most unvenerable fashion, revealing the calves under his cassock like spiny ninepins. With a foot Murtaugh scooted a low wooden stool beneath the priest's nates to prop him up, but the more dignified perch did nothing to resolve the issue at hand. For the combustible Cashel, however, there was no quandary at all. "I'll be scragged and gibbeted first!" he bellowed, and confident of allies added, "My friend Phelim here will have something to say about this." He pounded the barkeep on the back, who fought to keep his balance, muttering, "I wouldn't have a widder woman." Then taking heart, he asserted, "The girl is anyhow a sack of cats. The dead man is welcome to her."

"But he's a gobshite Jew!" bawled Cashel, looking now to his sons for encouragement. The two of them wagged their heads in dumb accord but appeared more interested in than appalled by the situation. Cashel then uttered what he must have assumed would put the controversy to rest: "Nor ain't the man even baptized!"

Katie replied almost dismissively that Father Farquhar could certainly remedy that, though the priest showed no sign of compliance. On the contrary, summoning something of the gravity of his office, he submitted, "One should look, in extremish, to the welfare of the soul rather than the rites of the flesh."

At that the apparently moribund peddler reared up one more time. "Give to me for a blessing Katie's hand," Pinchas rasped, "and it wouldn't leave from this life in despair mayn neshomah, my soul." Then seemingly spent from the effort the words had cost him, he fell back again onto the soggy quilt, his eyes rolling into his head. He flopped a moment, twitched, then lay still.

Katie spoke for the priest's ear only, "If it's a crime to wed us, sure it's the greater not to honor his dying wish."

With his face still screwed up in thought, Father Farquhar could be heard quoting various opposing church canons to himself. At length he confessed, "Thishishmost irreggaler," as Katie advised him to take another sup off the sponge. He did so and shuddered like a palsy, after which the scales seemed to have fallen from his glassy eyes. "Leave ush make haste then," he announced, "for the lad's essence is already in his teeth."

"Bollocks!" sputtered Cashel, dropping his bulk into a chair beside the deal table. "You'll put the heart crossways in me." Behind him Phelim Mulrooney, muttering "Feck the lot of yer," took the occasion to slip out the door. But Father Farquhar, having turned toward the patriarch, was now become the voice of reason: "It's the one vow they'll be making this evening," he stated, his speech surprisingly lucid, "for the nuptial bed of this marriage will be the grave." A momentary grin rent his wadded face. "Then the relict may go to her second husband as pure as from her father's side."

Cashel threw up his hands in a gesture of defeat. "Marry him, then bury him," he grumbled. "Then somebody make me my supper."

The priest rubbed his palms together. He was evidently energized by the prospect of presiding over a wedding rather than administering the viaticum once again, though the distinction here was admittedly a fine one. Swiftly he dispensed with the baptism, splashing the peddler's face with brackish water from the chipped basin the girl had provided. "I baptize you in the name of the Father . . . ," et cetera. Katie had hauled Pinchas to a sitting position, his back against the splintered boards, but before she'd finished patting dry his snuffling features with her apron, the curate had moved on to the nuptials. He was asking the bride and groom if they had come of their own free will to give themselves to each other in marriage. Would they raise their children according to the law of Christ and his church? Here Pinchas was aware of having entered a degree of apostasy beyond anything he'd known to date. All religions were opiates of course, but some residual sense of the magnitude of this particular trespass seemed to rankle in his vitals; it might take one of Katie's sodium clysters to purge it. But what was he thinking? Love was the physic that dispelled every ill sensation the body was prey to.

Father Farquhar was saying, "Do you, Kathleen"—he looked to her sire, who grudgingly supplied "Fiona Aoife"—"Kathleen Fiona Aoife Keough, take as your lawful husband"—the bride provided the peddler's name—"to have and to hold from this day forward, for better or for worse, for richer or for poorer, in s-sickness"—his tongue tripped over the word—"or in health, to love and to cherish till death do you part?"

She did, and Pinchas's heart became a living flame. When the priest repeated the formula for the lovelorn peddler, he replied with a resounding "I do!" Much too resounding in fact, because his sudden robustness awakened a shuffling skepticism among the witnesses.

Next came the exchanging of the rings, and Cashel objected to Katie's transferring the ring that once belonged to her mother from her own finger to the sheeny's extended digit. She ignored her father even as she pressed upon the peddler a curtain loop brought by her hapless ma from Ireland in anticipation of curtains that never materialized. Pinchas encircled her finger with it like a quoit. Then Father Farquhar proclaimed, "What God has joined together, let no man put asunder," and the pale groom, lifting his bride along with him, rose up from the bedding with a self-congratulatory "Mazel tov!" He pulled her to him and kissed her full on the lips, the contact banishing—just as he'd expected—all fear.

It was a banishment on the heels of which the newlyweds themselves were soon to follow. For Cashel was also standing and, even as the gawking Tighe exclaimed "A bleedin' miracle," shouted, "We're played for patsies, lads!" Thus rallied, they would have set upon the peddler in a body had not his defiant bride stood between the groom and his assailants.

"It's too late, Da," said Katie, radiant in the assurance of her new estate. "Deny him and it's myself you're denying as well."

"So be it!" her father roared.

It would not do in any event to murder the Jew in front of a holy man, however dissolute he might be. That could wait. And if in the meantime the Keoughs lost their appetite for homicide—since their father's death soon after from fever or drink would dampen the brothers' bloodlust—they might satisfy themselves with malicious pranks; though the pranks themselves would diminish in cruelty and decline into habit with the years, when it became clear that nothing was going to drive the peddler from the neighborhood.

Not that Pinchas hadn't wanted to take his bride far away from that festering slough. During the time he'd spent as the guest of her family, the Pinch had become nearly deserted: a handful of hollow-eyed survivors still reeled and debauched in the streets, though in their halting danse macabre they were already three-quarters ghosts. Some slept, for convenience sake, in coffins rather than beds. But the peddler had no money for travel, and the roads around Memphis were anyway barricaded, the bridges burned; refugees from the city had been shot on sight. Thrust into the night with no more than the clothes on their back—and Pinchas's borrowed at that—the newlyweds clung to each other, their eyes smarting from the carbolic acid dumped into the seething Bayou, its surface mantled in dead fish. Of course there were other parts of the city where the houses were built of stone, where crape myrtles bloomed and people died in their beds, but there was no place among those for a pauper and his disinherited bride. And in any case, Katie surprised her new husband with her stubborn refusal to stray from what she called home.

"But Katie, ziskeit," Pinchas had demurred, as admiring of her iron will as he was daunted by it, "the Pinch is geshtank, a shitcan."

"Then we'll fill it up with Easter lilies," she assured him.

They found shelter on their wedding night in the Court Street Infirmary, where the mortally ill squirmed under mosquito netting like weevils trapped in spiderwebs. Their bridal banquet was brined cabbage ladled from a tin dinner pail by a nun. In the morning, turned out on account of their good health, they took up what they assumed would be temporary quarters in an abandoned tenement above a boarded-up saddlery on Smoky Row. (They would remain there, but for a brief excursion into the Underworld, for the remainder of their days.) It was in that apartment, in an iron bed vacant of corpses, with the tar barrels still smoldering beneath their window, that they finally consummated their marriage. That's when Pinchas discovered, to the delight of his ardent bride, that he was the victim of a persistent satyriasis. It was a condition that left the couple unable thereafter to rid themselves of a bashful self-consciousness in each other's company. (At least until, after the decades of their failure to conceive, Pinchas began to lose courage and heart.) Their heady pleasure in one another, plus whatever they managed to scrounge in their forsaken district, was nourishment enough during the period of their honeymoon.

Nor had Pinchas used up his fund of ingenuity in winning Katie, but was inspired to a further audacity in his desire to provide for her. When the first frost signaled the beginning of the end of the epidemic, he prevailed upon the Lowenstein brothers, whose wholesale dry goods business occupied an entire city block, to extend him a line of credit. Despite their distaste for the unwashed Ostjuden in general, the staid merchants were impressed by this one's initiative and drive; and the immigrant came away with an inventory of railroad boots and brass-studded denim pants, silk ribbons, thimbles, combs, and almanacs. Equipped with two sixty-pound packs, strapped fore and aft to steady his balance, Pinchas staggered out to travel the Delta roads; though not before his wife, easily her husband's equal in resourcefulness, had culled from his stock a selection of mourning goods: black-trimmed calling cards, black crepe. She placed these items in the unboarded window of their squatted building at prices low enough to lure a few hearty souls into the ravaged neighborhood. By progressively lightening her husband's load before each of his forays, Katie built up the business over time to the point where it was no longer necessary for the toilworn Pinchas to go peddling anymore.

By then the city had once again begun to show vital signs. The din of steam compressors, train whistles, and trolley bells could be heard even from the blighted North Main Street. Cotton bales replaced the caskets stacked along the carious wooden sidewalks, which were themselves replaced with stone, and the stagnant channels of Catfish Bayou were transformed into covered culverts. The Negroes, who had been the city's unsung guardians during the fever, were sent back to their prior squalor, and while people of quality never really returned to Memphis, the streets were made safe enough for decent folk to promenade. Meanwhile Katie's clever husband had gotten wind of a legal provision called adverse possession: it seemed that, by paying taxes on a property whose owner had vanished, the squatter might assume the right to ownership himself. Moreover, the bankrupt city was happy to encourage the resettlement of an area it had essentially written off, just as the state had written off the city by repealing its municipal charter. Weaned from his dependence on the Lowensteins, Pinchas now purchased discounted goods straight from the factory warehouses. As proprietor of Pin's General Merchandise— he'd dropped a syllable from his name to give it an American zing—the former peddler set about making improvements, knocking down clapboard walls to resurrect them in mortar and brick.

He was not alone in his effort to revive the neighborhood; others also arrived to take advantage of the rock-bottom real estate deals. One of the first was another itinerant peddler, who upon encountering Pinchas declared in Yiddish, "Tie me by all four limbs but put me among my own!" Sighing over the quaintness of these wandering Jews, Pinchas felt obliged to inform him that he himself was meshumed, an apostate, living in an unholy union with a gentile woman.

"So long as you got your health," replied the peddler, Mose Dlugach by name, hardy and quite well fed for a traveling man. A little wary of welcoming competition, Pinchas warned him that the town was prone to frequent bouts of pestilence. Doffing his homburg to scratch his pate, the peddler had offered a humble solution: "If I will sell shrouds, then no one will die."

He opened a secondhand shop at the corner of Winchester and North Main and sent for his family in Szeged as soon as he was able. More followed, dispersed after widespread pogroms in the wake of the czar's assassination: a wife joined her husband, a brother his sister and brother-in-law, and so on, until the Pinch was reconstituted as an East European ghetto–style enclave in the heart of the South. Ultimately the neighborhood earned the seal of approval from the city fathers, who viewed their Hebrews as a solid mercantile class. This attitude endured despite the street's eventual invasion by a gang of fanatical Hasids, whose riotous spiritual exercises resulted in a rending of the fabric of time.

ca. 1880–1911

Not long after North Main Street was paved and the bridge over the river completed, after an Otis hydraulic lift was installed in the Cotton Exchange and a Negro shot for accepting a job as a postal clerk, the merchant Pinchas Pin received a letter from a niece in the Old Country. It seemed that, during a peasant rampage in the village of Blod, his brother had been murdered, his body left to marinate in a barrel of kvass. His sister-in-law, having witnessed the atrocity, lost her wits and had since been confined to an asylum in Dubrovna, where she died soon after of disregard. What's more, in an unrelated incident his brother's son Muni, arrested for Bundist activities, had been deported after a yearlong imprisonment to a labor camp in the Siberian wastes. Pinchas didn't know whether it was the news itself or the way the news underscored his utter estrangement from his family that disturbed him the most. In his agitation he was especially moved to learn that his nephew, whom he'd understood to be a pious yeshiva boy, had become a militant revolutionary. The nephew's fate piqued his uncle's conscience, aggravated as it already was by the compromise of his youthful ideals for the sake of a livelihood. While no special request was included in the communication—it simply stated that, as a surviving relation, he ought to be informed—still Pinchas believed he might be in a position to help the lad. He appealed to the North Main Street Improvement Committee, which in turn made the case to the congregation of the Market Square Synagogue, a place Pinchas seldom set foot in. Nevertheless, prayers were said and a collection taken up (if a bit sanctimoniously), and the funds, converted to rubles, were stitched by the tailor Bluestein into the lining of a cheviot topcoat.

In a cold katorga compound, below the entrance to a mica mine somewhere east of the town of Nerchinsk, Prisoner 71640 (conspiracy, fifteen years) received a parcel in the mail. This was unprecedented. A trustee had dropped the parcel in his lap in the mess hall, its postmark indecipherable, its contents fairly spilling out of the tattered brown paper. It contained some tins of currant jam, sliced pineapple, and sardines, all of which were promptly snatched up by covetous convicts. Under the cans, however, was a folded topcoat of some lightweight gunmetal material wholly unsuited to the glacial climate. Nevertheless, as no one bothered to confiscate it, and as it signified his persistence in the thoughts of someone beyond the Siberian immensity, the prisoner pulled it on over his worn quilted jacket. Another layer of insulation wouldn't hurt. But in a week the coat had become a haven for lice; a sleeve, caught in the gears of the ore separator, was ripped to shreds and the tails burnt when he backed against a cast-iron stove. It made him look like a clown, the coat, though clownish was a countenance the prisoner found it convenient to exploit once the lining fell out.

In order to take a dump in the sulfurous latrine, you had first to tamp down the shit that protruded from the holes in the planks laid over an otherwise open trench. The shit was packed so hard and tight beneath you that it tickled your ass as you sat, and there was seldom any available wastepaper to wipe with. Still, such moments were among the few that afforded the convict any respite from the harsh routine. This was the prisoner's situation as he sat with his pants around his patchy boots, idly meditating upon a loose thread at the hem of his topcoat. Intending to snap it off, he wound it around a finger and gave a tug; then the stuttering thread opened a seam from which fell, along with some cotton batting, a number of thin glassine envelopes. The envelopes, when he leaned over to inspect them, seemed to contain Russian currency in various denominations. The prisoner finished his business with an efficient grunt; then swiftly, before anyone else entered the jakes, he stooped to gather up the packets, stuffing them into his pockets along with a letter that was similarly wrapped.

It took his being sentenced to isolation for some trivial infraction of the rules before he found the privacy to read the letter and take stock of his fortune. The isolation cell was a miniature stone dungeon in which one could neither fully stand nor lie down, but its narrow grille admitted the light of a summer during which the night seemed never to fall. The sunlight illuminated a wall emblazoned with religious graffiti painted by inmates with powdered feldspar and beryl from the mine, so that the cell, despite its constriction, had the air of a shrine. By this brightness the prisoner was able to read the letter's greeting, in its homey Yiddish script, from one Pinchas Pin of North Main Street, America: "Honored Nephew, please find enclosed the means by you I'm sending to come . . ." But the body of the letter made no more sense to him than did its opening salutation. He read it again, until the language began to stir in his entrails the beginnings of what felt like a symphonic episode. The jarring music, however, communicated not one jot of meaning to his sluggish brain. Moreover, he ached in every joint and fiber from hunkering in such cramped quarters, and his fingers, stiff as claws from the years of wielding the shovel and pick, could barely count the rubles in their envelopes. Once more he read the letter: ". . . the means by you I'm sending . . . ," until it struck him that "you" was he, Prisoner 71640, né Muni Pinsker. Then the music, converted at length into words, woke up his fears from what he'd hoped was their perpetual slumber.

Escape? Who escaped? There was Shishkov the sharper, found frozen in a fetal attitude not half a kilometer from the camp; and the patricide Alyosha, who was torn apart by sled dogs in sight of the watchtower, his agony backlit by the setting sun. There was Osip Katzenelenbogen, a political, who made it as far as the bank of the swollen Lena, where he was caught and returned to the camp to run a gauntlet of his fellow convicts. Their anger was stoked by the starvation rations they'd received as a collective punishment during the time following the zhid's attempted flight. In the end his already decalcified bones were shattered and Osip was left to drag his broken body between the barracks and the mineral sluice for the brief balance of his days. But the fact remained that Pinchas Pin of North Main Street, America, had sent a parcel to his nephew Muni, a human being. Tahkeh, how could you tell?—when he was harnessed by day to a horse collar that rubbed blood blisters on his scrawny chest as he hauled a cartload of ore up a slanted shaft. He breathed air that was either so cold that it crackled like paper or scorched your sinuses with its reek of excrement and carbonic acid. He never cared whether he was eating bugs or pearl barley in the soup they called "shrapnel," and his teeth were as loose in his gums as headstones in mud. His body was so inured to filth that scrubbing himself in the bathhouse drew blood. Once he'd helped a fellow hide a convict who'd dropped dead of heart failure, so they could share in the extra rations for the three days it took the putrefying corpse to betray them. But on the other hand, he was light-headedly surprised, this Muni Pinsker, to find himself still alive in another summer, when the snow had retreated far enough to reveal the arsenic green moss underneath.

Almost involuntarily he began to collect the tiny pots of salt from the log canteen, squirreling them away among the fir branches his mattress was stuffed with. Other items he secreted in that lumpy mattress were bought, no questions asked, with hard currency: the mess kit, the tinderbox, a wire noose for snaring game. With gradually increasing histrionics he started to demonstrate the symptoms of derangement that overtook the mine workers as a prelude to total collapse. He spoke aloud to himself in a nonsensical hybrid of Russian and Yiddish, and pretended to read fortunes in the globules of fat he scooped from his gruel on a good day. More than once, though he could barely stand at the end of the working day, he coaxed his toothpick legs into a kind of spontaneous scarecrow gavotte. No one paid him much attention, so accustomed were the other prisoners to the extravagant behavior of convicts on their way out; though Ilya Popov, former editor of the leftist *Proletarii*, himself stricken with silicosis, saw the method in Muni's antics and slipped his fellow traveler a clamshell compass with a sundial before he died.

Then it was nearing autumn and the soft ground was hard again; the rivulets from the melted snows that had mired the transport sledges and made the taiga impassable were dried up. That's when Muni swallowed all the salt he'd been hoarding. The insult to his system brought on a hectic fever that got him transferred to the infirmary, an aboveground facility outside the camp "zone." Its wards—each guarded by a single sentry seated with a shotgun beside an iron stove—featured every species of real and imaginary affliction. No disease was quarantined: convicts suffering from typhoid lay next to those turned yolk-yellow from jaundice; pneumonia victims rattled their last beside imposters who worried superficial wounds into life-threatening infections. There was little actual treatment, few instruments, and no anesthesia for surgery, and small medication beyond the bottles of alcohol drunk up by the orderlies mustered from among the patients. Nor was there any barbed wire surrounding the infirmary grounds, since who, having gained a berth without shackles in the sick bay, would (even given the strength) want to leave?

Muni lay gibbering on his cot, despite his broken fever, in a self-scripted delirium, raising himself on occasion to perform his St. Vitus rigor. The strategy was intended to get him judged dokhodyag by the skeleton staff: a lost cause convict in the throes of his final agony; and it appeared to work. The stranger his behavior, the more it seemed he was ignored by the population of that raving pesthouse. Moreover, so drowsy was the round-faced sentry that Muni could almost believe that what was left of his topcoat, notwithstanding its clanking from the provisions he'd sewn inside it, served as a cloak of invisibility. Thus emboldened, he contrived, after a week of conspicuous malingering, to sidle by breathless degrees out of the ward, slip along a corridor, and pad down the stairs into the chill October night. He plunged into a stand of larches and paused with a stampeding heart beside a patch of black ice that had survived the previous winter. Though he'd tied the earflaps of his flannel cap tightly under his chin, the cold had already penetrated the several layers of his clothing; his eyes watered, his nostril hairs become bristle-stiff, and frost invaded his lungs. He took the compass from the folds of his coat and tapped its glass face, but the needle would not come unstuck. Neither was he assisted by the stars that glinted metallically through the branches above him, resembling nothing so much as the vaulted ceiling of the mica mine. But there was a pale lavender light in a corner of the sky: that would be the east, and it was away from the light that the fugitive's steps must tend.

He slept by day, shivering in burrows dug into clay embankments with a sliver of spruce. He ate from his little store of rubbery fish preserved in the stinking oil he'd pilfered along with a bolus of congealed fat; he smeared the fat on the hardtack he rationed himself over the numberless days. He chewed wrinkled berries hard as goat turds sprinkled over a salad of thistles and mushrooms tough as rawhide. Through nights that grew ever longer, he stumbled across the bone-brown steppe and up through sparse timberland, blundering into treacherous ravines. His garments, ragged to begin with, hung from him in shreds, his footcloths working their way out of his galoshes, his hair and beard matted with twigs. He wasted hours building fires, chipping away at the flint from his tinderbox until the sparks ignited the kindling and moss. Often the vicinity of nightfall would threaten to turn the fire into a beacon, and Muni would have to abort his progress; but without the periodic warmth and drying out the fire afforded there would be no progress at all. Shivering in holes lined with ash branches and willow shrubs, he poked his head out to see now a foraging bear, now a party of forced-marching convicts or a patrol perhaps looking for him. Some patrols passed practically under his nose and Muni wondered that they hadn't sniffed him out in his blind; but the sled dogs were not retrievers and his marginal subsistence left only the slightest of trails.

At some point Muni realized that the search parties no longer seemed to be in pursuit, and guessed that the time allotted for hunting the runaway had elapsed. Or had he actually wandered beyond their range? Muni waited to feel the relief that never came. He grieved that he had no way to measure his transit, no program for reaching Irkutsk, which was the terminus of the Trans-Siberian railroad some five hundred kilometers west of the mines. He was a speck in a vast mapless terrain, and after so many detours around crags and unfordable torrents he was unsure that he was even traveling in the right direction. Still, the nearly continuous gloom of winter had not yet set in, and the sun, however shrouded, still gave some faint indication of which side of the earth it rose upon.

He nibbled roots, ate a scallopy fungus that he sometimes vomited up, sometimes evacuated in a helpless diarrhea. It hadn't occurred to him that hunger and exhaustion could so far exceed what he'd already been accustomed to. Then the snows had commenced, submerging the landscape in a polar desert, burying as well the dying flora that provided Muni with occasional nourishment. Wildlife was scarce and entirely unavailable to one who lacked the skill to lay traps. Once or twice, spotting a hedgehog or guinea fowl, he chased it, expending energy he could no longer spare; he found the carcass of a musk deer and cooked what remained of its fetid meat, which he choked down and instantly threw up. In the chill mouth of a cave, where the elements had preserved it, he came upon the corpse of a man. It wore the vestiges of a sheepskin burnoose and bore on a creased blue cheek the Cyrillic tattoo that marked it as an escapee from an earlier era. Muni wondered if his own corpse would age as well. He chewed bark, sucked icicles, and began effectively to starve. Sometimes he remembered the currency tucked in his galosh and had to snicker over the cruel joke his unknown uncle had played on him. Intermittently snow-blind, he wondered if the nothing that wasn't there was equivalent to the nothing that was. In this way the fugitive's own logic confounded him.

Though the number that had replaced his name in the camp had faded from his mind, his own given name had little more sonority. Words had become so remote that Muni would occasionally pronounce some phrase aloud ("Administer to the prisoner one hundred flagellum pletes!") just to ensure that he still had a voice, though he frightened himself by the shattered silence. He exhaled a powdery moisture that stiffened his beard and fell to the ground in a shower of crystals, with a sound the convicts called "the whistling of stars." Now that the ground had grown too hard to dig, he burrowed in snowdrifts and told himself the snow was fleece. He woke to find the exposed parts of his body distended and without sensation, then stamped his feet and beat his arms with his fists until the stinging began and feeling started to return.

After a storm, while treading a shallow defile where the snow concealed a thin skin of ice over a spring-fed stream, he fell through. By the time Muni had managed to scramble back onto the bank, the water had sheathed his trousers in ice. Unable to feel his extremities, he had the disoriented impression of being unconnected to the earth; he was desperate for a fire but the ice inhibited his movements like a suit of armor. Still he managed to squat and strike sparks with the flint wedged between his gelid mittens. He succeeded in igniting a scrap of birch bark, which he dropped in some nearby underbrush, but no sooner had he fanned the brush into flame than an overhead bough released its burden of snow on top of him, snuffing out the fire. Half-buried himself, he was a stranger to his hands and feet, which he endeavored to locate with filmy eyes. The numbness that swiftly invaded his limbs would soon engulf his heart and still its stammering, and anticipating that moment Muni let go a voluptuous sigh, relinquishing the small affection he had left for the world.

He wandered in and out of consciousness, vaguely aware of being attended by creatures whose fur-trimmed hoods framed shadows where their faces should have been. That was in the forest where he was jounced on an inclined litter pulled by beasts with branched menorahs protruding from their heads. Later on he perceived in more lucid moments that, now that their hoods were thrown back, the creatures did have faces of a sort, though the faces seemed to be missing essential features. There were open wounds in place of noses, eyes drooling onto collapsed cheeks like traveling snails. Their chamois-mittened hands, which pummeled him in an effort to restore sensation to his deadened limbs, were not mittens at all but nubs bearing only the stumps of absent fingers. Satisfied that he was either dead or dreaming, Muni drifted until the nerves in his fingers and toes began to send howling dispatches throughout his spent anatomy. Then he woke up to the realization that he was not in hell but on a pallet in an octagonal wooden structure, smoke curling from stoked embers through a hole in the roof. Rather than abducted by a tribe of gargoyles, he had been rescued by the inhabitants of a far-flung colony of the mutilated and misbegotten. They were survivors, the burned-out offscourings of a disease that had run its ruinous course. But while the malady was no longer communicable, it occurred to Muni as he began to recover that leprous deformation might be just the disguise for an absconded brodyag, a fugitive such as he.

His emotions still deep-frozen, Muni felt neither gratitude nor revulsion toward his hosts, as they applied their poultices to his frostbite and pried a revolting broth between his crusted lips. For their part the colony's population neither ostracized nor made to absorb their guest, but once they'd restored him to reasonable health simply tolerated Muni's presence. He observed no discernible order to their society, no special roles assigned: those capable of doing did while the rest endured. They raised enough beets and marrows during the short growing season to see them through most of the winter. Occasionally they slaughtered a reindeer from their cadaverous herd, using its hide for the clothing they seldom changed. They caught trout in a nearby stream, which they salted and froze and pounded into a meal mixed with moss to make flapjacks. Once in a while they might procure from an itinerant prospector a horsehead, which they would boil and feast on for days. They slept together in clumps for warmth in their slapdash yurts and the crouched lodge—stinking of sour milk and gangrene—where Muni was housed. The noises they made in the night alternately terrified and fascinated their guest, who was unable to distinguish between their unchaste baying and cries of anguish from the pain of their strangled nerves.

Once he was on his feet again, though still shaky, Muni did try to make himself useful: when he was strong enough, he began to accompany the village's hunting and fishing parties, attempting the basics of setting snares and drilling holes through the ice with an outsized corkscrew—operations for which he showed little aptitude. Though wary of the fugitive—for they were under no illusion that he was anything else—the natives were not unfriendly. Some, like Fyfka the Reptile, so-called for his crocodilian skin, and Grigory Popp, with his warty lesions and saddle nose, made companionable overtures. Grigory had himself been a hard-labor convict, turned out of a camp lest he contaminate others, and so was well disposed to sympathize with Muni's plight. Then there was Esma, a Buryat girl with a blacksnake braid, who kept her burnt-almond face kerchiefed like a bandit to hide the rictus of her mouth and ulcerous jaw. She, it seemed, had conceived a particular fondness for the fugitive, which she demonstrated in moderately aggressive gestures. The most conspicuous of these was her habit of rubbing against him at every opportunity, a development that Muni found especially disquieting at night, when he lay for warmth among the others in a squeamish intimacy. Then he might feel her spare hips pressing against his backside, her lobster claw teasing his spine.

It was enough to make him think better of lingering longer in their community, but the season of snowstorms was upon them and it would have been suicide to continue his journey before spring. Besides, the villagers would have been obligated by their code of hospitality to hinder his premature departure. So Muni stayed on, gathering strength, while the brutal weather forced the colony into a period of hibernation.

Dogs and reindeer shared the crowded shelters, compounding their noxious atmosphere. No one ventured outside except to fetch wood or relieve themselves, and a stranger approaching the village would have observed few signs of human habitation. All that was visible above the snow were enameled mounds, black plumes coiling from the smokeholes like tassels on a Tartar's helmet. In the absence of the sun in its midwinter retreat the inhabitants led a troll-like existence, which is not to say they were idle: their long naps were often an excuse for indiscriminate sporting in the dark. Collectively afflicted with tapeworm, they gorged themselves on their bilge-like bouillon and the gamy venison rissoles with kneaded roe; they drank measureless cups of tea laced with monkshood schnapps. They told tales of werewolves and flesh-eating Baba Yagas by the light of the fish oil lamps. And there was music, when the leonine Attila broke out his concertina and accompanied a windup victrola playing polkas and scratchy quadrilles. Then those with feet would dance despite the cramped space, music and drink having whipped them into a bacchic frenzy.

Throughout the weeks the eager, drop-footed Esma continued to moon over Muni. But the trinkets with which she embellished her frowzy garments and the immodest glimpses she allowed of her scaly flesh did little to promote her suit. Still she persisted in her indiscreet advances, which the fugitive was compelled to eschew in a manner that could only be interpreted as rejection. So disconsolate had Esma become that Fyfka the Reptile, in his capacity as unofficial starosta or elder, felt obliged to intervene. "Why you don't give to the girl a tumble," he urged in some polyglot tongue near enough to Russian for the guest to compehend. When Muni replied that he would rather not, Fyfka assumed he was being coy, which was at least part of the truth. For even had the girl resembled his own species, the fugitive would have had scruples; he had after all never known a woman, and (Hebraic taboos aside) had yet to recover enough of himself to feel equal to such an occasion.

Muni tried to plead diplomatically that the girl was just not his type, but the elder put it to him that the situation was urgent: she was wasting away for want of the young man who could boast all his digits and toes.

"How can you tell?" blurted Muni, who immediately wished to retract his thoughtlessness. But the damage was done and from that moment on his welcome—as borne out by the entire community—was officially outworn.

In the meantime a thin band of sea-green light had appeared on the horizon promising the return of the sun: it danced, the light, inside the ice cake that served as a windowpane like a filament in a glass bulb. A speckled snow bunting was seen to perch on a frozen midden, at which sign Grigory Popp and Grinka Spivak, jowls hung with nodules like bunches of grapes, began helping to provision Muni by way of expediting his departure. Having no need of it, the untouchables returned to him the money they'd held in safekeeping, which astonished the fugitive, who'd never missed it. When he offered them compensation, the gesture was viewed as an insult.

They saw him off in a purga, a blizzard, with the assurance that spring was just around the corner. There was no special ceremony to mark his parting, though he was escorted by Fyfka the Reptile and some of the others (leaning on crutches, paddling in wooden crates on runners) past the boundaries of their village. In fact, he was led far enough beyond the belt of mixed forest and steppe surrounding the settlement that Muni couldn't have found his way back even if he'd wanted to. Somewhat resentful of his abrupt send-off, once he was alone again amid the limitless Siberian barrens, he began terribly to miss his unclean hosts.

They had equipped him well, outfitting him in a fur-trimmed parka, trousers with a white fox lining, and moccasins with reindeer-hoof soles. They'd furnished him with a cedar sledge, lashed to which were a tent and animal snares plus several weeks' worth of foodstuffs. There was a flask of vodka tasting of turpentine, a brick of black tea, and a sleeping sack made from muskrat pelts. They gave him as well a partial map of the territory, insisting it was all he needed, since by the time he'd traveled beyond its edge he would either have crossed the frontier or expired.

They cautioned him to follow the sun (what sun?) due west, but owing to the irregularities of the region it was difficult to maintain an undeviating direction, and often he had the sense that he was traveling in circles. The snowflakes battered him like hailstones, though after his first frightful nights in the wild the squalls began to abate. Muni knew that haste was essential: with spring the swollen streams and mudslides would make the distance to Lake Baikal impassable. Moreover, the lake itself, practically an inland sea, must be frozen solid during his passage or else he would have to traverse the hundreds of miles around it. But he was hard pressed to summon the necessary urgency; his destination—Memphis, America, home of the deliverer to whom he owed (he supposed) some recompense—evoked in him no feeling of any kind. The mindless impulse to cover ground, to put one foot doggedly in front of the other, was all that now characterized his trek.

He scrambled over slippery transverse ridges, inched along shelf-like cornices, threaded clefts between palisades and perpendicular crags; he crossed a jagged penumbral mountain and skirted a gorge scarred by viridian tarns. When the landscape permitted, Muni shod his feet in the klunking racquets the lepers had bequeathed him. Once in a boggy declivity he stumbled upon the timber-sized ribs and tusks of some mired prehistoric behemoth. As he paused to ponder it, he spied through its ark of bones a pair of dogsleds zigzagging down the snow-blown slope he'd just descended. They were likely a party of trappers who, in this country of outcasts, would perhaps welcome a wayworn brodyag. On the other hand, there were bands of bloody-minded peasants who mounted posses in the hope of capturing runaway convicts with bounties on their heads. Rather than wait to find out which they might be, Muni bounded forward, tearing off the hobbling snowshoes in his flight. It was then that the bent pines beneath him, casting off their blanket of snow, stood to attention, and Muni fell victim to the impromptu airborne event that he would later relate to a girl in a tree. A sprung projectile, the fugitive was sent sprawling beneath a cloudbank, sliding over the hatch-marked ice; while behind him the dogsleds crashed into the frozen littoral of Lake Baikal and sank like the chariots of Pharaoh's army.

In his pious youth Muni would have viewed the event as an instance of divine intervention, but it never even occurred to him that God's reach could extend this far. Bruised and aching in every joint, he assessed his situation: his food and equipage were strewn behind him over the steppe and the broad lake he slowly picked himself up from would take days to cross. He'd never make it. But neither was turning back, and perhaps en-countering his undrowned pursuers, an option. His salvation, it seemed, was only a temporary reprieve, but still goaded by a kind of residual loco-motion, Muni staggered on through veils of pea soup. The wind swirled the snow in filigree patterns over the grizzled plane of the lake, while the ice soughed and yawned like an ancient ship's rigging. He had no idea how long he'd been walking or in what direction his leaden steps had taken him, though he was aware of having nearly outdistanced his body's capac-ity for movement. For all he knew he'd strayed beyond the margins of the known world into some uncharted dimension. It was a notion reinforced by the spectral light, like an orange in a nest of spun sugar, which had appeared just ahead of him. He was drawn toward it, the light becoming beacon-bright, the beacon declaring itself as a metal brazier beside which sat a shaggy character holding a trident.

He was wearing a fur cap and sheepskin coat fringed with plaited thongs, sitting on what looked to be an oblong drum. He had a flat, squint-eyed face with a complexion like cracked mud, a beard as fine as milkweed floss. As Muni approached, the old man acknowledged him with scarcely a grunt and redirected his attention to the hole he'd carved in the ice. Having ceased his forward motion, the fugitive now felt incapable of budg-ing another inch; weary beyond measure, he plunked himself down beside the brazier, its kettle on the boil. The embers that warmed his cheek also drained him of his last ounce of energy, and seated cross-legged on the obsidian tabletop of the lake, Muni dropped his chin to his chest and fell fast asleep. He awoke after an indeterminate while to find himself bundled in fleece, a steaming cup of tea set before him. He sipped, wincing at the syrupy consistency and taste of tar, but vile as it was, his stomach wel-comed the thermal liquid, which left him feeling somewhat revived. He felt buoyant in fact, and weirdly indifferent to his predicament.

"Do you know maybe the way to Irkutsk?" he asked the old man al-most disregardfully, since he suspected there might be no way back to the world from there. At that moment there was the splash of a fish breaking the surface of the water in the hole. The fish—like a transparent bladder, its bones and viscera visible through isinglass skin—was instantly skew-ered by the fisherman upon his three-pronged spear. Then the old man held it over the brazier, where its sweating essence caused the embers to spit flames.

"Irkutsk," the man at last flatly responded, pronouncing the word like a preliminary attempt at a foreign language. Then he showed the chipped sprockets of his liver-brown teeth and let go a hyena laugh. He stripped the flesh of the fish from the bone and tossed the feathery spine toward his guest, who snatched it out of the air and began greedily to suck at the few scraps of meat that remained. Meanwhile the fisherman, still chewing, had dumped the contents of his brazier into the hole, from which rose a roiling cloud of vapor. Unnaturally nimble for his years, he whipped Muni's fleece out from under him—which sent him tumbling— and tossed it along with the brazier onto a hand-carved toboggan. Having battened down his gear, he started off hauling the toboggan across the ice, using his trident like a pilgrim's staff. With an instinct perhaps more canine than human, Muni scrambled to his feet and followed.

As they tramped through ranks of fog dense as waving draperies, the old man never once turned around to look at him, and Muni wondered if his guide was even aware that he had a shadow. He wondered why he should think of the old man as his guide. Every so often the fisherman would pause to consider, as if he'd arrived at some invisible junction; then he would turn so sharply to left or right (according to what internal sextant?) that Muni thought he was trying to shake himself free of his follower. But while it took all his stamina just to keep up with the old man, the fugitive was determined for no apparent reason to hang on.

In that interminable yellow mist there was neither night nor day nor any way of predicting when the old fisherman would—every once in a very great while—come to a halt. Then showing no signs of fatigue, he would unload the spider-like brazier and sprinkle fish oil over a few foul-smelling pellets to build a fire. He would extract a fat sturgeon from his creel, sear it on his trident, and attack it with slavering bites. A sound he made while relishing the fish suggested articulate syllables: "Ogli" was what Muni heard, and he seized upon it for the fisherman's name. Then it was Ogli who tossed scraps to his hanger-on, after which he brewed the acrid tea in a tin cup that served double duty as samovar. He would take a sip and nod as he passed the cup to Muni. That the fugitive did not gag was a minor triumph for which he was awarded a degree of refreshment, but the tea also seemed to augment the unreality of his circumstance.

Somewhere, he sought to remind himself, there was a body politic; there was a czar and his coterie, complete with mad priest and hemophiliac son; there were Draconian laws and massacres, Jews and revolutionists—all of which seemed illusory to the wanderer at this hyperborean end of the earth. Not that the frozen lake, which knocked and creaked and thundered like distant cannonade, had much in common with the solid earth.

After his meal the fisherman, his slit eyes lit like phosphor, would commence to beat his drum with puckered fists. The pulse of the instrument felt like a corollary to Muni's own heartbeat: until he feared that if the beat ceased so would his heart. Ogli's weather-cured features were made the more grisly by the ruby light of the brazier and the stringy hair that whipped his face. His spindly limbs moved in some spastic approximation of a dance, like a marionette trying to disentangle itself from its strings. When he'd completely encircled his follower, intoning sounds that ranged from guttural to rooster, Ogli would sit down on his drum with a hollow thud. Unprotected from the buffeting winds, eyes closed and body motionless, he would appear to have fallen asleep. Concerned that the old man might be in danger of freezing, Muni would poke him experimentally in the ribs. Then Ogli's eyes would flash open, and, whinnying with laughter, he would spring from his drum, pack up his goods, and proceed apace, with the drooping fugitive straggling at his heels.

Maybe it was the stimulus of the bitter tea or the hypnotic effect of the tinkling silver discs sewn to the fringes at the back of the old man's coat—which, he couldn't have said—that kept Muni slogging forward. All he knew was that nothing stood between him and being forsaken to an inhuman solitude but this indigenous loon, whose behavior was anything but reassuring. Once, without turning or breaking stride, Ogli opened a flap at the rear of his breeches to release a steamy turd, which Muni had to dodge to keep from stepping in. Another time the old man retreated so far into his postprandial trance that no amount of the fugitive's prodding could bring him around. It was as if his spirit had departed his flesh, leaving behind a body as brittle as a dried-up puffball; if you poked too hard the frame would fold in on itself and crumble to dust. Then awareness returned, and, with his characteristic cackling, Ogli sprang from his drum and continued on his way. Muni followed, lagging farther behind, craving more of the bilious tea for its restorative properties, though the tea had begun to have diminishing returns. When his legs did finally give out, Muni sat down on the lake's frigid moonstone and waited to die. He'd already lost sight of the old man in the encompassing murk. Now the wind slashed his face like a swarm of razors, penetrating his garments till he shuddered uncontrollably. Closing his eyes, he was almost wistful at having traveled so far to perish so purposelessly. When eventually he opened his eyes again, he saw erected in front of him, as in a grainy photograph, a portable yurt of red felt. Crawling inside he found the fisherman curled under a fur blanket fast asleep. He was snoring, farting, filling the tiny shelter with fulsome odors, but as he also exuded warmth like a furnace, Muni nuzzled against him and was soon asleep himself.

He was awakened by the naked Ogli leaning over him, chanting a string of gibberish. Having unbuttoned Muni's coat and shoved his sweater and singlet to his chest, the old man seemed to be performing some kind of surgery: he was digging with crooked fingers in the pit of Muni's stomach, tickling him as he scooped out what were either intestines or sausage links slathered in sauce. In a tortured pantomime, his loose flesh and genitals flapping, Ogli wrestled with the slimy mess as with a serpent. Assuming he must be dreaming, Muni wanted with all his heart to wake up to some life he could call his own. It was a desire that would not survive the rest of the journey to his destination, where it would take a cataclysm to rouse it again. It would already have ebbed, that deep yearning, by the time he'd scrambled out of the yurt and stumbled into the sandy cove below the forested cliffs above the lake; it would be further dissipated as he gathered the whortleberries and goose eggs he wolfed down in deserted povarnias. What little remained of his fervid desire would dissolve in the churning waters of the Angara, where he boarded the ferry that took him upstream to Irkutsk. Once arrived, Muni would make for the maidan, the thieves' quarter, to purchase a forged identity card on the black market. The card would cost him more than the phony passport he'd also have to secure. He would get himself shaved and reappareled, his appearance having earned him stares more agitated than those he bestowed in return, so staggering was the experience of being back in the precincts of men. When he rode the train over the Urals, the very concept of desire would become as alien to Muni as Siberia itself, and he would wonder why he persevered: why not make Moscow his terminus and pick up where he'd left off? Even the kulaks were openly advocating rebellion these days. But by then it would be too late to do anything other than continue traveling, paying bribes and crossing borders, booking passage in the steerage section of the SS *Saxonia* at Bremen, which set sail for the port of New York. There he would pass as if blinkered through its confusion of tongues, then board another train that would carry him across yet another continent, or at least a sizable slice of it, to Memphis, Tennessee.

But at the moment when he bolted from the yurt, the desire was strong in him to put land and sea between himself and the crazy fisherman. Slipping on the damp ice, he blundered away from Ogli, who was in the process of pulling on his parka over his hoary head. When Muni had emerged from the lifting fog, he turned to see his guide dragging his sledge back into obscurity, trailed by cracks in the ice that was beginning to break up around him. Then the fugitive stepped in the nick of time onto the far shore of Lake Baikal, where it was already spring.

I was reading to Rachel when I noticed that her eyes were getting heavy, so I flipped ahead in the book until I found the passage. "'Later on in a bookstore on Main Street,'" I read, "'a scrawny, hook-nosed lad'"—lad was my own edit as the text said, unflatteringly, nebbish—"'a lad named Lenny Sklarew chanced to open a fat volume called The Pinch . . .'"

Her eyelids fluttered open and she sat up abruptly, unheeding the sheet that had fallen from her breasts (their nipples like tiny berets). "Give me that," she said, snatching the book away from me to peruse the page. She returned it in a moment with a harrumph. "Lenny, you're such a card," she assured me, having apparently seen no reference to her bedfellow in the text.

"Yeah," I replied, recalling a caustic rejoinder from some old noir film, "the Ace of Spades." Then I quickly checked the book again to make sure that I was still there.

ca. 1912–1921?

In Memphis Muni worked for his uncle Pinchas in his general merchandise and did odd jobs in and around North Main Street. Across the way, at the new Idle Hour Theater, a Keystone Cops two-reeler called *Cohen Collects a Debt* premiered, and blind Helen Keller spoke on behalf of the Wobblies at the Lyceum off Court Square. A famous evangelist challenged the devil to a wrestling match at a tabernacle erected in Riverside Park, and a black boy, accused of raping a white woman in a Gayoso Avenue brothel, was lynched and dismembered. Muni Pinsker fell in love with the wirewalker Jenny Bashrig, and against every law of decency on or off the books, got her with child. Then he abandoned her to chronicle the history of the Pinch. The history included incidents that took place after the timeless time that was brought about by local fanatics through a regimen of spiritual exercises and prayers. It also included events that preceded and followed that great enchantment, including the fate of the book after Muni had stopped writing it. He wrote with his brain ablaze, as if fueled by the mephitic tea he'd sipped long ago on a frozen lake; wrote in the hope that, in the writing, the task would ultimately reveal to him his reason for pursuing it.

He described an incident involving the blacksmith Oyzer Tarnopol and his prodigal son Hershel, who was swallowed by a fish. This happened a few years after the father and son had come to the Pinch via the port of New Orleans. They'd come to Memphis because Oyzer had heard it said that the city still maintained a large number of livery stables full of draft horses. These were the horses that pulled the fleets of municipal ice and refuse wagons, and they would require an endless supply of iron shoes. But by the time father and son arrived on North Main Street, they discovered that much of the transport labor had already been mechanized. Moreover, the bulk of the metal work that had been Oyzer's mainstay in the Old Country was now performed by machinists in factory shops. It was a situation that further aggravated the blacksmith's already virulent temper.

His temper had not always been so foul. Back in the village of Hrubeshoyb on the River Wieprz, where his family had dwelled for generations, Oyzer had been a principled householder and good provider; he was a gentle if strict father to his son and daughter and an attentive husband to his wife, the baker Pesha Sarah. But late one afternoon in the month of Nissan, as he and his son returned from a fishing expedition (little Hershel trailing behind him toting a string of spiny-finned perch), Oyzer heard shouting and saw smoke. From below the brow of the hill above the river he could spy the street of the Jews with its shake roofs burning. He watched a gang of peasants overseen by uniformed Cossacks looting shops and torching houses, including his own. He saw them beating his neighbors and worse, and lest his son see it all as well, held the boy down and covered his eyes with a hand. But Hershel did see—through the visor of his father's thick fingers—what the hoodlums had done to the women (among whom were his mother and sister) who had been dragged into the street. He also observed his father's terrible fixed expression as they lay on their bellies in the eel grass, and when the cries of the martyrs became unbearable, the blacksmith turned his heavy head toward Hershel and saw that he saw. Afterward he could not forgive his son for being a witness to his cowardice.

In America, to which they fled after the pogrom, the blacksmith cursed his son along with his failing livelihood. He cursed his neighbors even as they tried to ease his destitution by bringing him small jobs. "Tinker's tasks!" he groused, when they asked him to repair a damaged sausage stuffer or lard press. In fact, he might have made a tidy living had not his self-defeating temper driven potential clients away.

To offset their poverty and further stoke his father's ire (which he preferred to the blacksmith's neglect) young Hershel took to thievery, stealing tinned victuals and various other essentials from the shelves along North Main. Aware of the hardships the boy endured at the hands of an irascible father, the shop proprietors were likely to turn a blind eye to his petty thefts. There was some tacit consensus that his modest burgling was a kind of insurance against greater encroachments, and there were those who even admired the dexterity of his sticky fingers. Hershel's father, however, was not grateful for the provisions his son laid in at the forge, serving as they did to emphasize the blacksmith's inadequacy. But his curses and throttlings did little to discourage the boy. The more he was punished, the more Hershel seemed to step up his delinquent activities, compounding plunder with random pranks. In the end he was more of a nuisance than even the yokels who sometimes invaded the Pinch to bedevil the Jews.

A day came, however, when something seemed to break in Oyzer Tarnopol. One minute he was at his anvil tapping at the twisted barrel of a toy gun (a dainty job beneath his dignity), the next he let go of his hammer, which caused a minor tremor as it struck the earth. He stood a moment with limp arms, his bullet head sagging as if the thick shaft of his neck could no longer support it, then dropped his considerable bulk onto a workbench. Maybe his sudden lassitude was due to the infernal heat of the forge on that mid-September afternoon, or maybe it was the appearance of Zlotkin, the junkman, so wasted with age that he must have thought he had nothing to lose by invoking the blacksmith's wrath.

"Your boy, the ganef, that he took by me the shmattes from my wagon," he was complaining, when the blacksmith abruptly wilted and sank onto his bench. The junkman was peering curiously at Oyzer when the culprit himself wandered in with an armload of secondhand clothes. Seeing his father in this uncustomary posture, he demanded of the fossil Zlotkin, "What you did to my papa?"

"I didn't do nothink," stated Zlotkin, who seemed disgusted by the blacksmith's woebegone attitude. In truth the whole of North Main Street had grown so accustomed to Oyzer's explosive temper as almost to rely on it as a natural feature of the neighborhood. Shrugging his bony shoulders, the junkman shuffled out the open doors of the smithy, snatching back his clothes from the boy as he left.

"Papa?" asked Hershel tentatively, still braced for the inevitable volley of curses, the boxing of his ears that would follow Zlotkin's charge. He was waiting for the branched veins to stand out on his father's broad forehead as he rose to deal with his son. Once, he had lifted Hershel by his unruly hair and the boy felt his scalp come unstuck from his skull, admitting whole galaxies of pain.

But the hulking blacksmith remained slouched on his bench. "It smells from your mama's challah, the hearth," he said at last, an unprecedented exhaustion in his voice. Hershel looked toward the glowing firepot, which exuded as usual the trenchant stench of burning coal.

Though it fascinated him at first, in the days that followed, the son found his papa's chastened behavior even more unnerving than his late evil humor. Hadn't the boy become the neighborhood scapegrace less from cupidity than the wish to provoke a father whose attention he could command in no other way? He would take the blacksmith's abuse over his quiescence any day. Rascal he might be but no fool, Hershel knew his father's emotive torment was a last defense against paralyzing despair, and it was the son's job to keep that torment alive.

With a mind ordinarily geared to capers and practical jokes, the boy set about hatching a serviceable plan. It was nearly Rosh Hashanah, the Jewish New Year, when the entire population of the Pinch paraded beyond the trolley lines out to Catfish Bayou and tossed into it the crumbs representing their sins of the past twelve months. Although the blacksmith had long since dropped all pretense of religious observance, the tashlikh ceremony was a custom he'd always insisted on performing back in Hrubeshoyb. They'd made a family excursion of it every year along the myrtle-thronged banks of the River Wieprz. Thus did Hershel decide to take advantage of his papa's docility by persuading him to take part in this year's ritual.

His idea was that, since the unpardonable sin that fueled his father's fury now seemed only to weigh him down, perhaps a symbolic unloading of that sin would allow the rage to return. It was worth a try. So on the day in question he dissolved the yeast and mixed the flour and milk himself; he kneaded the dough in the trough but didn't wait for it to rise. Molding it into a substantial glob, he delivered it to the blacksmith, who received the lump of dough like a convict receives a ball and chain. Then, a little intoxicated by the new power he wielded over his father, Hershel goaded Oyzer into the train of citizens marching to the banks of the bayou. There he pressed the blacksmith to heave his burden into the murky inlet, where a large, stipple-scaled fish leapt up to swallow the dough before it even entered the water.

Despite the miscarried gesture, Hershel waited for his father to be transformed back into the man he'd been before the junkman's visit, or even—halevai!—back before the destruction of his home and family. But if anything he appeared even more deflated, as if he'd jettisoned what little was left of his spirit along with his burden of sin. The brawny blacksmith now seemed as vacant as a passive clay golem. He still pottered bare-chested about the forge in his dangling suspenders, listlessly busying him-self with whatever work came his way. (Ironically, there were more jobs since his customers seized any excuse to view the spectacle of a tame Oyzer Tarnopol.) But he could scarcely muster the strength to pump the bel-lows or manipulate his hammer and tongs. His inefficacy made his son's freebooting among the businesses of the Pinch all the more needful, but Hershel's forays went far beyond mere expedience. On a spree, he stole items that had no practical application—bust food, secret society buttons, a Heidelberg electric belt; he engineered dangerous pranks involving gun-powder. His out-of-hand antics culminated in the theft of a cumbersome shot-metal clothes wringer from Pin's General Merchandise. Its employee, Muni Pinsker, recent refugee from a Siberian labor camp, fed up with the kid's terrorizing of the neighborhood, gave chase. He pursued the boy as far as the bayou, where Hershel leapt from the bank and was swallowed by a bloated fish grown immense on the misdeeds of North Main Street.

Or so Muni reported. Nobody disputed him though neither was he especially believed. Since the arrival of the Shpinker Hasids, who conducted their mystical experiments above a Commerce Avenue feed store, the citizens of the Pinch were aware of goings-on that did not comport with the prosaic routine of their days. But even Muni wasn't entirely convinced that he'd seen what he'd seen. "It's a fact even if it isn't true," he'd declared to Jenny, further confounding himself with the qualification "or vice versa." He wasn't in any case too surprised when Oyzer Tarnopol came into his uncle's store in his stained leather apron to purchase a jointed bamboo rod and reel. Every morning after that the blacksmith was seen to set out for Catfish Bayou, where he baited his hook with a rubber frog, cast his line into the still water, and sat on the muddy embankment all day. And every evening he returned empty-handed to his ill-lit rooms above the smithy. Still, he persisted even during the period immediately following the earthquake, when a breach in its banks caused the bayou to be nearly drained. With something akin to his old energy the blacksmith flung himself into shoring up the rupture, rallying others to pitch in until a dike was constructed and the shallow basin replenished again. Then, while most residents of the Pinch seemed to go bughouse in the wake of the quake, Oyzer Tarnopol continued sitting his stationary vigil beside the bayou with his rod and reel.

Owing to the peculiar time zone that the district occupied after the earth's upheaval, the prehistory of the Pinch was as available to Muni, from his current perspective, as was the present. In fact, past and present were often indistinguishable, jumbled as they were with visible auguries from the future. As a result, Muni could include in his chronicle, alongside an account of Mrs. Elster's dancing fever, an appearance by the demagogue Davy Crockett haranguing the tipplers in Bell Tavern; and Yankel Zlotkin hondling malbushim (soul garments) to the lawless flatboat fraternity— half men and half alligator—that tyrannized Smoky Row. Then there was the shiftless kid who found Muni's "history" in a used book store on Main Street, its contents bleeding into his own late twentieth-century neighborhood; and the golden child of Mr. and Mrs. Padauer, who was stolen from his bassinet by marauding shretelekh and replaced with one of their own.

The shretelekh are a largely innocuous class of Jewish elemental, though known in their caprices to hinder as often as help a human being. Mostly, however, they prefer to remain, unless disturbed, in subterranean habitats—cellars, caves, grottoes, and the like. This particular tribe had dwelled for some time under Market Square Park, in and out of the crannies and tunnels beneath the roots of the great patriarch oak. Only once before the quake had they ventured as a body aboveground. That was when they'd surfaced in order to rid themselves of a superannuated member of their society, a decrepit old specimen who'd long outworn his usefulness. With the hog-tied party in tow, they skulked (knee-high and semitransparent) about the tenements of North Main Street after midnight, surveying the fresh crop of newborns in their cradles. They settled on a crocus-curled, angel-faced little kaddishel, the offspring of Rose and Morris Padauer, a weary-winged couple with an apartment over Dlugach's Secondhand. Poor in spirit as well as pocket—she a footsore hausfrau, he a luckless traveler in ladies' corsets and stays—the Padauers had always felt that their beautiful child was an anomaly; he was more good fortune than humble folk such as they seemed entitled to. They were therefore disheartened but not entirely surprised to find that the boy had turned overnight into a shriveled homunculus; though how he'd gotten himself trussed like a Passover pullet remained a mystery. In any event, after the shock had worn off, they continued to care for the "child" as their own, which they after all believed him to be.

For his part the obsolescent little imp, who came to be known like his predecessor as Benjy, had had enough of geriatric abuse at the hands of his own kind. And Mama Rose and Morris were indulgent parents, sensitive to his delicate condition, indignant at the kaynehorehs, the "no evil eyes," that some spat in his direction when they wheeled him by in his stroller. Despite their slender means the Padauers appareled their creature in sailor suits and flannel drawers; they made sacrifices to ensure him a protein-rich diet full of boiled brisket and herring with smetana—a welcome change from the blue mold and lichen that were the regular fare of the shretelekh. They powdered and diapered him after the spells of incontinence his diet sometimes induced, bought him a windup Kabongo African dancer and a wooden pelican on wheels. Although he remained misshapen, Benjy thrived in the Padauers' charge and even regained the ability to walk, albeit at an unsteady bowlegged waddle. If he occasionally balked at playing the part of his adoptive parents' little manikin (he was after all several centuries old), he understood that infantilization was a small price to pay for the pampered existence he enjoyed.

So he persisted in the imposture and considered himself fortunate. As for the Padauers, why disabuse them of their fond delusion? The guardianship of their special child gave them a unique status in the community as universal objects of pity, and besides, they seemed genuinely devoted to the counterfeit boy. For all this Benjy was grateful after his fashion, and even sought to reward his foster family's generosity. Though what conjuring powers he'd once laid claim to were mostly depleted, he could still provide them with certain luxuries that would otherwise have been beyond their reach. Morris Padauer, returning with his paltry profit from the road, liked to refresh his spirits with a drop of brandy, and Benjy was able to ensure that his de facto papa's flask remained bottomless. He assisted Mama Rose's unending efforts at rendering goose fat by making certain that the schmaltz never ceased to overflow its jar. While he couldn't produce the pot of shekels that his species had been rumored to possess in more storied times, he could see to it that the pennies in Rose's piggy bank were inexhaustible. The Padauers never knew the source of these small blessings but came to accept them as gifts complementary to the abiding gift of Benjy himself.

Meanwhile the Shpinker Hasidim, a ragtag quorum of celibate bachelors, performed their penitential rites with a wanton zeal in their shtibl above the hardware and feed store. Under the auspices of their venerable rebbe Eliakum ben Yahya they initiated liturgical practices regarded as heretical if not downright obscene by lay observers, practices that ultimately resulted in a neighborhood apocalypse. The earth shook, the waters rose, and the ground opened beneath the great oak in Market Square Park. The tree toppled crown-foremost into a yawning chasm, so that its muddy roots were upended, and the creatures inhabiting those roots were thrust suddenly into the galvanic air. Thus exposed, they scurried from their perches and scattered abroad into the shadows. A few hung on around the flooded North Main Street to further nettle the already arsy-varsy lives of its citizens, but most, with an aversion to water, abandoned the Pinch. They went in search of places where no one would recognize them for what they were.

The outcast Benjy Padauer caught sight of them from his elevation atop the geyser that had erupted beneath him in the backyard of Dlugach's Secondhand, where his mama had been hanging out clothes. Riding the crest of that fountain, he suffered a pang of anxiety that the shretelekh might be coming back for him. Then the pang was superseded by the pain generated from the hot waterspout that was scalding his keister through his knickerbocker pants.

When the spout subsided and the temblors ceased, a dazed Rose and Morris Padauer carried Benjy to Doc Seligman to be treated for his burns. The good doctor had set up an impromptu clinic behind a standing hospital screen in Market Square Park, to which the majority of the neighborhood had retreated after the quake. Despite the trauma of having lost their homes and livelihoods, the survivors seemed for the most part in an unaccountably convivial mood. Families with salvaged tea urns and featherbeds occupied their outdoor dormitory like castaways on a charm-bound island.

Physical injuries among the local population had been thankfully slight, but even the superficially wounded insisted on battlefield dressings, which they wore like badges of honor. Thus was the doctor, though capably assisted by a humorless Miss Reudelhuber, exhausted from his labors. His cotton-wool hair was matted, his varicose cheeks puffing like gills, when the Padauers presented their aged child, the seat of whose pants was still smoldering. Rallying somewhat, Doc Seligman welcomed them as he folded the privacy curtain around them and asked Miss Reudelhuber to please fetch a basin of cool water. He yanked down Benjy's trousers against the "peanut's" (his mama's term of endearment) croaking protests, and sat him in the basin, which sizzled from the immersion of his scarlet tush. The peanut emitted a sigh like a rattle; then the doc raised him up and rubbed an aromatic ointment on his blistered nates, while the Padauers looked away, respectful of their child's modesty. The doctor, applying a gauze plaster with a frown, was not so tactful.

"Good as new," he pronounced, resisting an urge to give the little oddity's bandaged bottom a patsch before helping him lift his pants. Then, perhaps realizing the irony of his pronouncement, he added sympathetically, "You folks ain't yet too old. Why you don't try for a human child?" Upon which the doc, clearly regretting what he'd said, began to busy himself with his instruments.

He hadn't meant to let the cat out of the bag, though it wasn't as if the bag hadn't already been poked full of holes. This wasn't his first examination of the Padauers' stunted entity; the parents had brought him to the doctor early on with the question of why he didn't seem to grow. An old-school physician cautious in his diagnoses, Seligman had allowed for the rare possibility of a premature aging syndrome for which there was no known cure. He'd suggested they seek confirmation from specialists, whose fees the beleaguered couple could never have paid. Besides, Seligman's judgment, speculative though it was, was good enough for them. But that night in the park, his weariness infected by the uncommon lucidity of the postseismic environment, the doctor let slip a truth the whole community took for granted: that the Padauers' prodigy did not belong to the race of men.

Husband and wife exchanged evasive glances, each trying to hide from the other what they had failed to hide entirely from themselves. Attempting to conceal his stubbly beard behind an upturned piqué collar, Benjy mumbled apologetically in his froggy voice, "Nobody's perfect."

The senseless jubilation that had overtaken the Pinch in the aftermath of its earthshaking event served only to salt the Padauers' wounds. Morris, in his chinless despondency, and Mama Rose, heavy-laden with the freight of her saddlebag hips, seemed in that moment to have lost their knack for comforting each other. At one point Morris even put the question in plain words to their peanut, "Benjy, what kind of thing are you?"

His response was a half-hearted bleat: "I'm a red-blooded American boy?"

It was perhaps the electric atmosphere itself that renewed the Padauers' motivation to find a solution to the mystery of their charge. Having given up on gleaning enlightenment from the medical community, however, they thought they might consult with clergy. They ruled out the stuffy Rabbi Lapidus of the Baron de Hirsch Synagogue as too insensible to preternatural affairs and chose instead to seek the crackpot wisdom of Rabbi ben Yahya. Like the rest of the neighborhood they'd shared a skepticism bordering on animosity toward the Shpinker fanatics. But as all parties now agreed that the Hasids' ritual antics were responsible for shifting the planet's tectonic structure, the Padauers had revised their attitude; they wondered if the Shpinker rebbe might have some special knowledge concerning the origin of their ill-made little shaver.

They gave the Dlugach boys a few coins to row them as far as Commerce Avenue, where they disembarked at Hekkie's Hardware & Feed. At the top of an exterior staircase they were admitted into the loft above the store by an idiotically grinning young Hasid. Behind him a chorus line of his fellows had linked arms in a frantic kazatsky, chanting psalms and balancing bottles and books atop their heads as they danced. In a corner a solitary disciple waltzed with a Torah scroll wrapped in a corset cover trimmed in Valenciennes lace. (Mr. Padauer recognized the style of the garment as the Esnah Ingenue from the catalog of a company he represented.) The room itself, with its floor like a deck listing to starboard, was strewn with penitential paraphernalia—trays of tacks for rolling in, a cat-o'-nine-tails—that had apparently fallen into disuse. There was a long table piled with books at the head of which sat Rabbi Eliakum ben Yahya, instigator of the providential new order. His eyelids were swollen and heavy, his complexion chlorotic, his beard spilling like cinders from a scuttle over his vest. The cushions that held him wedged in his throne-like chair looked to be all that kept him from pitching into the revelry.

Nervously the Padauers approached the rabbi, each holding on to one of Benjy's nipper-like hands.

"Rebbe," said Morris, not wishing to disturb him, though how could he not be disturbed by his disciples' buffoonish behavior? "Rebbe, this is our son."

The rabbi's thick eyelids wavered as his fingers groped for the snuff-box on the table before him. Taking a pinch, he stuffed it up a hairy nostril, sneezed, and wiped his nose with his beard. Then, slightly revived, he reached for Benjy, whom he lifted with a wheeze onto his lap. The Padauers' little curiosity went stiff, wincing at the old man's sour breath and piss-pot odor as the tzaddik proceeded to bounce him on his knee. Unforbearingly, Benjy submitted to the inspection of his turtle-shaped head and pointy ears, but when the old man stuck a fat finger in his mouth, he clamped down reflexively with one of his few remaining teeth. Seemingly unfazed, the rabbi pried himself loose and returned their bogus child to the custody of his parents.

"These type shretelekh," he uttered, "they ain't known to have a poisonous bite." He nonetheless offered the offended finger for a disciple to kiss.

Morris and Mama Rose looked at one another dispiritedly, but Rabbi ben Yahya wasn't finished. In a phlegm-filled voice from deep in his throat, he began to list all the things Benjy was not: he was not from sitra achra, the provenance of demons; he was neither lantekh nor kapelyushnikl, who hailed from horeh khoyshdekh, the mountains of darkness, and were no damn good. Theirs was a member of a relatively harmless race of underground folk—"and this one, the pitsvinik, he got left in him no mischief at all."

It was Rose who first attempted to state the obvious: "Then the peanut is not"—which Morris undertook to complete—"our son?"

"Cholileh," said the rebbe. "God forbid."

The noise in the room had reached a pitch that precluded conversation, the dervish dancing of the enraptured disciples causing the building to tremble as from another aftershock. In the midst of it the Padauers raised their voices to ask the rebbe if he knew what might have happened to their original offspring, him of the flaxen curls.

Eliakum ben Yahya cupped a hand to his tufted ear so that they had to repeat the question, but again he was unable to hear. After failing a third time, Morris, in his frustration, shouted, "What should we do now with *him?*," indicating the creature.

"Him?" said Rabbi ben Yahya, sinking back into his former torpor. In fact, he appeared to be quite unwell. "Why not show to him a good time?" he breathed. "Is playing now they tell me on the Hotel Peabody rooftop the New Pygmy Minstrels, that it's fun for the whole family I'm led to believe."

Then he closed his eyes and the downcast Padauers, taking hold of little Benjy again, had to agree they could use a night out, which they hadn't enjoyed since their courtship days.

Even as his uncle chased after his wife's ghost as far as Market Square Park, Muni Pinsker sat on his cot in his odorous underwear chronicling the event. He didn't need to be in the park to observe the episode. If he left his narrow room at all, it was only to fetch another inkwell or nib or more stationery; he visited the watercloset when necessary, shared with Pinchas the food that Mrs. Rosen sent across on a tray suspended from the pulleyed clothesline, then hurried back to his room. In the scribe's ranging mind, experience and narrative occurred with a simultaneity that made it impossible to know whether the act prompted the story or the story the act.

Tonight Muni munched a stale rugelach from the dish he'd taken to the kitchen to offer Pinchas, who was absent, but Muni never missed him since he followed his uncle's every movement in the history he was busy

composing. Or was it the reverse? His uncle did whatever Muni wrote that
he did. Along with ongoing events the nephew recorded others that came
before and after, which also somehow happened concurrently: such as
General Bedford Forrest's cavalry charge through the doors of the Gayoso
House Hotel, and a monthlong camp meeting on the bluff, where the bull
pen was filled with straw so that attendees who got the holy shakes would
not be injured—all of which took place even as the butcher Makowsky
and Bluestein the mohel merrily prepared to circumcise young Nathan
Halprin's heart.

These things Muni cited while remaining holed up in his cell for an
indefinite time, time itself having become as still as standing water. The
length of his tangled hair and beard attested to the fact that time still
flowed, however, and the music from the fiddle outside his window was
both doleful and demoniac.

At the news of Katie's untimely passing imparted to him by Jenny
Bashrig, who abandoned the Pinch soon after, Pinchas Pin never budged.
He stayed fixed to the kitchen chair he'd sat vigil in for weeks. Banished
from the bedroom by a wife who didn't want him to witness her suffering,
he had wondered if his obedience were due to consideration or cowardice.
Still he'd trusted her to the care of Doc Seligman and the watchful Jenny;
told himself that when the crisis passed, as it must, she would welcome
him back into her presence, where he would find her hale and lovely again,
and less cruel. But that outcome had not ensued, and so Pinchas was
determined to remain obstinately unmoving until such time as Katie's fate
was reversed. After all, there had never been a satisfactory diagnosis, and
an affliction without a name was no affliction at all, and therefore had no
power to vanquish its victim. So, mulish, he sat and waited beyond the
time when garments should have been rent, mirrors turned to the wall,
the burial society called in to wash the corpse. Never mind: tradition no
longer figured in Pinchas's frame of reference, just as illness and death
had no place in the present-day Pinch. His neighbors, with their chronic
complaints of shingles, piles, furuncles, goiters, and fatty hearts, were not
complaining anymore. They had surrendered to an epidemic of unbridled
felicity that supplanted illness and death; dying they would now have regarded as bad form.

The lights that streamed through the kitchen window from the ju-
bilee beyond made auroras of the waving chintz curtains, while Pinchas

continued to sit in dull denial. Grief at this stage was its own anesthesia: he felt nothing. Oh, maybe some bitterness, as when he suspected that his wife's malady was his punishment for failing to lie with her as her husband these past several years. But if so, hadn't he been punished enough? "Katie, come back already!" he shouted, then had a laugh at the sheer idiocy of his outburst; then forced himself finally to his feet and went to see if she might have obeyed his summons.

He was met at her door by a sickly-sweet odor that filtered into his nostrils and penetrated his guts where feeling began to return. The resulting pain was exquisite, as when (wrote Muni) frozen limbs begin to thaw. Stumbling into the bedroom, he found a blue marble woman—her ice-gray hair threaded with rust—laid out in her nainsook chemise as on a tomb. But before Pinchas could fall upon her as his pain dictated, a thing happened that would have violated the limits of his freethinking consciousness, had that consciousness not been already so savaged: for Katie's spirit—he assumed it was her spirit though it wasn't in the least diaphanous and looked instead uncommonly alive—had begun to detach itself from her dormant body and, once free, rushed directly out of the room. Pinchas watched her departure, wondering if he were the catalyst, that even in the tranquility that had succeeded her suffering, his wife preferred to elude his regard. But so urgent and quick did her risen shade appear that it rendered all but superfluous her supine form; it was in every way the animated likeness of the original, which confused Pinchas as to whether you could even say that the ghost was deceased. And as *dead* was still not a concept he was able to attach to his wife, Pinchas managed to overcome a disabling anguish and lumber after her out the door and down the hall.

"Katie, my dove," he called to her, "this is foolishness, no?"

He had some vague intention of overtaking the apparition, because the more distance her spirit put between itself and his wife's remains, the more permanent did that separation become. He realized as well that this logic, unique to the moment, was at the same time entirely groundless, though it must have some basis in reason—mustn't it?—since Pinchas was a reasonable man.

"Och, Katie," he cried, "I'm loving you beyond logic!" and would follow her, dead or alive, wherever she led. Or so he believed.

Once outside, Pinchas sloshed into the canal that the neighbors declared had its source in Eden, whose surface the shade walked briskly across. For their part his neighbors, if not playing at being shopkeepers and artisans, could be seen prospecting with strainers for the nacreous dream residue that bobbed like manna atop the shimmering stream. The jeweler Gottlob led his goose of a daughter through seasons that changed from one block to the next, bundling and unbundling her in her peacoat accordingly; the pharmacist Blen waved a butterfly net from his wherry to try and snatch a monkey-faced ziz bird out of the air. The North Main Street Improvement Committee was convened in the back of Makovsky's to propose names for emotions that no one had previously experienced. So preoccupied were the citizens of the Pinch with their manifold phenomena that they scarcely noticed the bespectacled merchant in pursuit of his wife's fugitive ghost.

On the crest of the little hill that was formed by the great oak's uprooting, Katie paused a moment as a breeze stirred her auburn hair and pasted her chemise against her well-knit bones. Above her in the violet sky a cloud hung from a crescent moon like a rag from a scimitar; an owl hooted and the merchant's phantom wife ducked without a backward glance below the surface of the earth. She sank among the inverted limbs that extended into the fissure as if she were descending a staircase. Having mounted the hillock behind her and peered over the brink into darkness, Pinchas balked in his pursuit; he'd come (it seemed) as near to the abyss as his tether would stretch. Weak from days without eating and further debilitated by a fathomless sorrow, he was snapped back to a plausible sanity: Katie's ghost was not Katie; the wraith swallowed up by the earth's open maw had nothing to do with his beloved wife. Hysteria had given way to a soberer rationale: he was a retail merchant again, and rather than follow a shade into the sunless unknown, Pinchas elected to turn around and retrace his steps back home.

He left the park and again confronted the spectacle of a neighborhood he perceived as a perverse impersonation of itself. But no sooner had he arrived at the bank of the canal than he realized that he'd succumbed to a stunning failure of nerve. Katie's specter had more vitality than the corpse growing stiff back in the apartment to which he knew he couldn't bring himself to return; the ghost had the greater claim to his allegiance, and Pinchas hated himself for having turned around. Isolated from his preposterous community by grief, he belonged to neither this world nor any other. Deeply ashamed, he stepped into an empty coracle moored to a hitching post in front of Poupko's Hosiery and began paddling toward the place where all the lunacy had begun.

Mr. and Mrs. Padauer were leaving as Pinchas arrived. As they passed him on the landing above Hekkie's Hardware, they were debating whether it was actually possible to travel beyond the borders of the Pinch.

"Mama," Mr. Padauer was saying, "it's like there's around the neighborhood a Shabbos boundary, and can't nobody come in or go out."

"But we got special an exempt from the rebbe," she countered, to which her husband concurred, though he had no recollection of having received such a thing.

Pinchas stepped undeterred into the dusty shtibl, where the Hasids were behaving as if it were Yom Kippur eve. They were performing the kaporeh ritual, twirling roosters by the spurred ankles above their heads. So rapidly were they twirling the chickens that the birds had begun to function as propellers, lifting the chanting fanatics into the air while feathers fell all around them like snow. Pinchas had to duck beneath the elevated disciples' kicking feet as he approached the slumbering rebbe, with whom he had never before stood on ceremony. Still, he was a little daunted by the old man's waxy countenance and stertorous breathing. But in his desperate need for answers, he gave the holy man's shoulder a vigorous shake, until his lids began to open like jimmied clamshells.

"My Katie died and her ghost went in the hole in the park," he stated defiantly.

"So you say," replied the rebbe with a yawn, automatically reaching for his snuffbox.

Taking his response for indifference, Pinchas felt himself becoming incensed; he was on the verge of blaming the old kocker for his broken heart and demanding to know what he was going to do about it, when he remembered that Eliakum ben Yahya was not responsible. He and his band of zealots might be blamed for turning the Pinch into a sort of supernatural funfair, but he'd played no apparent part in Katie's demise. No one was culpable, he reminded himself in an effort to calm his outrage, though he still couldn't manage to rule out his own guilt. Then Pinchas became aware that the rebbe was posing a question.

"So why you didn't follow her?"

"What?" said Pinchas, who'd heard him perfectly well.

The rebbe emitted a restive grunt. "Why you didn't go after her?" he repeated.

"To what end?"

"Tahke, to bring her back."

Again Pinchas was near to erupting with rage, until he realized, again, that the real target of his anger was himself. Hadn't he gone to the park with that very purpose in mind before the madness of his resolve stopped him cold? Nevertheless he felt obliged to restate the irrefutable. "She's dead!"

"So go where go the dead and bring her back."

This was too much; he was being mocked. He'd compromised his integrity by seeking an audience with the old charlatan only to be humiliated for his trouble. "It's what I deserve," he supposed. But on the other hand, why had he come here if not for confirmation that the laws governing the conventions of the ordinary were in abeyance. And where wouldn't he go to fetch back his Katie?

"You 'fraid?" Pinchas was dimly conscious of the rebbe inquiring.

"You damn for sure right I'm afraid!" he barked.

"But you been there before," reasoned Rabbi Eliakum. "You should know from the way back already."

Pinchas peered at him in perplexity before grasping the old man's reference; everyone knew the story: how the young pack peddler had been rescued from his entombment during the Fever. He'd told it so often, leaving open the issue of whether he'd been actually dead and resurrected, that he'd practically leached the tale of any truth, but now the memory recurred in all its stark veracity: Katie had saved him then and had given him now an opportunity to return the favor. Wasn't that what the rebbe implied? But it had been so long—not since leaving his country of origin—that Pinchas Pin had been called upon to take himself into the unknown.

Seeing how he was torn, Rabbi Eliakum, with a heavy "Oy," endeavored to raise himself to his feet. Some of his Hasids, spent from the aerial exertion of twirling their chickens, had dropped from the ceiling to lie in a blissful heap among the cross-eyed birds. The rebbe made an exasperated gesture with his bearded chin as if to say they were beyond his influence now. "I'll go with you," he asserted. Then taking up his walking stick and a small siddur, which he slipped into the pocket of his caftan, he began to scoot haltingly toward the door. Even through his own forebodings Pinchas could see that the old man was in no shape to play his guide.

"Rabbi, you're not well," he cautioned.

"A nekhtiker tog," pooh-poohed the old tzaddik. "Nonsense, a nice stroll will do for me good."

Once on a visit to the Pink Palace Museum with Rachel, while standing in front of the case containing a pair of shrunken heads from Borneo, I tried pitching my voice.

"Oy," I made one of the heads to say, and the other, also in an old man's voice via Rachel, replied, "You're telling me."

An item now, you might have seen us together around town: at a poetry reading at the Bitter Lemon Coffeehouse or an Italian film about a plague of boredom at the Guild Art Theater. We made a road trip at Rachel's suggestion into the Delta, a pilgrimage to the crossroads where bluesmen bartered their souls to the Devil, and to the grave of William Faulkner, where we shared a fried pie. We watched the sun set over the river, which left an indelible rose madder impression on my brain, even without the agency of LSD. Then we repaired to my apartment—never to hers; I'd yet to be invited to spend the night at her place—where we fooled around and I read to her aloud.

I guess you could say I was happy. Hadn't I waited all my days for such a girl? Still, there were times I wished I could get even closer to her, to penetrate her heart's core as they say. Though wasn't it enough that, to put it crudely, I was getting laid? So what if Rachel never quite responded in kind to the zeal of my attentions; never mind that her caresses often seemed almost maternal, as if she was moved less by desire than compassion. Not proud, I would take what I could get. Besides, I had sufficient enthusiasm for the drum-tight hollow of her abdomen and the scent of her tar-black hair, the spicy compartments of her mind, to compensate for whatever was lacking in her participation. The fact of our lovemaking was enough for me to build a small universe upon.

The sap from my arrested adolescence surged like an aneurysm whenever she touched me. Meanwhile The Pinch *had receded from primary experience to the dimensions of a regular book; its pages ceased to swallow me whole as they had before my association with Rachel, whose history I would sometimes investigate as eagerly as I had North Main Street itself.*

"When," I'd asked her somewhat hesitantly, "did you lose your virginity?"

"Well, there was the unicycle when I was thirteen, and again . . ."

"Again?"

". . . at fifteen, a boy from the planet Mongo . . ."

"Never mind"—becoming mumpish—"I don't want to know."

"What's the matter, Lenny? Can't you take your own medicine?"

She was right of course, since even with her I tended to trade mostly in double-talk. Still I refused to let her off the hook: *"Were you ever—and you should know I stand ready to avenge you if you were—abused?"*

"No," she said demurely, *"but there was the guitar-playing cantor at Temple Sinai—I was his pet—who asked me once if I wouldn't mind spanking him. I remember I was so flustered I told him I had a cold."*

What was her greatest disappointment? When, after having her tonsils out at age eight, she'd written to Neil Sedaka to come visit her in the hospital and he didn't show. Once she caught her big sister in a primal embrace with the country club golf pro and wrecked their moment by laughing until she spat up. She was a daddy's girl until he suggested a fix-up with an old friend's son, the feckless heir to a radiator steam trap industry. She had a thing for animals: her favorite TV show was Zoo Parade, her favorite book National Velvet, which had surpassed even Anne Frank's diary as a teen-age passion. She traveled in Israel and Egypt the summer after high school graduation with a boyfriend who claimed not to have had a bowel movement during their entire month abroad. Despite her practical bent (she'd been treasurer of a Brandeis College political action committee and worn a gas mask to an uneventful demonstration), she thought she might like to die like Joan of Arc.

Then it would be my turn, though her interrogations tended to be less specific, as when she asked, *"So Lenny, why are you such a—to put it mildly—such a case?"*

"Blame it on my childhood."

"Your childhood."

"As you know I was snatched from my cradle by a buzzard that dropped me on the doorstep of a London blacking factory . . ."

At which point during that particular exchange she had stiffened and turned away from me. I sat up in bed to find her staring at the opaque glass of the window that gave back the reflection of her seal-sleek body. My eyes slid down her breast and clung to the nipple like Harold Lloyd hanging on to the face of a clock.

"You're not really an authentic human being," she mused, and in case I hadn't got it that she had my number, "are you, Lenny?"

"Me?" I said, dodging the subject lest she think she'd struck a nerve. "I'm an open book," I insisted, reaching for the book and opening it to the place where we'd left off reading—the part where old Yoyzef Zlotkin, who sorted tin at Blockman's junkyard, developed the faculty for what is called kfitzat ha-derekh, or the seven-league leaping of the way.

"I interviewed his granddaughter Mindy Gerber last week," put in Rachel, albeit a bit mechanically. "She graduated from White Station High School and went to Yale on a full scholarship, one of the first women to take a PhD in physics. All she recalled of her zayde was a disagreeable odor."

In 1855, according to Muni Pinsker, Mayor Israfel Baugh and Dr. Roscoe Dickinson settled their feud with pistols for two, coffee for one, behind the slave pen on Exchange Street. In 1924, Clarence Saunders of Piggly Wiggly fame built a palace of pink marble out on Central Avenue, and in the thirteenth month of 1913, a month that included all others, the blacksmith Oyzer Tarnopol, in his frustration, threw his anvil into the soup of Catfish Bayou. It was a ponderous anvil that took what remained of the blacksmith's once fabled strength for him to toss it, and the colossal splash caused a shower of displaced fish to fall all about him. Walleye, garfish, and even a Cretaceous alligator flopped in the mud at his feet, though none appeared to have swallowed his lost boy.

Poking about the bank inspecting the fish, the blacksmith did unearth a beaver-felt shoe he recognized as having once belonged to his son Hershel. Contemplating it awhile, he reasoned (aware that his reasoning was skewed) that perhaps the fish that took the boy might return for what it had left behind. So he hung the shoe on his hook and cast it into the muck. Still no luck. Then Oyzer did a thing that would have been unthinkable during his ferocious days. Though he set no store by religion anymore, and assumed that God had as little use for him, he went to visit the Shpinker rebbe. Why? Because that's what North Main Streeters had done—furtively, to be sure—whenever the absence of all other options left them wondering if there was more in heaven and earth than they cared to believe.

Oyzer's neighbors, starry-eyed from an excess of belief, ogled him from atop the sandbag seawall as he trudged through hip-high water on the way to ben Yahya's shtibl. But the rebbe wasn't there. His disciples, however, were still in residence, behaving more like a mob in a tavern than daveners in a holy place. Their monkeyshines ceased abruptly upon the entrance of the terrible blacksmith.

"You can tell me please where is Rabbi Eliakum?" inquired Oyzer, his hangdog humility annulling his bull neck and barrel chest.

The schnapps-soaked Hasids looked at one another. Surely the blacksmith's subdued condition was further proof (if they needed it) that the messianic age had arrived. One of the Shpinkers, reclining on the floor with a dead chicken for a pillow, informed him to the amusement of his fellows, "He went in the Cave of Machpelah."

Another, plucking a still-wriggling fish by the tail from Oyzer's pants pocket, chimed in, "He went like Akiva in Abraham's bosom alive." Others got into the act, enjoying the fact that the blacksmith could be teased with impunity; they gathered round him, continuing their taunts: "The rebbe went in Gehinnom to lasso with his tefillin the devil Asmodeus." They danced around him, a manifest version of the internal demons that had harassed him throughout the years. At some point the blacksmith's neck tendons began to swell and he trembled in all his limbs, seeing which the disciples left off their sport. They grew quiet again, bracing for the violent outburst that was surely at hand, but all Oyzer released was a spate of hot tears.

So daunting was this display that it convinced at least one of the Hasids, a rodent-faced lad with a pronounced overbite, to abandon the high-handed antics in favor of pity. He attempted a serious explanation of the rebbe's disappearance—"When is exposed the hidden saint, his work here is done"—then looked dismayed that the explanation sounded so much in line with the taunts.

With no reason to tarry, the still-sniffling Oyzer turned to go, when the earnest disciple seemed possessed of a realization: "No more is he the blacksmith," he proclaimed, indicating their visitor with a gesture. "The fisherman is he become!"

"The fisherman!" echoed others of their minyan, as if a veil were lifted and the blacksmith's true identity revealed.

The earnest Hasid had moved to the long table upon which lay a double-crowned Torah scroll. Reverently peeling a negligee from the scroll, he began to unroll the vellum parchment until he found the passage he was looking for. "Toyreh is the best of merchandise," he declared, producing from a pocket a pair of pinking shears. Then like a haberdasher cutting fabric, he guided the scissors in their munching progress across the passage and held the clipped fragment of scripture aloft. The others seemed disappointed that the fellow wasn't instantly atomized by a fist of lightning but accepted his demonstration as more evidence that a new order obtained. All was permitted.

"The Toyreh one studies in this world," stated the rodent face, "l'havdil, it's nothing compared to the Toyreh one studies in the next." The implication being to all within hearing that they hadn't seen anything yet. Then coming forward he pressed the passage into Oyzer's thick mitt. "Fisherman, put in your pipe this and smoke it."

Of course Oyzer did not smoke or drink or engage in any kind of profligate activity; his remorse had always been sufficient to fuel his immoderate wrath. But despite the dubious authority of the Shpinker disciples, cantankerous in the absence of adult supervision, he began to think of himself as "the fisherman." As if that designation relieved him of the onus of being Oyzer Tarnopol. Plucked from his cheder at an early age to become his father's apprentice, he'd forgotten the little Hebrew he knew, and so was unable to read the scripture he'd been given. But it nevertheless assumed for him a talismanic cachet.

Early next morning—a morning like the others that came and went without advancing the calendar date—the fisherman was back at the bayou. Dawn, he recalled from his days along the Wieprz, was an optimum hour for angling, though that was the extent of his knowledge of the pastime. The fog hung like lace tatting over the water, on the other side of which Oyzer was able to descry some figures emerging from a large conduit. This was the conduit that the old Gayoso Bayou, converted after the yellow jack plague to a sewer main, spilled out of into the Catfish cove, and from its mouth appeared a procession of spectral figures. A fever blister of a sun shone through the fog, illuminating the blind fiddler Asbestos as he picked his way at the head of a plodding file of colored men. Pausing in the sludge outside the tunnel, the musician clamped his cane between his teeth, removed his instrument from the gunny sack, and began to improvise a humoresque. It was a mercurial air in marked contrast to the dirge-like pieces he was generally heard to play around North Main Street, and the men seemed to scatter in time to its sportive rhythm. Some made for the shanties north of the cove while others stepped into pirogues and paddled for the narrow channel that led into the Wolf River tributary. A little stimulated by the music himself, Oyzer stuffed the passage of scripture into Hershel's shoe; he snagged the shoe once again on his hook—a hayhook he'd optimistically fastened to the end of his line—and cast it over the pond.

At once a gigantic fish broke the surface with a three-story splash and struck the bait before the shoe had a chance to hit the water. The horse-hair line grew taut and the spool spun rapidly as the fish ran free with the beaver-felt lure. The resulting tug nearly pulled the cork grip from Oyzer's hands, yanking him forward at a stumble into the shallow water as he tried to hang on to his rod. With only a rudimentary experience of the sport, he understood that he was seriously outmatched, giving up already the farcical misnomer of "fisherman": a wretched smithy was all he was.

"Palm the rim," came a harsh smoker's voice from behind him.

Oyzer strained to look over his shoulder, where a pink-eyed rustic in a dusty sack coat was standing.

The man spat a stream of tobacco juice. "Palm the rim of your spool to give it some drag," he said, gesticulating with his hand. "Use your thumb."

The blacksmith applied pressure with his cudgel-sized thumb to the reel's rotating spindle and felt a slight retardation of the big fish's head-long run.

"Now play that sucker," said another more nasal voice. "Click and pawl."

Oyzer turned again to see that Pink-Eyes had been joined by a lantern-jawed gent in a battered straw skimmer.

"He ain't got no clicker, Ethel; that's a cheap-ass Alright reel."

"Should of bought hisself a Orvis multiplier; them's got a slide drag for easy retrieval of your got-dang game fish."

"Myself," said the original kibitzer, "I'm partial to the Pflueger direct-drive, which it'll let you feather your line with a forefinger."

"Had me a Pflueger oncet," countered Ethel, "but the got-dang bird's-nest device couldn't keep the line from snaring."

"You should try shometime the Koshmic quadruple," came a third voice that Oyzer, facing forward again, recognized as his neighbor Alabaster's, speaking as usual through a chomped cigar. "With the fifty-pound tesht I uzhe it, and alwaysh with the woolly booger lure."

There commenced a heated debate concerning the virtues of woolly boogers versus mayflies, caddises, midges, and hare's-ear nymphs, but by then the blacksmith wasn't listening anymore. He was struggling to maintain some traction against the prodigious fish pulling with the might of a man-o'-war at the end of his line. Resigned now to contending with the fish not as an angler but as a stiff-necked Jew, Oyzer was able to draw again on some portion of the blacksmith's strength. He'd managed to slow without halting the free run of the fish toward the channel outlet by applying pressure to the reel, but was unable as yet to summon enough force to reverse the clockwise revolution of the crank handle. As a consequence, leaning backward at an inordinate angle with his heels dug into the mud, the blacksmith was in a stalemate with the powerful fish.

He was aware that a growing number of spectators had gathered behind him, heard snatches of advice he ignored, knowing in his bones that he must bring in the fish on his own or not at all. The fog had lifted and the sun shone forth on a brilliant late spring (or early fall) day. North Main Streeters had ventured beyond the enchanted zone to mingle with a few gentile citizens alerted to the blacksmith's struggle. As Oyzer gripped the handle of the still turning reel, the cane rod was nearly bent double from the tension, but miraculously it did not break nor did the line snap. Miracles notwithstanding, however, what was called for was simple brute strength. But while the veins stood out like cordage on his ham-sized forearms, Oyzer was unable to wind the spool in the opposite direction. He groaned aloud, his red face contorted in the anguish of his effort, but the handle on the reel would not be moved.

In describing the deadlock from the confines of his narrow room, Muni Pinsker evoked epic contests with legendary denizens of the deep, associations that lent velocity to his pen. But the thoughts of Oyzer Tarnopol, who shared no such associations, were elsewhere: he told himself that, had he interfered on that black day back in Hrubeshoyb, he could only have succeeded in getting himself murdered alongside his wife and daughter, thus leaving his son an orphan—and that, however, was finally no excuse. Meanwhile the blacksmith's neighbors, Jew and yokel alike, had tied an anchor rope around Oyzer's thick middle and hauled on it as in a tug-of-war to prevent his being pulled farther into the drink.

Morning gave way to afternoon then evening—the orange sky deepening to plum—then morning again, the first day; and still the blacksmith held fast in his struggle with the fish. Sweat streamed in runnels from his brow, tiny blood vessels bursting in the whites of his eyes, which he squeezed shut; he clenched shut his jaw, though he opened his mouth periodically to receive the chicken soup that Mrs. Rosen insisted on spoon-feeding him. The neighbors, heaving at the hawser that kept him from pitching forward into the bayou, spelled each other, comparing fish tales of their own as they rested before taking another turn. Then another evening and morning, the second day; and Oyzer's neighbors began to show signs of fatigue and restlessness, some wondering why they'd left the scintillant waters of their canal to assemble by this noisome sump. Most of the goyim, grown bored with the marathon encounter, had begun to wander off, as what had they been waiting for anyway? The lunker, presumably stalled below the surface, had yet to reappear, which made one question whether it even existed. Most likely the big Yid had snagged his hook on a scuttled flatboat. By the third evening the blacksmith's trunk-like legs were sunk to his thighs in the gumbo, so that he looked to have been planted there, more an immovable fixture of the landscape than a man.

Oyzer himself, his every sinew and nerve on fire, his brain an ember, wondered whether the fish remained on his line, or was it that—his thoughts unraveling—the dead he'd deserted were attempting to pull him under? How he'd resented his son for whose sake he'd refrained from taking his own life, though staying alive was surely the punishment he deserved. But with Hershel vanished, what reason was there not to surrender? Maybe it was time to follow the sins he'd flung into the bayou. Ever fewer of his neighbors now manned the rope that held him against the opposing tow, and the suction of the mud he was lodged in could scarcely offset the leverage he'd lost. Soon what strength he had left would fail him, his heart would burst from the strain, and he would be dragged into the water to perhaps become food for the very creature he battled with. It would be a welcome end. But in the meantime he owed it to the family he'd betrayed to prolong his agony.

There was no telling how much time had passed—another day and night?—when suddenly in the gusty late afternoon the line went slack. With the cessation of tension the blacksmith fell backward into the sludge, along with the handful of neighbors still tugging at him from behind: the fish must have slipped the hook. But standing on the bank in back of them were Oyzer's initial observers, volunteering a different conclusion. The pink-eyed one said, "Thang's done turned around," and the lantern-jawed other, "Git up now and wind your reel like a scalded devil." Because the lunker had apparently doubled back and was swimming straight toward them, the broad V of its wake ruckling the surface of the coffee-colored water. Muddled and covered in slime but not quite defeated, Oyzer hauled himself to his feet and began to crank the previously unyielding handle. He cranked with a galloping alacrity that caused smoke to emanate through the vents of the aluminum reel and the braided line to smolder from the friction. He cranked until his shoulder was practically thrown out of joint and another circuit of the handle seemed beyond his powers of endurance. At that point the line grew abruptly rigid again, and calling on some reserve fund of strength (donated in part by the chronicler Muni Pinsker in his description), Oyzer locked the reel and heaved the rod upward. Crying "Gottenyu!" he thrust it into the air until the titanic fish hung suspended from a slender bamboo wand as curled as a shepherd's crook. Seeing how he wobbled so unsteadily, nearly impaled by the hilt of the rod wedged against his gut, others came to the blacksmith's assistance.

He hadn't set out to catch a mythical monster, but there it hung: awesome and shuddering, a dreadnought of an aquatic vertebrate, oily water pouring from its massive silver flanks. It was risen only partway out of the bayou, the great saw-toothed fan of its dorsal fin only half exposed, its thrashing tail concealed beneath the churning surface, gills puffing in and out like the bellows in Oyzer's forge. The diminished crowd of onlookers was swiftly reconstituted, the hardier pitching in to help uphold the rod as if rallying to raise some mammoth primeval standard. But as they held it aloft, the monster, its eyes dull as old chrome, opened its jaw to show a double row of needle-sharp teeth before sliding back into the turbulence. In its place was another fish, smaller but still monumental, its torpedo-shaped flanks louvered with breathing tiger stripes. Then that one also opened its mouth and slid back into the cove, leaving a lesser giant still on the line. Lifted high enough above the water to reveal its cankered underbelly, its forked tail slapping the air, that fish too slipped back into its element, leaving behind it young Hershel Tarnopol hanging by his collar from the rusty hook. He was grinning around the piece of paper clenched between his crooked teeth, his legs cycling slowly in his baggy plus fours; in his hands he held a large round loaf of baked challah bread.

Several of the men rushed forward to help disengage him from the hook. As they lowered him, Hershel shifted the bread to his left hand in order to dip his right into the breast pocket of one of his assistants. When they set him down in front of the blacksmith, whose body was still heaving from its Homeric exertion, the boy's feet (both of them shod) made squelching sounds in the mud. Removing from his mouth the biblical passage with which Oyzer had baited the shoe, he said sheepishly, "Straight from the hearth, Papa," as he offered his father the golden loaf. Then, with the wisdom he'd acquired during his confinement in the fish, Hershel began to read the Hebrew script in a stentorian voice.

"'Can you draw out Leviathan with a fishhook, or press down his tongue with a cord? Can you fill his skin with harpoons, or his head with fishing spears? Lay hands on him; remember the battle—but never do it again!' Job forty-one, one." And assuming a dignity he had not previously been known to possess, the son enjoined his father the fisher-smith to "Ess gezunterhait, Papa. Eat in good health."

With a sigh that rocked his entire frame and admitted a seepage of tears, Oyzer took a bite of the warm challah baked in the heat of a monster's bowels. It had a cottony texture that tasted of sweet divinity and ashes, and melted in his mouth before he could swallow. In that moment the blacksmith forgave his son for having forgiven him. Then the stationer Seymour Lipow, noticing that his breast pocket was empty of his seven-jewel Swiss, shouted that he'd been robbed, and Hershel took off at a sprint. His bandy-legged father gave chase, roaring after him: "Marinated imbecile! When I catch you I throw you back!"

Somewhere there was a war. There was also a mass jailbreak from the county clink at Auction and Front Street and a surefire cure for pellagra concocted in a basement on Beale; there was an evening when Rose and Morris Padauer took along their proxy son, Benjy, to dinner and a show on the roof of the Peabody Hotel. They might have chosen a venue more suitable for children—a circus or a zoo—but the old rebbe had assured them that the roof garden cabaret specialized in family entertainment. So, despite their desolatation over the plain truth that their child was not their child, they took the old man's advice. Of course, if they were honest they would have had to admit to experiencing as well a measure of relief: for the unsightly specimen they'd nurtured these several years had not, it seemed, sprung from their own loins. In the interim, however, they'd lavished so much fondness on the wizened little chap that, regardless of

Benjy's tenuous relation to humanity, it was too late now to withdraw their affection.

To save money—since Mama Rose's pillaged piggy bank had disbursed only a pittance—they spared themselves the trolley fare by walking the dozen blocks to the hotel at Main and Monroe. Crossing the unmarked border between North Main and Main Street proper, they realized yet another instance of relief. Because once they'd begun to stroll beyond the neighborhood, the world reverted blessedly to three dimensions, as opposed to the dizzying multitude observable in the Pinch. The last to find out what everyone else already seemed to know, the Padauers felt like strangers in their own community, and so breathed easier at having left it for a turn.

"Mama," said Morris, admitting a roguish smile as he swung one of Benjy's horny hands in his own, "I feel like we keepin' company."

"Fresh!" chided Rose, flushing vermilion while squeezing their creature's other hand.

On the Peabody roof they were seated by a maître d' with a permanently arched brow at one of the farthest tables from the stage, below a parapet hung with paper lanterns. The air was pervaded by the caustic scent of citronella from the candles on every table; the potted palms stood about like discreet chaperones. Looking around, the Padauers tried to quell the sense that the other patrons were of an altogether better class than they; they were further disturbed to find no children in evidence at all. They consoled themselves that it was in any case a warm summer night, the stars low-hanging fruit above their heads.

They would have liked to order, say, a plate of mamaliga or noodle pudding but were served instead the singularly unkosher entrée—chicken-fried steak and pinto beans stewed with ham—that came with the bill of fare. (The haughty waiter in his waist-length jacket advised them there were no substitutions.) Unaccustomed to worldly pleasures as they were, the Padauers were nevertheless determined to enjoy their evening out. So they sipped their sweet tea, into which a neighboring couple were pouring something from a brown paper bag, and speculated on the ingredients of a menu item called shoofly pie. They rubbed the sparse thatch atop Benjy's outsize head and solicited his assurance that he was having a good time. ("I'm havink a ball," he croaked, though you wouldn't have known it to look at him.) Then they applauded enthusiastically when the penthouse curtain parted and the New Pygmy Minstrels pranced onto the low stage.

High-stepping in procession around a semicircle of chairs, they played a ragtime number whose base melody the Padauers identified as, remarkably, the fraylekh standard "How Does the Czar Drink Tea?" They played an array of instruments—clarinets, bass fiddles, snare drums—with exaggerated gestures and flourishes, marching about the raised platform long enough to give the audience an opportunity to appreciate their gnomish anatomies and outlandish garb. Their burnt-cork features beamed from globular heads like faces painted on balloons, balloons from which dangled stringy torsos and bantam legs. Shod in spangled buskins, they wore top hats and spike-tailed coats stitched together from swatches of calico, croker sacks, and colored glass. When the general hilarity was subdued enough for the tune to be heard, the bandleader, no taller than the others but perfectly proportioned, signaled the troupe to halt. "Gemmun," he called in a nod to Negro dialect, "be seated." Though forceful enough, his voice was that of a child, as were the soft honey curls that peeked from under his tall hat in contrast to the minstrel makeup.

Once seated, the players performed another spirited number, this one a syncopated but ill-disguised version of "Zing, Faygele, Zing." The Padauers exchanged puzzled glances, wondering that the goyim didn't lose patience with such a hybrid program—though in fact the audience, unacquainted with Old Country klezmer, seemed to accept the performers as a variety of authentic blackface minstrelsy. Then the bandleader doffed his stovepipe, releasing his profusion of curls, and presented himself as "Your humble interlockator." Again the juvenile voice was at odds with his authority, as he begged permission to introduce "two chaste and elegant gen'lemen." "Mr. Tambo," he called, and a sprightly little musician leapt forward from one end of the orchestra, shaking his tambourine. "And Mr. Bones." Another pygmy musician sprang forth from the opposite end of the chairs, clacking knucklebones. "In their inimminable Ethiopian pah-de-do." Upon which the interlocutor surrendered the stage to Tambo and Bones, who bowed to one another, bumping heads.

Tambo (earnestly inquiring): "Mistah Bones, yo' mammy and pappy, am dey siblinks?" The dialect was Negro but the accent pure Galitzianer.

Bones (just as concerned): "Nu, Mistah Tambo, do y'all still have from nature a 'fection for it, despite what it done to you?" Again Negro with a Litvak inflection.

Tambo: "How mizzable am our lot, Mistah Bones. Plagues we got, pogroms, the Ku Klux Klan . . . Sometime I tink we been better off not to be born."

Bones: "But who has dat much luck, Mistah Tambo? Not one in a thousand."

Their dialogue accelerated to a rapid-fire exchange, each joke graduated in saltiness ("Do y'all with your wife make love doggy style, Mistah Tambo?" "I sit up and beg while, tahkeh, she rolls over and plays dead, Mistah Bones"), punctuated with rim shots on the drums. So shocked was Rose Padauer that she clapped her hands over Benjy's ears but couldn't help sharing a furtive smile with her husband.

The antic pair concluded their routine with a brief skit involving a change of gender by Mr. Bones, who adopted for the part a princess petticoat and a sheitl wig. (He's a lady in a café who lets fly a fart then tries to deceive the other patrons by scolding the waiter: "Stop dat!" The waiter: "Absolutely, madam, which way were it headed?") Then the minstrels struck up a raucous choral rendition of "When Mose with His Nose Leads the Band," to which Tambo and Bones commenced to dance.

Their capers began as a combination of cakewalk and (as the Padauers perceived) a mother-in-law dance of the type seen at Jewish weddings, but soon progressed to acrobatics bordering on the hyperkinetic. They were joined by other band members juggling their instruments and spinning dreidls that disappeared in multihued whirlwinds. Bedlam reigned onstage until a Lilliputian trumpeter blew some shrill notes on a spiraling ram's horn, and the interlocutor reappeared with his winsome face scrubbed clean of burnt cork.

"Ladies and mentschen," announced the squeaky-voiced trumpeter, "we now present for your delectification the kindshaft phenomenum Master Splendido, hypnotist and animal magnet extry-ordinaire."

The minstrels performed another roistering walkaround, playing a march tempo version of "Nokh a gletzl vayn" while circumambulating their featured entertainer, before exiting through the sequined curtain. That left the audience to admire the comely boy who stood before them, having swapped the interlocutor's tatterdemalion for a silk-lapeled coat whose tails swept the floor.

As Mama Rose removed her hands from his ears, Benjy fidgeted in the face of all he beheld. Suffering their hijinks, he couldn't help but gloat over the situation of his former brethren, who'd cast him out of their underground kingdom only to be cast out themselves by the aftermath of the quake. He could picture with relish the collapsed catacombs that sent them scrambling up into the province of mortals, where they were met with a flood that dispersed them even farther afield. Seeking a more hospitable environment, they had apparently forsaken their habitual meddling in the lives of the Jews to assume this ludicrous imposture on higher ground. But while he might take some satisfaction in their reversal of fortune, Benjy harbored no lasting resentment: they'd merely done to him what they'd done to generations of antiquated ogres; countless like him had been switched for rosier human types and left to soldier on as best they could in the upper atmosphere. But you could bet your second sight that few had found accommodations as favorable for a haimish ever after as were his with the Padauers. Even now, when forced to acknowledge his alien origin, they continued to treat him as their cosseted ward, and he regretted that the skimpy gifts he was able to give them were so unequal to the attentions he received in return.

Now, however, he was in a position to give them the supremest gift imaginable: he could reintroduce them to their stolen child. It would be the greatest sacrifice a fake kid could make for his adoptive family. But the shretelekh were an essentially selfish breed, not known for a generosity of spirit, and the substitute Benjy, who couldn't even recall his original name, had never supposed himself to be better than the rest.

Meanwhile the callow headliner, Master Splendido, had invited volunteers from the audience to step onto the stage. Charmed by his cherubic face and piping voice, a goodly number accepted his invitation, the gents helping the ladies onto the platform where all took the chairs vacated by the minstrels. The volunteers were a largely youthful contingent in dinner jackets and cotton voile frocks, slightly lit and eager to participate in whatever frolic was requested of them. Master Splendido wasted no time in exploiting their receptiveness. He addressed the house, reeling off his credentials without a trace of the former mock dialect: "Ladies and gentlemen, I am Splendido, who was initiated into the mysteries by the stupefying sorcerers of Sfat . . ." The audience was as transfixed as they were amused, if only by the distinction between the child's reedy voice and the inflated claims he made. The performer removed from a coat pocket the small tin figure of a grass-skirted African dancer and turned the key in her back. Then he held the shimmying doll at their eye level as he paced back and forth in front of the row of volunteers.

"From this moment everything I say, no matter how stupid, will become your reality. But first, go to sleep . . ."

At their table Rose and Morris Padauer were as spellbound as the volunteers, for they'd recognized the windup doll as the very twin of the one they'd replaced for the unshapely replacement of their kidnapped baby boy. Surely a coincidence, since it was as absurd to believe they could have begotten a Master Splendido as it was to think they'd spawned the little bogey seated between them. The boy onstage was nothing like the infant they'd lost—except for his fair hair and beryl blue eyes, the snub nose, the poppy petal mouth . . . Between them their surrogate child saw his guardians in the process of making a stupendous connection, dismissing it, then tentatively beginning to entertain it again. Benjy sucked his vestigial tooth: a reckoning, he understood, was at hand. The Padauers had perhaps only to declare themselves for a joyous reconciliation to unfold before the assembled, leaving the cast-off "peanut" hung out to dry.

But thunderstruck as they were, Mama Rose and Morris remained seated lest they disrupt the proceedings—they were that cowed by their circumstances. It's true that Mrs. Padauer had started up without thinking from her chair, but Morris, himself drained of color, restrained her with a hand to the wrist, saying, "Mama, we cooled already our heels this long . . ." Her full bosom aquiver, his wife resumed her seat; their reuniting could wait (could it not?) till after the show, though in the meantime both she and her husband might plotz from anticipation.

Charged by the hypnotist to sleep the sleep of the guiltless, the row of volunteers had instantly slumped against one another like weary travelers in a station waiting room. Sauntering to the front of the stage, Splendido assured his rapt audience that the subjects were now entirely under his control. "I can change them any way I want," he boasted. His voice, no longer merely beguiling, had acquired a touch of the petulance consistent with his age; it was a little chilling given the powers he laid claim to, and the cabaret patrons laid down their utensils, their dinners growing cold on their plates.

"You, sir," said the hypnotist, tapping the shoulder of a natty gentleman sleeper, who was jerked awake at the touch. "You were created by the echo of a voice from the black heaven and are now infested with demons."

Straightaway the young man tumbled from his chair, his lacquered hair losing its wave as he began to roll around the stage. Thrashing and flailing as if attempting to escape his own skin, he was heard to utter words in languages that (the hypnotist submitted) were conceived before the creation of Adam.

Leaving the possessed gentleman to his loquacious seizure, Splendido began tapping the other volunteers. "You and you and you," until all the rest were awakened, "are swine."

The lot of them lurched from their chairs and, negligent of their evening finery, began scrambling about the stage on all fours, grunting, snuffling, and rooting about as if for truffles. Readdressing the possessed man, the hypnotist proclaimed, "By the secrets I stole from a nest in the cosmic tree, I command the demons to flee through your left big toe." The man was propelled into the air as if yanked by the foot in question before falling limply onto the boards. Then via some invisible transit, his demons seemed to have taken up residence in the swine, who emitted bloodcurdling squeals as they spilled from the stage and circulated among the tables. The audience snatched up dishes and bunched their skirts, craning their necks to watch the bewitched volunteers racing toward the surrounding parapets. They clambered onto the low walls, where they reared up on their hind legs, teetering perilously above the streets, until Master Splendido called out to them, "Be as you were!" At his direction they stepped backward from the walls as one and, uttering residual oinks, returned to the stage, where they resumed their chairs and again fell immediately asleep.

Shaken by what they'd witnessed, the spectators dabbed their faces with napkins and murmured among themselves in a susurrus of hushed conversation. Onstage the hypnotist, having reawakened and dismissed his volunteers, doffed his high hat to take a bow. The applause was irresolute. "Mama," whispered Morris a bit uncertainly, "it's a rare little pisher we made," but Mama Rose could barely nod her head to concur.

Released from their trance, the volunteers, apparently amnesiac, looked perfectly composed as they took their places again at the candlelit tables. Their fellow patrons, however, regarded them suspiciously. Then Master Splendido began to move among them, menacing now despite his pink cheeks and dewy curls. In fact, most of the audience avoided making eye contact as he toddled past them, asking, "Who would like next to be transmogrificated?" Nor did he seem especially discouraged that no one was willing. When he'd strolled to the farthest tables, he paused beside the Padauers and smiled at them like, they felt, the breaking dawn. "Would you care to join me on the stage?" he asked warmly, and Rose and Morris squeezed hands under the table. Between them the pretend Benjy was acutely aware of their contact, and he cringed in his knowledge of what he believed they were thinking: they were thinking that the wonderful boy had recognized them as well, and was summoning them to a surprise reunion where all would be revealed; the audience would stand and cheer the happy occasion. Benjy's heart (or whatever crabbed organ still pumped the green ichor through his calcified arteries) sank as he watched the half-pint sorcerer help his family to their feet—she in her frumpy tub frock and he in his shabby gabardine suit.

Diffident but full of expectation and exchanging secret grins, Mr. and Mrs. Padauer trailed behind Master Splendido back onto the stage. There they stood looking tenderly at the Tom Thumb mesmerist, who had already removed the grass-skirted figurine from his pocket and turned the key. Despite his poor eyesight and distance from the stage, Benjy was nevertheless able to lip-read the word the volunteers were mouthing in unison: "Zuninkeh." Darling son. But the doll had already begun to wiggle her hips and Splendido, an unkind expression distorting his pretty features, to utter his trance-inducing suggestions. Then, still sharing their inane grin, the Padauers sank into the chairs—all but two of which had been removed by pygmy assistants—and were sound asleep.

The hypnotist wasted no time in rousing them again, rapping their heads with his knuckles till Rose and Morris sat abruptly upright.

"Feeling kind of amorous, are we?" asked Splendido. Mama Rose made a flirtatious moue in response to which her husband raised and lowered his monobrow suggestively. The spectators succumbed to a nervous tittering. "Perhaps you will give to the audience a lesson from romance."

The couple needed no further encouragement. At once they were entwined in a heedless embrace, clinging to one another with grappling arms and legs as if seeking wrestling holds. Morris planted suction-cup kisses over his wife's face and fleshy neck, popping a button at the top of her bodice in his passion; while Rose, her coiffure askew, grabbed hanks of her husband's ebbing hair in her fists. Every blatant moan he extracted from his wife elicited another endearment from Morris: "Hartzeniu! Sweet hamantash!" The audience was in fits, though some shifted uncomfortably in their chairs, moved to concupiscence by the heat of the demonstration. At one point the pygmies wheeled on a gauze-curtained hospital screen, which Master Splendido, making a show of discretion (it had after all been billed as a family revue), placed in front of the lovers. But the sounds emanating from the shadow play behind the curtain provoked even greater gales of laughter than had the couple's groping in plain sight.

At the back of the house Benjy seethed, the public humiliation of his foster parents having brought him to the brink of tears. The sensation had no place in his emotional repertoire; sympathy was not a common function of his species. His time among mortals, aggravated by the insults of his outdated age, must have softened him, which was itself a cause for indignity. He was further incensed when a pair of minstrels reappeared to accompany the lustful cries of the Padauers with screechings and tootings on their fiddle and flute. This sent the audience into convulsions. Benjy suspected that what he was seeing was not so much entertainment as a type of revenge. The pipsqueak hypnotist was after all a meshumed, a convert, gone over entirely to the tribe that had abducted him. He'd recognized his original begetters and was punishing them for the threat they posed to his disowned identity. Rather than embrace them as a returning prodigal, the little renegade had chosen instead to reject his birth parents outright: their degradation would put the lid on that rejection and by extension his rejection of humankind.

Such was the case, based wholly on instinct and enlightened self-interest, that the aged outcast had constructed against Master Splendido. Then it followed that, instead of making himself the instrument of their reconciliation, the greatest gift Benjy could give to Mama Rose and Mr. P. was to save them from their natural son.

He slid from his chair and began a resolute if splay-footed approach to the stage, bent on a showdown with the wicked child. It would be a duel between conjurors, with Benjy summoning the array of powers he'd inherited as a veteran shretele. There was the ability to shape-shift and render himself unseen, though colitis and lumbago had taken their toll on those faculties. (The most he could command in the way of invisibility now was to make himself a bit blurry about the gills.) There was the talent of invoking mind-bending incantations in occult tongues, none of which he remembered, or calling on animal helpers, though even friendly dogs shied away from him these days. He could still sour milk at a glance and tie the hair of sleepers in granny knots, but such skills would be of little use here. So what was left but a sixth sense that had small value now that the other five were so severely impaired? By the time he'd managed to scramble onto the stage he realized that he was virtually unarmed. Regardless, Benjy—he owned the name now that its previous possessor had forfeited it forever—intended somehow to unmask Master Splendido for the imposter he was.

The cabaret audience was still in stitches over the mounting crescendo of the Padauers' dalliance behind the curtain, so no one paid much attention to the diminutive newcomer who'd lately taken the stage. In the interim a dwarf vocalist had joined the musicians, integrating Mama Rose's rapturous *oy*s into a song whose refrain went "I wanna be an oy oy oyviator." Busy conducting the whole cacophony, the hypnotist had also yet to remark the intruder; then, out of the corner of an azure eye, he did. He ceased the rhythmic waving of his hands and faced the shrunken atomy, removing his hat to make a sweeping bow.

"Paskudnyik," croaked Benjy, "a thunderbolt in your pants if you don't release from your spell these good people."

Master Splendido seemed to welcome the challenge. He'd already withdrawn the tin doll from his deep pocket, but Benjy was much too shrewd to be seduced by her hoochie-kooch. He ignored the hypnotist's injunction to "Watch Jemima dance" and instead looked the kid straight in the eye. He steeled himself to do . . . what? Maybe head-butt him in his kishkes, the beautiful boy, with his blue eyes flecked with gold like tiny fishes swimming in circles, the circles themselves spinning like pinwheels. Peering into them, the old hobgoblin, centuries old in fact and very sleepy, lost all consciousness.

"What looks here like a miniature Methuselah," pronounced the hypnotist in the fullness of his authority, "is really a chicken."

It would have been diverting enough just to leer at the little eyesore who'd dared to defy the child phenom. But to see him now as a docile subject dropped into a squat, beginning to cluck and flap his elbows like wings, sent the audience into an orgy of belly laughs and guffaws. That the hypnotist's subject did actually manage to stay aloft for some seconds in his maniacal flapping only increased the general mirth. Then Master Splendido invited the spectators to toss any spare change they might have in their pockets and purses onto the stage. A hail of coins showered the ensorcelled Benjy, who, waddling awkwardly here and there, proceeded to peck at the scattered pennies and dimes; he paused just long enough in his foraging to raise his chin, shaking his head to facilitate the sliding of the coins down his gullet. So loud was his contented squawking, to say nothing of the peals of rooftop hilarity, that the symphonic climax of the couple behind the screen was drowned out. Nor was it observed that the man and wife had warily poked their heads through a gap in the curtains.

"He's too gristly for roasting," judged Splendido with respect to the chicken, "but he might make a tasty soup."

He clapped his hands and a party of pygmy minstrels, stripped now to grass skirts with bones through their noses, carried out a large zinc boiler possibly commandeered from the cabaret kitchen. It sloshed over when they set it down on the boards, steam coiling out like hooded cobras. Then, pursued by the pygmies, the pseudochicken ran gabbling and squawking about the stage as aimlessly as if he'd lost his head. In the end he was tackled and bound hand and foot with lengths of rope, though he struggled in a welter of imaginary feathers. In the throes of his furious resistance, however, Benjy became dully alert to a fact of his trussed condition: how it was analogous to his plight on that memorable night some years ago when he was smuggled into the Padauers' apartment. The realization was sobering enough to rouse him from his trance. An awareness of his present circumstance returned to Benjy as it had for his foster parents, whose tempestuous trifling had jolted them back into a consciousness of their whereabouts. Of course they had no recollection of what had happened or how they'd arrived at such a pass; nor did they recognize the author of the event as anything more than the puerile principal of the evening's program—who, with the help of the near-naked minstrels, had hoisted their little Benjy above the cauldron and was about to drop him in.

This the Padauers could not abide. They hesitated only a moment, as if trying unsuccessfully to recall some unrelated issue, then shared a mutual shrug and, with their clothing still immodestly disarranged, charged forth from behind the screen. Mama Rose went teeth-first for the hypnotist's tender calf while Morris grabbed his throat and a fistful of his golden locks with tenacious fingers. Taken off guard, Master Splendido lowered his hands to defend himself, leaving the unsupported weight of his victim to slump onto the crown of his hat, shoving the stovepipe over his ears and eyes. His assistants—their bare chests like saloon doors on spindle legs—backed away from the frenzied interference. In the succeeding fracas Benjy was left to tumble onto the planks, where he wriggled like a bug from a chrysalis as he shucked off his bonds. Besieged by the Padauers, Splendido had lost all pretense of his magisterial presence; blind now and powerless to fend off his assailants, he'd begun to bawl like the child he was. At length his whimpering incited his tribe to regroup and make an effort to come to his rescue. The aborigines that had already taken the stage were joined by the costumed strutters, all of them swarming over the couple who'd disabled their young headliner. Semi-recovered from his ordeal and seeing his family in danger, the self-liberated Benjy trotted headlong into the fray; promptly tossed out, he turned about and headed back into the scrimmage again undismayed.

The audience, having assumed that everything thus far was part of the act, were confused by the current turn of events. If they'd been previously well disposed toward the entertainers, they were dumbfounded now to the point of outrage. With the defeat of the Confederacy always fresh in their memories, it was not in their nature to sit idly by while Caucasians—albeit of Hebrew extraction—were torn apart by cannibals. However misguided their motives, a score of the diners abandoned their tables to storm the stage, some producing concealed weapons (such as a sword unsheathed from a cane) in the process. Standing beneath a pergola twined in artificial grapevines, the treble-chinned maître d' signaled frantically to the waiters to intercede, while the waiters waved back in amiable helplessness.

But the shretelekh are finally not a confrontational race. The present kerfuffle notwithstanding, they much preferred flitting stealthily among mortals, creating discord then becoming scarce. So rather than make a stand against such wholesale insurgency, they scattered. Some slipped back behind the sequined curtain; others dove through skylights and bulkheads in varying stages of anatomical evaporation. They took with them their stolen child in his crushed stovepipe, who for all his talents remained perfectly discernible: a royally spoiled and squawling brat.

Indifferent to their own scrapes and abrasions, Mr. and Mrs. Padauer made to soothe their little goblin, Mama Rose straightening his sailor collar as Morris smoothed the part in his few remaining hairs. Benjy fairly purred at their petting. On the walk back from the Peabody Mrs. Padauer began to hum one of the jaunty minstrel airs (was it "Under the Matzoh Tree"?) while her husband asked her teasingly, "Mama, did we have tonight enough fun?" Then he stopped at a newsstand to purchase, for the first time in his life, a Havana cigar. They strolled home slowly in the cool of the evening, since Benjy's short legs were especially bowed from the weight of the coins he'd swallowed. But after he'd used the WC—the loot having proved a much-needed laxative—he winnowed and washed the coins from his movement and presented his mama with a bulging piggy bank.

While Pinchas Pin was otherwise occupied, the czar was overthrown and the revolution that the merchant had waited for for so long finally happened. The so-called Sodomites of South Memphis, sworn enemies of the Pinch, released a sheet of raw ooze and filth from Carr's tannery into the bayous around North Memphis; but that was before Pinchas's time. Alvin "Shipwreck" Kelly sat on a flagpole above the *Commercial Appeal* building on Second Street as a crowd watched from Court Square then grew bored; but that came much later. Meanwhile, on the night he and his improbable companion Rabbi Eliakum ben Yahya set out in pursuit of Katie's absconded spirit, Pinchas was less concerned with this world than the next.

When he and the rabbi arrived by dinghy at the shore of Market Square Park, the inverted tree at its center was illuminated by a jumble of lantern-lit shacks. They were small, jerry-built shacks nestled amid the network of gnarled roots that had reared up in place of the great oak's undulant branches. The shacks were made of the kinds of odds and ends from which the Jews constructed their sukkah booths, though to Pinchas's knowledge it wasn't Sukkot. Or rather, it was Sukkot, Passover, Purim, and Hanukkah rolled into one. For just as on holidays the Jews acknowledged themselves to be living contemporaneously with their biblical forebears, so in this new dispensation did all the holidays occur at once. And through the fabric walls of the booths, some of which dangled like lockets from ropes and chains, Pinchas could see the silhouettes of North Main Streeters at their tables observing simultaneous celebrations. The sight halted him a moment in his tracks, though it only took a tug at his sleeve from Rabbi ben Yahya to bring him back to the mission at hand.

"Did you think I forget!" fumed Pinchas, who needed no prompting.

"Touchy touchy."

Pinchas sighed, sparing a worry for the frail old man who'd offered himself as his safe passage to the underworld. He'd always judged the tzaddik and his followers to be frankly insane, and now, when the old dotard should have been on his deathbed dispensing holy madness to his disciples, here he was leaning on his cane at the edge of an abyss. He was meshuggeh all right, as must be the dry goods merchant who had agreed to follow his lead.

Always Pinchas had regarded himself as a forward-thinking man, who, had he lived in the age of Spinoza, would also have been declared a heretic. But his wife's untimely end had reduced him to a fool like the rest of his demented neighbors. The rebbe had explained it all so plainly in the boat on the way to the park: how, thanks to the interference of himself and his fanatics, below was now above, and vice versa; existence was turned on its head. This afforded the individual a rare opportunity, since one could now enter the afterlife (which in this instance came *before*) without having to die. By the same token, those who expired during this erratic interlude were not officially defunct. Katie had perished at an opportune moment . . .

At which point Pinchas had shouted, "Shvayg!" and held his ears; for his yearning after his departed wife finally wanted no explanation. It wanted only her foggy green eyes and washed-out terra-cotta hair, the swan's-neck curve of her spine in her taffeta waist; it wanted her flashes of temper, her terrible jokes ("They say Saint Paddy chased the snakes out of Ireland, but he was the only one who saw the snakes"), her roast potatoes like kidney stones. In the absence of Katie's animate presence, Pinchas's desire for her had overwhelmed his grief and stunned him with the force of an apoplexy. Then it had set him in motion.

Throwing away his cane, the rebbe leaped with a single bound from the lip of the crevasse into the roots of the tree. With an agility that seemed to Pinchas indecent in one of his dropsical and dilapidated years, he lowered himself as far as the base of the sunken trunk; then crab-like he began to scramble down its incline until he was swallowed up by darkness. Leaning over the edge of that obscurity, Pinchas froze. How pointless it would be—he reasoned—if in the course of chasing after his lost wife, he should lose himself. But frightened as he was of the descent, he found he was even more frightened at the prospect of losing sight of Rabbi ben Yahya. So the merchant, no young man himself, overcame once again the rational turn of mind he'd set such store by and, exhaling a prayer, made the thrilling leap into the roots.

He caught hold, absorbing the bruising impact with his chest and chin, and astonished at finding himself still in one piece, hugged the tree for all he was worth. Then, with extreme caution, he began the treacherous downward climb. Steep as was its declivity, the thick trunk was studded with hollows and knobs, so there were no end of ridges and footholds to hang on to, and the cool loamy scent of the earth was somehow beckoning. Even now Pinchas was skeptical that the tree, in its inversion, could serve as an artery between two worlds, but once he'd begun his descent he seemed to have left (along with his logic) his fears largely aboveground. He gave himself up entirely to this penumbral element, which presumably had a logic of its own—one he hoped to discover as he inched his way down the long incline. It was an endless descent that provided him plenty of time to contemplate his objective: for Katie's runaway soul, in its corporeal aspect, was—he believed—inextricable from his own. He had the sense that, sinking farther into the earth, he was sounding the depth of his devotion, which ought not—if he were worthy—to have a bottom.

He was deep enough now that the hole above his head had shrunk to the size of a penny embossed with a silver sliver of moon. Though the coin had no capacity to shed light into the fissure, the spores and slick mosses that Pinchas encountered appeared to give off a phosphorescence of their own. An orchid-like flower sprouting from a knothole shone like a gas burner. There was sufficient light to give the merchant fair warning that he should halt and let pass the fiddler Asbestos, who was tapping his way out of the mouth of a broken sewer tunnel. The fiddler was followed, as he groped his way round the tree trunk and into a similar segment of sewer pipe on the other side, by a raggedy column of Negro men. Each had an arm on the shoulder of the one in front of him so as not to be left behind in the dark, as they disappeared into the far conduit. Farther down, there was more traffic and Pinchas had to make way for a party of elemental creatures (some still in costume) with a pouting human child in tow. Back from their theatrical exile, they skirted the tree's broad diameter and burrowed into an oval grotto on their way to reclaim their native haunts.

Though he must have been by now many fathoms beneath North Main Street, Pinchas had yet to arrive at the spreading branches that had tipped foremost into the crevasse when the oak was toppled. The nubbly trunk itself seemed interminable, and where, by the way, was the old rabbi who'd volunteered to be his guide? For some reason Pinchas refrained from shouting after him, afraid perhaps that his raised voice might cause a cave-in. Or was it that in the quiet of his descent he rather cherished the solitude?

Then he'd reached a depth where the darkness was absolute. The tree bark had become less coarse, more slippery with bubbling sap; there were whole stretches where, still hugging the trunk, the merchant was unable to find a purchase. In addition, exhaustion had begun to overtake him in every limb, and he wondered again how such precipitous folly could result in the recovery of his bride. He was slipping more often, barely hanging on until his gumsoles could snag on a protuberance or his fingers grab hold of another indentation. Still Pinchas had no thought of turning back; the climbing up would in any case be more arduous than the climbing down, and the oblivion that awaited him if he fell was no more menacing than the oblivion he'd already penetrated. Then his foot struck what seemed to be a solid bough projecting from the trunk and, completely spent, Pinchas folded onto his haunches, sitting down at long last and dangling his legs. But before he could draw a breath in relief, his stomach lurched into his throat and his brain was swamped by a wave of total disorientation; bereft of his internal compass, he found himself hanging by the crook of his knees whose strength was close to giving out. In a moment he would drop into the abyss and God (whose authority the merchant disdained) help him.

At that juncture a hand grasped his arm and hauled him upright, where he was seated on the bottommost limb of the patriarch oak. "Aliyah tzerichah yeridah," came the singsong voice of Rabbi ben Yahya, who, perched on a neighboring branch, appeared to have aged a decade or so in reverse. "To ascend you got first to *de*scend," he chirped. "What took you so long, Reb Pin?"

His heart kettle-drumming in his ears, Pinchas looked out over the park and the street beyond, and had no idea where he was. Then gradually it dawned on him that this was the Pinch, though this particular incarnation looked to have awakened from the sublime dream of itself to a threadbare reality. The houses and buildings from his elevated vantage were smoke gray against the heliotrope sky, the park itself appearing neglected, the neighborhood deserted though unaltered by natural disaster. With a groan the dry goods merchant began creakily to lower himself from the stout branch. The rebbe dropped neatly to the ground beside him, his billowing caftan covering his head as he landed. When he swept it back, Pinchas saw there was color in the tzaddik's pursy cheeks, his wispy beard become robust and full. Even his previously deflated skullcap rode his head like a proud cupola.

"Nu?" said the rejuvenated old man.

"It's a ghost town," asserted Pinchas, but the rebbe begged to differ.

"We are here the ghosts. Is waiting, this place, for the world to get tired from magic."

Pinchas squinted at him. "You don't make no more sense down here than you did up there."

"What makes you think this ain't 'up there'?"

Then Pinchas felt again the hot pain of his loss boiling up from his chest into his throat. "Katie!" he cried, and heard his voice echoing through the empty streets and alleyways surrounding the park.

The rabbi rested a hand on his shoulder. "Go home already," he said.

The merchant let go of one last sob, pushed his eyeglasses back over the hump of his nose, and was calm. Though he hadn't run since who could remember, Pinchas began to lope down the gravel path past the dry fountain, out into Second Street and over to North Main, gaining momentum. He ran beneath unflapping awnings past vacant shopfronts whose dirty windows showed his reflection with its lanky legs pumping like pistons. Arrived at the grimy portals of Pin's General Merchandise, he burst through the front door and bolted up the stairs through the parlor and into the kitchen, where he found his wife seated at the table, singing a cradle song ("Oh hush thee my lapwing . . .") as she peeled the skins from a bowl of spuds.

Looking up at him with her emerald eyes clear of clouds, she said, "Sometimes I think my whole life was about potatoes."

In his head he'd already rushed forward to take her in his arms, so what held him stalled and still hesitating in the doorway? Winded from his sprint, Pinchas swallowed the heart that had heaved into his throat again. "Katie," he replied, "I don't believe you are all-the-way dead."

She was nowhere as pale as the blue marble woman he'd left in their marriage bed, though her complexion was still a bit tallowy, the bones still prominent beneath the flesh. Here and there about her fingertips and split ends were signs of a transparency that might, if uncared for, spread to the rest of her anatomy. Ignoring his remark, Katie reflected aloud that the illness that had taken her was perhaps a reprise of the one that took half the town in the early days of their romance. "Sure all our years together were borrowed from the distemper that returned to take back the years."

But Katie's symptoms were not those of the yellow jack; Pinchas rejected her theory out of hand, and in so doing summoned the courage to dismiss it with an emphatic "Feh!" "Speakink of which," inching a gingerly step closer to the enameled table, "to take you back is why I came here."

"Back to where?" asked Katie, tilting her head quizzically.

It irked Pinchas that the question should deserve consideration. But the quiet of this abandoned North Main Street did have a seductive quality, peaceful compared to the carnival aberration that the postdiluvian neighborhood had become. In truth, this alternative version was more faithful to the original, homelier and less rigorously demanding of one's energies. In its recent manifestation everything in the Pinch was so hugely important, whereas here only Katie mattered.

Just then a voice was heard at the open window, and husband and wife looked to see Rabbi ben Yahya standing outside on the fire escape, smiling in all his abnormal good health. "Excuse me my lack from discretion," he said, "but I wanted to see with my own eyes you are safe."

Jerked from his brooding by the interruption, Pinchas wondered that the rebbe, who with his minions had turned the whole cosmos inside out, should worry about being discreet. Apparently satisfied that things were in order, the old Hasid said a bit flightily, "So good-bye and good luck," and turned to leave. But Pinchas, realizing to his chagrin that he had no earthly notion of how to get back to the world, lunged for the window. "Rabbi," he asked in a panic, "where are you going?"

"Where else?" replied the blooming ben Yahya. "To pray. Should be nice and quiet, my shtibl, without all those tochesleckers hangink around. Oh," pivoting his head to whisper by way of an afterthought, "you should know by your Katie that her days are still numbered."

"What are you saying?" gasped Pinchas. This was cruel and unreasonable.

"Once it gets the habit from wandering, the soul," the rebbe shrugged, "nishtu gedacht, it's a hard habit to kick."

Pinchas shuddered as if the earth's tremors had started up again. "Rabbi," he blurted in desperation, "I will need still from you a guide."

Stepping deftly onto the horizontal ladder, the holy man mentioned in parting the condition that qualified his own return. "If is allowed your wife to go back with you, then somebody got to, how you say, stand surety. Somebody got to stay here in her place."

The horizontal iron stair dipped his plump person toward the sidewalk—though how he'd mounted the thing in the first place was anyone's guess.

Still languidly engaged in her labor, Katie had shown small interest in their conversation. Was this then her postmortem punishment, wondered Pinchas, to peel potatoes in this unpeopled purgatory until the hill of skins grew to a height she could scale to heaven? But why should Katie be punished at all? She'd been an exemplary wife, endured with equanimity her life as a colleen among yentes only to expire before her time. True, their marriage had been without issue, for which she'd always taken the lion's share of blame; but if anyone was at fault it was Pinchas himself for allowing her to assume his portion of guilt as well. It was an attitude that had contributed in part to his neglect of her in recent years, but nobody died from a dereliction of affection, did they? No! thought the merchant, there was no rhyme or reason for her being here, and he was perfectly within his rights (by the authority that sheer chutzpah had vested in him) to fetch her back.

But there was nothing of penance about her activity; in fact, she looked, despite her sere and slightly pellucid countenance, quite self-possessed. Like Rabbi ben Yahya, the afterlife became her. It seemed almost a shame to drag her away, and Pinchas, torn now himself, felt the temptation to linger awhile amid the tranquil reassurance of the spice pantry, coffee mill, and brass-bottom tea kettle—household objects pleasantly divested of the totemic aura they'd acquired back in creation.

"Katie," began Pinchas, his brain near to exploding, "it's lonely here."

She placed the peeler atop the curlicued pile of skins on the chopping board and looked up. "Husband," she sighed, "you've a face like a slapped donkey's arse."

At that the merchant fell to his knees wringing his hands, scooting forward in that perpetual twilight until his chin was practically resting on the table between them. "I miss you!" he cried in a beseeching tone that seemed finally to get his wife's complete attention.

A wry smile spread across her features as, abruptly, she shoved the table into his chest, which knocked him sprawling onto his backside. Then she was standing over him, yanking the pin from her hair and shaking it out until it framed her head in a rusty corona. From flat on his back Pinchas admired how the points of her breasts poked like pear stems through the thin material of her chemise, its hem brushing his brow as she stepped across him.

"If you want me," she said, looking over her shoulder, coquettish for all her years, "you'll have to catch me." Then she fled the room.

"Oy," groaned Pinchas. It wasn't enough he'd come all this way for her, he had now to play with her hide-and-seek? But he was on his feet again, staggering after her, prepared to pursue her to the ends of eternity if need be. He plunged into the dust-mantled parlor where, hidden behind the door, she darted past him back into the kitchen. Turning about, he followed, chasing her several times around the table, which she managed always to keep tantalizingly between them.

"Didn't I climb already down a hole for you?" he pleaded.

"And didn't I one fine morning plumb the plague pit to find *you?*"

As he stood pondering the difference, she slipped past him again, though he'd reached out to snatch her waist. Or had his hands passed through her, grasping only vapor? Whatever the case, he'd begun to warm to their game, convinced that if he captured her spirit he captured everything. He chased her back through the parlor and along the narrow hallway with its flickering gas sconce, past the closet-sized room they'd once set aside for a nursery but was occupied now in another dimension by a scribe. The scribe was at that moment busy recounting how a harried husband chased the shade of his wife around the underworld . . .

Pinchas blundered into the bedroom at the rear of the flat, where he could barely perceive the outline of her shadowy form, standing there beside the iron bed in the coppery gloom.

"Katie, I never lost for you the yetzer," he told her breathlessly, "the wanting."

"Prove it," she challenged.

At that Pinchas became aware of a throbbing in his pants, the beginnings of a pride he hadn't achieved in an age. As he contemplated this signal event, Katie made to sprint past him again, but this time, holding wide his outstretched arms, he was quick to bar her way. She passed straight through him—a puff as from an atomizer—then stopped and turned around, husband and wife now facing each other in a reciprocal sorrow-stricken distress.

"Beg pardon," came the voice of Rabbi ben Yahya, who appeared at the window (the bedroom window beneath which was no fire escape) again. "This I forgot." Then he began to intone ex cathedra, "'Thy dead shall live, for thy dew is as the light, and the earth shall bring forth the light of shades.' Isaiah twenty-six, nineteen. Of course," he stipulated further, "Maimonides don't mention resurrection, while Nachmanides maintains that, after Judgment Day, the soul don't necessarily get back the body it had before . . ." His voice faded as his head disappeared below the windowsill, by which time Pinchas and Katie, who had already embraced, were no longer listening anyway.

The heat that met Pinchas upon holding his wife was torrid, as if he'd clasped a lighted bundle of kindling to fuel his own immolation: that was his mad thought as he lifted her, laying her gently across the creaking bed and crawling in after. He touched the warmth of her midsection, which yielded under the stuff of her chemise; felt, as he gathered her into his arms, the washboard ribs that illness had carved from her once ample frame, and exulted in her compliant palpability. Ablaze himself, he marveled that he wasn't consumed, that his limbs, which he shucked of his garments, remained wondrously intact—as did his wife's, whom he also feverishly stripped bare, while she returned his attentions with an equal appetite. Then what they exchanged along with their voracious kisses was the sense that neither was any longer the sole occupant of his or her own skin; so that Pinchas thought Katie's Gaelic outcry, "A choisel mo chroí!" issued likewise from his own lips, just as Katie heard herself bellowing in Yiddish, "A leben zolt ir!"

When they were finally able to peel themselves apart, gasping and glad to find that they were still capable of separation, it was morning, or whatever passed for it in that bravura atmosphere. The sun slanted through the bedroom windows like a boat oar dipped in gold; the reflection from the canal was a school of silvery minnows on the ceiling, and blue notes from a nearby fiddle dashed themselves against the furling wallpaper like birds that had lost their way.

"Katie," said Pinchas, "I think we are home."

"Lord save us," she replied, burrowing her head beneath his arm.

Now that the crisis of her infirmity had passed, Katie was visited by a parade of neighbors congratulating her on her miraculous recovery and bearing unbefitting gifts: nursing flasks, nipple shields, colic remedies. Among the visitors were a company of Hasids, hungover and shamefaced in the absence of their rebbe, greeting the merchant's wife with an obligatory "Mazel tov!" "HaShem that he tells us," said their rodent-faced spokesman in the tone of one citing a little bird, "you going to have a blessed event." Dismissing the news as more of the sort of twaddle they were accustomed to hearing from that quarter, Katie began despite herself to snicker then laugh out loud; she gave herself up to an unblushing salvo of horselaughs until she saw on the faces of the gathered fanatics that God has no sense of humor at all.

11
Man without a Country

When I wasn't at the bookshop or waiting around my digs for Rachel, I still hung out at Beatnik Manor, even though I had nothing to sell. While nobody told me to get lost, I sensed a coolness that made it abundantly clear that a Lenny Sklarew who wasn't holding was less welcome than the Lenny who was. This hurt my feelings, though not enough to keep me away, admiring as I was of the Psychopimps' counterculture bona fides. The most bona fide of them all was Elder Lincoln, master musician and erstwhile hustler, though these days he made his presence at the manor pretty scarce. Increasingly alienated from the band, he spent his time conspiring with the circle of young turks who'd gathered about him; he was talking a brand of black nationalism and violent overthrow of the system that exceeded the humbler objectives of the other band members. On the evening I took Rachel to the manor, however, Elder was there, seated in the parlor at his upright piano, striking keys and listening to the respondent hum of a steel tuning fork. With the garland of paper blossoms that a groupie had strewn in his puffy 'fro and the fork one tine short of a triton, he looked like some black Neptune perched astride his throne.

I introduced him to Rachel a bit anxiously, wanting to gain merit in her eyes by my familiarity with the player but a little leery of his legendary attraction for women. He raised his drooping lids a fraction by way of acknowledgment then tilted his head back toward the vibrating instrument. Hoping, I suppose, to score points with him, I mentioned in passing that I'd been reading about a blind street musician of the 1910s, a fiddler who used his busking money to pay the bail and court costs of jailed brothers. "And one time when the costs were too high, he contrived to break them out of jail. He wormed his way through the sewer system and popped up from a grate in a holding cell, then took out a dozen or more . . ."

But Elder was way ahead of me. "That would be the same celebrated fiddler used to read the whiplash stripes of former slaves like they was some kind of Braille? Sucker could hear like with his fingers the whole harmonic progression. Found his own groove in them grooves that later on the Delta bluesmen would put words to, and later still some snake-hip yokel with hair like Lucite paint sped up the tempo—and that's how the Southland gave birth to rock 'n' roll? Yeah, I heard tell of him."

Feeling scooped, I wanted to ask how Asbestos's music had made its way into not-so-common knowledge, but Elder wasn't done.

"As for them court costs you speak of, see, the cops used to round up your nigra"—he gave the word a cutting emphasis—"on bogus charges—adultery, say, or eavesdropping. Then the judge would fine them what he knew they couldn't pay. That's when the whip boss from the cotton plantation or the turpentine camp'd step up to defray the expense. 'Cept the nigra had to work it off like a pee-on in the field or the camp or the coal mine, where he was treated even worse than slavery times. 'Cause your endless supply of convict labor meant it was cheaper to work him to death than provide even the creature comforts you'd give a common slave. And as y'all can see from the treatment of our boys the sanitation workers, ain't much changed. However," he grinned the visual echo of his piano keyboard, "'everything under heaven is in chaos; the situation is excellent.' Chairman Mao said that." Then the grin collapsed. "That's your history lesson for today, young ofays. But what do y'all puff-the-magic-dragon-headed hippies care about history?"

"That's not fair . . ." I began feebly to protest, wavering between resentment and guilt. But Elder was no longer listening, and Rachel tugged at my sleeve that it was time to move along.

Still I was stung by the indictment; it was wrong to think I wasn't concerned about the current state of things. Didn't I want the revolutionary dictatorship of the proletariat as much as the next dude? I was aware that the mayor had backed off from a compromise, that strike leaders were being arrested on frivolous charges and the National Guard was staging riot drills. I knew there was a war on. But I was lately subject to a condition I hadn't previously experienced, which altered my attitude regarding the urgency of the political situation; it was a condition I hadn't realized how much I'd missed until it took hold of my heart and genitals: I was in love.

Rachel was pure oxygen, and while her association with me had seemed

to make her less conventional in manner and dress, mine with her secured me more firmly to the family of man. Menschlikeit is what Avrom
might have said I was acquiring, if Avrom were in the business of paying
compliments. It was a consequence about which I still had reservations,
since my role as Rachel's companion threatened to jeopardize the image of
L. Sklarew as unreconstructed misfit. And too, there were times when I
felt that, for all her Gypsy concessions to fashion, Rachel was still slightly
embarrassed to be seen with me in public. Unhygienic as was my apartment, she preferred to meet me there, and though I'd seen her place in
midtown—an ivy-clad greenstone edifice with a courtyard—I'd yet to be
invited to spend the night. These things were finally immaterial in the
face of what really mattered: that the girl could short-circuit my instinct
for self-sabotage with a finger to my lips; with a well-timed furrowing of
her brow she could break me of a lifelong habit of longing.

Whereas before we met I'd been in a stupor of self-medication—as
stuporous from books as from drugs if the truth be known—now I lived
in the real world with a girl and only occasionally resorted to reading a
book. Or rather *the* book, which we read together, so that with Rachel I
struck a fine balance between fiction and fact.

We read slowly, interrupting the narrative at random points to fool
around. Sometimes the narrative itself inspired a friskiness that broke
the rhythm of our reading; sometimes the friskiness, acquiring gravity,
overwhelmed the narrative's affecting influence. I might be reading aloud
a passage in which the barber Ivan Salky, asked to give a trim (close back
and sides) to the angel Ben Nez, took umbrage at the angel's patronizing
tone and clipped his wings—when Rachel, whose nakedness beside me I
never got used to, would interrupt to offer some item from her research:
"You know, Ivan's son Oscar started Salky's Paper Bag after the war,
which made him a mint. His wife, Sophie, is very active in Hadassah and
on the board of the Lightman Nature Preserve." Then I would thank
her for the edification and devour her with kisses. But much as I wanted,
I was never able to lose myself wholeheartedly in our lovemaking, since
the moment always came—often at the height of passion—when I remembered that I couldn't take Rachel back with me to Muni's street of
amaranthine time. That's when I missed the intimacy with characters
that were at least temporarily immortal, especially given the surplus of
mortality outside the book.

Because like I said, I knew well enough what was going on in the world. I knew about the Tet Offensive and Khe Sanh and Hue, and the major who said, "We had to destroy the village in order to save it." I knew, pace Elder, about the protesters murdered by the highway patrol at a bowling alley in South Carolina. I knew that *Life* magazine declared Jimi Hendrix the most spectacular guitarist on earth, and that 116 strikers were arrested in Memphis for sitting in at a council meeting at city hall. I knew that the Reverend Martin Luther King Jr., who some said had had his day, was coming to town to march. Sometimes I thought the state of the planet was bodeful enough to make you want to trade all of creation for an instant of righteous make-believe.

It was also around this time that other peripheral events had begun to intrude. No sooner had Lamar Fontaine allowed his attorney to secure his release from the county jail than he jumped bail and disappeared. The rumors of his relocation—on a houseboat moored off an island in Plaquemines Parish, in an ashram in Kuala Lumpur—persist to this day. Meanwhile, I'd already met some of Lamar's creditors, a horror show assortment of motorcycle outlaws with lurid tattoos, and had no desire to encounter them again. They would be looking for my landlord's cat's-paw, anxious for news concerning Lamar's whereabouts, and the fact of my ignorance would not deter them from trying to extract that information by any means necessary. I had no choice but to appeal to Rachel for temporary refuge, and despite the unspoken scruples aflicker in her hazel eyes, she obliged.

I came to her with only a toothbrush and a skittish grin. Leaving the Pinch, I deliberately left behind *The Pinch* in anticipation of a total immersion in all things Rachel. Her tidy apartment was located in a quiet old neighborhood whose sidewalks heaved and plunged above the roots of tall trees. The street was a stone's throw from the zoo, a fact in which Rachel delighted, and at night you could hear peacocks yawp and lions roar. The apartment's interior was impregnated with her scent of vanilla and roses, which clung to the clothes in her closet and the sheets on her bed, and tinged a little the taste of her chamomile tea. There were objects that affirmed her identity—reproductions of primitive art alongside the Chagall and Ben Shahn prints on the walls; a bookcase crowded with essential volumes: *The Thousand Nights and a Night*, Ginzberg's *Legends of the Jews*, *The Golden Bough* ("Wow," I said, "*The Bough*! Wow!"), *National Velvet*.

There was a small black-and-white TV with an antenna like a caduceus, a portable stereo and a stack of albums full of strange bedfellows—Barbra Streisand and Joni Mitchell, Stravinsky, Burt Bacharach, and Spike Jones; there was a fat marmalade cat named Jezebel that barfed lozenge-shaped hairballs into my discarded shoes.

Rachel would leave in the morning for the Folklore Center, then drive into the suburbs where the Jews lived to conduct her interviews, returning in the late afternoon. By then I would have made a token pass at house-keeping before browsing her library and lingerie drawer, handling books and brassieres invested with a taint of sanctity because they were hers. I watched a cooking show on daytime TV and tried to duplicate the recipes, though the incinerated loaves and imploded soufflés prompted Rachel to state a preference for takeout. Occasionally I attempted a cautious constitutional along the shady streets with the uncooperative cat on a leash. As a hideout Rachel's apartment seemed a safer haven than any I'd known, more so than even the bookshop or Beatnik Manor, both of which were off-limits till the coast was clear. Moreover, I believed that we'd turned a corner in our relationship. So what if her friends disapproved of me, if she took phone calls behind the closed door of her bedroom, from which I sometimes heard aggravation in her muffled voice. Relaxed as a convalescent, I thought without remorse that I was making a genuine bid for normality. Maybe there was a future in which I might return to school, avoid the draft, communicate with my parents—and Lenny Bruce would come back from the dead.

I felt like an urchin in a penny dreadful who's rescued from the streets and given a bath and a hot meal. Only instead of a jowly financier, my benefactor was a pretty girl, who allowed me to undress her and plumb her mysteries to the length and breadth of my tongue. After making love (and before our heads settled back into their respective entities) we would read to each other from her treasury of folktales—stories of tricksters who juggled their own eyes and stole magic hats from the gods—while the cat accommodated itself to the space between our adjacent bodies. In the mornings before she left Rachel brewed strong coffee and squeezed a medley of juices whose liquid incandescence caused (lifting my shirt to prove it) my extruded navel to glow. Then I would wave good-bye to Rachel from a window, which made her laugh: "You're like Penelope reminding Ulysses not to forget his lunch."

Early on I'd phoned Avrom to say I would be away from the shop due to a family emergency. I was disappointed that he failed to even inquire about the nature of the emergency ("Since when you got a family?"), letting me know through his fruity cough—which he may have exaggerated to pique my guilt—that I wouldn't be missed. We both understood that the job had more to do with charity (his toward me and mine toward him) than actual labor, but I did worry that he might need some looking after in my absence. I soothed my conscience by calling Old Man Zanone, who had the Planter's Peanuts shop next door to the Book Asylum and was himself a relic of Main Street, asking him to please look in on Avrom every once in a while.

Avrom's disinterest was the flip side of Rachel's persistent third degree; she was forever pestering me about my past—"and don't tell me you were raised by wombats or whatever."

"I have a family," I was finally compelled to admit, "of sorts." I had an obese mother, I told her, whose Valium addiction had left her in the vegetative state of a beached manatee; a father who, when he wasn't foreclosing properties, napped with an open *Wall Street Journal* over his face. This was all more or less true, though I tended to err on the side of less, but Rachel seemed to find the current version feasible enough.

"So you hate your parents because they're not . . . what? Sonny and Cher?"

"Who said anything about hate? I hardly know them." Having just made their acquaintance.

Rachel emitted the sigh that was her signature assessment of my character. "I'm fond of you, Lenny, really I am," cupping my jaw between her palms as if she intended to squeeze my face into two dimensions, "but you know, you're not all that special."

"Fankoo," I told her, my lips still squinched between her fingers, which I removed. "I appreciate your honesty."

She did this circumflex thing with her eyebrows by way of apology and made herself pliant again, leaning against me so I could fold her in my arms like a hero. We were seated on a stone bench in her apartment's courtyard, the air practically narcotic with the fragrance of honeysuckle and hyacinth. A blue butterfly played about Rachel's hair, the warm sun highlighting her unconfined breasts through a translucent blouse. "Must have been some awful trauma that made you want to erase your own past," she mused.

"Yeah," I confessed, "the trauma of boredom."

Then it turned out I had a limited tolerance for bliss. Like a fish that'd scrabbled onto dry land to become a person, I felt I'd evolved too fast, and wanted to turn tail and flop back whence I'd come. I loved the girl but missed the Pinch (the place and the book), and began to feel as if I were under house arrest. I tried my best to conceal my unease from Rachel, but it didn't help that she reminded me repeatedly that I shouldn't get too comfortable in her apartment: our arrangement was never meant to be permanent. The caveat made me painfully aware of how comfortable I'd become. Having determined that the solution lay in consolidating the book *and* the girl, I decided that enough time had passed; I would return to North Main Street and retrieve Muni Pinsker's desultory saga. If we resumed our custom of reading from it aloud, it might resolve my restlessness and at the same time placate Rachel's growing impatience with the space I took up in her flat. But when the bus dropped me off in the early morning at the corner of Winchester and Main, I discovered that my building was padlocked as if in solidarity with number 348 across the street. Ordinances advising *No Trespassing* were pasted to either side of the crumbling entrance.

Undeterred, I stepped into the vacant lot next to my building and shinnied up a budding mimosa tree to a second-story window. From a swaying limb I managed to raise the unlatched sash a few inches before it stuck; then I slithered into the room, in effect illegally breaking into my own life. Even standing amid the cuckoo's nest of my unshelved library, I felt like a burglar. I had a fleeting urge to organize the books, arrange them in uniform stacks according to subject and author; the exercise would unclutter my mind and provide a blueprint for an ordered existence. Because the truth was I felt no more like I belonged in those mildewy rooms than I did in Rachel's harmonious abode. Muni's homely beige book lay splayed open on the mattress where we'd left it. I stooped to pick it up, closing the covers as if afraid its contents might spill out, then tucked the book under my belt. As I ducked out the window back into the tree, I promised myself I'd return with a wheelbarrow to cart the whole library back to Avrom's.

I grappled down a branch of the mimosa until I felt my feet touch the weedy ground, but rather than drop back into the lot, I pushed off again with my toes. The limber branch tossed me into the air like a trampoline. I bounced high and, when the branch nodded back toward the earth, bent my knees and shoved off again. I let out a whoop, wanting just to keep bouncing—a human yo-yo—between North Main Street and the shell-pink firmament, but the bough snapped and I came crashing to the ground amid a furor of exploding dandelions. Rattled but unhurt, I rolled over to find that I'd landed on the open pages of Muni's book, which I credited if irrationally with having broken my fall.

I located a phone booth and dialed the office of Bernie "the Mouthpiece" Rappaport, who made it clear he had no time for anyone associated with Lamar Fontaine, whose flight from justice had left his attorney holding the bag. He explained the situation in brisk officialese, using jargon like "angary" and "writ of replevin" until I begged him to please speak in plain English. Then he told me that the former owners of Lamar's properties, which the scofflaw had failed to develop since their purchase, had invoked a legal loophole supporting their reclamation of the deeds. The tenants of said properties—of whom, to my knowledge, I was the only one—were to be promptly turned out.

Back at her apartment I fretted over my eviction to Rachel, who asked me, "Where will you go?" Which left me to understand that, assurances of abiding affection aside, she wasn't renewing the invitation to stay longer with her.

When later that same day I pounded on the door of the Book Asylum, mysteriously locked during business hours, nobody answered. I stood on the sidewalk with nothing but my bintl of belongings and the increasingly dog-eared copy of *The Pinch*, feeling that all doors had been bolted against me.

"Where's Avrom?" I asked Mr. Zanone in his flyblown nut shop next to the Asylum. (The irony of their juxtaposition was not lost on me.) He was an old codger, Zanone, whose stubble-dusted dewlaps trembled like udders when he spoke; his red-rimmed eyes blinked every time the mechanized Mr. Peanut tapped his cane against the window, where a silver dollar protected the glass from the cane's nickel tip. He told me that, after being discovered barely breathing on the floor of his shop by a passing pedestrian (a demonstrator who fanned him with his I AM A MAN placard till the ambulance arrived), Avrom had been taken to St. Joseph's Hospital.

I found him on a harshly lighted ward whose odor of mortification was only slightly mitigated by the tang of cleaning solvents. The rows of beds containing patients in varying stages of decrepitude were separated by folding privacy screens. Loomed over by a metal pole like the tree in *Godot* hung with transparent fruit, Avrom lay flat on his back in the adjustable bed. He was connected by tubes, hoses, and what looked like electrodes to a console of winking and ticking machinery. At first sight of him I was put in mind of the victim of some ghastly experiment—as if the machines, rather than sustaining him, had sucked the essence out of him and left in his stead the husk of a sick old man. But such a notion was gilding the lily in the case of Avrom, upon whom the worst had already been perpetrated. On the trolley table beside a beaker of water and a bowl of untouched pablum lay his thick glasses, which left his open eyes looking as vulnerable as poached eggs. I approached his bedside reluctantly, a little ashamed of my aversion to being in such close quarters with the ebbing geezer. His glaucous eyes, registering a visitor, rolled slightly in my direction, and in a voice just above a hoarse whisper he declared, "I ain't contagious."

Feeling guilty for having failed among other things to bring a gift, I asked him, "Avrom, what can I do for you?"

"Don't do for me no favors," he groused, and let loose a whistling exhalation.

"I thought I should ask . . ."

A turquoise-veined hand worked its way from beneath the sheet to clutch my wrist, which made me recoil as from a tentacle. "Awright," he said, "you can mind in my absence the shop." He made a gruesome sound in his throat that may have been intended for a chuckle. "I think will be permanent, my absence."

This last was pure melodrama, no doubt meant to reinforce my guilt. "You'll be up and around again in no time," I said, because wasn't that what you were supposed to say?

His fluid-filled lungs gurgled like water down a plughole, giving the lie to my blandishment. "And don't sell cheap the incunabula," he managed.

"Incunabula?" There were no incunabula.

I cautioned myself not to be fooled. Death was for Avrom an anticlimax; it was a sham even if it was real. If he expected me to honor his words with the weight of some final request, he was sorely mistaken. It was the age of

Sgt. Pepper and Benny Profane; my fellow freaks were milling peyote buttons in supermarket coffee grinders, cultivating their hysteria with pleasure and terror, and I too had other fish to fry. To quell the disquiet in the
pit of my stomach, I announced that, with all due respect, I would prefer
not to return to the bookstore.

He relaxed his grip on my arm but gave no indication that my answer
had discouraged him. "It's bashert," he muttered, actually showing the
teeth I was relieved to see were still in his head, "your destiny."

I inclined my chin at the word. "Since when have I got a destiny?" I
wanted to know.

A rattling cough, then: "It is written."

"Excuse me?"

"You heard."

"Where is it written?"

He was having such difficulty speaking now that I thought I should
leave him alone; there was no point in pretending that I didn't know what
he meant, but I still needed him to give me the news in no uncertain terms.

"In the book"—he coughed again raggedly—"that you took it already
hnh from mayn gesheft."

I could have said I'd taken any number of volumes from his business,
but I was ready to stop playing dumb. "I thought you didn't read it."

"So *hnh* I lied."

"Lied that you didn't read it or lied that 'it is written'?"

"What's the difference?" he burbled. "What you got *hnh hnh* better
to do?"

It wasn't the first time he'd accused me of purposelessness, but he
should understand that things had changed: I had plans, or at least plans
to make plans; I had a girl and was in no mood to accept a life sentence of
dismal seclusion in a cave of outré books. Did he think that, because he'd
been where he'd been and was going where he was going, his words had
some special gravitas? His flesh was yellow cheesecloth, his breathing the
sound of oil in a skillet, and I wished a nurse would come forward to insist
I leave the patient alone to get his rest. I fiddled with a control that raised
the angle of the bed in the hope it might take some pressure off his lungs,
and tilted a glass of water to his parched lips.

"Look." I sighed regretfully, while my heart knocked at my ribs with
a clenched fist. "I appreciate the symmetry and all. You check out, so to

speak, and bequeath your business to a poor aimless soul whose life then acquires meaning and direction. But this is your program," I said, sorry to have raised my voice, "not mine. Besides, what's so important about your farkukteh business that it should survive?"

Avrom uttered something so faintly I had to put an ear to his lips in order to hear.

"Pishn zolstu mit grine verem," he breathed, his chest whistling like a nightingale; and glad of an opportunity to show off how my education had progressed under his patronage, I translated, "You should go and piss green worms."

Satisfied that his benediction had been duly received, he closed his eyes, squeezing them shut. "Go already. Zanone's got the key."

As he relaxed into raspy snoring, his dentures slipped from his gums, further collapsing his face. I picked them up with a tissue and dropped them into the glass of water, which magnified them like some monstrosity preserved in formaldehyde. Unnerved by their frightful grin, I turned back to their toothless host and promised (though he was beyond hearing) to bring him books. I knew of course that for Avrom his books were less about reading than insulation; I'd have to bring back enough to build him a house, or a tomb.

Since it was after Asylum hours I locked the door behind me, a safeguard against the cops and outlaws who had probably lost interest in me anyway. I threaded the warren of shelf-worn volumes and ducked into the little cell at the rear of the shop, where I flung myself down on Avrom's sagging bed. It was a single bed, the one he must've slept in since the war, its covers disarranged, the fusty sheets gone snuff-brown with age. In homage to the old man I tried to put on the loneliness of his posthumous existence; certainly I was no stranger to loneliness. But who was I kidding? Even lying there across his crumb-strewn bed flanked by the chimney-like stacks of books, I couldn't imagine what it was like to be Avrom. For that I would have had to enter his past as far as Avrom had retreated from it. I would have had to let go of a girlfriend I wanted to believe I would lay down my life for, even if she regarded me as no more than a curious detour on the way to marrying her lawyer.

It was in any case cozy in Avrom's back room with its rust-ringed washstand and cheesy odor. The toilet gurgled behind a paint-peeling door in imitation of the absent occupant's clotted breathing; the lightbulb with its squiggly filament dangled over the bed like a teardrop containing a tiny hanged man. There was an old Bakelite radio on a shelf above the bedstead. I switched it on to a staticky local station, which announced along with the news of Memphis State University's tournament loss to Tulane that Dr. Martin Luther King and members of his Southern Christian Leadership Conference were en route to the city. It's a mean-spirited, inhospitable town, Memphis, I imagined telling the reverend: be advised. Then I took up the book with its crimped spine and tatty binding, and opened it to the joker card I used for a marker.

In the Russian bathhouse on Jackson Avenue between North Main and Front, Saul Plesofsky, his gravid belly concealing his parts like an apron, was pouring another bucket of water over a red-hot topaz the size of a honeydew. Shimmying among the ghosts released in the outpouring steam, the zaftig Einhorn sisters began to lose their towels. Meanwhile Mr. Blen, leaning over his pharmacy counter, gave the dyspeptic Feivush Metzker, in lieu of the usual bicarb, a powder made from the horn of the ram caught in the thicket on Mount Moriah. In his optical shop around the corner Milton Chafetz was fitting the Widow Teitelbaum with a pair of spectacles whose lenses were ground from the Tzohar, the stone radiating the primordial light that preceded the creation of the sun. The glasses, Mr. Chafetz assured the widow, would allow her to see objects at a distance of five hundred years.

◢ 12 ◣
Before the Revolution

In time Muni Pinsker had become so accustomed to having his needs attended to—his latkes delivered, his chamber pot scrubbed and returned—that he seldom looked up from his writing. Had he bothered, he might have noticed that a cradle on curved wooden rockers had been placed in his little room, and in it an infant lay sleeping. Sometimes the baby would wake up bawling, and Muni might be briefly distracted from his scribbling. But since his chronicle also included the tale of a child born late to Pinchas and Katie Pin, its cries were largely absorbed into Muni's narrative—as much absorbed in the composition as they were calmed by the tender attentions of its parents. Lately Muni's scribbling had accelerated, which is not to say that the scribe anticipated the story's end: a story that took place simultaneously in parallel epochs could only be resolved in infinity. Besides, if he stopped telling stories about the street mired in timelessness, the lives that inspired those stories might be curtailed. Then the Pinch itself might no longer exist, or at best revert to what it used to be. Still, Muni's scribbling acquired momentum, his pen careening across the water-scalloped pages as if he were writing downhill. Though occasionally, when a baby's whimper or its mother's cooing caused him to lift his head from his work, he might think his project was sheer mishegoss.

Then Muni would shrug and resume his account of Hershel Tarnopol relating to the leaderless Shpinker Hasidim the revelations he'd received during his tenure in the belly of a fish. Not to be outdone, the Hasids boasted how they'd employed the seventy divine names to build an invisible bridge over the North Main Street lagoon. Muni chronicled how Mickey Panitz, a lonely bachelor, was baited into a wrestling match with an angel of a lower order, but when Mickey prevailed, the angel, a poor loser, refused to bless him. He was consoled, however, by the Widow Teitelbaum, who practiced on him seductions described to her in a dream by Potiphar's wife—techniques that happily succeeded with Mickey where they'd failed with Joseph. Meanwhile a klatch of North Main Street wives had inaugurated a Ouija craze, appropriating a high priest's Urim and Thummim for their oracle. There was the fad among the kids of raising murexes, the snail that produces the Tyrian purple for prayer shawls, whose trails graffitied the sidewalks in rococo designs. Mrs. Alperin administered a clyster filled with honey from a hive in the inverted tree to her husband, whose voidance stank thereafter of Paradise, and Mrs. Cohen sold out of her stock of a material so fine-spun that thirty yards of it could be concealed in the closed palm of one hand.

The seasons, like the years, were experienced as a palimpsest: the spring that the Anshe Mishneh Synagogue was converted to a nightclub coincided with the summer of the Confederate reunion; the winter evening the mob burned Ida B. Wells's printing press overlapped an afternoon when Elvis, his pegged pants upheld by a hairline belt, stepped out of Lansky's on Beale, and the first breeze of autumn failed to disturb a hair on his oleaginous head. There was the cloudy day in February when Lenny Sklarew (whoever he was) opened a book in a shop on Main Street and read a passage in which a guy named Lenny Sklarew opens a book in a shop on Main Street . . .

Muni recorded what was happening in the neighborhood and its environs, and what happened was whatever he wrote, or so he believed. Once, pausing to take a forkful of the potato boxty Katie had left beside his bed, he observed in the doorway a bowlegged toddler. The waddling child had, thankfully, his mother's face and auburn hair (crested a little like an orangutan's), and was waving a mother-of-pearl teething ring. Another time, shifting from his bed onto the chamber pot that Katie swabbed out each morning, Muni looked up to see an auburn-haired little boy in a Dutch suit staring back at him with starry eyes. He noted also that the thunder mug he hunkered over was putrid and filled to overflowing, and that his hair, which Katie had kept cropped short, was thick as turf and grown over his ears; his beard was bristly, his writing hand with its fingernails like pincers cramped to paralysis.

The pages of his narrative lay in a heap on the floor at the foot of the folding cot. They included, along with tales of the pharmacist Blen, the blacksmith Tarnopol, and the Widow Teitelbaum, the tale of the young Muni Pinsker—who once (Muni read from a random page scooped from the helter-skelter pile) sat in a latrine in Siberia where a frozen coprolite tickled his bony behind. This was the same Muni whose father (on pages yet undredged) had carried him as a tot wrapped in a lint-white tallis to the cheder run by Yozifel Glans, whom the students called Reb Death's Head. It was a horror, that little school, where the Death's Head wielded his quirt indiscriminately, as likely to punish the boys for their pride of accomplishment as their inattention. He flogged them doubly on Passover that they might know how the Israelites suffered under Pharaoh's lash. But against all odds Muni flourished there, conceiving a deep-felt affection for his alef-bais and proving himself a precocious scholar.

Shortly after his bar mitzvah he was sent to a more reputable cheder in the nearby market town of Tzachnovka—where he slept on the hard study house benches—and thence, after some years, to the far-famed yeshiva in Minsk. The yeshiva was located in the basement of the Water Carrier's Synagogue, where Rabbi Yeshayahu, the renowned Chazon Ish, was in residence. He was a very old man who sat stock-still at his lectern, his blood-rimmed eyes closed in meditation or sleep; no one was ever sure which. (Indeed, days passed when he seemed to show no vital signs.) But while the Chazon Ish gave little actual instruction, Muni was undiscouraged; still girded in the sanctity of his studies, he was inspired by the saint's venerable presence to delve ever deeper into the texts of the Law. It was also during this period that, half-starved and light-headed from his dependence on so-called eating days, the student was occasionally distracted from his exegesis of some halakhic perplexity. Then he would undertake to write sacred verses of his own, and sometimes, in the absence of a Death's Head to scourge his vanity, fancied himself a youthful David composing a cycle of original psalms.

Muni might have thrived indefinitely in that austere environment had it not been for his study mate, Yoysef Tsentsifer. Yoysef was a spindly lad with a pronounced Adam's apple and curly hair that lifted his skullcap as boiling water lifts a samovar lid, but his mole-gray eyes were fierce. He had a maddening habit of concealing socialist tracts behind a volume of the Bava Batra and, worst of all, making disparaging remarks about the

Chazon Ish. While he knew it was probably pointless to attempt to engage the youth in the kind of rapid-fire dialectics that defined the Talmudic method, Muni nevertheless felt duty-bound to try.

"According to Rabbi ben Yona in Tractate Hagigah," he might begin, "the chicken, since it does not chew its cud, ought to be considered un-kosher. So why does Rava insist in Tractate Avot that the bird is pareve, neither meat nor dairy?" But Yoysef would merely counter with un-answerable questions of his own: "What is the status in a minyan of a man born with the head of a toad? Why may you not share your prunes with a victim of gonorrhea?"

At length, addressing him above the hermeneutical drone of the acad-emy, Muni had asked his mate, "Yoysef, with all due respect, what are you doing here?"

Making as if to shuckel over a portion of scripture, Yoysef replied in a prayerful singsong, "I'm marking time till the revolution." Then he indi-cated with his downy chin their neighbor Naftali Blinken, who he said was doing the same. "In the meantime he operates for the Jewish Workers' Union an underground press. And Pesach Kvitko, him with his falling-down britches, he distributes pamphlets in the back alleys of the Bog when he's not studying Russian at night. Wolf Kipnis over there is organizing already in the factories, and little Anshel Twersky, that's tripping over his ritual fringes, belongs to the HaShomer Defense League and is preparing to make aliyah to Palestine . . ."

The litany continued until Muni was convinced that all his fellows were leading double lives; they merely used the yeshiva as a safe harbor while fo-menting the overthrow of the established order. Muni Pinsker was perhaps the only authentic student in the school. Yoysef promised he would have his guts for tefillin if Muni breathed a word of what he'd been told.

The awareness of his solitary lot, however, only contributed to Muni's sense of self-worth. It scarcely bothered him that, other than the exas-perating dialogues with his study mate, he had such scant commerce with his own kind. Loneliness and even the chastity that stoked his pimples and an irritation below the belt—these were conditions that further dra-matized the martyrdom to his studies, and could also be exploited to good advantage in fables and poems. (The current involved a wonder child who, following a recipe from Sefer Yetsirah, pours oil on water to consult with the sages of old.) Such was his hubris, in fact, that Muni believed his compositions had attained a level of accomplishment that demanded an audience. There were a number of Jewish presses in Minsk that published a variety of texts ranging from the fanatically religious to the outright blasphemous. But was his "work" really ready for a popular reception? After all, no eye but his own had ever viewed his productions. What he needed, Muni decided, was a reader he could trust, one who wouldn't simply flatter his efforts. Presenting his poems to the implacable Chazon Ish would be like placing an offering before a waxwork; nor did any of the rabbi's rigid assistants inspire confidence. Then Muni lit on the idea of showing his work to Yoysef Tsentsifer, who was as close to an intimate as he had in that dreary city. Yoysef would certainly have no qualms about giving him an honest appraisal.

Since Yoysef's attendance at the yeshiva was intermittent at best, several days elapsed before Muni encountered him outside the synagogue's recessed entrance. The Water Carriers' shul, as if embarrassed by its hulking stone eminence, appeared to be sinking below the level of the streets. It squatted on the edge of the central market, whose square on that unusually sunny morning was rowdy with hucksters, brokers, and market wives. Pigeons warbled, geese honked in their cages; a Cossack in a crimson tunic, saber flashing at his hip, plied the crowds astride a velvet-flanked stallion.

"Pardon me," Muni urbanely accosted his mate, "but would you mind taking a look at these?" He held out a nosegay of irregular pages.

Raising an inquisitive brow, Yoysef plucked a single leaf from the bunch, some of which fluttered free. Muni scrambled to retrieve them while assuring the other that he could read the work at his leisure, but Yoysef insisted on reading a few lines there and then. Having done so, he smiled a sidelong smile and returned the page to Muni. Then he took a stiff page of his own from inside his jerkin, unfolded it, and handed it to the poet. To himself Muni read:

> She saw it all and she's a living witness,
> The old gray spider spinning in the garret.
> She knows a lot of stories—bid her tell them!
> A story of a belly stuffed with feathers,
> Of nostrils and of nails, of heads and hammers,
> Of men, who, after death, were hung head downward,

Like these, along the rafter.
A story of a suckling child asleep,
A dead and cloven breast between its lips,
And of another child they tore in two,
And many, many more such stories
That beat about the head and pierce the brain,
And stab the soul within thee, does she know.

The tag at the bottom of the printed broadside identified the lines as an excerpt from Bialik's "City of Slaughter." Muni's heart was still thumping when he looked up questioningly from the verse.

"What's the matter, Pinsker?" asked Yoysef. "You never heard from Kishinev?"

Of course he'd heard of Kishinev, and Gomel and Durashna; massacres of Jews were nothing new under the sun. They were acts of God, were they not, and little could be done to deter them. "There have always been pogroms," Muni submitted, irked that his own verses had been so summarily dismissed. "They're eternal as"—he felt suddenly compelled to say—"the Covenant."

At that Yoysef laughed so heartily that he had to hang on to the bill of his cap. He made to turn away but, on second thought, hauled off and socked the young poet in the jaw.

Muni lay on the granite flags ogled by a fishwife or two, while a gust of wind disseminated the pages of his literary oeuvre. They wafted over cabbage bins and settled in baby carriages, one page plastering the face of a legless ikon artist until he scrunched it up in his fist. Not long after that Muni got word of a disturbance in his hometown of Blod. During Passover, fueled by the usual rumors of ritual murder and goaded by the police, the peasants had gone on a rampage. In a letter full of rhetorical flourishes composed by Reb Death's Head himself, the student was informed that his parents and sisters had suffered tragically at the hands of the barbarians. Estranged as he was from his family, Muni borrowed a few rubles from the academy fund and traveled to his native province. The wretched huddle of wooden houses that comprised the shtetl looked as if they'd been picked up in a whirlwind then dropped in a heap on the barren ground. Citizens were bandaged like mummies, leaning on pokers and hobbling in splints. Once arrived, Muni discovered that his younger sister, Puah Lippe, had been defiled before the eyes of his mother, who'd lost her wits. His hapless father had been missing since the outbreak of the violence, but on the very eve of Muni's return his body was found fermenting in a barrel of kvass.

It wasn't until sometime after he'd returned to Minsk that Muni began to succumb to pangs of conscience. Hadn't he been a fundamentally dutiful son? He had after all sat shivah for his father and helped facilitate his burial; he'd assisted his big sister, Zilpah, in installing his unstrung mother and her younger daughter in a Dubrovna asylum run by the Society for the Poor and Sick. But while he assured himself he'd done all in his power, that his responsibilities were faithfully discharged, Muni was unable to resume his studies with his former equanimity. He tried meditating on the words from *The Pomegranate of Ibn Zimri*: "The Torah is fulfilled only by one who offers his life for it"; instead he brooded over reports that a handful of Jews in Olevsk—teamsters, patch tailors, a glazier, a clerk— had taken up clubs to defend themselves, only to be shot by soldiers from the local garrison for attacking the attackers. He attempted a midrash on the occupations of the Messiah while He tarried in the Palace of the Bird's Nest, but the exercise seemed frivolous to him now. He could hardly concentrate, and, improbable though it seemed, he missed his study mate, who'd been truant since his return. There were topics he would have liked to discuss with Yoysef.

Muni looked for him in the narrow streets where conversations among the laborers grew hushed whenever he passed by. He crossed an iron footbridge over the open sewer of the Svisloch River into the teeming Bitza District at dusk. Soot from the tanneries and sugar refineries blanketed the crooked passages in black snow; rank perfumes mingled with the odors of boiling noodles and pitch. Ladies with unspooled hair, wearing wrappers like draggled fog, beckoned from eroded doorways. University students, themselves on strike in sympathy with the conditions of the factory workers, loitered in the noisy courtyards and teahouses. It was among them that Muni eventually located Yoysef Tsentsifer, seated at a table in a seamy tavern—the first Muni had ever entered—along with both male and female comrades.

"Look at what the red heifer dragged in," greeted Yoysef with his trademark mixture of antagonism and mirth. The pretty girl at his side yawned like a cat, then winked at the tense newcomer. "Nu, Reb Pinsker, what can we do for you?"

In the first instance Muni didn't know; then he did. "You can tell me how to volunteer for the Jewish Labor Bund."

◢ 13 ◣
The *Floating Palace*

A drunk in a shabby mackintosh stumbles from the audience into the sand-and-sawdust ring. The ringmaster, attired in white jodphurs and scarlet tailcoat, is announcing through his bullhorn the high-wire act of Mademoiselle La Funambula. He's visibly disturbed by the intrusion of an inebriated member of the audience, who's pantomiming his desire to perform. The crowd of nearly a thousand in the floating amphitheater is confused but entertained by the unscripted trespass. The ringmaster tries to shoo him away, but the drunk lingers on the margin, leaning against then grabbing hold of a guy wire attached to a platform high above the ring. As the ringmaster continues his spiel, the intuder swings onto the cable and manages by clumsy degrees to mount it, wobbling and lurching in a bungling attempt to maintain his balance. Alerted by the laughter of the audience, the ringmaster turns about and blows his whistle. A pair of burly roustabouts come running in to grab the drunk before he does himself an injury. They bob for his ankles, but kicking and squirming, the man evades his would-be captors and continues his lubberly progress beyond their reach. Ringmaster, roustabouts, and audience are helpless to do anything but watch the fool in his reckless ascent up the inclined cable. There's a universal intake of breath as the man pitches frantically to and fro, losing items of his wardrobe—the mackintosh, the porkpie hat—in the process. Then somehow he's managed to gain the platform some forty feet above the ring, where he sheds the rest of his garments and shakes out a head of crow-black hair to reveal the lithe form of La Funambula in spangled tights. The crowd goes wild.

She proceeds to cavort on the wire, returning to the platform for various props—a unicycle, a pair of stilts—while far beneath her two men and a gargantuan lady position themselves to spot her in case she falls.

The three of them compete for the ideal placement, though no one pays them much attention, all eyes riveted on the girl prancing in the amber followspot.

She skipped rope, turned cartwheels, and somersaulted through a tasseled hoop. Children gawked and women covered their eyes, peeping through parted fingers; godly men expressed shock at the briefness of her costume, then surrendered to fantasies. Journalists penned tired bromides—"she's more a creature of the air than the earth"—and cited the dramatic contrast between the grace of her aerial daring and the limp she exhibited as she plodded out of the ring. And it was true that, capering above the upturned faces, she was beyond the reach of memory and heartbreak, always just a giant circle away from a total liberation from the terrestrial sphere. But Jenny Bashrig had no wish to liberate herself. Like the poet that the sad clown had read aloud to her, she was less in love with the products of eternity than of time.

Not that the circus had much in common with ordinary time. Plying the river from Dubuque to New Orleans, Forepaugh & Broadway's Floating Carnival of Fun weighed anchor at towns fixed to the regular calendar. But after a run of no more than three days in any designated port of call, the circus was launched again like the Flying Dutchman in a perpetual navigation of the Mississippi. The river flowed and the towns stood still along its banks, where time passed, while the river remained impervious to its passage. For Jenny, the equilibrist, this was a fine arrangement, the balance between rolling river and stationary shore, a state of affairs much more preferable than, say, a North Main Street stuck in its everlasting chronological rut. She'd become adept at observing the bluff reefs, falling chutes, and shoals, and could interpret what lay beneath dangerous dimples on the surface of the water as well as the roustabouts that doubled as deckhands. Her fondness for riding the river was rivaled only by her excitement on disembarking at the cities and towns, when the entire company, mounted on horses, elephants, velocipedes, and a thundering calliope, paraded through streets thronged with rubbernecking locals. She liked sampling the bazaars of places with names like Festus and Andalusia, places not always welcoming to circus folk. Over time her sea legs had become steadier than were her same halting limbs on dry land,

and the wire was never so compliant as when she felt the slap and sway of the *Palace* in its watery berth.

Of course the great floating extravaganza had seen better days. The old packet boat that towed the barge and menagerie behind it was in a constant state of disrepair; its kingposts, hogchains, and stern wheel had been replaced so many times that the vessel could no longer qualify as the original *Yellow Wren*. (Defaced by weather or wags, the name painted across its bow now read *Yellow W en*.) While it still maintained a few showy staterooms for its principals, the *Yellow Wen* seemed to anticipate its own wreckage: the plush banquettes had long since given up their stuffing, the gingerbread trim broken off to feed the high-pressure engine when fuel ran low. The ancient boiler pulsed like a dilated heart; pistons sputtered and would have come to a shuddering halt were it not for the occasional nudge from a passing bum boat. The grand saloon was converted to a mess hall, where performers practiced their juggling and the less carnivorous beasts—the ones not confined to the trailing menagerie scow—roamed free. Excluding the bedlam, however, when viewed from a levee at night, the moonlit Carnival of Fun in its musical progress constituted a siren-like tableau, luring small-town boys to swim out after it and sometimes drown.

Jenny had never meant to outshine her partners. After all, the Piccolomini Brothers—not really brothers but comrades involved with one another in a way Jenny didn't at first understand—had voluntarily taken her under their wing. Impressed with her natural ability, they helped develop her talents until she was equally proficient on the bounding wire and the tightrope. Dubbing her Mimi Piccolomini, they broadened their repertoire to accommodate her, introducing various properties: unicycles and stilts. But Jenny, a quick study and already accomplished after her years of self-taught endeavor, soon surpassed the skill of her mentors and, without trying, upstaged them. Finally the Piccolominis, complaining of chronic seasickness, took their injured vanity and left the Carnival of Fun at Vidalia for a spot in a circus that thankfully traveled overland.

After that Jenny retired Mimi and, graduated now to center ring, carried on solo as La Funambula, Mistress of the Air. There were other mistresses of the air: Rosa Bunch in her hourglass corset, spinning like a whirligig from her swivel loop, and Yvette, who hung from a single trap by her fuchsia hair. Each regarded herself as a prima in her own right and in that capacity snubbed all other claimants to the title. La Funambula was snubbed as a matter of course, but never wholly integrated into the circus community, she was spared much of the usual venom. In any event, so preoccupied was Jenny with the demands of her midair ballet that she scarcely noticed the cold shoulders she received on the ground.

Marital status notwithstanding, the lordly ladies of the floating circus each had her circle of admirers, sometimes several at a single destination. The sons of senators and cotton barons showered their favorites with flowers and bonbons after every show. Heated competition among these young gallants sometimes moved them to fistfights and even duels, outrages that translated into boasting rights for the ladies in question. Naturally the young men gave their offerings in the hope of receiving favors in return, and while a few of the ladies did reciprocate amorously, all were deft at keeping their suitors at bay. Such artful teasing, however, only increased the tensions that stoked the disorderly atmosphere of the *Yellow Wen*, and many an embarkation was marked by jealous husbands flinging bouquets and bijouterie overboard.

Jenny, who shared tight quarters with Madame Hortense the Female Hercules, had no room for housing her own gifts, the loving cups and potted viburnums she gave away to the sideshow performers. She had no more need of tchotchkes than of romance, the pain of which she had not the least wish to repeat. Besides, Madame Hortense (whose weightlifting apparatus increased the steamboat's draft by a foot) had conceived a maternal fondness for the wirewalker, and as Jenny's self-appointed protector kept the predators at arm's length.

It was the last of its kind, the Carnival of Fun, a relic from the days when showboats featured canebrake troupers in temperance comedies like *Ten Nights in a Bar-Room*. While nearly every other touring company or tent show had taken to the rails, Forepaugh and Broadway persisted in the novelty of their riverborne spectacle. With hyperbolic publicity and the promise of shared profits they'd lured a boatload of bally broads, kinkers, and clowns on board the *Wen* and the *Palace* that followed in its wake. Later on, as the carnival evolved into an authentic circus, first-class animal and aerial acts were added to the ranks. But in the end, for all its variety the floating "argosy of wonders" was a losing proposition. Salaries aside, the maintenance of the porous packet absorbed the lion's share (sometimes literally) of the season's revenue, and even the draw of a loop-the-looping automobile could barely compensate for the cost of steam-heating the amphitheater. To say nothing of the repairs to damage caused by the river itself—the fogs that led to collisions with driftwood, the runnings aground on islands and sandbars. There were medical bills due to accidents and injuries incurred in attacks by the natives of the towns where they played. No matter that the circus went to excessive lengths to convince the yokels of the show's inherent morality, going so far as to label the menagerie living relics from biblical times: the hippopotamus was "the blood-sweating Behemoth of Holy Writ," and so forth. Let there be a rumor of godless fornicators among the troupe, and the citizens, under the influence of sanctimony and drink, would rise up to punish the heathen. This was especially the case south of the Mason-Dixon Line, where the show people were often assumed to be of a debased Yankee persuasion. Then pitched battles would ensue, when the company had to defend themselves with guy stakes against knives and firearms.

Nor were the townspeople always satisfied with directing their malevolence toward the human performers. There were the boys that threw pepper between the bars of the gorilla's cage or fed plug tobacco to the black bear. There was the time in Morganza, Louisiana, when Celeste the elephant, spooked by urchins who poked a broom in her hindquarters, bolted from the parade and crushed an alderman's wife underfoot. When the town demanded vengeance, the circus had no recourse but to bow to public sentiment. Perfectly tractable now, Celeste was led by the bull handlers to the railyard, where a seven-eighth-inch chain was wrapped round her neck and she was hoisted into the air from a railroad derrick. The chain snapped and Celeste fell to earth in a stupor but made no resistance as a second chain was secured. When she was raised again, she sighed, died, and in keeping with the age-old protocol of lynchings, was dismembered, her bones and tusks displayed as trophies in the courthouse and barbershop.

As a first-of-May performer (and a Jew), Jenny was no stranger to the role of intruder. What bothered her more was the clamorous adoration of her fans, which could throw off her timing. For even a run-down riverboat exhibition was hailed by the rustics, starved as they were for entertainment, as heaven-sent. (Never mind that its artists might be judged pariahs from hell.) As La Funambula, who danced on a rope woven from a witch's hair in the caverns of the djinn—or so claimed the ringmaster, Mr. Ephraim Peavey—she was viewed as a magical creature, and courted accordingly by hayseeds and gentry alike. What jerkwater Galahad wouldn't want to pluck the sylph in her chiffon kilt out of the air and fetch her back to terra firma for a souvenir? (Even if on earth she was a bit of a klutz.) But Jenny had no truck with magic: the wire was the wire, the earth the earth, or anyway the promenade deck of a coal-belching steamboat. Unlike the ethereal La Bunch and Yvette of the iron jaw, who held court in their staterooms, she was content to hobnob with Madame Hortense in their stuffy cabin. There the lightly mustachioed strongwoman would read her tarot cards and massage her feet, which were always sore. (The thin doeskin pumps that allowed her toes to grope and steer along the cold-drawn steel left her soles sensitive to the sharpness of the wire.) At home with marginal types, she cultivated the company of various ten-in-one oddities, some with topknots and plates in their lips, a fraternization that consolidated her outlier status.

So Jenny enjoyed the best of two worlds. Though Mr. Peavey might assure the audience that the upper atmosphere was her exclusive element, it wasn't. True, there was nothing quite like a romp on the wire; few planetary pleasures matched the rapture of executing a midair flifus or one-wing crab. But Jenny took similar solace in reclining in a canvas deck chair watching the children and diapered chimps swarming over the boat. She liked observing the kingfishers perched on a floating bough: how they scattered like roof shingles flung by the wind when the paddle wheel walked over their perch with a crunching racket. During nights that the rousters said were dark as the inside of a cow, they passed timber rafts and coal barges, vessels visible only by the light of their bull's-eye lanterns, and by lantern light Jenny conned the poetry that Bonkers the clown was teaching her to read. Above the ring she suffered the yearning of her admirers below, though she remained proof against their overtures even when they belonged to her own touring caste.

He had christened himself Bonkers in an ironic counterpoint to his melancholy mien. During the specs, when the clowns disported themselves about the ring en masse, he wore a chimney-pot hat and tattered swallowtails like some ruined aristocrat, which in point of fact he was. His original name was Marmaduke Fortinbras Armbrewster the Somethingth, black sheep offspring of the potted meat Armbrewsters of Davenport, Iowa. Cut off without a sou after his expulsion from Princeton, he'd discovered in himself a talent for confidence swindles; but when his face became too familiar to the local constabularies in the river towns where he plied his trade, he boarded a steamboat hauling a cargo of gaudy misrule. He exaggerated his decadent pallor with greasepaint, accentuated the soot-gray bags under his eyes (from one of which leaked a diamond tear), and donned a sponge rubber nose. While his detractors (and there were many) claimed he'd merely swapped one bogus identity for another, the more sympathetic believed that in Bonkers the young wastrel had found his true nature.

As it turned out, he had an aptitude for clowning. Athletic despite his dissipation, he incorporated complicated pratfalls into his gags; he climbed ladders that leaned against invisible walls and, during the walkarounds, carried a board on his head that remained fixed even as he reversed direction. But what made him a favorite with the crowds was his acquisition of a mangy goat he'd won in a crap game from a farmer in Vicksburg who'd already forfeited his shirt. He called the goat Medea and claimed she was a sorceress transformed by a rival into a unicorn. (She had, projecting from her shaggy forehead, a single off-center horn.) Bonkers was seldom seen without Medea, who nipped at his backside during his act and employed her horn in rude ways to impede his progress—this to the shock and delight of the audience. But outside the ring the goat was as brooding and aloof as her master. There was even something menacing about her that caused the circus folk to keep their distance and the big cats to recoil in their cages. Tethered to the pipes on the boiler deck, Medea would bleat disconsolately throughout Bonkers's all-night larks ashore, from which he returned in the mornings weak-kneed and ruddy-eyed.

Perhaps it was her own detachment in the midst of such knockabout company that drew Bonkers to Jenny Bashrig. Or was it the challenge of breaching her self-possession? Owing to his doleful eyes and buttery tongue, he was accustomed to easy conquests, but Jenny seemed immune to his charms. When he learned she was unlettered, however, the clown may have thought he'd hit upon a source of vulnerability and offered to school her. Jenny's watchdog, Madame Hortense, was skeptical, having lately seen ominous signs in her tarot spread.

"Your Star, which is among the greater secrets, is crossed by your Magician card (sometimes called the Juggler), and the Wheel of Fortune is in opposition to your trump card, known as the Fool . . ."

"What are you talking about?" asked Jenny, who'd already advanced from the *Whiskers and Wagtail Primer* to a poem that Bonkers had translated himself. It was written, he alleged, by a French poet under the influence of opium.

In answer to Jenny's question Madame Hortense, whose relation to cartomancy was purely instinctual, had to admit that she really hadn't a clue.

Nevertheless, when she wasn't playing footsie with Professor Hotspur (whose pygmy elephants she lifted above her head in her act), the stronglady kept a weather eye out for anyone or thing that might endanger the equilibrist. This included the danger of falling from the wire, beneath which she took up her self-assigned station during Jenny's cynosure turns. Still wearing the full Wagnerian regalia from her own act, she would stand in the darkened ring far below the girl in the dancing amber spot. She was often joined there by a loitering Bonkers and his goat, though the latter was clearly impatient with her master's vigils. To this unallied company was eventually added another, a more furtive figure in top boots and flared trousers, who—while he lingered on the ring's perimeter—was nonetheless braced for any mishap.

The third party was Lem Kelso, whose nom de guerre was Captain Cumberbund, though he'd be the first to admit he wasn't any kind of a captain. A trainer of wild animals who could face down a Burmese panther with perfect aplomb, he was pathologically shy of the ladies. In consequence the ladies took every opportunity to tease the tow-haired lion "tamer" (who would assure you the beasts could be trained but never tamed), flaunting their attractions in ways guaranteed to raise a cardinal blush on the young man's cheeks. The blush would persist like hives for days, embarrassing him so that he kept to his berth on the menagerie scow. He was in any case more comfortable in the company of his cats and beyond the allure of the women, who were to his thinking a puffed up and immodest lot. Then Jenny Bashrig arrived with her infernal blend of earth and air, and the lion tamer was entranced; while for her part, Jenny, a connoisseur of every variety of daredevil, was largely indifferent to the animal acts.

He'd hired on to the Carnival of Fun as a candy butcher and might have remained content in that role, such a far cry from digging potatoes on a dirt farm. But always fond of animals, he offered his assistance to Giacomo Bondi, the cat man, and quickly progressed from being useful to indispensable. Bondi styled himself a member of the school of "bring 'em back alive" white hunters, whose every encounter with jungle beasts was staged as a life-and-death conflict. He was liberal in his use of the bullwhip and viewed his act as a demonstration of the power of his will over that of the brutes in his charge. He was also a drunk whose cruelty extended beyond the ring, so that his sullen animals smoldered in their resentment. Then it wasn't wholly unexpected when, audaciously sticking his head for the thousandth time between the jaws of a Bengal tiger, he emerged without it.

In the succeeding mayhem young Lemuel presented himself as not only prepared to take over the care and feeding of the cats, but ready to exhibit them in a caged act as well. He'd closely observed his mentor's methods and learned from his example everything that one ought not to do. Given the go-ahead—as what choice did management have?—he set about culling the broken animals from the spirited, overseeing the sale of the "seat warmers" to zoos. Having picked the brain and plundered the medicine chest of the resident vet, he ministered to the ailing and abused: he dosed Oliver the costive Nubian lion with an aloes physic, then borrowed a shovel from an elephant handler to remove the results, and he nearly lost a finger rubbing cocaine on Ethelred the tiger's toothachey gums. In teaching them tricks he substituted reward for punishment, and was sensitive to his critters' mercurial moods. He nursed their offspring with warmed bottles when a mother's milk ran dry. For having turned a brood of sulky and unpredictable felines into a pride of obedient beasts, Lem Kelso was dubbed Lancelot Cumberbund by Ringmaster Peavey, and promoted from fairy floss peddler to captain of the cats. He still carried the whip and pistol into the circular cage, but an occasional flick of the wrist was sufficient to signal a lion to fake an assault, and the blanks in the revolver (which the animals were used to) made a crowd-pleasing bang. Such confidence did Captain Cumberbund demonstrate in the cage that his bashful countenance outside it made him something of a figure of fun. That and the general suspicion that he was a virgin.

Of Lem Kelso's leering after Jenny, Madame Hortense was distinctly aware, but she regarded him as harmless. Bonkers, however, with his marked-for-death demeanor and his distempered unicorn that even the lion tamer steered clear of, was another story. Though he was courtly in his manner toward the rope walker, no one would have mistaken his intentions as honorable. Kneeling beside her deck chair to help her with difficult words as she read, he practically singed her cheeks and throat with his hot absinthe breath, while Medea took unforbearing bites out of his pant legs. The Malay tumblers would cluck their tongues as they flip-flopped past, and even the india rubber man shook his attenuated head. No one, it seemed, trusted the dissolute clown with the delicate usage of a featured headliner.

Irrespective of the educational benefits, Jenny was amused by the boozy Bonkers, judging his overdone declamations—"The worm is in the fruit!" "Il pleure dans mon coeur!"—as mere affectation. She took his advances no more to heart than the scraps of news that now and then reached the Carnival of Fun. Pancho Villa's insurgents might kill American passengers on a train in northern Mexico, German U-boats sink American merchant vessels, an anarchist take a potshot at J. P. Morgan—such things happened in places moored to history, whereas the *Yellow Wen* was adrift in time; it flowed with the river, having escaped the depredations that landlocked society was heir to.

Still, Jenny had her moods when she wondered if she'd only swapped one population of loose screws for another. And at night in her berth across from the volcanically snoring Female Hercules, she dreamed dreams that were an antidote to an excess of pageantry. Such as the recurring one in which the circus wintered in a decayed urban ghetto. Then she would wake to the strange sensation that the dream belonged not to her but someone else. She felt similarly remote from Madame Hortense's relentless attempts at playing sibyl with her cards.

"The good news," Madame H. had ruminated one morning over the current constellation, "you got Strength in your astral influence; that's the card with Samson coldcocking a lion. But you got also Lightning in the place of your final outcome . . ."

Upon which Jenny clapped her hands over her ears. "Sweet mieskayt, enough! Please spare me your predictions. This is the circus: there's no past or future, only the here and now. Anyhow, I'm not a child; I can take care of myself."

But the stronglady was not appeased. Mother hen that she was, she warned her cabinmate, even as she massaged her instep, that her cavalier attitude in regard to the clown was driving him, well, bonkers; she was playing with fire.

"Fire," pronounced Jenny, who'd learned the habit of uttering sphinx-like phrases from the clown, "is my element."

Madame Hortense groaned and nearly pinched Jenny's foot in two between her thumb and forefinger.

"Ouch!"

"You watch yourself, girlie," admonished the stronglady, tucking her massive hands into her cavernous armpits, while outside their compartment the windjammers could be heard rehearsing "The Battle of Shiloh." The music was augmented by a chorus of bleats, brays, and howls from the menagerie, the whole clamor muted in the shoosh of the paddle wheel.

To her list of worries on behalf of the equilibrist, Madame H. added her anxiety over Jenny's unconcern for the superstitions that were de rigueur among the aerialists. (If someone patted you on the back, you must then be patted on the stomach; you must never place a costume on the bed . . .) As a consequence she made it her business to look out for the girl. In her helmet, brass bra, and leather girdle, Madame Hortense stood beneath the wire in the center ring, flanked by a pony act in one end ring and a human pyramid in the other. There she received the shabby clothes the drunk shed on his way to becoming La Funambula, clad in sequined lamé. The stronglady also endured, in the same ring, the presence of Bonkers the clown, seated astride his mock unicorn, and the lion tamer lurking at the margins.

But Jenny seldom faltered. She executed full gainers with flawless precision from the pedestal to the wire, threw herself backward through a crepe-papered hoop; she did a running forward somersault, the most perilous feat in the rope-walker's playbook, because your feet must lead the arc over your head and find the wire before you can see where to place them. It was during such a leap on a particularly sultry evening that the rigging slipped, staggering La Funambula's velocity, so that when her feet struck the wire, her momentum thrust her forward into the netless air.

Forty feet below, Madame Hortense was braced to receive the falling body in her arms, nor did the other watchers stand idly by. Goaded by a boot heel to her flank, Medea bolted forward with her rider as the lion tamer lunged from the ring curb. The stronglady, knocked from her formidable pins by the goat, toppled onto the clown, whose mount was then flattened beneath the combined weight of its rider, the doughty madame, and the madly scrambling Captain Cumberbund. Tucking in the nick of time, the plummeting equilibrist landed hard amid the scrum of her would-be rescuers, and rolled off into a balletic stance amazingly unharmed. She took a bow and made her exit with a spring in her limp, while the stunned crowd remained silent, uncertain as to whether the event called for laughter or cheers.

Risen to her buskined feet, Madame Hortense was enraged by the ineptitude of the rival spotters, whom she snatched up in either hand and flung into the stands. The goat, realizing that her single horn was no match for the pair on the stronglady's helmet, retreated of her own accord.

The tale of La Funambula's plunge became legend, increasing her popularity, which increased in kind the jealousy among her fellow artists. Although it had been an accident, they tended to view her tumble as a further attempt to grab the spotlight from her competition. Even Madame Hortense remained grumpy about the incident, as if Jenny were to blame for her public humiliation.

"It's a good thing you got knocked over," Jenny cajoled her, "or I'd've been spit on the tusks of your pointy cap."

Unamused, the stronglady moped and began to spend more time in the company of her sometimes paramour Professor Hotspur, his gaunt frame reduced to skeletal from the pressures of their association. Her absence from Jenny's side left the field open to the advances of the clown, who observed to her in his mellifluous voice, "So your giantess no longer discourages Bonkers's oily solicitations?" He liked referring to himself in the third person.

Jenny was sitting with her feet propped up on the taffrail, while the clown leaned against it, the wind riffling his spiky hair, his wretched goat chewing peevishly at his bootlace. "It's Marmaduke Armbrewster's the oily one," she replied, because she was fond of him in her fashion. "Bonkers is just a big bluffer." Though on second thought: "Madame H. still thinks you're a rat."

Bonkers dug a hand in the pocket of his swallowtails and insisted he was misunderstood. "Doom knows no reprieve," he declared, producing a cruet of laudanum from which—popping the cork—he stagily took a sip, "but love."

"So tell me they ain't stuck on you, Sasha Groszniak the foot juggler and Birdy Valentine of the revolving ladder . . ." For it was the case that a suite of ladies fawned over the world-weary clown, while Jenny remained the primary object of his affection.

"O Death," he intoned, "pour your poison to revive my soul," extending his tongue to catch the last drops from the cruet, *gulp*, "careless if hell or heaven is our goal . . ." When Jenny had to snicker at his high-sounding bathos, Bonkers mimed indignation. "Your mirth retards my evil designs," he accused.

The girl issued an insincere apology.

"O Jenny," rallied the clown, wringing his hands in their overlarge gloves, "your breasts against watered silk are like a gorgeous armoire . . ."

The girl tilted her head toward the barely convex bodice of her shirt-waist. "It's percale," she said, and snickered again. She did, however, remove her feet from the rail and rearrange her skirts, having become self-conscious of her exposed petticoat.

Not as tickled by Bonkers's inveigling, however, was Captain Cumber-bund, who eavesdropped from a nearby companionway. It was whispered about among those who heeded such things—and the *Wen* was a seething gossip mill—that the clown's effrontery enflamed the Captain, not only for the liberties he took but also for the boldness he demonstrated in doing so. Because Lem Kelso's own obsession with the wirewalker had yet to lend him the courage to confront her with his suit. This was the same lion tamer at the crack of whose whip four-hundred-pound jungle cats would rear up and walk on their hind legs, balance on mirror balls, and leap through flaming hoops. Kismet, Sennacherib, Carmen of the basilisk eye and brindled fur, they even made as if to maul him, which was all part of the act; and afterward, when they'd been rolled back in their cages down the ramp onto the menagerie scow, the Captain would hand-feed them gobs of beef heart, snuggling and confiding in them his devotion to the marvelous girl.

One afternoon, at a moment of what in his anguish he must have mistaken for clarity, Captain Cumberbund donned his predecessor's ascot and removed one of Carmen's suckling tiger cubs from its cage. With perhaps the intention of making a gift of it to the wirewalker, he carried the feisty little creature over the gangplanks that connected the scow to the *Palace* and the *Palace* to the *Yellow Wen*. Along the way the children of the Flying Saragossas and the Royal Stamboul Rola-Bolas, the alligator children from the ten-in-one, left off their marauding to follow him. All sought an opportunity to pet the infant tiger with its foxglove ears and outsize paws. By the time he arrived at the steamboat's upper deck, the Captain's progress had been slowed to a standstill, beset as he was by the sons and daughters of the circus. It was all he could do to hold on to the squirming whelp and keep it from being wrested from his hands.

Leaving her cabin on her way to rehearse, La Funambula caught sight of the lion tamer and paused. Tightening the cord at the waist of her robe, she spared him a curious glance—a sightly young man in a pith helmet festooned with children—and was rather touched; while he, in the midst of the mob, lifted the tiger cub like an offering above his head beyond the reach of the pawing brats.

At that instant the boat was passing a stand of liveoak on the riverbank. Perched in their moss-hung branches was a party of harpy eagles, one of which was moved to take flight. Swooping down between the smokestacks and over the hurricane deck, it snagged the cub by its nape with barbed talons and tore it from the upraised hand of Captain Cumberbund. There was total silence among the children and their elders standing in the shadow of the eagle's wings—which flapped twice as the bird glided with its dangling prey above the trees on the shore. Not until it had shrunk to a spot against the sun then disappeared was the silence broken by Lem Kelso's sobs.

There were portents besides the bird and the Burning Tower that turned up in Madame Hortense's tarot readings. Awesome Arnold the human cannonball overshot the net and broke his neck. The surcingle came loose while Lady Equipoise was performing Mazeppa's Ride and she slipped from the rump of her Arabian with her foot caught in a stirrup. The horse made five circuits of the ring with its rider's cracked-open head throttling the curb before a shivaree of clowns were able to subdue it. The *Yellow Wen* docked at Rock Island, Buena Vista, and Prairie du Chien, and La Funambula continued to enthrall the spectators on her silver thread, thrilling them with near misses caused by the involuntary recollection of troubling dreams. In the interim Captain Cumberbund continued to eat his heart out over Jenny, its bitterness feeding his resentment of the degenerate clown.

Those who kept watch on the watcher said that the Captain's ears steamed at the sight of Bonkers and Jenny together, though so far no open unpleasantness had transpired between them. The clown declaimed his verses, whose words ("O rancid night of the skin, you have kissed my buttocks in your covert conspiracy!") may have sounded to the lion tamer like indecent proposals; and the fits of tittering those words provoked in the wirewalker were perhaps more galling than if they'd aroused her desire. There must have been times when the Captain came close to intervening. What a simple matter for a master of savage beasts to vanquish a mere buffoon. Was it an apprehension of how unwelcome his interference might be that stopped him? Or was it a morbid fear of Bonkers's goat? With an Abyssinian lion you were more or less sure of where you stood, but who knew what contagions that one-horned deformity might carry? (Never mind that, in her petulant nudgings and bleatings, Medea appeared to view the liaison between the aerialist and the clown as unfavorably as did the lion tamer himself.)

Meanwhile Captain Cumberbund was looking much the worse for wear. From loss of sleep and appetite his cerulean eyes were sunken, his straw hair beginning to molt, flared trousers drooping from his spare flanks like hound dogs' ears. In the cage his attitude alternated between recklessness and lethargy. Scarcely bothering to incite the cats to their sham aggression, he sometimes allowed them to nuzzle him like house pets, revealing the danger as only illusion. On those occasions the Captain was roundly booed by the crowd.

He watched the girl in the air, haloed in limelight, and saw an angel; watched the clown hanging on to the tail of a liberty horse while the goat rode the tails of his coat, and saw a devil that needed harrying back to the pit. "If I can't have her," he was heard to say to his cats, whose baritone growling may have echoed the Lord's own approval, "can't nobody else." Then on a windy night somewhere between Wabasha and Winona, he came upon the two of them on the afterdeck; he heard the girl scream as the clown threw his coat over her head as if to abduct her, and something in him snapped.

They'd been reading a slender volume of poetry together, or rather Bonkers had been reading to Jenny in French. The book was an *en face* edition and the clown, in his absorption, seemed less concerned with seducing the equilibrist than refining her sensibilities. Bending over her chair, he invited her to follow on the left-hand in English the despondent lyric he was reading in the original on the right-hand page. Jenny, however, was paying scant attention to either the written or spoken words. She was fatigued after a trying week that had involved her oversight of the repair of the flying frame and the dead man's rigging; she'd done double-duty, performing her matinee and evening turns then reappearing in the Babylonian-themed blow-off. So it was good to be voyaging again between stands; the brisk weather at this northernmost extremity of the Carnival of Fun's circuit suited her. She enjoyed the rhythmic rocking of the packet over the choppy river, the way clouds slid across the face of the moon like gauzy tights pulled from the globe of a lamp. And the drone of the clown's lugubrious voice in a foreign tongue was a fitting antithesis to the martial air of the brass band rehearsing "Billy Barlow" in the saloon.

Their evening ritual was something that, in truth, the girl had come to look forward to, and even Madame Hortense had learned to live with it—especially since Bonkers seemed to have decided it suited him better to languish for want of Jenny than to actually have her. (He was anyway consoled by a bevy of others.) Though lanterns abounded on board the *Wen,* he preferred to read by the light of a votary candle, but the wind tonight was too whipped up for the candle to hold a flame. So he kept striking matches, one after another.

"Votre âme est un paysage choisi," he read, signally twitching the rubber nose he'd yet to remove. Then noting Jenny's inattention, he construed, "It means you're a blowzy baggage."

Jarred momentarily out of her reverie, Jenny leaned her head toward the book to verify the translation, and as a consequence a loose strand of her hair was ignited by the match in the clown's cupped hand.

"O for a muse of fire!" cried Bonkers as he tore off his ragpicker's tailcoat and threw it over Jenny's flailing head.

It was then that the lion tamer, having just emerged from a hatch, was unhinged by what he saw and charged blindly forward onto the deck. With a roar that rivaled the window-rattling vibrato of his cats, the Captain locked his arms around the clown's midsection, and lifting him bodily, dragged the kicking Bonkers across the afterdeck and flung him over the railing into the foaming turbulence of the revolving paddle wheel. He turned around triumphantly, perhaps expecting the girl he'd rescued to run gratefully into the safety of his arms, but was met instead by Medea the goat who gored him in the calf with her single horn. As he bent to

clutch at the searing pain of his injured leg, the Captain was further battered by Madame Hortense, who hammered him to the deck with a closed
fist on her way to save the clown. Fresh from an assignation with Professor
Hotspur, she was wearing her marquee-sized kimono, which billowed to
reveal her ambiguous anatomy as she climbed over the rail.

Risen from her chair with her still smoking hair in wild disarray, Jenny
Bashrig looked on with a sinking heart. But distressed as she was on behalf of Bonkers, she was more aggrieved by the realization that, despite
his peril, the forlorn clown had never seemed to her entirely real.

Other members of the troupe, responding to Madame Hortense's "Hey
Rube!," vaulted over the rail from the texas deck and tumbled out of the
galleries. Apprised of the situation, they clambered out along timbers and
spars, though whether they meant to save the clown or simply get a better
view of his plight was uncertain. Kinkers and joeys, Hector the globe-of-
death rider, Dainty Nell the Elastic Incomprehensible—all perched in the
blustering winds on either side of the turning wheel, waiting along with
the stronglady for the blades to complete their revolution and end the
clown's forced baptism. The gibbous moon spilled mercury like a burst
thermometer, the band in the saloon played "Over the Waves," and up
popped the sodden Bonkers seated on a wooden bucket at the height of
the paddle wheel. He was reciting verses above the churning propulsion:
"Let him mark well who laughs at my despair," he cried, pulling a catfish
from the bosom of his shirt, sniffing it with his rubber nose before tossing
it over a shoulder, "with no fraternal shudder in reply." From a capacious
pocket he extracted an apple that squirted him in the eye before he could
take a bite. "Every moon is atrocious, every sun bitter; the flesh, alas, is
sad, and I have read . . ."

As the clown was swallowed up again by the moiling waters, Jenny
silently ended the refrain, ". . . all the books."

Stupefied by Bonkers's recital, the onlookers had made no attempt to
grab him, though surely they would not allow him to make a second pass
without releasing him from the wheel. Then the boat pitched violently
as it clattered over some river monster or submerged tree, an object that
could smash the rudders and fracture the keelson. Alerted to the crisis on
board and off, the pilot had already killed the engines, though the stern-
wheel continued its final rotation. This time, however, when the clown came

back around, he was no longer speaking, his body hanging in a mangled configuration from a paddle blade.

Madame Hortense later claimed that the Wheel of Fortune card from her pack, which was always promising some type of categorical change, had foretold everything, though the circus had no need of referring to any laws beyond fate. Marmaduke Armbrewster's remains were shipped back to his family in Iowa with condolences: he had sadly fallen victim to an unnamed occupational hazard. He was mourned briefly by the handful of ladies he'd dallied with, but beyond them there was little love to spare among his fellow performers for the clown-maudit. Reduced thereafter to the status of untouchable, Captain Cumberbund was otherwise left to carry on as before, but Lem Kelso's festering conscience found its physical corollary in the leg wound inflicted by the goat.

"The tip of your unicorn's horn is commonly known to be full of p'ison," pronounced Madame H., offering a morsel from her dubious store of occult wisdom.

The goat itself had vanished since the death of her master. Jenny Bashrig had looked high and low, but nothing remained of Medea beyond her abandoned tether. A shame, thought Jenny, who'd imagined the goat becoming her own steadfast familiar, like in that story about the Gypsy girl the clown had read her. She missed others of his stories, such as the one about the doomed lovers Tristan and Isolde, and the wirewalker Elvira Madigan and her officer in their (what did Bonkers call it?) *liebestod*. There was yet another story that Medea's disappearance had put her in mind of, about the goat who wandered into a cave that led to the Promised Land. But that one had been told to her in the top of a tree by Muni Pinsker, the scribe of North Main Street, before he left her to snuff out their unborn child on her own.

She missed the clown like she missed her original infatuation with all the circus ballyhoo. It was an earthbound sadness, however, that never reached the height of the tightrope, which more than ever she lived to mount. She relied less on props, disdained the parasol and the balance pole, performing increasingly risky somersaults and running leaps. She pirouetted high above the war in Europe and the champagne tastes of the absentee owners Forepaugh and Broadway, who were regularly cheating their employees out of their contracted wages. Beyond distraction,

Jenny scarcely flinched when the human blowtorch accidentally inhaled, incinerating his innards; or when the lion tamer entered the cage with his suppurating leg, whose infection incited in his cats a lust for carrion, and as instinct trumped affection they mauled their trainer. He bled to death, despite the ringmaster's best efforts to four-flush the horror away, before an audience of twelve hundred strong.

But when Jenny descended from on high, she was often made aware that she wasn't the only one who'd grown disenchanted with the Carnival of Fun. There was talk in several quarters that the circus was hexed. It was a notion Madame Hortense corroborated in her readings, assuring La Funambula that the Hanged Man card lay athwart her immediate future.

"The hanged man I saw already yesterday!" Jenny snapped at the stronglady, who had, come to think of it, not one womanly feature and was maybe, she surmised aloud, "what they call a morphodite?"

As she spoke Professor Hotspur, having come to their cabin door holding flowers, turned turkey red and beat a retreat. Then seeing a bangle-sized tear stream down the cheek of Madame Hortense, Jenny relented. Nevertheless, she threw the cards overboard, though they blew back in her face like in that story she'd read under Bonkers's tutelage, the one in which the little girl falls down a rabbit hole.

A week or so later, just south of Herculaneum, the boiler blew on the *Yellow Wen.* In the hope of reaching Cape Girardeau before morning, the rousters had allowed the pressure to rise beyond what the safety valves could contain. The needles on the gauges spun like teetotums and the middle boiler exploded, launching the pilot house like a missile over the wooded shore. The packet was blasted to splinters amidships, sparks from the resulting fire raining like phoenix feathers over the midnight river. There was no time to lower the lifeboats, leaky at best, and performers and crew alike jumped overboard from the decks just ahead of the flames. Some, already alight, sizzled in the current, while those that weren't pulled under by the suction from the sinking vessel clung to crates and tea chests amid the burning debris. Set adrift, the *Floating Palace* continued careering downstream with the menagerie scow wallowing behind it until it ran aground on a sandbar. The scow plowed into the rear of the *Palace,* causing the cages and stalls on board to be smashed apart, releasing in turn a stampede of terrified animals, many of whom promptly drowned. But in the years following the disaster, hardshell religionists from the nearby towns might spot in the surrounding scrub a camel or rhinoceros, a Barbary horse or a Nubian lion with a nettle-snarled mane, and believe that Noah had unloaded his cargo thereabouts.

Jenny, who'd started life in America after having been fished from the wreckage of a steamboat, realized that she'd come full circle. But that didn't mean it was time to go home. Instead, she thanked Madame H. for saving her life, as she had the lives of a dozen others, and parted company with her for good. (The stronglady had elected to join what remained of Professor Hotspur's pachyderm act on the vaudeville circuit, where she became known as "the Human Bridge" over whose chest the elephants routinely paraded.) Along with a clutch of survivors from the Carnival of Fun, who'd clung to one another since the calamity, Jenny took up with the Great Southern Circus, which was no more than a flivver-drawn mud show. Tracked down by a scout from the Sells-Floto Spectacular, however, she was offered a contract and once more given a spot above the center ring. The sadness that dogged her in the back lot and the pie car and invaded her Pullman berth still couldn't touch her on the wire. But the dreams that seemed to belong to someone else continued to disrupt her equilibrium during her more death-defying stunts. Especially the dream in which the earth is propelled through space by means of a paddle wheel: when its blades are sideswiped by the wheel of heaven, which turns in the opposite direction, they interlock and both wheels come to a grinding halt.

◢ 14 ◣
Artist in Clover

Mine is a wild and savage heart that cannot be confined by this airless dungeon,
was what I was thinking, as I sat ensconced among the soiled cushions in
Avrom's office chair. Still dopey from having read late into the previous
night, I was hidden from view of the customers (of whom there were as
usual none) by the books stacked on top of the broad metal desk. Outside
was Main Street, whose heyday had come and gone, its commerce bled
by suburban shopping centers to which the white citizens collectively
flocked. They'd abandoned downtown Memphis, leaving it in its decline
to the poor colored populace whose prophet had come to the city to lead
a march. The march would be composed of the persecuted and dispos-
sessed, and shouldn't I—who paid such lip service to championing the
underdog—be in their number? But that would involve leaving Avrom's
deep-cushioned chair where I was nestled so comfortably, and despite my
wild and savage, et cetera, I was at peace for a change.

I'd read last night with that intensity that obliterated the distinction
between being inside and outside the book. I attended the marriage of
Twinkl Saltzman and Firpo Belzer under a canopy fashioned from the
giant Og of Bashan's foreskin. I inspected Jakie Epstein's scrapbook in
which the revenants in his group portraits, photographed with a Buster
Brown box camera, figured more prominently than the living subjects.
I kibitzed a debate between Doc Seligman and the pharmacist Mendel
Blen concerning the virtues of natural versus unnatural miracles, and the
means of measuring the half-life of love. It broke my heart when Katie
and Pinchas Pin pulverized one another in their erotomania, though after
that I confess the narrative began to sputter a bit. At the point where the
municipal workers come with their crosscut saws to level the upstanding roots of the inverted oak, the story seemed to limp to a standstill;

it receded from eyewitness experience back into a fable I could scarcely believe, and released from credulity, I fell asleep. I woke in the morning at the rear of the shop with a sense of tranquility I hadn't known since my pill-popping days. When had I stopped popping pills?

Just then the telephone rang, which came as a surprise; I couldn't remember ever having heard a phone ring in the Book Asylum and wasn't even sure where the thing resided. As the ringing continued, I located a jack in the wall and followed a wire that trailed under a bale of sheet music and led to a dusty pedestal atop which sat an ancient ebony instrument. Lifting the receiver as gingerly as you'd defuse a bomb, I heard a voice it took me a second or two to identify. "So you found me," I conceded, because I'd assumed that in Avrom's shop I was as good as incommunicado.

It had after all been some thirty-six hours since I'd spoken with Rachel, whom I admittedly hadn't tried to contact, since after sending me packing it was up to her to make the next move: I had my pride. And while I didn't realize how much I'd missed her till that moment, I nevertheless perceived the call as an interruption.

"Were you lost?" she inquired, only slightly sardonic.

"Since the Creation."

"Listen," ignoring my emphasis, "can you meet me at the B'nai B'rith Home across from the park in an hour? There's something I want to show you."

Ordinarily a summons from Rachel would have spurred me to immediate action, but her peremptory tone—she spoke as if nothing was altered between us—left me feeling frankly mutinous. Moreover, the shop itself seemed to hedge me in, its shelves quiescent as a library at the bottom of the sea: Prospero's drowned library which you had to dive fathoms to read. Above the surface all bets were off; uncertainty was the order of the day. But there in the depths of Avrom's shop I'd developed the knack of breathing the submarine atmosphere.

Still I spritzed my face and armpits in the sink, locked the shop, and caught a bus down Poplar Avenue as far as Overton Park, whose lion-crowned gates were the end of the streetcar line back in the day. I got off the bus at Tucker Street and walked up a short semicircular drive, where I was met by Rachel standing in front of the B'nai B'rith Home for the Aged. It was a low, bunker-like building bordered by acacias, its entrance flanked by potted nasturtiums beside which, looking equally vegetable,

were parked a pair of seniors in wheelchairs. There was a hint of chloro-
form on the breeze, a setting designed to accent Rachel's vivacity. In the
brief time since I'd seen her she'd trimmed her bangs, which made her
look like Cleopatra or Grace Slick; she wore a short suede jacket over a
corduroy smock and, despite the balmy morning, her leather boots.

I flung my arms about her.

"He's not here," she stated flatly, patting my back as if to encourage a
burp.

"Marry me," I heard myself saying, squeezing harder, but when she
failed to return the pressure I relaxed my embrace. "Who's not here?"

"Tyrone."

Concealing my disappointment at her lack of enthusiasm, I took a breath:
"Let me guess," I said, my thoughts leaping ahead of themselves. "You got
him transferred from the state asylum and now he's run away . . ." Phrases
like "dragnet" and "all-points bulletin" came to mind.

Released from my hold, Rachel gave me a look. "Earth to Lenny," she
said patiently. "He goes to the park to paint."

You might have thought that after so long a confinement he'd be in
dread of the out-of-doors, but there, across the way, sat the artist in a folding chair behind an easel in the shade of the bronze doughboy statue. An
attendant stood at his shoulder, a stout woman with a plum-colored face
wearing scrubs, the flesh hanging like wineskins from her folded arms.
Scattered in the grass about the easel was a murmuration of flower children seated in lotus positions, playing penny whistles and weaving clover
chains. The month of March, having run the scales of the seasons, had
settled this morning on picture perfect: yellow daffodils and forsythia,
pink dogwoods, azalea, crab apple, redbud, and tulip trees, all seemed
to have burst into blossom only moments ago. Despite the warmth, however, Tyrone was bundled into a duffle coat, a watchcap pulled nearly to
the hooded lids of his soft shamrock eyes. His attendant, who seemed
to recognize Rachel—this was evidently not her first visit—announced
somewhat skeptically, "The chirren have 'dopted him."

I looked over his shoulder at the painting in progress, its bold pri-
maries having little in common with the pastel hues of the surrounding
meadow. The composition repeated the moonstruck themes I'd grown accustomed to from Muni's book: a street of unlikely juxtapositions and
historic anachronisms, merchants and members of long-extinct races

mingling in front of flyblown facades. But where that brazen Pinchscape might ordinarily have enthralled me, today it only gave me the willies with its mad departure from the morning's serenity.

Bending close to the artist, Rachel asked him (a little patronizingly, I thought), "Are you happy here, Tyrone?"

Previously so slow to respond, he replied now without hesitation in a voice that, cracking like an adolescent's, sounded almost sane. "Isn't everybody?"

Given the source, I found his answer rather chilling, but Rachel allowed herself a sigh of satisfaction. I supposed she'd earned it. After all she'd been instrumental in bringing about the artist's improved situation, in making sure he had available the choicest materials: a stretched cotton canvas on a lyre easel (she had me to know), a watercolor palette and squirrel hair brushes. She had indeed been a busy girl. She'd conducted her interviews and written a grant that would enable her to conduct even more, and was composing a monograph based on her research. The monograph, a projected oral history of North Main Street, was the initial stage of what she hoped would result in a book—a book that might be viewed as a kind of practical companion to the one Muni Pinsker had written. That one she'd invited me to donate to the Folklore Center's archive.

Regarding Tyrone with an almost proprietary benevolence, she whispered to me that it might be possible to put together a show of his paintings at the center. "The naive art thing is really catching on."

I couldn't help admiring her even as I suspected that her interest in Tyrone's work was not entirely selfless. Meanwhile Tyrone, uncorked, had become almost conversational.

"There's thirty-nine occupations that if you do them on Shabbos you're punished with death," he submitted without looking up from his painting, "and Fannie Dubrovner was guilty of the worst"—the hippies appeared to be communally holding their breath—"which is to spin the wool while it's still on the goat." I recognized the reference from Muni's text, but the rest was unfamiliar. "She sweated lice, Fanny, that sizzled in the oven where God put her without a kitsl or a kiss . . ."

I saw Rachel shudder and thought, good, maybe she's beginning to understand that Tyrone isn't Mr. Dick. The painter went on offering unsolicited information: "Sanford Nussbaum carved the Lord's name on a donkey's hoof / and laughed to see it jump over the synagogue roof . . . ,"

while one of the hippies took scrupulous notes. Another, a girl with a pen-
dulous bosom swinging freely beneath her gossamer shift, rose to drape
a clover necklace over Tyrone's head. He looked up to give her an ap-
praising glance, his eyes ticktocking back and forth with the sway of her
breasts, and thoughtfully remarked to his audience or himself, "Moses
and Aaron."

"He means a nice rack," I interpreted for Rachel, who simpered as if to
say that the phrase needed no translation. The attendant rolled her eyes as
if to imply that her job might be more than she'd bargained for.

We walked to Rachel's car, which was waiting at the curb in front of an
old hotel with awninged windows overlooking the park.

"So what do you think?" she asked as she unlocked the door.

I was thinking that, appearances notwithstanding, there was no place
that Tyrone Pin would ever really belong, and his vulnerability made me
a little sick to my stomach. But as Rachel's question had no special reference, it merited only a general response. "I think you would have to be out
of your mind not to be crazy in this world," I said.

She awarded me a tight-lipped grin. "Or vice versa," she replied.

I tried to return the smile, wanting so much to parlay the moment into
an intimate exchange: we were bonding again over a lunatic who was the
living connection to the vanished Pinch. But a perverse impulse refused
to let me take advantage of her ebullient mood. "Do you imagine that you
brought him back to the Garden?" I said. Her grin reversed itself. "He's
damaged goods, Rachel. When all's said and done, he's just a poor defec-
tive shell-shocked ex-GI."

She looked puzzled: "Thus spake Lenny Sklarew." But rather than
object, she narrowed her eyes to examine me through the bore of her
inquisitive squint. "Since when did you become such a scold?" she asked,
not without a note of respect; then gently lowering her voice, "What's eating you, Lenny?"

What wasn't eating me? I'd lost my apartment, my employers, and
even, it seemed, my relation to the book that had all but eclipsed my own
past—though that last was perhaps a blessing. But shouldn't the book's
loosened hold on me allow for a tightening of Rachel's?

"Avrom's dying," I said, and felt instantly ashamed: I was exploiting
the old man's condition to gain pity for myself. All the same, it seemed
to work. I made a noise like I was trying to clear my throat of my heart,

and Rachel took my hand; she drew me round to the other side of the car, deposited me in the shotgun seat, and drove me home with her to her greenstone building.

She undressed in the window outlined by the spiky sunlight whose beams appeared to emanate from her pores. She revealed herself in full consciousness of the gift she knew her body to be—its skin smooth as a blanched almond, her navel like a tiny knot in a balloon. Dayenu, I said to myself, because it would have been enough just to behold her, even had she not begun to crawl into the bed. She crawled like she was stalking me, scaring the cat, which leapt from the pillow, and began to unbuckle my belt. With every button she unbuttoned, zipper unzipped, she uttered a gasp, as if my pasty flesh and bones were some great surprise. Her lips performed lamprey-like kisses, suctioning my nipples, my thighs, my organ, which rose with comical alacrity like a jack-in-the-box, the only part of me not behaving like her victim. But once drawn into the arena of her sensuality, I wasn't so passive anymore. Then we were indivisible, bucking and writhing as if we shared the symptoms of some saint's disease—a sublime seizure that purified us of contaminents in the blood, such as fear. When it was over, I told her I'd ejaculated a crazy glue that would cement us together for all time. So I was bewildered at the ease with which, immediately after, she disengaged her body from mine and said she had to get to work. I couldn't account for her abruptness, but later that afternoon, slouched again in Avrom's "siege perilous" (perilous because it was so hard to get out of), it dawned on me she was saying good-bye.

◢ 15 ◣
Party in the Park

Muni glanced again at the kid in the doorway who'd outgrown his Dutch vestee suit, his knees smudged and raw below his short pants. One stocking had fallen down around his ankle and his rust-red hair fanned his brow in an unruly cowlick.

"Where have *you* been?" asked Muni, or rather he mouthed the words in silence: because it had been so long since he'd conversed with another person that his voice box had lost the knack of making sounds. But the boy seemed to have no problem reading his lips.

"Nowhere," he replied.

There should have been no more need of asking the second question ("Where is your mama and papa?") than the first, since everyone's fate had already been recorded in Muni's hill of loose pages. So why couldn't Muni himself, the instrument of that record, recall what he'd inscribed? He glanced at the heap of manuscript turning sepia on the floor, then back at the boy with his faraway eyes, and realized that something was amiss: he'd awoken, it seemed, from his protracted dream and could no longer recall a single word of what he'd written. The recognition sucked the air from his lungs.

Starting again from scratch, from *nowhere*, Muni inquired, "Who are you?" and this time his voice was audible, if only just.

"I'm the boy," replied the child with an offhand precocity, "that my papa made with my mama's ghost. That was before it came back in her own body again, the ghost."

It took all the patience Muni could muster to express any interest, so great was his wish to spend his sympathy on himself. "You don't say," he muttered; then he stood up, which was no easy undertaking, since he hadn't stood in a very long while. He was aware of the odor his unbathed body exuded through his grubby underdrawers, the itch of his scalp and beard. His knee joints shed cobwebs and creaked like unoiled machinery; his brain felt as if an hourglass had turned over in his skull. Taking the boy's hand less out of kindness than the need to secure his balance, the weary scribe set off with him in search of his mother and father.

They didn't have far to look: turn left out of the neglected nursery, shuffle to the end of the hall, open the door into the wrecked bedroom, and there in the collapsed iron bed, scattered over the disheveled sheets, was the dust of Katie and Pinchas Pin. Muni was unable to identify it at first. Despite being slightly incandescent, as what wasn't in the Pinch in those days, it might have been egg cookie crumbs left over from a late-night snack. But a reference to his handwritten chronicle back in the nursery revealed to Muni not only what had happened but also that there were telltale clues to what was coming all along. Because one of the distractions Muni had suffered repeatedly during his marathon scribbling—distractions he'd incorporated into his text—was the noise of Pinchas and Katie's rampant copulation from down the hall.

Not that anyone in the Pinch could have been accused of conventional behavior, but the proprietor of Pin's General Merchandise and his resurrected bride made noises such as their nephew had never heard in the years prior to the quake. His sleep, back in the days when Muni still slept, had seldom been interrupted by anything other than the music of the blind musician who accompanied the girl who danced on the clothesline, before the girl went away. But for all their unreserved devotion to their infant son, the physical appetite of Katie Pin for her husband, and his for her, had increased exponentially since the boy's birth. In fact, their enduring gratitude for the gift of the child was sometimes overwhelmed by their delight in their newfound lasciviousness.

Pinchas could reason that their intemperate relations were part of a healthy regimen. For he had it on Rabbi ben Yahya's authority—and he was willing now to credit the rebbe with some authority—that Katie's time on earth was imperiled, and hadn't their steamy union in the underworld proved to have revitalizing properties? Didn't the shtupping quite simply restore her to life? Meanwhile Katie, for her part, wanted desperately to lengthen her days for the sake of their son. Moreover, there was the mutual conviction that they were making up for lost time. But in the end their rationalizations mattered little in the face of the unabashed randiness that compelled them to fling themselves hammer and tongs into each other's arms.

Though each was likely to blame the other for initiating the frolic, it was usually Katie who made the first move. That might consist of no more than a shoulder shrug or a finger teasing a lock of her hennaed hair—or perhaps the scratching of an armpit, since the gesture required nothing overtly erotic, only some slight indication of the instigator's corporal presence. Then they would come together, husband and wife, in a blind heat that caused their clothing to smolder until they tore off whatever they wore. Their bodies collided with a jarring impact that generated hairline fractures that would result later on in a splintering of bones. They tried to control their urges in a responsible fashion, to coordinate their reciprocal itch to correspond with the times when their child was asleep. But as Tyrone grew older and his napping more irregular, there were long periods when the boy was left on his own. The Pins weren't too terribly concerned: he was a solitary kid capable of amusing himself, more wedded to fancy than material interests. (His most abiding occupation consisted in the vigilant observation of his cousin Muni at his writing.) Their periodic abandonment of Tyrone, his parents reasoned, was an unavoidable consequence of their serial abandonment of themselves, which is not to say they were able entirely to escape a measure of guilt.

So when they weren't fornicating to beat the band, Katie and Pinchas Pin were attempting to atone for the times when they left their child to his own devices. Coming back to themselves after their spent passion, they would coddle and indulge their son. They gave him toys he seemed to outgrow as fast as he received them, plied him with Mrs. Rosen's compotes and choice cuts of Makowsky's manna-fed flanken that, with his bird-like appetite, the boy scarcely touched. They took him for strolls along the canal to view the sights that beggared belief, stopping in at various storefronts, some no more than painted facades, where they introduced him to the neighbors' children. But Tyrone showed little interest in the other kids—whose games included exorcisms and a variation of hopscotch that involved skipping over whole calendar cycles. On their side the kids, all older than he, were wary as well of Tyrone, who wasn't so much timid as remote. Plus, he was the only kid on the street who (despite the stalled clocks) was still growing in stature and advancing in age, a dreamy boy at a moment when no one else seemed to have need of dreams.

The cautious attitude with which the neighbors regarded the child was extended to his parents as well. It was true that the Pins had been the objects of jealousy and idle talk in the past, but back then Pinchas's status in the community was unimpeachable, and his wife's affability had always tended to stem the loshen horah, the gossip. Besides, Pin's General Merchandise was the long-standing anchor of North Main Street. Now, however, all anchors had been weighed, and from their bobbing vessels and supernal vantages the population deemed the Pins a suspicious lot: their bliss was not the same as the street's.

For Tyrone's sake Katie and Pinchas tried to maintain a pretense of normality. They represented themselves as solid citizens in a neighborhood whose permeability to wonders mocked the very nature of solidity. Still, Pinchas reasserted the proprietorship of his business while Katie took charge of her kitchen, the nursery, and the care and maintenance of the obsessed nephew. She helped out in the store, where her husband tried to push his damaged commodities. They didn't seem to notice how they were perceived as violating the very spirit of the neighborhood, taking the part of earnest merchants when others only played at business. Where Pinchas endeavored to flog his waterlogged flannels and yachting caps, Leon Shapiro might offer, along with a factory rebate, an imp encased in a soap bubble, and Mr. Abraham peddled the philosophers' stones the kiddies played potsie with. The currency they exchanged was more likely to be secrets than hard cash. But there were other reasons their neighbors signaled against the evil eye whenever they saw the Pins, other reasons why the Pins embraced their standard inventory with such a will.

Because, despite her lickerish vitality, Katie had begun to show signs of decomposition, and out of sympathy her husband had also developed symptoms. Her fair complexion, once dusted in freckles like cinnamon in milk, had acquired a pastry-like flakiness, bits of which dropped into the lap of her apron dress. The dress itself hung from her brittle bones as from a hanger. Her formerly russet hair, discolored and dyed, began to fall out in hanks, revealing patches of scalp the texture of coconut shell. Her green eyes had faded to oyster gray and ran with a viscous humor. The more she appeared to be actively decaying, however, the friskier she became, as if that insatiable hunger might redeem her wasting flesh. But each coupling took a further toll on both her and Pinchas, who was likewise beginning to come apart. Still they yentzed with an ever more fevered determination, further decimating the selves their desire was meant to preserve.

"Katie," Pinchas had at last to admit while facing a merciless mirror, "let us face it, we are starting to rot."

To which Katie replied with a transparent optimism, "Bollocks, we're only shedding skin."

But with every orgiastic release she experienced, Katie also felt the efforts of her soul attempting to escape its moldering confines. She had glimpsed it seeping out of herself like a bubble from a pipe, an amorphous rose blob suggesting the outlines of a young Irish bride. Then it was Pinchas's job, sharing as he did her perception, to stuff his wife's herniated neshomah back into whatever fissure it emerged from. But it was a dim and elusive entity, Katie's soul, and Pinchas, in the groggy afterglow of their prodigious coition, was often slow in attempting to retrieve it. As a result, the thing had managed on several occasions to detach itself from her person. And once it ventures forth from its mortal frame the incorporeal is selfish: it feels no warmth or responsibility toward its former substance or much attachment to anything else on earth, be it husband or son. It feels only the mindless instinct to wander in the direction whence it came, and Katie's soul might have fled halfway back to yenne velt, the other world, had not Pinchas managed to recover it in time. But occasionally the husband questioned his own selfishness in not allowing his wife her spiritual freedom. Besides, that oft-repeated effort of retrieval had worn him pretty thin and unseated his own restless spirit, which had also begun to look for a way out of its disintegrating skin. The situation had made Muni think, as he related it in his ongoing chronicle, of the escape artist Harry Houdini, who strove to release himself from straitjackets and sausage casings.

So it was only a matter of time before the ghosts of Katie and Pinchas Pin gave up their ravaged bodies, which continued for a while to pummel one another into a glimmering dust.

Still, their nephew wondered if he could have written their end differently, if even now it might not be too late to change their destiny: they had been in such an agony over leaving behind their only child. But when he reentered his privy-sized room, shadowed by the odd little boy, and gazed again upon the heap of his manuscript, its pages appeared to him as so much spindrift from an already receding tide. Soon, he thought, they would completely evaporate. Also scattered about the floor were a few long-abandoned toys—a wooden caboose, a tin frog, an Indian headdress from which Muni, stooping, plucked a red feather. He returned to the bedroom with the boy at his heels and used the feather to sweep the luminous crumbs from the rumpled sheets into the open palm of his hand. The boy watched him with unblinking jade-green eyes. Muni made a fist around the crumbs in his left hand—where they hissed like the interior of a nautilus shell—and with his right reached for the boy's, whose small fingers entwined Muni's own.

"I remember when they had faces," he said.

"I wish I did," replied Muni, beyond consolation. He put on his estranged clothing and led little Tyrone down the stairs through the largely liquidated store, then out onto the raised sidewalk above the canal that no longer deserved its name.

Vacant now of vessels except a foundered few, the grand canal of North Main Street was mostly dried up, the once steely blue body of water having separated into standing pools. The dregs of the lagoon were exposed: spittoons and smashed hogsheads, the legs of a supine piano protruding like a belly-up beast from the shallow residue. The air was no longer as tonic as it had been in Muni's written version, where the atmosphere partook of the bracing climate on the first day of creation. The street was not quite the street of his composition, which had renewed itself daily, so that every morning you had to reacquaint yourself with the drama of your surroundings: the melancholy of the Floradora girl in the ad painted on the wall of Grinspan's Cigar Store, the grace adhering to the wrought iron volutes of tailor Bluestein's sewing machine . . . The dilapidated storefronts had lost their look of scenery suspended from a rigging in heaven and appeared as if about to collapse. The sidewalks were barren of people, giving the impression that the never-ending festivities that had so absorbed Muni Pinsker in his role as chronicler were finally over.

But the festivities, as the boy and his unkempt cousin discovered, had merely moved west to Market Square Park, which was where Muni had been headed in the first place. It was his duty to his aunt and uncle and their surviving offspring to consign the dust of Katie and Pinchas Pin to the hole in the park, the one with no bottom in which the great oak was upended. That way their remains might follow where Muni assumed their spirits had led. He never questioned the sense of this conviction; in his logy and discomposed state it was the only logic the former scribe felt he had a hold of, though it also soothed him somewhat to hold on to the hand of the unquestioning little boy.

Entering the park, they encountered the gathered tribe of North Main Street, assembled as they'd been on that night—yesterday and long ago—when the earth had spasmed and split its seams. This evening they were joined, however, by a crush of strangers. Some were dusty farm families from the open market in the wagonyard off Commerce Avenue, others from the town in their Sunday best, a few brandishing torches though it wasn't yet dark. Muni was surprised to see that his neighbors mingled so freely with the outsiders, who had kept their distance from the Pinch since the quake. The general mood seemed to extend the holiday attitude that had prevailed throughout the pages of his chronicle, though his co-religionists looked to have relaxed their exultatation, tempered now to a bland expectancy. While some were still costumed in vestiges of fancy dress—the Widow Teitelbaum in her harem pants, Eddie Kid Wolf in his samite robe—most wore their typically drab, out-of-fashion apparel. The children toddled about willy-nilly, their expressions suggesting they'd just waked up from a vivid dream they were trying without success to recall.

Muni was greeted with a cordiality that gave no hint of his long seclusion. Mr. Elster chucked Tyrone under the chin with an arthritic hand, while his dumpling wife exclaimed a bit cryptically, "Every child brings its own luck." Others remarked with admiration how the boy had grown. The bruiser Kid Wolf snatched him up and set him astride his thick shoulders for a better view of whatever it was the crowd had gathered to see. Tyrone went wide-eyed at the sudden separation from his cousin but soon enough became acclimated to his elevated seat. He was further calmed, it seemed, by the grin he received from the stunted grotesque seated next to him on the stooped shoulders of Morris Padauer. Muni had to stand on tiptoe to look past the wintry garb (though the season was unequivocably spring) of a cluster of Shpinker Hasids for a glimpse of the spectacle, if spectacle there was. He noted with interest that in the midst of the fanatics, looking decidedly refreshed from his underworld sabbatical, stood their sable-trimmed rebbe, Eliakum ben Yahya. What Muni saw beyond them, beneath the roots that had replaced the broad boughs of the inverted oak, made him tighten the fist that gripped his aunt and uncle's crumbled remains.

For next to the pit, out of which sprouted the roots like Hydras' heads, was a cedar-staved nail keg, and on the keg stood a hatless black man, his wrinkled dome wreathed in a horseshoe of gray wool. His pants bagged around his spare shanks, and his homespun shirt was buttoned to the throat. His smoked lenses had been removed, so it was hard to tell in the failing light whether his eyes were sunk in their hollows or simply not there. Had his hands not been tied behind his back, he might have serenaded the crowd on the fiddle that someone had hung about his neck by one of its broken strings. Around that same wattled throat there dangled a noose. The rope extended from the Negro's neck straight up into the leafless tangle then downward again at an incline, its tasseled end resting in the hands of a man in a hood like a dented dunce cap and a white linen robe. The man, his beefy face unvisored and flushed with the pride of his office, resembled a jolly monk about to ring a bell. That's when Muni noticed that other cowled figures, a few of them holding rifles, were interspersed throughout the gathering.

Between the bell ringer and the nail keg stood another man whose white robe boasted the insignia that identified him as a figure of some rank in the Knights of the White Kamelia. This one, his badger face also exposed, cleared his throat as if tuning an instrument.

"Ghouls and goblins of the Invisible Empire," he bellowed, "Anglo-Saxon brethren and sistern of our hallowed Dixie, we are gathered here this evenin'—"

"This ain't no weddin', Lawyer Poteet!" shouted a voice from the crowd, provoking laughter. Others chimed in to the effect that he should can the speechifying and get on with the main event, but the speaker would have his moment.

"To avenge the evil wrought on our citizens by these ape-like creatures of jungle darkness"—Asbestos turned his head toward Lawyer Poteet as if he hadn't quite caught the gist—"and make a example of the vile species that would defy our laws and miscegenate," tasting the word, "with our women."

There was more laughter, since it was obvious to the audience that, had it ever been the case, the old Negro's miscegenating days were long over. Some of the assembled yawned demonstratively; a bonneted woman distributed sandwiches and soda pop to her family from a hamper. Then Muni was suddenly moved to ask himself what day it was: for he had the marked impression that this evening—against whose chartreuse sky the park was thrown into stark relief—was fixed to a particular calendar date: rather than containing other days, this one had the distinct character of a Friday evening, when all good Hebrews should be in shul.

The Grand Syklops of the Memphis Klavern continued reciting the laundry list of crimes against nature that the nigra was guilty of, though there was no mention of Asbestos's specific offense. At one point, spurring his hobbyhorse onward, Lawyer Poteet strayed into territory clearly intended for the ears of Muni Pinsker and his kind, declaring that Caucasians were the true Israelites (you could read it in the Bible) and America the prophesied site of the regathering of the tribes. The Jews themselves (again quoting scripture) were a mongrel breed, "satanic, poisonous, and parasitic."

His neighbors shifted apprehensively, while Muni came only by degrees to understand what was happening. It had been a rocky passage back from the story he was writing to the one he was living, despite their being in theory one and the same. How, he wondered, had these interlopers come to invade the sovereign precinct of the Pinch? (The interlopers seemed to be asking the same thing with regard to the Jews.) Were such lumpen bumpkins as these really capable of pulling off any authentic mischief? Surely Boss Crump's hirelings would appear on the scene in time to break up the mob and put an end to their shenanigans (though Mr. Crump's handpicked high sheriff, Longwillie Tatum, could be seen mingling among the robes in a sheet of his own). Maybe it wasn't too late for the scribe to hasten back to his room and devise a different course of events, but the prospect of writing anything at all now seemed beyond his powers, and besides, like everyone else Muni was glued to the spot.

That Lawyer Poteet's general vitriol had descended into ad hominem abuse ("This'n's proof skunks fuck monkeys, pardon my French . . .") implied that his speech was winding down, and a hush fell over the crowd. The bound Negro, who had seemed almost incidental to the proceedings, was now the focus of everyone's rapt attention. In the twilight the torches flared more brightly, prompting Muni to remember a phrase: *auto-da-fé*. So maybe Asbestos would prove as good as his name. But a nod from the Grand Syklops to his henchman reminded Muni that fire was not the chosen method of execution; this was a lynching pure and simple, a time-honored tradition of these peculiar southern states. And the locus they'd selected for the event was a sure way of demonstrating that the ghetto had lost its inviolability. The blind musician cocked his frosty head this way and that, presumably from the discomfort of the rope. Or was he listening for unheard melodies?

"God bless y'all white folks," he murmured, his scratchy voice, though just above a whisper, still carrying in the silent dusk. "You done climbed the ugly ladder and never miss a rung."

It was then that the girl in her sequined leotard flashing the last rays of the setting sun began to slide headfirst down the thick rope.

She had thought of him often during the jumps from show town to show town, had always missed his spooky music; none of the windjammers had ever adjusted their rhythms to suit so well her aerial turns. Lately she'd missed the old-timer like she missed the river itself and wondered why his fiddle couldn't be added to the brass jig band that played the side-show. She imagined him taking his place alongside the ensemble of darky musicians, such as Calliope Clarence, who played his Apollonicon with a sickle grin. The blind fiddler could play in the band and double-stage as a bumbling auguste, like the whiteface Negro clowns who were as thoroughly assimilated into the circus community as the freaks.

She knew that back in Memphis his days were numbered: he'd been marked (and marked again) for blue ruin since the time of his maiming on the north Mississippi plantation where he was born into bondage. He'd told her the tale: how he had the misfortune to stumble upon the overseer involved in an unspeakable act in the corn crib. "I ain't seen nothing!" he protested to the cap'n, who assured him that *nothing* was what he would see from then on, and straightaway proceeded to gouge out his eyes with a penknife. The master, enraged at this wanton destruction of his property, dismissed the overseer and thereafter made of the blind pickaninny a house pet, awarding him—when he'd observed him admiring it with grazing fingers—the gift of a spruce trade violin. Demonstrating an innate aptitude for the instrument, the boy expressed his gratitude by taking to the open road with his gift, only to be returned in chains soon after by patrollers. The overseer, rehired for his redoubtable efficiency, flogged the boy and salted his wounds in a bath of brine. Unable to relieve the pain that inflamed his back, the blind boy displaced it by stroking the wounds and welts of others, thereby touching nerves whose oscillating vibrations he translated to the strings of his fiddle.

The next time he ran away he was put in stocks, and the time after that branded with an iron, during which procedure his refusal to cry out earned him the honorific that stuck. After his fifth or sixth attempt at escape it was noticed, when the serial fugitive was stripped for punishment, that he'd begun to mature—an observation that inspired the cap'n, always handy with his blade, to geld him on the spot. A generation or two later, when the blind man came to guide other fugitives through the tunnels that the old bayous were converted into after the fever, it was said he stuffed nugget-sized stones into the hollows of his eyes; legend had it that the stones allowed him to see in the dark. But the cops who finally apprehended him at his illicit business, and the mob that wrested him from the hands of the cops, aware of the rumor, never recovered any such stones.

If Jenny were honest, she would have had to admit that her reasons for wanting to retrieve the fiddler from his station in the Pinch were mainly selfish; her motives had more to do with missing the company of his eerie music than securing his safety. Then, too, the dreams that had saddled her with an unwieldy ballast on the wire caused her to teeter precariously in the direction of her old hometown. None of which excluded the providence of her arrival at the eleventh hour, when she stole into the roots of the tree in the park and did what came naturally: peeling off her garments to the costume beneath and lowering herself headfirst down the rope, she began to spin.

She performed a series of one-arm planges, looping her hand in the rope and flinging her body up and over her shoulder as if throwing herself repeatedly into a sack of air. She executed cunning jackknifes and dislocations, rolled herself up into a ball, hung by her ankles and knees. As she caracoled above the crowd, the rope swayed and the noose twirled like a lasso about the Negro's neck until it was lifted clear off over his head—though, riveted as they were by the acrobat, no one seemed to notice. Some of the assembled held their breath while Jenny gyrated in circles; others, such as Muni Pinsker, could not have drawn a breath if they tried. In fact, so staggered was the retired scribe by battling emotions that he was on the point of passing out; he had to pound his chest with the heel of his empty right hand, as in the prayer of repentence, to coax his lungs into filling again. Then the pain of his breathing brought hot tears to his eyes. What did the girl intend with her unscripted exhibition? he wondered. Did she mean to beguile the crowd until the condemned man could be spirited away? If that was the case, she had badly miscalculated, because the spectators were so spellbound by her performance that no one—even had they been so inclined—stepped forward to rescue Asbestos, who remained standing patiently atop his nail keg, his face upturned despite his sightless eyes.

The merest meniscus of a moon had appeared in the lapis sky, prompting the Hasids among them to begin mumbling the Rosh Chodesh blessing. The sequins on Jenny's costume, catching moonlight, seemed to throw sparks, which a few of the fanatics tried to snatch out of the air. Between their antics and those of the girl on the rope, most of the spectators missed the rueful blue chord soughed by a breeze on the remaining strings of Asbestos's fiddle. But the chord was apparently loud enough to snap the Grand Syklops's attention back to the task at hand. He bade his fellows hoist him to a height from which he could replace the noose around the fiddler's unresisting neck. Lowered again after tightening the knot, Lawyer Poteet gave the nod to his henchman—"Klaliff Peay!"—who yanked the rope taut and tied it off on a nearby hydrant. The minstrel's stick legs appeared to execute a two-step in the air above the keg that the klansmen had kicked over; then, only inches from the ground, the legs grew still. Transfixed, Muni Pinsker was unaware that his clenched fist had opened and the dust of his aunt and uncle—at least that which hadn't already been trodden underfoot—was dispersed by the mild evening breeze.

◢ 16 ◣
Hostage to Destiny

The day was bright and the blades of the ceiling fan stirred the cool spring air in the shop, raising the dust in miniature twisters about the floorboards. The radio announced that Senator Eugene McCarthy had defeated LBJ in the New Hampshire primary; Walter Cronkite was urging negotiations to end the war; and I had been gloriously seduced. So why did I feel like I was in helpless freefall? Because, if I wasn't Rachel's lover anymore, then what was I? "Gornisht!" I proclaimed aloud. I'm nothing—and heard my old boss remarking, "Look who thinks he's nothing." Where was his therapeutic abuse when I needed it?

Not that I couldn't get along on my own. I had my resources, didn't I? My memories, though they seemed these days to have dead-ended around the time I came across Muni's book. Since then I'd done such a good job of covering my tracks that I'd almost managed to hide them from myself. This was of course only a temporary amnesia, the lingering effects of a period of wretched excess; it would pass. Then I remembered how the population of the Pinch—after the tree in Market Square Park had been hauled off for cordwood and the crater filled with tons of gravel from a convoy of dump trucks—how they seemed to have jointly misplaced the past. One morning they looked around and the world was no better than it should be: the neighborhood was a slum, its primary thoroughfare strewn with drenched unmentionables and broken furniture (and perhaps a drowned hippogriff). They shared a universal hangover that felt as if it might last the rest of their days. Like me, they'd become marooned in the present.

Muni's book lay on the desk in front of me, looking as nondescript as ever, though the hard reading I'd subjected it to had given the binding some character. I recalled the first time I'd opened it to that random passage—

somewhere toward the middle or was it the end of the book?—when Lenny Sklarew makes his shambling entrance into the chronicle. So far I'd steered clear of that chapter, not wanting to encounter some fate incompatible with the one I might choose for myself, assuming I had a choice in the matter. Now, however, I wondered what the text could reveal beyond an account of Lenny opening a book to read about a moment when Lenny opens a book. Like Moses receiving the Torah in which he reads the story of Moses receiving the Torah, world without end . . . ("Look who thinks he's Moses.")

I opened *The Pinch* to where I'd left off the night before, at the part where the trucks came and went from the park and the merchants of North Main Street began again to contact wholesalers and contractors beyond their neighborhood. I read that another artesian well had been located in a sand aquifer by means of a water witch in Orange Mound, that the Reverend Billy Sunday accompanied Sheriff Hoss Tatum, Longwillie's cretinous son, on a "still" raid in the Loosahatchie Bottoms. Machine Gun Kelly was captured in his skivvies in a bungalow on Rayner Street, and Lenny Sklarew . . .

The door chimes jangled and I looked up in the vain hope of seeing old Avrom hobbling back into the store. The goldbrick, he'd been exaggerating his symptoms as usual. What need did he have of dying anyway, when his closeted residence here in the Book Asylum was just as good as? But instead of my old boss there appeared an elderly colored man attired in a back-numbered suit that practically swallowed his meager frame. His face was dour, his cotton-boll hair, when he'd doffed his hat, center-parted like opposing waves.

An actual customer.

"Can I help you?" I asked, because it occurred to me that, shipwrecked as I felt, I needed to make some scratch. I was down to pennies since Lamar had taken a powder, and I hadn't received my starvation wages from Avrom in weeks. Nor was there anything in the drawer of the antique cash register beyond a little silver and some paper-clipped IOUs. Then it interested me that, aside from my native distrust of private enterprise, to say nothing of my battered heart, an entrepreneurial impulse seemed to take hold. Was this what Muni Pinsker had felt when he quit his writing (or the writing quit him) and took over the operation of Pinchas's store?

"I need a good book," I thought I heard the man say in his deliberate cadence.

Eager to show my familiarity with the Harlem Renaissance, I began naming titles from the canon. "We've got *The Blacker the Berry* by Wallace Thurman and *Nig* . . . ummm . . . *Negro Heaven* by Carl Van Vechten—" when he interrupted me.

"I said *the* good book."

I looked at him quizzically. "You mean the Bible?"

"Yassuh. I lef' home this morning without mine."

Prying myself out of Avrom's chair, I inquired, "Any particular edition?"

"The good news edition," he asserted, as if to say, is there another?

I nodded, though I hadn't a clue what he meant, and went to the Religion shelves. From a row of Tanakh, Pentateuch, Vulgates, and Masoretic texts I chose a Revised King James version published by the Gideon Society. He snatched it from me and began thumbing its pages with urgency.

"'So God created man in He own image,'" he read aloud. "'In the image of God He created him.'—Genesis one, twenty-seven." He gazed a moment over the rims of his spectacles, seeming to take my measure, then began frantically riffling pages again. "'Is this not the fast I choose,'" he intoned, stabbing the page with an index finger, "'to loose the bonds of wickedness and undo the thongs of the yoke, to let the oppressed go free?'—Isaiah fifty-eight, six." His authoritative delivery suggested he might be a preacher, and I was his congregation of one. "'Let justice roll down like waters and righteousness like an ever-flowing stream.'—Amos five, twenty-four," he practically sang, when I remembered it was the day of the big march in support of the garbage strikers. The reverend was apparently priming himself for the occasion.

Having satisfied himself with these passages, he returned the scripture to me so forcefully that I had to take a step backward to receive it. He continued to stare at me, his quince-yellow eyes boring auger-like into my own.

"'Then fool,'" he pronounced, "'not nex' year, not nex' week, not tomorrah, but this night thy soul is required of thee.'—Luke twelve," upon which he turned and scuttled out of the shop without bothering to close the door.

"But it's not night," I objected at his parting, albeit idiotically. I hit the NO SALE key on the register and wondered why it was my lot to be always hounded by sanctimonious old gadflies. I understood well enough the moral imperative I was meant to draw from his visit: Who cowers in a shop nursing his nebbish ego when history is calling just outside the door? Stop already with the lotus eating and join the struggle for justice and equality; there are larger issues afoot than self-centered concerns that "don't amount to a hill of beans in this crazy world." And so forth. But I was far beyond being susceptible to such a conspicuous pricking of conscience.

Nevertheless, when I set down the Gideon Bible on top of the single edition of *The Pinch*, I had the troubling notion that I was laying a trump card over an inferior suit. I got up to close the door, but instead of pulling it to, stepped over the threshold and pulled it shut from outside. Then I began to follow the right reverend gent down Main Street.

Though he was nearly a block ahead of me I kept him in view, following past the discount clothiers, package stores, newsstands, and five-and-dimes ranging from business as usual to locked up tight. Squad cars outnumbered ordinary vehicles in the street, and the nearer we got to Beale the denser were the sidewalks with quick-stepping pedestrians carrying signs. I saw the reverend take out a pocket watch then pick up his pace, scurrying down a sidestreet where he melded among others flooding the alleys on their way to the gathering place of the march. That's when I lost sight of him, surrounded as I'd become by the hordes of people pouring into the intersection in front of the brick-domed pile of the Claiborne Temple. This was at the junction of Pontotoc and Hernando Streets just a few blocks off Beale.

Then, without the reverend for a bellwether, I experienced an abrupt failure of nerve. What the hell did I think I was doing so far from my hill of beans? Still, the atmosphere was unthreatening, even festive, the crowd reassuringly inclusive of every stratum of the Negro community: mothers with babies in strollers, skinny boys from the neighborhood in kneeless britches, pigtailed girls in jumpers turning cartwheels. There were ministers straightening clerical collars, business types adjusting horn-rims and foulard bowties. Strikers attempting to shepherd whole families were themselves called to order by designated marshals sporting megaphones and pumpkin-colored armbands. Smartly dressed ladies in stiletto heels accompanied aunties with cumbrous bosoms, their flinty-faced husbands in tow. Teenagers chanting the names of their high schools along with their opposition to the mayor were greeted with complicit nods from their elders. The only other white faces I saw were a smattering of union leaders and a group of tense women holding a banner reading *Rearing Children of Good Will Workshop*. But even the police helicopter flying low overhead seemed to contribute to the field-day mood.

While I consoled myself that I was ignored by most, caught up as they were in the general exuberance, I was aware of attracting a number of stares, some of which seemed a bit chilly. Again my resolve began to waver. Was this really my fight? I reproached myself for my pigeon heart, though I couldn't have been the only one who detected unbenign elements in the throng. Among the omnipresent placards proclaiming I AM A MAN and NO DREAM DEFERRED were less circumspect slogans such as MAYOR LOEB EAT SHIT. The latter were brandished by unsmiling youths regarded misgivingly by the older marchers. A child riding the shoulders of a man in combat boots carried a branch dangling a noose with a sign attached reading LOEB'S HANGING TREE. But just when I was close to succumbing to a paralysis of irresolution, someone slapped my back, and I turned in alarm to be hailed by none other than Elder Lincoln. He was wearing a puff-sleeved paisley shirt, a beaded headband encircling his 'fro like a fence around a billowy black cloud.

"Hello, buckra," he said, flashing his keyboard grin. "You lost?"

I was maybe a little gladder to see him than the situation warranted, and he perceived it.

"It's awight, young white folks"—did he even remember my name?—"you among friends."

You couldn't have proved it by the phalanx of young men in their Invaders jackets backing him up. One of them wearing a sideways baseball cap had torn a stick from a pasteboard sign and was slapping it menacingly against his thigh. Another, the beetle brow I recognized from Beatnik Manor, asked pointedly, "What's this crackerass mo'fuck doing here?"

Observing how his right hand was fisted in a black leather glove, I was ready to declare myself a gate-crasher pure and simple, then make my apologies and slope off into the wings, when Elder spoke up again.

"Be easy, Sweet Weeyum, the man's here to see we get justice. Anyhow," shading his eyes toward the sun peeping out from behind a dissipating thunderhead, "this a zippadee-doodah kinda day." His genuine high spirits, it seemed to me, overruled the inherent sarcasm in his voice.

Then I was among them for better or worse, and we'd begun to push through the crowd that had itself started sluggishly to move forward. For the word had come down that Dr. King had finally arrived, and we could see the commotion up ahead where a white Continental had just peeled away from the curb. I could even make out the crowns of a few snap-brim fedoras and the tops of a couple of bare heads belonging, I supposed, to the dignitaries of the movement. One would be the reverend doctor himself, the knowledge of whose presence gave me a nameless sensation. They'd said he was played out, that Memphis was anyway an annoying diversion from more pressing concerns, but there he was and I felt my ganglia crackling like spark plugs.

He would be flanked by his retinue, among them his lieutenant, the hefty one with whom he was always shown arm in arm: Abernathy. I knew Abernathy and had heard of others—Kyles, Jackson, Young—heroes of a people who had only recently stepped out of the shadows. But I was ignorant of the identities of most. Of their trials—compared to which my own were kreplach, as Avrom might have said—I knew next to nothing; and again came the feeling of having trespassed an affair that was none of my business. But the smaller I felt, the larger seemed the moment I was in, and buoyed by the energy around me I couldn't help it, I began to exult a little in the largeness of the event, wishing that Rachel could see me now.

As the march had started in earnest, the marshals strode up and down the line shouting through their bullhorns to stay in formation, keep the sidewalks clear, though no one seemed to pay them much heed. People were spread out all over the pavement, their haphazardness more akin to an unofficial parade than an orderly demonstration. The upstart clouds had parted, prompting the marchers to remove their coats and jackets, and I too welcomed the sunshine that dissolved the slight chill I'd felt earlier on. As we turned the corner into Beale, I relaxed in the moving current, and though I knew that negotiations between the city and the workers had failed, that Dr. King's coming to Memphis was in fact a last resort, I thought I sniffed a shared sense of victory in the wind. I had an urge to take Elder's arm but feared the gesture might be a liberty too far. Nevertheless I began to feel secure in the company I was keeping, its immediate members making their way through the crowd with more haste than the crowd itself was advancing toward Main Street. It was a joyful but restless multitude, everyone wanting, it seemed, to get closer to the front, anxious perhaps to be nearer their prophet, but Elder's bunch with their sly expressions were pushier than the rest. Their obtrusiveness provoked the occasional irritated glance from their fellow marchers, and Elder, the adult among them, must have sensed the tension, because he assured me (or himself?), "My boys have done waited a long time to fix the world."

Tikkun olam, I thought, which was Pinchas Pin's term for the efforts of the Shpinker Hasids to repair the rift between heaven and earth—though I thought also that Elder's "boys" hadn't waited half so long as most.

The signs bobbed above the heads of the marchers, many of whom had begun spontaneously to sing "We Shall Overcome." Members of the procession joked with those standing by on the curbs, beckoning them to "join us, brothahs," and here and there some vagrant would hitch up his trousers and toddle into the flow. There was even a cohort of idlers with conked hair and flashy suits hanging out in front of a pool hall who stepped into the passing humanity, so that I began to think the whole colored race might be eventually swept into that mighty stream. No pretense was made of staying in line, everyone strolling at his or her own pace (with the exception of the Invaders, who continued to muscle their way forward). I understood that the destination was the Civic Center Plaza, where speeches would be made before the crowd was dispersed and sent back to whence they'd come. Still it was easy to imagine that the whole Negro nation was on its way to entering Beulah Land. Then an extraordinary thing happened: Elder Lincoln linked his arm in mine.

"I mon' edumacate you, son," he announced. I recognized the condescension whenever he resorted to minstrel show dialect, and as for the paternal term of address, Elder—his name notwithstanding—wasn't much older than me. All the same, his sudden bonhomie gave me a charge. "Gon' introduce you to the various genus and species of the nigra," he continued, his words turning heads despite the surrounding din. "Now that one," pointing to an ashen-faced old party wearing his sign about his neck like a mug shot tag, "that's what you call your common or garden shine. Don't matter they ain't much shine to the boy. And the lady there," indicating a sallow-skinned woman in churchy attire, "she's what you call a mustard seed. Them deacons with their process hairdos, they arnchy niggahs, not to be confused with the dicty. And over there you got your standard-issue spade." He seemed to be pointing at random now, closing one eye as if taking aim over the barrel of his forefinger, a bitter edge having entered his voice. "You got your dinge, your boogie, the eight-ball, the ink, Uncle Mose hisself, and that one"—he grabbed my chin with his free hand to direct my attention toward a slack-jawed character in a shower cap—"that's your bluegum niggah—an extremely dangerous variety with a poison bite."

I didn't see why he felt the need to harass me with his commentary; it was unfair given the clear commitment I'd made to the cause. Offended, I searched for some topic that would prove I knew more about negritude than he gave me credit for.

"Elder," I said, "remember the lynched fiddler you said your grandma had relations with?" He made a face as if shocked at the reference. "Well, he couldn't have been anybody's daddy 'cause he didn't have any balls."

The musician scratched his scalp vigorously and flashed his ivories. "You didn't know the colored man's 'nads is uniquely re-gen-er-*a*-tive?" he replied, then instantly retracted his grin.

Meanwhile Elder's crew were behaving more like a flying wedge than members of a disciplined protest, shouldering people out of their way as they forged ahead. Elder himself looked a little troubled by their increasing aggression, though he nonetheless lurched forward with them, and I with him. Fact was, everyone was walking slightly too fast for a body of that size: people bumping into one another and tripping over each other's heels. Did they mean to overtake the leaders they were drawing ever nearer to? We were practically in arm's reach of the vanguard that included the standard-bearer himself, though surely nothing could go wrong on a march led by him, his very presence guaranteeing the non-violence of his creed. Even so, there was more cause for distress than the brazenness of my companions.

Some of the kids had broken ranks to run onto the sidewalk and beat with sticks on the plate-glass windows of the pawnshops along the route. They swatted at the hanging brass balls like they would at piñatas. At first the shop windows shivered but resisted the battering, which may not even have been intended to break them; then one of them cracked, glass splinters showering the sidewalk, and that was all it took. The previously elated faces of the marchers in my vicinity changed instantly to expressions of agitation and dismay. There were mixed cries, mostly rebukes of the young vandals, though some, as if finally released from constraint, egged them on: "Smash them suckahs, chillen!" It was the signal for wholesale pandemonium. The police, whose presence had been reasonably measured in the early stage of the demonstration, swarmed from all quarters. They moved in to cordon off the street between the mass of the protesters and the vandals, some of whom had begun attempting to loot the shops. Nightsticks were produced and one young tomfool dragging a sousaphone out of Cohen's Loans was clubbed to a jellied pulp. A line of cops in gas masks and full riot gear had appeared at either end of Beale between Main and Third Streets, thus corralling the procession. Now there was the sound of shattering glass all around us, as the police began shooting canisters of Mace into the crowd. Screams went up, as much (I thought) in desolation over the aborted march as in fear, while a squad of the faithful formed a circle around Dr. King and his party to escort them out of the fray. Ignoring the calls of the marshals to walk don't run, people began to take off in every direction, some knocked down and trampled in their flight.

The wail of sirens filled the space in the brain where rational thought might have occurred. Seeing was no longer believing: the cops left off beating the marchers only to smash the cameras of journalists. Then I saw Sweet Weeyum give the nod to his cronies, who smirked like this was the moment they'd been waiting for, and pulled bandannas over their faces. With his gloved hand Sweet Weeyum drew from inside his jacket a cobalt-blue bottle with a muslin tassel protruding from its mouth. He struck a match as Elder (shouting "Nah-uh, homes!") reached out too late to detain him, and hurled the lighted bottle in a lofty arc through the broken window of Schwab's General Store—whose interior blossomed with a *poof* into petals of mandarin flame.

Straightaway the heat were all over him. "Like stink on a monkey," I heard Elder say in a mournful valediction, before he set his jaw and jumped on the back of one of the cops. The cop hunched his shoulders and flailed to no effect with his baton in an effort to shake himself free of his attacker, his eyes bugging behind his plastic visor from Elder's chokehold round his throat. Having laid out Sweet Weeyum, several of the other officers came to the aid of their comrade and made to pry the Negro from his back, but Elder hung on tenaciously. They commenced to pummel him, the *whump whump* of their truncheons on his buttocks and shoulder blades lending a sickening backbeat to the shrieks that filled the surrounding air. I looked about for the rest of the Invaders, who were nowhere in sight. The drifting smoke from the tear gas was beginning to scald my lungs, and, coughing convulsively, I pulled my collar over my nose; I wiped my streaming eyes with a shirtsleeve and waited to be convinced that what I witnessed was actually happening.

The cop had fallen to the pavement with Elder still on his back, his legs clinching the man's utility-laden waist while his fellows continued their cudgeling. They pounded him, the "apeshit nigger!," with an abandon so indiscriminate that some of their blows struck the downed patrolman as well. Then, when it seemed that their battery was unavailing, that no amount of punishment could make Elder let go of his nearly asphyxiated victim, one of the cops—his angular jaw grinding gum—pulled out his semiautomatic. The gun went off with a hollow clap, a plume of rose-pink mist spouting from Elder's head. It jerked, his head, as if he were trying to work a kink from his neck before he lay still on top of the cop, who rolled out from under him speckled in blood. Then I wish I could say I was compelled by impulse, catapulted into action by the gun's report, but I fully understood the pointlessness of my action as I leapt astride the back of the cop who'd pulled the trigger. I rode him a few tottering steps of a heartsore piggyback before a chandelier burst in my skull.

Back before his Jenny had returned to the city, when he was still compiling his history, Muni Pinsker—remembering the future—described a skinny kid shelving books in a used book store on Main Street. The kid's name was Lenny Sklarew and he was about to misplace a volume called *The Pinch*. Muni paused a moment in his writing, wondering if this nishtikeit character really existed, or would ever exist. "And what's he doing in my book?" Then the scribe inhaled the tainted air of his room and proceeded to recount Lenny's adventures without giving his claim to legitimacy a second thought. That was Muni's method: what was drawn from life and what was imagined were consubstantial.

There were few details of Lenny's biography worth documenting, the facts so sketchy that Lenny himself came to forget them in time. He grew up in a ranch house in an East Memphis suburb, so far from the river that the river was only a rumor. His parents were joiners, acquisitive types disappointed by the boy's lack of ambition. ("Can he really be ours?" they sometimes mused.) He was a poor student, had few friends, and spent his waking hours reading novels and watching black-and-white movies on TV. Owing to a severe case of cystic acne during adolescence, he suffered from a shamefacedness for which he compensated with wisecracks and bluster. Often he felt he didn't deserve to be loved. Conversely, due to inveterate dreaming, he conceived the notion that he was the hero of his own bootless life. Once, having called his own bluff, he joined a mass demonstration in support of striking sanitation workers. When the march disintegrated into chaos, Lenny, caught up in the melee, was hit over the head by a cop. He came to strapped to a gurney in the back of an ambulance attended by a pair of bantering paramedics.

"So Adell," he heard one of them saying through the ringing in his ears and the crackling of a shortwave radio, "you know what happened to the nigger who looked up his family tree?"

"Wait, Ricky, don't tell me; I believe I do know." A grunt, presumably the sound of Adell thinking. "Okay, I give."

"A gorilla shit on his face."

There was a reciprocal wheezing and hooting that passed for laughter. Then Adell: "I got one, Ricky. Wha'd the sheriff call the nigger that was shot fifteen times?"

Replied Ricky without missing a beat, "Worst case of suicide I ever seen."

"Aw, Ricky, you anus."

More wheezy laughter and Lenny opened an eye, the other swollen shut and sealed with dried blood. He saw the two paramedics seated on an aluminum bench alongside him in the joggling ambulance. One had a head like a royal-pink egg raddled with purple veins, the other an elongated equine face, though Lenny couldn't tell whether his perceptions were accurate or the result of his murderous headache. They were wearing matching navy polos with EMS emblems.

"Looks like our agitatin' boy is still among the living," averred the horse face.

"I'd speckalate," said Ricky, "that this'n's done contracted your jewrish strain of jungle fever."

"Hey, Ricky-tick, y'ever hear about the jew lady asked her husband to 'Give me ten inches and make it hurt'?"

"Naw, Adell, I ain't."

Adell rubbed his palms at the prospect of a joke his partner hadn't heard. "He fucked her twicet and threw her down the stairs."

The laughter this time was more lukewarm on Ricky's part, who countered, "You know what happens when a jew walks into a wall with a hard-on?"

While Adell pondered, their patient, despite his intense pain and prostration, offered by way of an automatic response, "He breaks his nose."

The medics exchanged looks, then leaned over Lenny in tandem.

"He seems to be ezibiting vital signs," was Adell's studied opinion.

"Better get to work on him pronto, Tonto," pronounced Ricky. "You know the drill."

"Look, listen, and feel," Adell recited by the book, the two of them becoming suddenly all business.

"First clear his airway," said Ricky, pulling rank. "Head tilt, chin lift, jaw thrust. I'll do the poopillary."

Following orders with perhaps more zeal than the situation called for, Adell yanked Lenny's head into a number of unnatural positions, while Ricky turned the patient's unbruised eyelid inside out. Lenny struggled against their good offices as best he could given the unyielding snugness of his leather restraints.

"Fucker's done gone into seizure," advised Ricky, "prob'ly the result'a nerlogical impairment. Adell," his partner stood to attention, banging his sconce on the ambulance ceiling, "administer traykl intubation and use your large-bore combitube." Smiling a bit diabolically, Adell began trying to shove a plastic tube into Lenny's throat, though his victim whipped his head back and forth to avoid it. Meanwhile Ricky was preparing a king-size hypodermic needle, sparing a wink of his piggy eye for the wounded young man as he gave it a squirt.

At that point the ambulance, its siren blaring, began an uphill climb, the abrupt ascent causing the medics to momentarily lose their footing. They braced themselves against the sides of the van as the trauma lights flickered and a defibrillator fell from the wall. Then the van hit a pothole and the double doors at the rear, which had apparently been inadequately closed, swung open. Regaining his balance, Adell must have assumed that Ricky would tend to the doors, because he persisted in his attempt to stuff the tube down Lenny's throat; but Ricky grabbed his arm.

"Whoa, bubba," he cautioned, "we're headed uphill with the doors wide open." Adell seemed puzzled that his partner should be thus stating the obvious. "I say," repeated Ricky more declaratively, "we're riding uphill with the doors wide open and the stretcher's starting to slide." He cut his eyes toward the floor, underscoring the motion with a bobbing chin until Adell, a little slow on the uptake, finally took the hint, releasing the lock on a caster with the toe of his boot. "And," he added, in harmony now with Ricky's sham alarm, "the got-dam thang's fixin' to roll out the back of the van!"

It didn't roll quite far enough on its own to satisfy the medics, however, so Ricky shouted to the driver over the screeching siren, "Pedal to the metal, Cooter, we're 'bout to lose this guy!"

Duly alerted, the driver stomped the accelerator, causing the ambulance to jolt precipitously forward and the gurney with its pinioned patient to shoot out the vehicle's rear end.

It landed in the street with a tumultuous clattering that nearly jarred Lenny's bones out of his skin and kicked what wind was left from his diaphragm. Its accordion frame having collapsed to the level of the curb, the stretcher began traveling downhill, gaining speed as it headed west along Madison Avenue, veering into the traffic headed east. Lenny wrestled in vain against the straps that held him, his panic anything but blind, since his good eye—its lid peeled back by the medic—stared helplessly into the oncoming traffic. Then a curious thing: he was launched beyond fear, utterly defeated by the sheer moronic opprobrium of his predicament. Fear was no longer an issue, for so complete was his immobilization that he felt oddly secure, as if bound to a mast in a storm. The cars honked and swerved to miss him, their windshields hurling shards of sunlight, sleek ornaments pointing like warheads from their hoods. But as the stretcher gathered momentum, Lenny experienced only an abysmal shame at how his situation mocked the ill-starred significance of this day. What had he thought he was doing in the first place—a muddy-brained white guy with only the flimsiest claim to a social conscience, or any kind of a conscience at all? Did he think he could dabble in history like he'd dabbled in romance?

The gurney rattled down the avenue at breakneck velocity past an automobile showroom, a rubber die workshop, a YMCA. Keeping pace with it—Lenny thought he observed—was the demon Ketev from the Left Emanation, tumbling alongside with his calf's head impaling his fetal-curled body on the horn that sprouted from his brow. Cars skidded, one sideswiping another; tires squealed and horns caterwauled; pedestrians looked on balefully, while Lenny's skull throbbed to the point of rupture with the magnitude of his disgrace. When the gurney careered beneath the turning juggernaut of an A&P truck and jumped the curb, its passenger almost welcomed the yowl of his shattered bones and the Lenny-shaped indentation he anticipated making in the metal foundry's brick wall.

On returning to the Pinch Jenny Bashrig, formerly La Funambula, found a neighborhood past its prime, its citizens gathered in the park to observe a public enormity. She never paused to question the psychic connection that had drawn her back at that evil hour; there was no time for idle conjecture. Without scrupling she climbed into the branches of the upside-down oak in the forlorn hope that someone might rescue the fiddler while she distracted the mob. But that had not happened. And when she descended to find the crowd dispersing and the sad-sack scribe waiting there with the moon-eyed boy beside him, she knew that she'd already said so long to the circus. It was a fact to which she would never be wholly reconciled.

Taking stock of her old lover's uncouth condition, she had only this to say: "You look bad enough to make an onion cry."

For his part Muni endeavored to coax his mouth into speech, but so far no words had emerged. It was frightening out there in the open air without a text to follow, and he seemed incapable of improvisation. He could guess that for Jenny the long absence was perhaps an unbridgeable gulf between them, though for him it was as if no time had elapsed at all.

He saw that her dark eyes were brimful of tears, her features (sharper than ever) drawn tight with grieving. Unable to speak he stepped forward to lift the shawl, which dangled from her hand, and drape it over the shoulders that her scanty costume left bare. Then he stepped back swiftly lest the gesture be taken amiss.

"Jenny," he managed finally, "what should I say?"

She considered. "You can say, 'I'm a prick with ears.' Say, 'I should sicken and remember.' Momzer, you should be eaten alive!" she shouted. She choked on an effort to release another curse, for want of which she resorted to slapping his cheek. She slapped him forehand and back, his head swiveling left and right with each cuff, so that he had at last to grab hold of her in order to subdue the buffeting. He held her firmly, folding her in his arms for fear she might come apart from her violent sobs. They stood like that for a time, both of them racked by her grief, until Jenny's body began gradually to grow slack and cease resisting. But even then Muni didn't let go. With his nose buried in her hair, he sniffed the miscellany of fragrances—pine tar, hibiscus, chimpanzee—that she'd brought back from her travels; while his cheeks, still stinging, were further lashed by the strands of hair working their way out of her bun.

Then suddenly reawakening to the cursed place they were in, Jenny cried, "Get me out of here!" As Muni began to escort her from the park, she took one last look behind her at the upstanding roots which creaked from the gentle swaying of the hanged man, a breeze teasing an Aeolian murmur from his fractured instrument. An armed Klansman was stationed in the shadows beneath him to discourage anyone who might want to cut down their ill omen too soon. As she turned back toward Muni, a quote from the drowned clown's store of favorites escaped Jenny's lips: "An oasis of horror," she breathed, "in a desert of boredom."

Heartened by her utterance, which was at least in the realm of communication, Muni dredged up a platitude of his own. "They say," he ventured, "that if so wish the righteous, they can make a world. Likewise the putz, if he don't pay attention, can lose one. A world, that is."

Jenny allowed herself one more sniffle, then no more. "A philosopher yet," she said bitterly.

Near the entrance to the park she paused to collect the carpetbag she'd stashed under a bench. When she stood up again, she pointed to the fey child that was still holding Muni's hand and inquired, "What's this?"

Muni explained that Tyrone was the boy that Katie and Pinchas Pin had had late in life before their dual demise.

Smiling wanly, Jenny licked a finger, thrust it into the blaze of the boy's ginger hair, and made a sizzling sound. The kid didn't return her smile but nevertheless raised his limpid eyes in acknowledgment.

"When I left," said Jenny, with delicacy, "Katie was dead already. Since when do dead ladies have babies?"

In response little Tyrone admitted, "I don't think I'm a hundred percent human boy."

Jenny harrumphed. "Life swarms with innocent monsters," she remarked, for despite all she was proud of the education she'd received during her voyaging.

"I have to pish," said Tyrone, as if to prove he had also the needs of an ordinary child, though looking at him neither Muni nor Jenny was fooled.

The North Main Street they encountered as they trudged back from the lynching was a detritus-clogged artery, its commercial establishments in a shocking state of disrepair. The proprietors of the shops and residents of the lodgings above them stood brooding over their broken surroundings, as if the death of the Negro had recalled them to the unimpassioned rhythm of their days. Where had they been for what amounted (when they were able to gauge the interlude according to a standard calendar) to years? The earth itself looked to have aged in their absence, its surface shelf-worn and unsparingly lived upon, though their neighbors appeared much the same. (Some even looked, despite their joylessness, to have improved in their general appearance.) All were aware as never before that a vital and prospering city was spread out around them, which the Pinch had failed to keep pace with. Why, wondered some, had they not decamped before it was too late?

"A shmutsik dump" was the judgment heard frequently as the merchants went through the motions of reclaiming their sidetracked livelihoods. "We're poor!" the families complained, having apparently never noticed before.

Muni's courtship of Jenny Bashrig, whom Mr. and Mrs. Rosen had

welcomed back into their household with open arms, was a brief and diffident affair. Neither pretended that the second chance they'd been afforded
was a continuance of the passion they'd known in the days before the
quake; their renewed sympathy for one another had little in common with
the infatuation that had shaken them beyond sanity at the top of the tree
in Market Square Park. That jarring romance belonged to a prelapsarian
period that neither Muni nor Jenny could clearly recollect, a variety of
forgetfulness they had in common with the rest of North Main Street.
What they shared now was a mutual sorrow, both believing they'd shelved
their own particular sadness to mourn what the other had lost, then discovered in that unpretty process that much of what they'd lost was the
same. In the event, they soon made a tentative peace with one another and
found in their reacquaintance that something of the original fondness had
endured. For a couple without fountain pen or balance pole to cling to, it
was enough.

When Muni said, "Marry me already?," Jenny replied, "Why not?,"
then squashed the reasons that tried to give voice. They were wed, after
registering with the proper authorities, in a private ceremony in Rabbi
Eliakum ben Yahya's chambers above the feedstore, with only Tyrone, the
Rosens, and the rebbe's handful of disciples as witnesses.

Their choice of the old holy man was largely a practical decision, since
his rogue offices could be had cut-rate as compared to the inflated services of the established synagogues. (Some of which, in their lordliness,
alleged that nuptials officiated by ben Yahya were not authentically sancti-
fied.) Also, the couple felt frankly sorry for the old man, whose bluff good
health had begun to deteriorate rapidly since his return to the Pinch. The
salubrious benefits of his underworld furlough were short-lived, and it
appeared to anyone who noticed his corky flesh and the troughs beneath
his lusterless eyes that he'd come back from the afterlife to die. In the
meantime he was being neglected by his disillusioned followers; so maybe,
thought Muni and Jenny—united in their good intentions—a wedding
would lift his spirits.

The occasion, however, was a little soured by the stiff-necked presence of the Hasids, who had become ever more doctrinaire since their
rebbe's return: they withheld their "Mazel tovs" at the crushing of the
goblet, as there could be no real mazel until the Messiah came; frowned

at the lopsided halo that the old man, with his waning powers, made to appear above the bride and groom's heads. While music was in any case absent in the ghetto since the death of the fiddler and the pawning of the Widow Teitelbaum's gramophone, they no longer deemed it kosher to chant or dance. Since the end of that murky period that they regarded as the failed result of their mystical experimentation, they had become increasingly rigid in their adherence to the letter of the law. Attempting to impose their intolerance on one and all, they policed the neighborhood (though the shopkeepers shooed them away like flies); they routinely accused individuals of having committed sins punishable by HaShem with chancres and bloody flux, and even tried to organize a rabbinic court to excommunicate Ivan Salky for having donned the phylactery of the arm before that of the forehead.

For all that, the rebbe performed the ceremony with perfect solemnity and a minimum of rheumy suspiration. Then, postponing their honeymoon indefinitely, the retired wirewalker and the former scribe set up housekeeping together, and Muni became a merchant by default. While his uncle had died intestate (his remains consigned to thin air), no one thought to dispute the nephew's right to proprietorship of the store. Besides, given Muni's reluctance to adapt his inventory to the changing times, Pin's General Merchandise never offered much in the way of competition. Not that anyone was getting rich. The economy at that time was a primitive affair, primarily dependent on a system of bartering, as the businesses had only just begun to replenish their coffers with coin of the realm. While most of the items exchanged on the street were fairly worthless, occasionally someone would bring in an object of value, something washed up in the receding floodwaters: a kiddish cup (found in Petrofsky's cellar) that the prophet Jeremiah had hidden after the destruction of the Temple, a nutshell bearing a microscript attributed to an angelic hand . . . But there was of course nothing of equal market value to trade for such objects, which were seldom recognized as sacred in any event.

The just-married Jenny Pinsker, if only to keep from looking back, threw herself into her labors upstairs and down, and in the tradition of the young Katie Pin before her, proved as able a business partner as a wife. It was she who kept the books and appeased the creditors; who prevailed upon her husband to either update his stock or else be relegated to some

quaint relic of a notions emporium—advice that Muni, resistant to in-
novation, only acceded to in the face of threats. Jenny threatened at every
setback to return to the circus, though in truth those years were becoming as unreal to her as Muni's time as compulsive scribbler was to him.
Moreover, her affection for her husband had seriously compromised her
center of gravity, further impaired by the often unbearable arthritis that
distressed her gimp leg. Old Doc Seligman, who was suspected in his
hemorrhoidal dotage of abusing his own medicine chest, prescribed her
various analgesic powders that she was given to chasing with a finger or
two of peppermint schnapps. It was a habit she'd picked up in her travels.
When Muni expressed concern, Jenny twitted him that "Der shikker
is a goy," and assured him it wasn't in the nature of a Jewish daughter
to become a drunk. Meanwhile she'd conceived a fascination for the
insular little boy who occupied the former scriptorium and was after all
an orphan like herself. She recited at his bedside the verses she recalled
from the clown's somber catalog until they'd faded from her memory,
then fell back on trying to entertain him with tales of the big top. On
occasion Muni might supplement her stories with his own account of
walking to America from the Siberian wastes, an event you might have
thought he'd completed only yesterday. More than the stuffed derma
and brisket that the ever-solicitous Rosens incessantly plied the newlyweds with, it was the broken record of those stories on which they endeavored to nourish Tyrone.

At least until Mrs. Rosen warned them, dripping sweat into the pot of
soup she'd lugged up the stairs, "they going, the bubbeh mayses, to stunt
the boy's growth."

They deferred to her wisdom, though there was no telling how much
of his guardians' maunderings Tyrone had digested. His physical growth
was normal at any rate, and while his emotional maturity may have lagged
behind, growing up was not a priority in the Pinsker household. Moreover,
Tyrone had found his way into his own cache of narrative, the one he'd
been poring over since before he learned to read. It was almost as if his
actual literacy had little to do with deciphering the ragged manuscript
that Muni had abandoned in the former nursery.

He attended to those pages with a sedulity not dissimilar from that
with which the Shpinker Hasids read Torah—that is, when they weren't

out exhorting the street to read it as well. They circulated in the neighborhood like missionaries, admonishing all and sundry to forswear their
getting and spending in favor of studying sacred texts; they should live
in the Book rather than the fallen world. But the only book the merchants of North Main were interested in was the one that kept their accounts, which were more often than not in the red. The fanatics would
have them meditating on the sacrifice of Isaac and the sack of Jerusalem,
but the population of the Pinch was otherwise occupied with Mrs.
Bluestein's Mah-Jongg circle and the dance marathons Rabbi Lapidus
had been pressured into hosting at the Menorah Institute. They were
distracted by Greta Garbo and John Gilbert in *Flesh and the Devil* at
the Idle Hour Cinema and by Representative Eustace Butler's attempt to
introduce in the Tennessee House a bill outlawing gossip. They were
troubled by the arrest of Tillie Alperin's scandalous daughter, caught
smuggling booze under her skirt into the Green Owl Café, and by the
crash of the New York Stock Exchange. Though with respect to the headlines announcing that hard times had arrived, the North Main Streeters
were likely to reply, "When wasn't it hard times in the Pinch?" Then they
might give one another a sidelong glance, as if subject to a phantom spasm
of memory recalling a time no one would have characterized as exactly
"hard."

Were Jenny and Muni happy? It wasn't a question they would have
bothered to ask, so absorbed were they in the specifics of their new life
together. Had they stopped to take account of their situation, they might
in fact have been surprised by the unqualified nature of their attachment.
It was an affinity that depended on neither chemistry nor looks—Jenny
was losing hers, and Muni, while trimmed and shaven in his commercial
aspect, was never a beauty. Even touch was not essential to their alliance,
though the occasional clip or pinch leading to a conjugal tumble remained a staple of their days. But at the heart of their union was a dogged
devotion—enhanced by an unwritten contract to reduce the past to make-
believe—that seemed to grow even as their energies flagged.

Muni's in particular were increasingly limited, his lungs having never
been entirely defrosted of arctic rime. No amount of eruptive coughing
could rid him of it, though he brought up a good deal of glutinous matter in his expectorations. Dr. Fruchter, whom the doddering Seligman's

patients had begun to consult, diagnosed consumption: "The Jewish disease," he remarked somewhat smugly, a self-satisfied, musk-scented man; "a fine old tradition amongst our people." (Muni allowed that he was not that keen on tradition.) Priding himself abreast of the latest treatments, Fruchter assured the couple that nothing short of a stint in an Adirondack "cure cottage" could delay Muni's inevitable decline. There was naturally no question of the Pinskers amassing the funds for such a retreat; and besides, the climate and prescribed exposure to the elements sounded too much like the katorga to the one-time fugitive. Jenny nursed him on his bad days as best she could, despite being run off her feet with waiting on customers and attending to domestic chores. Owing to her schnapps and morphine cordials, however, she sometimes performed her duties in a sleepwalker's fog: La Funambula become La Somnambula, as Mose Dlugach's wisenheim sons observed. Like everyone in the Pinch, Jenny and Muni had made plans: they would salt away enough cash to buy a place—a house with a yard and a tree—in one of the better neighborhoods farther east, where the business would ultimately follow. But like everyone else they could never quite get a leg up. In time they relinquished their pipe dreams along with their neighbors, who pinned their hopes on their children and resigned themselves to dying in harness in the Pinch.

Suspended awhile in the neighborhood, the process of aging was accelerated now as if to make up for its time in abeyance, and after a lengthy moratorium death had begun to visit North Main Street like a minor pestilence. Even the optimism of President Roosevelt's inauguration speech did little to curb the incidence of mortality; people were passing away at a rate that seemed like retribution for having lived so long. Sparber the undertaker had become the most well-to-do man in the Pinch and arguably the most popular, since the funerals he arranged gave the community its best outlet for recreation. The bereaved would pile into the few available local vehicles and follow Sparber's freshly waxed Phaeton hearse out to the Jewish cemeteries on the city's periphery. Businesses would close for the day (as what business was there to lose?), and the burials would be followed by picnics under the elms. For the impoverished and unaffiliated, there were processions on foot to the nearby potter's field. Since it was generally acknowledged that nobody among that immigrant generation left the Pinch other than in a pine box, a fond bon voyage was bade to those who managed to depart it in any fashion. There were even some so envious that, during the penitential prayer on the Day of Atonement ("Who by fire and who by water / Who by sword and who by wild beast . . ."), were heard to utter under their breath, "How about me?"

As a consequence, Tillie Alperin's departure from scrofula, Sam Alabaster's from a fatty heart, and Mr. and Mrs. Elster's from exposure to fumes after cleaning their carpet with carbon tetrachloride, were regarded by many as blessings in disguise. "It's for the best," some said when Milton Chafetz died of a stroke after reading his own obituary—a printing error—in the *Hebrew Watchman;* they said the same when Cantor Bielski perished from complications resulting from holding his bladder throughout a reading of the Megillah, and when Oyzer Tarnopol reputedly succumbed from spontaneous combustion. "He's well out of it." Thus was the street's population eroded. Where there were no widowed spouses or sons and daughters to carry on the business, shops were repossessed by the bank and thereafter left vacant, so that the complexion of North Main took an even more derelict turn. The joke was that the earthly Pinch itself was done for and had ascended to a better place, where a heavenly version of the neighborhood rejoiced in a seller's market.

While the bond between husband and wife in their apartment above the general merchandise was strengthened by a shared affection for their charge, tasks and frequent ill health kept them often preoccupied. So the boy was left, as he had been much of his life, to his own amusements. Though they reminded themselves that he was a product of his peculiar origins, Tyrone remained a conundrum to his adoptive family. Not a bad-looking kid—his green eyes when wide open were beacons—he seemed to them as backward in comprehension as he was periodically possessed of a quick (if eccentric) intelligence. Though his limbs were well enough formed, he was stingy of movement and had small interest in playing outdoors with others. Which was a moot point in any case, since there were really no kids his own age to play with; and while the older ones refrained from bullying Tyrone, they tended to keep their distance, though whether from wariness or disdain who could say. He was an indifferent scholar at the Christine School (named for the late Miss Christine Reudelhuber), where nothing in the standard curriculum seemed to rouse his curiosity. Regarded as a queer fish by students and teachers alike, he was nevertheless tolerated for his inoffensive nature. He seemed for the most part imperturbable, even during the onset of adolescence, when his interest in the opposite sex was never seen to extend beyond a dispassionate appreciation of their limbs in motion. Though capable of expressing a measure of gratitude toward his guardians, it was only the perusal of Muni's untended manuscript in the former nursery that truly engaged him.

It should have been a forbidding proposition, construing those pages, even as the boy's reading skills advanced in proficiency. Not only was the writing crabbed, the pages water damaged, smeared with food, and stained in their latter portion with gouts of blood, but the language itself often strayed from a pidgin English into Yiddish and back again. Latin characters were occasionally replaced by the hooks and hangers of Hebrew script. But for Tyrone, reared in a Pinch that everyone else seemed to have forgotten, the language was somehow no deterrent to his concentration. To watch him at his reading—his free hand waving as if in time to music, the fingers as if squeezing flesh—was to believe he had only to cast his eye over the text to feel he was present at the events it described: such as the moment the butcher Makowsky cracked a walnut with his teeth and released a nitzot, a spark of the divine, which set fire to his beard without consuming his face. You could imagine his acute identification with the bitterness of Pinchas Pin, who was unable to give his wife a child, and the joy when a child was born to the merchant's Katie posthumously and precircumcised.

There never appeared to be any special method to Tyrone's reading: wherever he dipped into the narrative, that was a beginning and wherever he stopped was a terminus, since the events contained in Muni's "book" seemed to be happening all at once. They were events that, for the boy, took precedence over anything that occurred beyond the Pinch—be it the kidnap of the Lindbergh baby or the institution of the Nuremberg Laws. When not immersed irretrievably in the book, Tyrone could be a more or less functioning foster son, though his obedience was a variable affair. Conscripted on occasion to help out in the store, he performed his assigned tasks—folding winter-weight underwear, stacking odorless galvanized iron commodes—with a benign inattention, scarcely noticing the comings and goings of customers. You'd have thought he viewed the store and the down-at-heel street, when he bothered to look, from a vantage outside time.

Muni and Jenny were of course aware of Tyrone's rapt attachment to that mishmash of untitled pages—the results of a bout of derangement the merchant had no desire to revisit—and it gave them cause for concern. For Muni there was a particular guilt, feeling as he did that his own former shut-in existence might be his legacy to the boy, who was on his way to becoming a reclusive young man. But neither husband nor wife had the heart to try and separate him from his ruling passion. Still it pained them that, except for school (where his attendance, they would learn, was sporadic) and the odd errand on which he was dispatched, Tyrone stuck so close to home. In fact, the older he got the less was he inclined to leave his tiny room, where he was occasionally seen doodling with Muni's discarded pen on the backs of the unnumbered pages.

"It ain't healthy," fretted the merchant to his wife, "that the kid's all the time in the genizah," which he'd taken to calling the nursery—a genizah being a place for the disposal of obsolete books and papers.

Replied Jenny, "I think he took a look at being a grown-up, then decided to turn back."

Surely the boy must have been alert to the troubles that were rife in the household. But so what if his guardians suffered from their respective maladies, exacerbated by overwork; in the stories he read—and sometimes confused with the ones they'd told him—Muni and Jenny remained hale and blooming. If Muni suffered a massive hemorrhage that Dr. Fruchter was pleased to identify as "Rasmussen's aneurysm," Tyrone could still imagine his foster papa as a dirty-faced tyke, riding Getzel the belfer's shoulders through the slushy streets of Blod on the way to Reb Death's Head's cheder. And if Jenny, due to the virulent effects of her paregoric cocktails, succumbed to a self-lacerating fit of itching, the boy could still see her swaying to her off-key lullabies; if she woke up screaming from a recurring nightmare in which she was strapped to the wheel of a paddleboat, he pictured her clogging on the back of a five-gaited black stallion.

Muni remained bedridden with an unhopeful prognosis after his return from the hospital, and Jenny attended him despite her own chronic nightsweats and shallow breathing. (So sensitive had her skin become that she could bruise from the sound of the whistle at the coffee factory.) But even then Tyrone was not disturbed: the mutually diminished condition of the merchant and his wife had little to do with a past that held dominion over the here and now. Then, on a dove-gray morning in February, drowning in a deluge of bronchial bleeding, Muni Pinsker expired with a rosy bubble on his lips. "Moykhl" was the word his wife thought she heard when the bubble burst, meaning Sorry.

"I can tell you're sorry," chided Jenny, who for an instant was back in the yard of Dlugach's Secondhand having just rolled out of a carpet. Then she drained her teacup of the narcotic cordial that tasted of hemlock from the admixture of her tears.

In their single-minded pursuit of commerce, husband and wife had neglected to pay dues to what remained of the local landsmanschaft; neither had they purchased burial insurance from the peg-legged little man who peddled policies in their shoddily reconstructed neighborhood. And while the community had always taken pride in caring for its own, lately their fiscal austerity made the citizens reluctant to absorb any extra expense. So Muni was interred in the municipal boneyard just beyond the culvert that had once been Catfish Bayou. It wasn't an exclusively goyishe parcel, however, since a portion of hallowed ground had already received Yoyzef Zlotkin, the Widow Teitelbaum, and the honorable Eliakum ben Yahya (whose disciples made a saturnalian show of mourning, which they discharged themselves of in a day). The city provided transport for the casket that included a county official, a well-meaning functionary who took it upon himself to conduct a token memorial service. Told that the deceased was an immigrant, he went beyond the dictates of his office in extolling the loved one's patriotic devotion to his adopted homeland. A marker was promised though none had yet to appear.

Only a small cluster of neighbors showed up for the funeral. Among them were an aged but nicely turned-out Mama Rose and Morris Padauer, who'd lately moved into a house on Alabama Street. (The house was a gift from their undying son, Benjy, who ran a lucrative loan-sharking operation out of an office above the Green Owl Café.) Also in attendance was

Hershel Tarnopol, displaying the chins and dignified paunch of his position as district ward heeler, his fur lapel still torn in tribute to the recent demise of his father. Supported at either arm by the Rosens, Jenny looked as if disfigured by grief, her abdomen so distended from noxious fluids that some wondered if, despite her years, she was big with child. Dismissing the poor turnout, the widow assured the assembled, "It don't matter where they put his bones," since his soul was tucked safely away like a pressed posy among the pages in his young charge's possession. And no one would try to wrest those pages from Tyrone.

Though the store had by then gone mostly to wrack and ruin, Jenny made an effort to hold things together for the sake of the boy; she wanted, if superfluously, to protect him even beyond the self-imposed fortress of his own solitary withdrawal. But the damage to herself was irreversible. Mourning for Jenny took the form of outrage: now that Muni was gone, the sanctioned intimacy they'd shared as man and wife had dwindled in her mind to small change; it was bupkes when compared to the cataclysm of forbidden love they'd known before the quake. All the tenderness of their domestic life seemed to her to have been a charade. It was an evil thought, perhaps owing to the toxins that were ravaging her body and brain. Their effects had created a gulf between the widow and the current North Main Street, the one on which she dwelled in the hermitage of a dingy apartment with a largely oblivious kid. To his credit Tyrone was not so remote as to be wholly insensible to Jenny's deterioration. He might sometimes coax her to take a sip of Mrs. Rosen's fortified borscht, then wipe away the pink mustache it left on her upper lip, and once he placed in her lap the fat scrapbook bulging with her yellowing press releases. But instead of contemplating the photos and encomiums as she had in the past, Jenny tossed them onto the glacier of pages in Muni's genizah.

The unburdening of memories must have left her the more vulnerable to instinct; because one dim day, far from the Pinch in her thoughts, Jenny mounted the slant wire again and began her drunken ascent into the glaring spotlight. Uncharacteristically temperamental, she cursed the riggers for shining the spot in her eyes so that she had to climb the cable blind—though her naked toes had thankfully a foresight of their own. It was the steadfast Mrs. Rosen, bringing over a tray of vinegar meats to feed the orphans, who found her prostrate on the stairs beneath the hanging bulb.

For Tyrone, who had little occasion to leave his room, the absence of his guardians was a vacancy, not a vacuum. Since they had always seemed to him more vital in the book than in the flesh, he scarcely missed them. He never wept when Jenny was buried beside her husband, in a funeral slightly grander than Muni's since the Rosens had provided refreshments. Nor did he register the news some months later that the potter's field was being plowed under to make room for a new subdivision. (The disinterred caskets, slated for transferral to other cemeteries, were subsequently lost in a welter of bureaucratic cross-purposes.) Such information appeared to make no more of an impression on Tyrone's consciousness than, say, the wreck of the *Hindenburg* or the refusal of the US government to permit the refugees of the steamship *St. Louis* to disembark on its shores. Cousin Muni and his wife were anyway well enough preserved in the stories where nobody ever seemed to be gone for good.

After the bank foreclosed on Pin's General Merchandise, Tyrone, whose high school career had degenerated to the merest pretense, became a charity case in a community that could no longer afford to be charitable. A space was made available for him in the Rosens' basement for which, now that he was of age, he was expected to pony up a nominal rent. The money came from various odd jobs, which he performed so ineffectually that his employers—Zipper's Fine Wines & Spirits, Hekkie's Hardware & Feed—complained they had hired a saboteur. Still, since he scarcely ate unless reminded, families passed him around at mealtimes in a version of the Old Country's eating days. It was not a sustainable situation, and when Tyrone was called up in the years following the attack on Pearl Harbor, there was a guilty sense of relief on the street. No one, however, was deceived: all knew that the young misfit was ill equipped to go to war.

The displacement of Tyrone Pin's sensibility that began with his separation from Muni's draggled pages was advanced in the hedgerows of Normandy and the snowfields of the Ardennes, and completed at the gates of Dachau. He survived in body primarily because others, amused by his recitations from a storybook nobody recognized, looked after him as they might have a child consigned to their care; they treated him more like a mascot or a lucky charm than a fellow GI. Such a previously taciturn kid, he'd been concussed into a kind of chattering competition with the noise of the Big Berthas and the ack-ack guns; he was jarred into loquacity by the hail of body debris raining down upon their pup tents from yet another artillery barrage. His chatter took the form of the stories he murmured like a constant prayer, a chant that kept time to their footslogging progress across the wasteland of northern Europe. But the foolish music of his tales was finally unsuited to the nether region they stumbled into on the eve of the armistice. There the stories that had once diverted the soldiers seemed an obscenity in a place where the little sense the stories made was lost.

The soldiers were no longer listening anyway, occupied as they were with inspecting boxcars full of corpses and vomiting over the sight of walking broomsticks with skin as sere as the wings of bats. It was a nation of dry bones with claws, unable to digest powdered eggs but still capable of tearing a camp guard thrown into their midst limb from limb. The soldiers had no time to attend to Tyrone, though his vaporing did catch the attention of at least one coat-upon-a-stick, and that one, having nobody of his own left to care for, conceived—though he couldn't yet feed himself—a desire to look after the pixilated GI. The survivor—formerly Avrom of Slutsk when he remembered his name and later the languages, including English, that he'd once been conversant in—Avrom, who must have been as starved for illusion as for nourishment, went so far as to follow the narisher mensch across an ocean to America.

There he found him, no longer so talkative, painting pictures in a basement storeroom, on butcher paper, plywood panels, plaster walls, and whatever else came to hand. As a kid Tyrone had evinced only the slightest interest in drawing or coloring; words were his pictures even before he could read. Now it seemed he'd returned to a childhood that he'd never left far behind in order to revive a latent instinct. Or was it an original instinct that he'd only just developed? Because his designs—devoid of drunken soldiers wearing masks as they shoveled mounds of putrefaction in striped pajamas—expressed a dazzled, perhaps willful innocence. He'd begun with a box of thick wax crayons, drawing crude images out of the stories he no longer seemed able to relate. Seeing that these compositions were his single enthusiasm, no other concern having seized him since his return, the Rosens encouraged his efforts. From their own spare pockets they provided him with supplies: brushes and an easel, water-colors, egg temperas, and oils. Ignorant of all method and technique, he daubed, slashed, and stippled his illuminations on coarse and hostile surfaces until they began to achieve startling effects. By the time Mrs. Rosen ushered his first and only visitor down a creaky flight of stairs, Tyrone had converted their basement into a garish Lascaux.

Having found at the end of his odyssey only a paint-splattered shmegegi instead of the bruited miracle street, the survivor couldn't conceal his disappointment. "Dos iz efsher der Pinch?" he asked, incredulous. Where was the book that Tyrone had quoted from chapter and verse, the one he'd cited as history, atlas, and gazetteer, which had assumed a Grail-like aura for Avrom? He pressed the artist for clues to its whereabouts and was met with abstracted unconcern. Led so far by figments and sick fancy, the survivor experienced a mounting anger, directed as much at himself as Tyrone; he became possessed of a determination to retrieve some tangible keepsake for his trouble. At length he proceeded to bully the redheaded mooncalf into an instant of clarity, which vanished as quickly as it arrived, but not before Avrom had been enlightened. Alone by starlight he dug a hole beside a neglected sapling that showed little promise of ever growing taller. The sapling stood in an otherwise treeless plot of ground that had once been a park, where Tyrone had buried Muni's manuscript like an outworn Torah scroll before leaving for the war.

Around that time the Rosens' deli went belly-up, as had so many other North Main Street businesses. Families that owned their run-down buildings survived by renting rooms to the transient poor; they became landlords and hoped the sacrifices they'd made on behalf of their children hadn't been futile, while their children seemed to be waiting for the excuse of another war to leave the Pinch. (Impatient, they made trial excursions as far as the Pig-N-Whistle to sample pork barbecue, the Dreamland Gardens to drink Purple Jesuses.) Tenants rather than proprietors, the Rosens were evicted from their premises and reduced to living on a picayune pension in two rooms above Futterman's Bail Bonds on Monroe. Bereft of their hospitality and judged non compos mentis by his neighbors, Tyrone Pin was deemed a neighborhood liability: an agency was contacted and papers signed, committing him to the state asylum at Bolivar. Having pursued the artist from an inferno to his fool's paradise (and having cleared no end of bureaucratic hurdles along the way), the refugee Avrom Slutsky lacked any compelling reason to stick around. Neither did he have a reason to move on. A scholar and dreamer during the time that had preceded the great interruption, he leased a commercial space with an option to purchase on a shoestring loan from the Hebrew Immigrant Aid Society. There he began the unprofitable operation of buying and selling used books.

He sat at a desk in the midst of his cluttered shop, where his moodiness tended to discourage the occasional browser, and commenced a task even more thankless than his chosen trade. He began to translate the cross-bred language of Muni's exhumed manuscript—worm-eaten despite the gunny sack it was buried in—into a negotiable English, his own becoming less rusty in the process. It took him five years. Then willing a functional dexterity into his shaky hand, he made a fair copy of the yet untitled book, which he called (what else?) *The Pinch*. He gave it the albeit tongue-in-cheek subtitle *A History* and oversaw its printing at his own expense at a local press. It was also Avrom's idea, frankly an afterthought, to include as illustrations reproductions of the pictures the unhinged GI had painted with a holy vengeance on his return from overseas.

The general belief was that the bookseller had been scrupulously faithful in his redaction of *The Pinch*, but there were those who later suggested he took liberties with the original text. They argued that, frustrated with an inability to wring from Muni's manuscript his fascination on first hearing its contents in the lager, he invented bits for his own amusement. He tampered and perhaps even perversely inserted himself and his assistant as characters. Avrom would of course have vehemently denied the allegation: it was shtuterai, patently ridiculous. The passages foretelling his own arrival in Memphis—along with so many other prophecies—had after all come as no surprise to him, who had lost the capacity to be surprised: "For me," he might have said, "the future came already and went." And as for the intrusion into those pages of the feckless kid who came to work in his shop: that one, he would have had you to know, existed in the book's printed edition long before he'd turned up in the flesh at the Book Asylum. Regarding that issue the bookseller had responded with typical insouciance even to the inquiries of the employee himself: "It's the gilgul, stupid."

"The gilgul?"

Then Avrom had wearily explained the mystical process of the transmigration of souls, a concept he naturally had no truck with; on the other hand, he allowed for the necessity of some spiritual recycling in this day and age, when the availability of Yiddishe souls was severely depleted.

The employee, one Lenny Sklarew, had sighed in bewilderment, then gone back to alphabetizing the shelves.

When he'd delivered *The Pinch* to Shendeldecker the printer, who ran off the job on his greasy old six-cylinder rotary press, Avrom was glad to wash his hands of the thing. The labor of preparing the book for print had left him exhausted—a klippah, a husk. Why, he wondered, had he taken on the project in the first place? Why, for that matter, had he come to this Bluff City, America? If he experienced any gratification in having rendered Muni's folly accessible to the common reader, he never located it in any part of his being. He made no effort to publicize the undertaking for all its pains, or even to acknowledge its existence, and had a customer decided on some stray impulse to buy the thing, he would have sold it for a song. When the volume was in fact discovered in a random stack by his employee, he disclaimed any personal connection to it, the completion of his self-assigned task having absolved Avrom of his commitment to *The Pinch* for good and all. Though his employee, confounded by his own appearance in its pages, thought he detected otherwise.

Lenny believed that his boss took a measure of pride in his possession of the book, just as he did in his ownership of the shop and all it contained. It was a proprietariness that extended as well to his sometime assistant, over whose fly-by-night progress Avrom maintained a paternal (if cranky) interest. An interest that went beyond his curiosity, no doubt already satisfied, concerning the character of the kid in the book—the one who swallowed the pills that made his brain swell like a hypertrophied heart and fell out of moving vehicles.

He came around on a ward in St. Joseph's Hospital at about the time that Avrom, his organs failing, throat percolating blood on another ward in the same facility, passed out of this world. Lenny himself had sustained an impressive array of injuries—cracked ribs and skull, shattered knee, internal bleeding, et cetera—that kept him confined in bed tethered to tubes, ropes, and pulleys and moored to a catheter for better than a week. The injuries would have lingering aftereffects that served to get him declared 4-F by the local draft board. It was a deferral that the late Elder Lincoln would have advised him was undeserved: an arbitrary decision on the part of a committee that had an ample pool of black youth to draw from for its steady supply of cannon fodder. But Elder was no longer around to stoke Lenny's guilt. Nor, as it turned out, was Avrom, whom Lenny—garbed in an open-backed hospital gown and escorted by a portable pole with its dangling saline drip, surrounded by an aluminum walker—had gone looking for as soon as he was able. But on the wing where he'd previously visited him, the former employee was informed that his choleric old boss was already departed, carted away and buried in an East Memphis memorial park at taxpayers' expense. Lenny would plan, then postpone, pilgrimages to his gravesite ever after.

The crisis of identity that had predated Lenny's day in the streets was naturally compounded by physical trauma and the liberal doses of morphine and painkillers that were afterward prescribed. Having forgotten his prior loss of memory, you could say that the patient suffered from a double amnesia, not that the condition deeply concerned him in his fuddled state. At some point he was visited by a small delegation from the band known as the Psychopimps, who assured him he was not to blame for Elder's death in a tone that suggested he might well have been. But if their tidings penetrated the convalescent's cloudy mind at all, they registered only as a muffled tympanum in the brain. Likewise the news of Dr. King's return to Memphis, his valedictory speech punctuated by thunder and lightning after which he was said to be giddy as a child, and his subsequent assassination—though the rumbling from that event would eventually reverberate in the patient's gut until his lunch backed up and spewed into the bedpan. Later he became aware that there was rioting all over the map, and thought it odd that his city, source of the wound that infected the rest of the nation, should remain so eerily quiet. It was during that lull that Lenny, leaning on a metal cane, with raccoon eyes and zipper-like stitches over his brow, was delivered an exorbitant bill and discharged from the hospital. He returned to the Book Asylum on a Main Street nearly deserted but for the patrolling reserves in combat gear.

He could have gone anywhere, become anyone, a notion that perhaps played a part in persuading him to take refuge in the bookstore. Whatever the case, reentering the shop was as close to a homecoming as any Lenny was likely to know. And if there remained some doubt as to Avrom's final wishes with respect to his store, that doubt was put to rest by a phone call on the very afternoon of Lenny's return. Still muzzy, he wondered before answering if the caller might be Rachel Ostrofsky, which was the first he'd thought of the girl since his hospital release.

"Is this Leonard Skla*rew?*"

The emphasis on the final syllable came across as fleering, but Lenny nevertheless confessed that he was he. The unfamiliar voice introduced itself as Philly Sacharin, a nephew of the North Main Street alumnus Sol Sacharin of Sacharin's Buffalo Fish, and also coincidentally a junior partner in the law firm headed by Bernie Rappaport. He seemed confident that the information would carry some weight with his addressee. Unlike the ordinarily harried Bernie, Philly gave the impression of a cooler customer; he informed Lenny with glib assurance that the book-dealer had been in touch with him before his final illness, and that his "gift"—the passing along in writing of a shop leased these several decades from Midsouth Select Properties Incorporated—amounted, should he accept it, to Lenny's very own mausoleum.

"You want to keep up the old man's fixed-term?" piped the lawyer a little gleefully over the wire. "We'll get your transfer certified with all due haste. All you gotta do is first sell your soul to Midsouth Select to the tune of a zillion shekels in improvements. They want the worn-out heat pump and swamp cooler—whatever that is—replaced, plus an upgrade of the drywall and insulation, and while you're at it why not install a new septic system, which they stipulate. Then there's your sidewalk maintenance . . ."

He continued rattling off a bewildering variety of technical terms—"prescriptive covenant," "peppercorn rent, which you can forget about it"—further demonstrating his command of contract law.

"Ever hear of Jewish lightning? That's when you torch a place for the insurance."

Lenny thanked him kindly, satisfied that, insofar as it had been Avrom's to give, the shop was his. Astonishingly, he found that he welcomed the news with all its attendant headaches—which, now that the big headache of his concussion had begun to subside, failed to intimidate him. The Book

Asylum was a bulwark against the ill winds that wafted over the planet, a shrine to Muni Pinsker's chronicle, which lay before him on the desk where he'd left it and was Avrom's real legacy. It was altogether fitting that an individual waking up from injury and shock might seek comfort in such a place; emerging from the wreckage of his heart and bones, he might, from within the confines of his very own business, begin to reconstruct himself. He could start by shifting into an underutilized pragmatic gear and hatching a plan; maybe devise a strategy that would allow him to be both alone and not alone, to invite a portion of the public into *The Pinch* and perhaps acquire some revenue along the way.

Forget the boho outlaw, a role that seemed to have run its course; Lenny remembered that he was essentially a bookworm, and as such had intuitions based on a lifetime of reading. Without the slightest idea of how to implement his plan, however, he contacted Philly Sacharin, hoping to prevail upon their mutual allegiance to North Main Street for some advice. The lawyer offered no encouragement but, admitting he had only scant knowledge of the publishing industry ("Not my bailiwick"), vouchsafed a suggestion: his wife was a shikse socialite whose circle of acquaintances included a local author of some renown. He agreed as a one-off favor to put Lenny in touch with her. The woman was delighted at a chance to demonstrate her noblesse oblige, and through her flighty offices secured the bookseller an audience with the author at his home out on the Parkway.

Unwilling to let the book out of his sight, Lenny photocopied the entire volume with the last bit of cash from Avrom's till; it was this unbound bundle of pages he hoped to press upon the author in his book-lined study. Something of a celebrity, the author appeared to his visitor as the very model of a modern man of letters: patch sleeves, briar pipe, august jaw affecting the spade beard of one of the colonels from his acclaimed multi-volume history of the Civil War. Clearly impatient despite the slow decanting of his treacly speech, he asked Lenny, "What kind of thing is this?" The question may have referred as much to the unkempt bearer of the bundle as to the pages themselves.

Lenny wondered if he was expected to tremble as before the great and terrible Oz. Finally invited to sit down (he'd been teetering on his cane), the bookseller mumbled something about North Main Street when the author cut him short, assuring him: "You don't have to tell me about the Pinch." Lenny suspected that his was the Pinch of Davy Crockett and Big Jim Canaan, a wild and ungoverned place still barren of Jews, but did not say so. The interview was hardly a success, though at its abridged conclusion the put-upon author received the book as if in tribute from the tense young man. He riffled its contents, arched a brow over the illustrations (black and white in their Xeroxed version), then promised to take a look and deliver a judgment even as he waved his visitor away.

Lenny could guess what the author anticipated—some vain amateurish history with at best a little anthropological interest. And when weeks passed with no news from that quarter, he began to think the busy man would not bother to keep his word at all. Meanwhile the Cotton Carnival proceeded in the shadow of the fixed cloud that hung over the city, and the demolition of Beale Street progressed in the name of urban renewal. A local Reform rabbi blasted the congregation that had turned its back on him for his defense of the garbage strikers, then retired soon after in despair. There were more riots, bloodshed; the segregationist George Wallace declared himself a candidate for president and named as his running mate General Curtis LeMay, who said, "I don't believe the world'll end if we splode a nuculer bomb." Midsouth Select Properties Inc. dunned Lenny for rent and threatened him with eviction, and the hospital demanded prompt remittance of their bill. Lenny managed to forestall immediate action on the part of the latter by submitting partial payments with cash acquired from the sale of an occasional book. (There was of course no question of peddling drugs anymore, since the onetime vendor knew better than to apply to sources still smarting from having been burned by Lamar Fontaine.) Then, long after he'd abandoned the hope of hearing from him again, the author sent Lenny a letter.

Dear Mr. Skarew,

I'm afraid this reader's tastes tend too much toward the traditional to allow for a plenary appreciation of the liberties Mr. Pinsker has taken with narrative convention. Nor am I a fan of violating common reality with such liberal incursions of the preposterous; whatever claims the book makes to historical authenticity are patently absurd. However, I am not entirely unaware of certain trends in contemporary culture, and I suspect there are camps in which Mr. Pinsker's brand of whimsy might be indulged. I suppose there are even those who might take some pleasure in the calculated ingenuousness of the author's voice, despite its clannish ethnicity. That said, I found the inclusion in the text of a character I assume is yourself to be a needless contrivance: it's a gimmick clearly designed to give the work a "metafictional" stamp and seems a deliberate pandering to the fashion of the day. Still, though I judge the book to be finally a curio without enduring literary merit, it would be ungenerous not to concede that it nevertheless deserves its moment in the court of popular opinion, and I have forwarded *The Pinch* to my agent with that endorsement.

Yours, & etc.

P.S. I believe the illustrations, chimerical as they are, have also their own kind of currency in this climate and can't hurt the book's marketability (hateful word).

Lenny was contacted by the agent in the fullness of time. At the suggestion of her valued client she was passing the book along to an editor at a well-respected publishing house who she thought might be receptive. She cautioned the book dealer, though, that he shouldn't get his hopes up; the chances of a self-published volume being picked up by an established press were extremely remote.

Things happened thereafter with a startling alacrity. The agent, confessing her own surprise, got back to Lenny in a matter of days with the news that the publisher had made a better than reasonable offer for *The Pinch*. There were legal issues that needed ironing out in order to resolve Lenny's dual role as both executor and beneficiary of Muni Pinsker's literary estate (he should see a lawyer). Once the details were settled, he would receive half the advance upon signing the contract and half on publication of the book. While Lenny's head was still spinning from what sounded to him like an astronomical figure, the agent increased his vertigo with talk of print runs and marketing strategies. There had been some debate over just how to categorize the work, but it was finally decided the subtitle, *A*

History, would be retained, further qualified by the sub-subtitle: *A Novel.* Ambiguity, it seemed, was a selling point. Though the publisher intended to target "the obvious niche audience"—Lenny wondered who exactly that was—it had a broader readership in mind, and toward that end engaged an eminent writer—Jewish though not to an onerous degree—to tout the book's universality in a preface. The writer, unable to locate any biographical information about the author of *The Pinch,* was told all roads led back to a book dealer in Memphis; so he appealed to Lenny for a chronology of the major events in Muni's life. Having spent the publisher's advance on settling accounts with landlords and bill collectors and making initial improvements to the store, Lenny agreed, with his fledgling chutzpah, to provide the timeline for a supplemental fee.

The book was published the following autumn in a handsome, octavo-sized volume, its contents printed in an elegant Garamond type font on acid-free, Bible-grade stock. The title was embossed, the glossy dust jacket a reproduction of one of Tyrone's extravagant polychrome mirages, others appearing at intervals throughout the text. Removing it from its padded envelope, Lenny pawed the book and fanned its pages, hoping to revive something of the heart-stopping emotion he'd felt on encountering the original. (That particular volume had been filed away among the shop's labyrinthine shelves under History.) But *The Pinch* no longer seemed to belong to him. He had the awful sinking sensation upon cracking the spine of the newly minted edition that, in selling the book, he'd betrayed Muni Pinsker and the entire vanished community of North Main Street. The feeling was not much relieved when he turned to his own contribution, attached as a historico-biographical appendix:

Significant Biographical Events

~

1889—Muni Pinsker is born to Zalman and Itke Pinsker in town of Blod in the Russian Pale of Settlement.

1892—Enters as pupil in cheder of Reb Yozifel Glans, called by his students Death's Head.

1898—Transfers to more advanced school in Tzachnovka, thirty versts from Blod; Muni begins "eating days" and writing poetry.

1906—Enters yeshiva of famed Chazon Ish in Minsk, where he is exposed to radical politics.

1907—Passover pogrom in Blod: Muni's father is murdered, sister assaulted, mother left deranged.

1908—Joins Jewish General Labor Bund.

1909–10—Is arrested for distributing socialist paper the *Hammer*, accused of conspiracy, and sentenced to four years' hard labor and permanent exile to Siberia; marched to the mica mines at Nerchinsk, a journey from Moscow of more than five months.

1910–11—Escapes from the labor camp: walks from Nerchinsk to Irkutsk across frozen Lake Baikal; travels (funded by smuggled currency from American uncle) by train through Russia to Bremen; then by SS *Saxonia* to New York and train to Memphis, Tennessee.

1912–13—Works on North Main Street (the Pinch) in the general merchandise owned by uncle Pinchas Pin; becomes romantically attached to funambulist Jenny Bashrig; earthquake occurs.

1913–21 (an approximate span of years perceived by population as single cyclical day)—Stricken with graphomania, Muni retreats into room, begins writing chronicle of the Pinch in which events seem to happen concurrently if not all at once; after terminating pregnancy, Jenny joins circus.

Children of flooded North Main Street begin fainting at will: entering hiver-betim (deathlike trances), they emerge with occult knowledge; permutate letters of Tetragrammaton with alphabet blocks to summon cosmic monsters for the purpose of remembering fear.

Significant Historical Events

1881–84, 1903–7—Major waves of pogroms in Russia, mass emigration of Jews.

1887—Artesian well water becomes available in Memphis.

1894–99—Dreyfus affair.

1897—General Jewish Labor Bund formed.

1899—Blood libel trial in Bohemia (the Hilsner case); black millionaire R. R. Church funds Church Park and Auditorium, first Memphis park and entertainment center for African Americans.

1903—The Protocols of the Elders of Zion *published in the newspaper* Zamnye; *Kishinev pogrom.*

1900—Casey Jones leaves Memphis's Central Station bound for catastrophic train wreck at Vaughn, Mississippi.

1905—Failed Russian revolution; pogroms ensue.

1906—W. C. Handy writes "Mr. Crump Don't Like It" (later "Memphis Blues"); opening of Overton Park Zoo.

1908—Wild Bill Latura murders five Negroes in Ashford's Saloon on Beale Street, acquitted by all-white jury despite concern that such behavior might lead to killing white people; Mose Plough loans son Abe $125 to start Plough Chemical Company, also on Beale.

1909—Edward Hull Crump elected mayor of Memphis.

1913—Riots at Paris premiere of Stravinsky's Rites of Spring; *Mendel Beilis on trial in Russia for ritual murder.*

1914—World War I begins.

1915—Lynching of Leo Frank.

1916—E. H. Crump illegally "votes" illiterate blacks, pays city budget deficits with bond issues, protects political allies who abuse offices, ignores prohibition laws; Clarence Saunders opens first Piggly Wiggly self-service grocery at Third and Madison.

1917—Bolshevik Revolution: approximately 200,000 Jews murdered as counterrevolutionaries and bourgeois profiteers; Harahan Bridge completed over Mississippi River.

Significant Biographical Events

Millie Poupko's son Myron slices open big toe, inserts chit inscribed with name of God, sprouts wings; Izzy Grinspan's daughters pluck scales from dragon Rahav, use as mirrors in which to view future husbands.

Tinsmith Manny Schatz manufactures mechanical bird: inserts tongue of adder that causes automaton to speak prophecies suppressed since Babylonian exile.

The floozy Katya Bimbaum wears in her marcelled hair the mystic thirteen-petaled rose; rose plucked by Hershel Tarnopol for his papa's lapel, its radiance resulting in papa's combustion.

Zygmunt Tisch invokes as maggid (medium) the medieval cephalophore Rabbi Ashlag to interpret dream in which Theda Bara palpates his frontal lobe; in the absence of their rebbe Shpinker Hasids devise balloon raised aloft by lilin (aerial demons) spawned from Hasids' own seminal emissions.

Sam Alabaster uses, for fishing bait, a toxic worm that causes birds to fall from the sky by merely crawling over their shadow; Mrs. Bluestein invites ushpizin (spirit guests) from the Circle of the Unique Cherub to her canasta table.

Pantsed by dog-faced imps at belated bar mitzvah (revealing his petsel like a licorice whip), the aged changeling Benjy Padauer nevertheless succeeds in delivering his Torah portion.

Returned from underworld, Katie Pin celebrates renewed menstrual cycle; her child is born six weeks later.

Et cetera . . .

1921—Blind fiddler Asbestos, longtime fixture of North Main Street, is lynched after aiding and abetting convict escapees; Pinch resumes Central Standard Time.

1921–22—Muni abruptly ceases writing; retired from circus, Jenny Bashrig returns to Memphis; Muni and Jenny wed, become guardians of orphaned Tyrone Pin and proprietors of Pin's General Merchandise.

1918—Spanish flu epidemic.

1919—Treaty of Versailles.

1920—Henry Ford prints 500,000 copies of The Protocols of the Elders of Zion.

1923—Ku Klux Klan candidate Clifford Davis elected Memphis city judge; old Orpheum Theatre burns.

1924—Reunion of Confederate veterans in Memphis.

1925—"Fee system" of blacks sold into peonage exposed; New Peabody Hotel opens at Main and Monroe; Tom Lee, "a good Negro," rescues thirty-two people when excursion boat capsizes; Mein Kampf *published; Scopes "Monkey" Trial begins.*

1926—Last Valley Line packet boats retired from Mississippi River.

1927—Sacco and Vanzetti executed; The Jazz Singer, *starring Al Jolson, released; Mississippi River floods.*

1928—Jimmy Lunceford's Orchestra plays roof of Shrine Building; Bessie Smith at the Palace on Beale.

1929—Stock market crashes; Memphis adventurer Richard Halliburton lost at sea in Chinese junk.

1931—Cotton Carnival launched.

1933–41—German Jews stripped first of rights as citizens, then of rights as human beings.

1937—Amelia Earhart vanishes; Great Flood brings thousands of homeless refugees to Memphis.

1938—Two runs shy of Babe Ruth's record, Hank Greenberg walked rather than be given shot at home run. Kristallnacht.

1939—Germany invades Poland.

1941—Pearl Harbor.

1943—Warsaw Ghetto uprising.

1945—Victory in Europe; atomic bombs dropped on Japan.

1948—State of Israel established; Gandhi assassinated; WDIA radio station adopts all-black format.

1950—Senator Joseph McCarthy mounts anti-Communist crusade; Sam Phillips opens Sun Records Studio.

Significant Biographical Events

1922–28—After years of financial struggle and compromised health, Muni succumbs to pulmonary tuberculosis (1927); Jenny dies the following year from kidney disease aggravated by alcohol narcosis; young Tyrone, self-designated custodian of Muni's abandoned manuscript, becomes virtual charity case.

1944–45—Tyrone is conscripted into US Armed Forces, sees action after D-Day in northern Europe, witnesses liberation of Dachau.

1945–52—Tyrone returns to North Main Street enervated from battle fatigue, begins to paint; immigrant camp survivor Avrom Slutsky, having followed Tyrone to America, recovers Muni Pinsker's buried manuscript, edits and redacts text—which he titles *The Pinch*—and funds its printing along with the plates of Tyrone's illustrations.

1953—Over Slutsky's protests, Tyrone is declared mentally incompetent and confined to Western State Psychiatric Hospital at Bolivar.

1968—Book dealer Leonard Sklarew, legatee of Muni's printed book, sells rights to the venerable Frigate Press for publication as *The Pinch: A History;* a novel.

Significant Historical Events

1951—*Phillips records Ike Turner's "Rocket 88," first rock 'n' roll hit.*

1952—*Night of Murdered Poets in Moscow; Kemmons Wilson opens first Holiday Inn on Summer Avenue.*

1953—*Rosenbergs executed.*

1954—*E. H. Crump dies.*

1955—*Emmet Till murdered.*

1956—*"Million Dollar Quartet"—Jerry Lee Lewis, Carl Perkins, Johnny Cash, and Elvis Presley—jam at Sun Records; Elvis appears on* Ed Sullivan Show.

1958—*Stax Records's "Memphis Sound" organized.*

1961—*Eichmann trial.*

1962—*Cuban Missile Crisis.*

1963—*Martin Luther King gives "I Have a Dream" speech; John F. Kennedy assassinated.*

1964—*Beatles come to America.*

1965—*Malcolm X shot; American troops sent to Vietnam.*

1967—*Six-Day War in Israel.*

1968—*Martin Luther King and Robert Kennedy assassinated; massacre at My Lai.*

1969—*Despite designation as National Historic Landmark, Beale Street area demolished and buildings (with exception of Schwab's Emporium) condemned.*

1970s—*Bisected by Interstate 40 as part of construction for Hernando DeSoto Bridge, Pinch district becomes target for slum clearance.*

It didn't happen overnight, but against all reasonable expectations Muni's book struck a chord with the reading public. There was, apparently, still a reading public. The reviews, such as they were, were mixed: the favorable, perhaps influenced by the psychedelic ethos of the day, praised the kaleidoscopic nature of the narrative. Some said it evoked a kind of folk consciousness and even delighted in the book's refusal to conform to a specific genre. Soberer judgments—and these were in the majority—suggested that *The Pinch* was the product of a puerile sensibility and dismissed it out of hand. There were those, too, who complained that the surplus of "tribal" content was off-putting and exclusive. But somehow a gradual groundswell of word-of-mouth sentiment began to create a stir in various quarters, and the book—like an awkward dance step that turns out to be liberating—started to catch on. By the time Lenny received the publisher's biannual statement, *The Pinch* had made up its advance and begun to generate royalties. By the end of the fiscal year the book had attained a minor cult status, a paperback edition was in the works, and Leonard Sklarew was on his way to becoming solvent.

A few readers, when they discovered that both the Book Asylum and its young proprietor were extant, sought them out. At first Lenny had welcomed the pilgrims; the book's notoriety (and the capital it generated) had helped to assuage his lingering guilt, and he was willing now to bask a bit in its reflected glory. But for their part the visitors were unable to hide their disappointment on meeting the book dealer in person: an unprepossessing, thickly bespectacled guy growing a paunch and bookish in the extreme, with no hint of the restless miscreant from the text. Ultimately Lenny would have them to know that the letdown was mutual.

Another consequence of the book's growing popularity was a renewed interest in the geographic Pinch (which few Memphians had ever even heard of) as a historical site. The curious began to visit it, looking for traces of the old ghetto community from Muni's tales. Most, finding mainly ruins, passed on, but a handful of young artists, imbued with nostalgia for a place they'd known only in print, took advantage of the cheap real estate; they purchased loft space to convert into studios in an old coffee factory that had so far been spared the wrecking ball. Soon after, a coterie of utopian-minded friends, for whom *The Pinch* had become a kind of holy book, pooled their resources to make a down payment on one of the few remaining tenements on North Main. They lived there as a collective, renovating the apartments upstairs and opening a crafts shop on the ground floor. In the shop, along with feather earrings, macramé bracelets, and scented candles, they sold—in a nod toward an "oriental" theme—homemade hamantashen and chocolate Hanukkah gelt. Thanks to a growing host of *Pinch*-inspired tourists, the shop prospered, its success spurring another young entrepreneur to open a tavern in a face-lifted building across the way. In deference to the spirit of place he served draft beer from a samovar.

This vest-pocket commercial revival lured more foot traffic into the area, people milling about the sidewalks as if waiting impatiently for the further transformation of the street. Their presence attracted the notice of a group of progressive local investors, who became interested in redeveloping the district on an enterprising scale. They formed a consortium and submitted an ambitious plan to the city for construction of a number of edifices along both sides of North Main. Included in the plan was a self-imposed provision that the design of the new buildings—which would house an assortment of businesses and apartments—conform to the architecture of the original structures, thus preserving the flavor of the turn-of-the-century neighborhood. Newspapers and city fathers applauded the North Main Street Renaissance, as the development was called, and businesses jockeyed for a spot in what they now perceived as a prime location. When the ribbon was cut at the quarter's inauguration, the public, like runners at the start of a race, bolted into a street lined with retail attractions. Alongside the boutiques and period cafés (one called unavoidably Catfish Bayou) there were traditional artisans' shops, where visitors could observe cobblers, cigar rollers, pretzel bakers, and bespoke tailors at work on antique sewing machines. There was even a quality delicatessen with the gilt inscription כשר in the window, though there was of course no kosher fare on the menu.

Residents of the luxury apartments above the shops enjoyed a relaxed urban lifestyle in an appealing if somewhat artificial environment, a secure community of like-minded affluent types; this at a time when the rest of the city, as viewed from the rarefied vantage of the Pinch, still wallowed in a swamp of ignorance and rising crime. It's true that the street's advance-guard pioneers—the loft dwellers and tchotchke-mongers—were eventually priced out of the gentrified neighborhood; but there remained enough of a bohemian-inflected atmosphere to ensure North Main's continuance as a fashionable destination for citizens and tourists alike. Nor did the new Pinch forget its debt to the Old World milieu that had fostered its revitalization in the first place. The vestibules of several condominiums were decorated with murals displaying large-scale reproductions of the paintings of Tyrone Pin. (These included mildly sentimentalized versions of the inverted oak, lit like a menorah and hung with fiends and earlocked children in beanies riding rafts like giant afikomens.) The paintings themselves, enhanced by the legend of the mad artist, now fetched princely sums. The proceeds from their sales were placed in a trust established by Leonard Sklarew through the connivance of his attorney, Philly Sacharin. As executive officer of the Tyrone Pin Trust ("Pin money," its recipients called it), Mr. Sklarew, flush from the thirteenth printing of *The Pinch*, could allocate the funds as he saw fit. Needless to say, he made certain that the artist, himself unaware of his success and protected from curiosity seekers by the staff at his facility, would be well looked after until his death. Then there were donations to pet charities and causes, plus an endowment (supplemented by a memorial concert) that allowed the B'nai B'rith Home for the Aged to break ground for a lavish new Elder Lincoln Wing.

Perhaps the crowning element of the North Main Street Renaissance was the construction of a streetcar line, which stretched from the Pinch along Main Street proper as far as the refurbished Central Station on South Main. The new trolley had an old-fashioned character, featuring heritage-style wooden cars with reversible mahogany seats and brass handles. Along its route once-vacant commercial premises began to reopen, their tenants including famous-name chain stores, gourmet markets, chic bistros, and wine bars. The mercantile fervor that had infected North Main and its contiguous district also reawakened the dust of Beale Street, which began again, Lazarus-like, to show signs of life. In time its vintage restoration became the hub of the city's musical nightlife, and downtown Memphis, risen from its longtime repose, flourished like never before.

17
Envoi

I woke up in the hospital under a morass of memories I thought had been lost forever. Wishful thinking, I guess. They must have been dislodged from whatever wrinkle in the brain they were stuck in when I was hit on the head, then—after I was launched full-throttle into a solid brick wall—released altogether. Memories of wanting and misspent time, they weighed on me; disappointments crushed my ribs, pinched my left leg, stung me like hornets in every joint, to say nothing of the pain in my aching head. They left me defenseless to the clinical invasions of the hospital staff, defenseless as well when, from behind the privacy curtain surrounding my bed, the female person I recalled as my sometime girlfriend, Rachel Ostrofsky, stepped forth.

She was wearing her black boots and blue raincoat, a Spanish-fan barrette like an unfolding wing pinning back one side of her shimmery hair. Her expression was full of a solicitude I expected to dissolve along with her physicality. But morphine pump notwithstanding, it seemed she was no hallucination. Her glow was so palpable I wanted never to traffic in hallucination again.

"You're a memory come alive," I heard myself mutter.

"Kafka?" came a voice from in back of Rachel. "The quote is from Kafka, am I right?"

The voice belonged, after he'd edged to her side—natty in his navy blazer and the woodpecker's crest of his strawberry hair—to the diminutive party who'd decked me an age ago in the 348. I remembered (what didn't I remember?) that he was a law student and could be an even smarter aleck than me. I remembered also that Rachel had once referred to him as her fiancé, though who even used that word anymore?

"We thought we'd find you hounded by reporters," she said, with the

339

breezy air of somebody trying to put a good face on a strained situation. Nor did her "we" escape my attention.

They stood over my bed, Rachel and her companion (Dennis, wasn't it?), observing me like they might have a child they thought cute despite (or because of) its deformity. In one hand Rachel held a bouquet of purple flowers, in the other a newspaper. The paper was folded to a page displaying a grainy black-and-white photo, which she waved under my nose like smelling salts. "I started phoning hospitals the minute I saw it," she said, pooching a lip in token of how much the image had disturbed her. I extended a hand to still her wrist and felt her blench at my touch. It was an alternative paper, a hippie rag, and the photograph was of poor quality and a bit out of focus. But you could make out clearly enough, amid the chaos of the panicked crowd and the club-swinging cops, a frizzy-haired white guy collapsed in the gutter near a fallen Negro with a bloody head. It took me a studious second to recognize the victims of what the paper called "needless brutality."

I shut my eyes until the awful pressure in my chest was a little relieved. When I opened them Rachel was calling to a passing nurse to please bring her a vase for the flowers. The sharp-featured nurse fairly snarled as if to imply that her job description did not include responding to imperious requests.

There followed an awkward silence during which I wondered what Rachel had told Dennis about me. Whatever it was, his smug expression suggested he'd made his peace with it; I could only guess at the terms of the treaty. The nurse returned to hand Rachel, uncordially, a small water-filled Mason jar. Rachel placed the flowers in the jar, which was too shallow for their long stems and tipped over as soon as she set it on the nightstand.

"You shouldn't have," I said.

When she went to fetch a towel, Dennis scooted closer to the bed to ask, "Are you in pain?" the way a torturer inquires of his victim on the rack. I wouldn't give him the satisfaction of answering in the affirmative, but I suppose he could tell from my squinched brow that I was hurting, because he grinned; though he resumed his masquerade of compassion on Rachel's return. Squatting beside the bed to wipe up the spill, she made small talk, talk so trivial, in fact, that it was hardly worth replying to: she hoped I'd recover soon from my injuries, praised me for taking part in the march . . .

"I was only sightseeing," I assured her, suspecting that she continued to wipe the floor in order to avoid having to get to her feet and face me. "I had no business there."

Finally standing again, Rachel countered, "I disagree," though she might have mustered a little more conviction. She added for good measure that my participation in the march was plainly heroic. "Quixotic," inserted Dennis, his tone suggesting that the cause was lost all along: case closed.

It was then I felt the tears beginning to well up from some sulfurous source deep in my bowels. They'd always been my special brand of incontinence, the tears, and I bit my lip to try and hold them back, but the words that escaped my mouth gave me away.

"Rachel, what about us?"

She looked downright horror-struck before the pity set in. But rather than succumb to it, she straightened her spine and chose that moment to drop her bombshell. Ignoring the question that still hung in the astringent air, she stated with a forced informality, "Dennis and I have set a date." It was to be a midsummer wedding, a small interfaith affair with a rabbi and a priest, for which they'd already chosen an ideal location on the river bluff. "We'd be pleased if you came," she said disingenuously, while next to her Dennis bared his barracuda grin.

I was restrained by traction, catheter, and IV tube from inflicting further injury to my person. Murder and betrayal are the whole of the law, I concluded as I lay there bereft of speech. The monitor tangled in cords beside my bed blinked and whirred as if some jackpot had been struck: it was the signal for another pair of visitors to make their unannounced appearance from behind the curtain. This is your life, I thought.

Rachel and Dennis donned tepid smiles to greet them: the middle-aged man and woman shaking their heads in unison at the foot of the bed. "Oh, Lenny," lamented the gentleman, and heaved a ten-pound sigh. His eyes behind his library-frame glasses were puffy, his nose porous and pickle-shaped like my own; the receding tide of his crinkly hair left behind it a littoral of wrinkled pink brow. Foursquare in a madras sport coat, he was holding, like the tail of a fish past its prime, the same hippie paper (the *Glass Onion*) Rachel had brought with her. "Lennylenny." His sigh was seconded by the woman beside him, her attitude of condolence as subverted by her tangerine pantsuit as was his by the plaid sport coat. So far they'd refrained from advancing any closer, for which I was thankful, since the distance aided me in my effort not to recognize them.

"So Lenny," the man ventured at length, "how do you feel?"

Rachel had thoughtfully worked some mechanism that caused the bedstead to raise me nearer to a sitting position. "Never better," I managed, which was apparently the wrong answer, because the man practically barked, "Just what did you think you were doing down there?"

"Myron," cautioned his companion with a hand to his sleeve, but no sooner did she quiet him down than she too started in on me. "Aren't you even a little ashamed?" A neon vein pulsing at her throat.

From the bottom of my heart I admitted, "I'm a lot ashamed," but their still-nettled demeanor implied that they didn't believe me.

At that point Dennis cleared his throat and took a step in their direction, offering his glad hand by way of cutting the tension, and making conspicuous my failure to provide introductions. "I'm Dennis Kavanaugh," he said, confident of the good impression he made on his elders. "And this is Rachel," placing an arm around her waist, "my fiancée." Whereupon the newcomers reflexively adopted a civil manner. The sport coat introduced himself as Myron Sklarew, the patient's father, and cranked Dennis's hand heartily in return. "I'm Mrs. Sklarew," submitted his pantsuited spouse, "Lenny's mom," smiling sweetly as she pinched the tips of Dennis's fingers.

The law student launched without preamble into chatty conversation. Assuming common cause, he employed his best forensic vocabulary in describing the inconvenient position the garbage strike had placed the city in. Rachel, to her credit, kept mum, perhaps remorseful at having savaged my last article of faith with her announcement. Then, as it looked like Dennis and my putative father might be on the verge of bonding over their mutual contempt for the poor, she gently touched the arm of her intended; she reminded him they'd been about to depart. "We have a prior engagement?" Dennis looked at her as if this was news to him but acquiesced to her resolute features.

She turned to me before leaving to mention something about how the B'nai B'rith Home had assumed power of attorney over the estate of Tyrone Pin, some of whose paintings now sold for upwards of . . . , but I was no longer listening. Then she reached across the nightstand to give my hand a squeeze. Maybe it was a tender squeeze, fraught with the pathos of unrealized desire, but to me it felt perfunctory, the way an arthritic squeezes a rubber bulb.

I wanted to tell her I'd never wash my hand again but couldn't even summon that much spleen.

As soon as they were gone the alleged Myron Sklarew, somewhat placated, informed me, "I phoned Kenny Kurtz down at the *Commercial*—he owes me, Kenny—and asked him to call off his dogs. Otherwise you'd have been swarmed by journalists wanting the scoop on the only white face in that mob of schwartzes."

I thanked him.

"He told me nobody had yet identified you and we agreed it should stay that way."

Then his wife chimed in. "It's bad enough our own rabbi has to get involved with those"—she choked down the ill-bred language on the tip of her tongue—"but you Lenny, what did that mess have to do with you?"

"Nothing," I conceded.

There was a silence during which they put on their concerned faces once again and I thought I knew what was coming. They were about to relent and invite me to come back home, all was forgiven, and for a weak moment I thought I might cave in to their appeal. After all, they hadn't been such bad parents, just clueless like everyone else: add denying them to the list of things I was ashamed of. But instead of flinging wide his arms, Myron gave a nod to his wife who copied the nod with righteous chins and withdrew a letter from her purse. Her husband took the letter from her hand and stepped forward to give it to me. The return address on the envelope—County Draft Board 480, Shelby County Federal Building, Suite 369—said it all. Seeing that I made no move to open it, he leaned over and tore it open for me, bending my fingers until they pincered the page bearing its official stamp:

GREETINGS FROM THE PRESIDENT OF THE UNITED STATES.

It seemed I was being ordered to report for conscription into the Armed Forces of the United States of America. I was given a specific time to appear for a physical examination that would precede my immediate induction into the military.

"We spoke to the doctor," said Myron. What doctor? I'd been visited so far only by interns, who glanced at my chart, then at me, as if to verify they made a match before briskly walking away. "He says you should be shipshape in a matter of weeks. Plenty of time to heal before," glancing at the letter, "your call-up date."

Then he took a paternal tone, which my presumptive mother complemented with an expression that risked creasing her cosmetic mask. "Do the right thing, son," placing a hand on my scarified arm, "and we'll be proud of you." Don't, he didn't have to tell me, and you're nothing to us.

Gazing up at them from my procrustean bed, I replied, "Who did you say you were?"

I waited for the next round of visitors to appear from behind the curtain and bring me some fresh mortification: the living had had their turn, so how about the dead? Where was the ghost of Elder Lincoln come to demand I wreak vengeance on his killers? Where was Avrom—though I didn't yet know he was gone, his casket conveyed by pallbearers dispatched from the Shelby County Penal Farm—where was he, my old boss, come forward to dump a steaming burden of fate in my lap? But nobody else arrived, the world was scoured of ghosts, and the tears that once flowed so easily were as dried up as Rachel's flowers dying of thirst on the nightstand.

I was released from the hospital a couple of days after the slaying of Dr. Martin Luther King, feeling as fragile as Humpty Dumpty. Hobbling on crutches into the April morning, I was assailed by bright sunshine like a hail of thumbtacks, my eyes acutely sensitive since the blow to my head. Pink azaleas and yellow buttercups trumpeted their shrill colors from a nearby park, and I winced from the mordant scent of lilacs. The natural world, it seemed, was in the process of reclaiming the man-made, which looked to me to be in retreat, the city strangely quiet, the traffic sparse to nonexistent; and I, with my pallor and plaster cast, stitches like railroad crossties over the shaved patch on my skull, was a suitably walking wounded survivor of the uninhabited landscape.

My armpits and ribs ached from the pressure of the aluminum crutches as I made my way to the nearest bus stop. I engineered the precarious business of boarding the bus and rode downtown, where I dismounted on Main Street with equivalent difficulty. Negotiating the last few meters from the corner to the Book Asylum, I unlocked the door and swung across the threshold into the semidark. I inhaled the shop's attar of arcane philosophies, forgotten histories, and baroque tales, and was at once relieved. The tall shelves were ramparts from behind which I could look out onto the armed camp of downtown Memphis, where fatigue-clad Guardsmen with fixed bayonets patrolled the street on foot and in jeeps. I was under siege, which suited my mood, holed up as I was in Avrom's sanctum while the nation burned. Leaning the crutches against the wall, I lowered myself into my former boss's chair, then lifted the dead weight of my rigid leg until it rested on top of the desk. Also atop the desk, where I'd left it, was Muni Pinsker's "history" of the Pinch.

I hadn't the least temptation to pick it up, or so I told myself, though I poked it like the curious artifact it was. I blew the dust from its cover, then I picked it up, opened it, and pitched headlong into its splashy contents. It was evening in the book, an evening partaking of the properties of dawn, and a wedding was in progress on a flatboat anchored to no particular season in the North Main Street canal. The vessel was "floodlit" by the moon's reflection on a scattering of seraphic fingernail parings floating on the surface of the water. The canopy, sagging like a pelican's pouch from the load of children peeking out of its sling, was held aloft by a flock of hoopoes with the heads of sages. Gottlob the jeweler, late as usual, was paddling furiously out to the boat in his leaky tub to deliver the ring. Its stone was cut from a sacred jacinth by means of the Shamir, the worm that had hewn the blocks for the Temple in keeping with the commandment that no iron be used in constructing the altar of God. On board the boat the staid Rabbi Lapidus, a rooster tucked under his arm as a sign of fertility, charged the lovelorn to "be always heartbroken, mein kinder, for only then can you keep evil away."

A balmy, schnecken-scented breeze emanated from the oven of Ridblatt's Bakery, under whose awning shuffled a Hasid with his nose in a volume of Talmud. He stepped off the curb and ambled several strides over the water before he realized where he was and promptly sank. A few doors down, Pin's General Merchandise was dark, a sign on the door announcing CLOSED FOR FENCY YENTZING. Upstairs Pinchas and Katie Pin were in flagrante, while down the hall their nephew, Muni, gleeful in his unwashed underwear, was busy scribbling on the pages in his lap. Behind him stood a silent, ginger-haired child peering over his shoulder in an effort to see what he was writing, and beside the child hovered a scruffy old party in red suspenders, also rubbernecking. To the knobby blades of the old guy's wilted shoulders were appended a paltry pair of wings, no bigger than a chicken's, their pinfeathers as spotty as the fuzz on his ill-shaped head. I too was seized by a desire to kibitz and tried to sidle between the little boy and Avrom Slutsky, for the transfigured old gaffer was none other than he. But while the kid stepped aside the old man gave me a sharp elbow to the kidneys, turning to shout, "Gay avek! Get outta here!" The shout, which was familiar as his standard glottal screech, had at the same time the sonorous authority of a bat kol, a voice from on high.

"Awright," I sulked, "I can take a hint," and slammed shut the book.

Then I wondered: What just happened? Still reeling from my swift eviction from Muni's creation, I was neither here nor there; I came back only by gradual degrees to an awareness of 1968, to which I was banished. The shop now appeared to me less like a grotto than a moldy funk hole. If only, I found myself wishing, someone had come along to close the book's cover while I was reading. Then, while my body remained sitting at Avrom's desk, a hollow effigy no more substantial than a meringue, my spirit would have been happily trapped in Muni's pages—where, incidentally, the draft board would never find me . . .

Such was my reasoning as I turned to withdraw the envelope from the pocket of my leather jacket draped over the chair behind me. I removed the letter, unfolding it with curious anticipation like a map that might give me back my bearings, then entertained a maverick notion: What if I went to war? It was after all a young man's rite of passage since the dawn of history, to embark on the great adventure and return (if he returned) marked by an awful wisdom and a cauterized soul . . . And again I thought I heard the strident voice—a tinnitus no doubt prompted by my head injury—crying, "A nekhtiker tog! Are you nuts?"

I took a breath and carefully lifted my hampered leg from the desktop, planted it on the floor, and opened the drawer. A sepulchral odor rose from its interior. I rooted among the clutter of unpaid bills, the yellow fabric Magen David, a worn scrapbook full of buff-brown circus clippings, until I found a box of wooden matches. Striking one, I set fire to the letter.

I watched it burn until the flames threatened to scorch my fingers, then let it drift out of my hand. A flaking black carbon zephyr on orange wings, it lit on the desk atop Muni's weathered volume, which ignited. A frayed corner of the book cover had absorbed the flame like a wick, and the book was instantly engulfed. I was fascinated to see how it seemed to welcome the combustion. I might have smothered the little blaze with a sleeve, snuffed it out like a candle; it was nothing but a lambent flickering. But instead I watched, interested, as the flames sprawled across the cloth cover, hardly believing the book could be so rapidly consumed. Then the small conflagration spread to some stray volumes on the desk, which proved equally flammable, their sparks rising like blown spores dispersed to the nearby shelves, where a wall of books seemed to have been awaiting its own incineration. In a few seconds the shelves had burst into trellises of efflorescent flame.

I remained transfixed by the sight until the door flew open and a cadre of National Guardsmen charged in, presumably alerted by smoke issuing from the shop. Callow weekend warriors not much older than me, they stormed the premises as if they meant to battle the fire with their rifles; they held kerchiefs over their faces and began to rush here and there at cross-purposes, calling for buckets of water. Close to choking myself, I was nevertheless ignored in the mayhem, still lacking the will to lift myself from the chair. Then one of the tall shelves toppled over, crashing to the floor in a spray of glittering sparks, out of which stepped, God help us, my beatified boss, having apparently followed me from the pages of Muni's book. His pinions appeared to have grown considerably; covered now in an eider of frothy feathers, they even flapped a bit, fanning the flames. His countenance was more terrible than any of the crabby aspects he'd assumed in life: eyes flashing, hair floating (at least the few strands that were left to him), his scraggly beard curved like a cutlass at its tip. This was not a guardian but an avenging host, who loomed above me in utter indifference to the fact that I refused, despite my dread, to believe in him.

But there was nothing spectral about the talon-like hand he thrust into the desk drawer in front of me, extracting a pair of rusty scissors. He raised them above his head where they hung poised to settle scores with the young shmuck who'd torched his store and betrayed his legacy. I deserve this, I thought, and closed my eyes, still half-expecting I might wake up in my hospital bed. Peeking through my fingers, I watched in awe as the celestial geezer plunged the scissors not into my heart but my thigh, stabbing through the baggy pantsleg and cutting a seam in the plaster cast. Then clenching the instrument pirate-style in his gums, he ripped the layered plaster, which came apart like an opened cocoon, and liberated my leg. He raised me up by the sore armpits and shoved me toward the door, expediting my forward motion with a well-placed kick.

I stumbled coughing and half-blinded out onto the pavement, where I was greeted again by the unpeopled morning. Behind me the fire roiled, the shop's dusty front window splintering from the inferno inside as the soldiers beat their retreat out the door. There were sirens in the near distance, men and trucks only minutes away, though I knew they would arrive too late. I wiped my watering eyes with my sleeve and suffered shooting pains throughout my body, an infestation of pins and needles in my game leg, all of which served only to animate me the more. I proceeded in a southerly direction along Main Street, its stores closed and boarded up against looters, the thoroughfare barren but for the odd sentry or armored tank. A phrase came into my head: "The royal road to romance," which struck me as so comical that I tried a few warmed-over others. "He lit out for the territory with only the clothes on his back." A breeze fluttered my torn pantsleg in unison with a banner hanging over the street announcing the commencement of this spring's Cotton Carnival; a flyer taped to a lamppost advertising the Elder Lincoln Memorial Concert at the Overton Park Shell also waved. We flapped—the banner, the flyer, the flitting pigeons, and myself—like flags at a regatta, which somehow increased the hilarity of my circumstance. I had to stop and surrender to a fit of laughter, a whooping fulmination that escaped my seared lungs with a sound like a raucous sneeze.

"Gezuntheit!" came the sublime squawk from behind me. I might have glanced back over my shoulder at its source but instead stayed true to the words I'd spied Muni Pinsker scribbling on the page in his suffocating little room.

"Limping forward again," he had written, "Lenny never turned around to give a look on the angel with the scissors and the flames. He figured was nothing already but rubble and ashes, the bookshop, like the district a few blocks to the north that they called it the Pinch."

Acknowledgments

Portions of this book appeared in *Fiction Magazine*, *J&L Illustrated*, vol. 3, and *jewishfiction.net*, no. 14.

My thanks to Fiona McCrae and the very fine people of Graywolf Press, and as always to my steadfast friend and agent, Liz Darhansoff.

STEVE STERN, winner of the National Jewish Book award, is the author of several previous novels and collections of stories. He teaches at Skidmore College in upstate New York.

Interior design by Ann Sudmeier
Typeset in Ehrhardt MT Pro by Bookmobile Design &
Digital Publisher Services, Minneapolis, Minnesota
Manufactured by Friesens on acid-free, 100 percent postconsumer
wastepaper